The plunge becomes dangerous....

Tucking back his massive wings, Scree plunged downward. He narrowed his yellow-rimmed eyes to thin slits, and clutched the staff tight within his talon. Then he screeched the cry of the eaglefolk—a cry that meant only one thing.

Death.

The two intruders froze. Just as his prey always did. Inwardly, Scree smiled.

One of the intruders yelped in fright and threw himself behind a charred black boulder. A flame vent spouted fire and smoke right beside him, but he just huddled there, cowering.

The other one reacted differently. This one didn't run and hide, or stand still, paralyzed with fright. No, this person instantly pulled out a bow and nocked an arrow.

Scree didn't veer aside. This wasn't the first time he'd faced flamelon archers, who came up here hunting for action. Even if the bowman got off a shot before Scree reached him—which was unlikely, given Scree's speed—he'd never hit the moving target. And never survive to shoot again.

The bowman shot. Just as Scree had predicted, the arrow was easy to dodge.

Scree plunged again. Rage flooded his mind. He screeched louder than before, his cry echoing across the smoky cliffs.

By the time he saw the second arrow speeding toward him, it was too late.

READ THE WHOLE MERLIN SAGA!

MERLIN

BOOK 9

THE GREAT TREE OF AVALON

T. A. BARRON

PUFFIN BOOKS
An Imprint of Penguin Group (USA) Inc.

PUFFIN BOOKS

Published by the Penguin Group

Penguin Young Readers Group, 345 Hudson Street, New York, New York 10014, U.S.A.
Penguin Group (Canada), 90 Eglinton Avenue East, Suite 700, Toronto, Ontario, Canada M4P 2Y3
(a division of Pearson Penguin Canada Inc.)
Penguin Books Ltd, 80 Strand, London WC2R 0RL, England
Penguin Ireland, 25 St Stephen's Green, Dublin 2, Ireland (a division of Penguin Books Ltd)
Penguin Group (Australia), 250 Camberwell Road, Camberwell, Victoria 3124, Australia
(a division of Pearson Australia Group Pty Ltd)
Penguin Books India Pvt Ltd, 11 Community Centre, Panchsheel Park, New Delhi - 110 017, India
Penguin Group (NZ), 67 Apollo Drive, Rosedale, Auckland 0632, New Zealand
(a division of Pearson New Zealand Ltd.)
Penguin Books (South Africa) (Pty) Ltd, 24 Sturdee Avenue,
Rosebank, Johannesburg 2196, South Africa

Registered Offices: Penguin Books Ltd, 80 Strand, London WC2R 0RL, England

First published in the United States of America as *The Great Tree of Avalon: Child of the Dark Prophecy*
by Philomel Books, a division of Penguin Young Readers Group, 2004
Published as *The Great Tree of Avalon* by Puffin Books, a division of Penguin Young Readers Group, 2011

5 7 9 10 8 6 4

Patricia Lee Gauch, Editor

THE LIBRARY OF CONGRESS HAS CATALOGED THE PHILOMEL BOOKS EDITION AS FOLLOWS:
Barron, T. A. Child of the dark prophecy / T. A. Barron.
p. cm. – (The great tree of Avalon ; bk. 1)
Summary: In accordance with prophecy, Avalon's existence is threatened in the year that stars stop
shining and at the time when both the dark child and Merlin's heir are to be revealed.
ISBN: 0-399-23763-1 (hc)
[1. Magic—Fiction. 2. Avalon (Legendary place)—Fiction. 3. Fantasy.]
I. Title
PZ7.B27567 Ch 2004 [Fic]—dc22 2004044427

Puffin Books ISBN 978-0-14-241927-4

Design by Semadar Megged
Text set in ITC Galliard

Printed in the United States of America

A Word from the Author

AVALON LIVES. FOR CENTURIES, IT HAS BEEN celebrated in story and song . . . for its magic, its mist, and most of all, I think, its memory of a time of truth and healing amidst mortal sorrow. It is a story, and a place, that continues to grow—much like the Great Tree of this story, whose roots reach as deep as its branches lift high.

Like all myths that have rooted themselves in our hearts, Avalon continually sprouts new interpretations: new blossoms and boughs. This tale is one of them. The shapes and colors of these new versions may be widely varied, but they are all connected to the same tree, drawing life from the same ancient soil. So while it is fair to say that I have reimagined Avalon in these pages, it is also true that this tale is but a tiny twig on an immense and wondrous tree—a tree that is very much alive.

—T.A.B.

To Mother Earth,
beleaguered yet bountiful

With special thanks to
Denali Barron and Patricia Lee Gauch,
my fellow explorers of realms in between

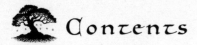 Contents

Part I

Part II

Part III

THE SEVEN ROOT~REALMS
of the GREAT TREE of
AVALON
BORN of MERLIN's MAGICAL SEED PLANTED in LOST FINCAYRA

T.A.B. 47 2003

GOBSKEN
FORTRESS

EVERNIGHT PEAKS
BEWARE OF DEATH DREAMERS

DOOMRAGA'S LAIR

VALE OF
ECHOES
LASTRAEL
(SHADOWROOT)

CAVERNS OF THE FLAMING JEWELS

DARK ELVES
BE HERE

LOST CITY
OF
LIGHT

VOLCANO
LANDS

RAHNAWYN
(FIREROOT)

EAGLE FOLK BE HERE

CRATER OF THE
CROOKED TEETH

RIVER OF FIRE

CLOUD
GARDENS
OF THE
FAERIES

BURNT HILLS OF THE FIRE DRAGONS

FLAMELON
FORGES

DANCING GROUNDS
OF
MIST MAIDENS

ANCESTRAL
HOME OF
MUSEOS

PALACES
OF THE
FLAMELONS

MAELSTROM OF MYSTERY

Y SWYLARNA
(AIR ROOT)

THE HARPLANDS

MALÓCH
(MUDROOT)

MUD HILLS

MISTY BRIDGE

THE SOUNDSWELLS

PLAINS OF ISENWY

MUDMAKERS
BE HERE

MISTY BRIDGE
ISLES OF THE BIRDS

VEIL
OF
ILLUSION

SHRINE OF LORILANDA

CLIFFS PERILOUS

SECRET SPRING
OF HALAAD?

HALL OF THE WINDS

AIRFALLS OF SILMANNON

GNOME
LANDS
OF THE
LOWER MALÓCH

BIRTHPLACE OF
SYLPHS

BEWARE OF BINKLES

CRAFTED
FROM THE BEST
AVAILABLE SOURCES
YEAR OF AVALON
1002
BY THE
EOPIA COLLEGE
OF MAPMAKERS

Born of a Seed That Beats Like a Heart

the celebrated opening lines of the bard Willenia's history of Avalon

AS ONE WORLD DIES, ANOTHER IS BORN. IT IS a time both dark and bright, a moment of miracles. In the mist-shrouded land of Fincayra, an isle long forgotten is suddenly found, a small band of children defeats an army of death, and a people disgraced win their wings at last. And in the greatest miracle of all, a young wizard called Merlin earns his true name: Olo Eopia, great man of many worlds, many times. And yet . . . even as Fincayra is saved, it is lost—passing forever into the Otherworld of the Spirits.

But in that very moment, a new world appears. Born of a seed that beats like a heart, a seed won by Merlin on his journey through a magical mirror, this new world is a tree: the Great Tree. It stands as a bridge between Earth and Heaven, between mortal and immortal, between shifting seas and eternal mist.

Its landscape is immense, full of wonders and surprises. Its populace is as far-flung as the stars on high. Its essence is part hope, part tragedy, and part mystery.

Its name is Avalon.

The Dark Prophecy

first revealed by the Lady of the Lake, Year of Avalon 694

A year shall come when stars go dark,
And faith will fail anon—
For born shall be a child who spells
The end of Avalon.

The only hope beneath the stars
To save that world so fair
Will be the Merlin then alive:
The wizard's own true heir.

What shall become of Avalon,
Our dream, our deepest need?
What glory or despair shall sprout
From Merlin's magic seed?

Prologue: One Dark Night

AFLAME VENT ERUPTED ON THE CLIFFS, BLAST-
ing the darkness like an angry dragon.

Then another. And another. All across the cliffs, among
the highest in Fireroot, tongues of fire shot upward, licked the air,
then vanished behind veils of ash and smoke. Rotten as sulfurous
eggs, blacker even than the black rocks of this ridge, the heavy
smoke swirled under cliffs and poured out of crevasses. Fire plants,
shaped like ghoulish hands, flickered strangely as they stretched
glowing fingers at anything that moved.

But nothing moved on the cliffs. Nothing but smoke, and ash,
and spitting flames. Nothing . . . except two shadowy shapes that
crept steadily higher.

It was night, and the two shapes, a pair of burly men, knew
well that darkness brought added dangers. Yet this particular
night had lasted for months on end, its blackness broken only by
the ceaseless fires of the cliffs. For this was the Year of Darkness—a
time long dreaded, ever since the Lady of the Lake had made her
infamous prophecy that all the stars of Avalon would go dark, and
stay dark, for an entire year.

Even so, the fact that night had swallowed all Seven Realms was not the most terrible part of the Dark Prophecy. No, far worse, the Lady had also foretold that in this year of darkness, a child would be born—a child destined to bring the very end of Avalon. The only hope, she had added, would come from someone else, someone she called *the true heir of Merlin*. Yet who that might be, and how he or she could ever defeat the child of the Dark Prophecy, no one knew.

"Aaaghh!"

The man's pained cry echoed over the cliffs. "Damn lava rocks. Burn me feet, they do."

"Shuddup, ye blasted fool!" spat his companion, crouching nearby. "Afore ye ruin everthin'."

The first man, still rubbing his feet through the burned-out soles of his boots, started to reply—when he caught sight of something above them, at the very top of the cliffs. "Look thar," he whispered, staring at a great tangle of branches, half lit by flames, that seemed to claw at the black sky.

"Where?"

"Up thar. A nest! I told ye we'd find—" He coughed, choking on a plume of smoke. "A nest."

The other man shook his head, sending up a cloud of black ash that had settled on his hair. "We ain't seekin' no nest, Obba, ye woodenbrain! We're seekin' a child. An' some sort o' stick, remember?"

"Sure, but thar's jest the place to find both, I say. Ossyn, if ye wasn't me dumb liddle brother, I'd chuck ye right off this cliff. A dead flea's got more brains!"

Ignoring his brother's growl, he went on. "Look, ol' White

Hands got us here all right, didn't he? An' promised us we'd find the child he wants. The one he calls the true heir o'—"

"I don't give a dragon's tooth *what* he's called, just as long as White Hands pays us good as he promised. What's yer point?"

Using the sleeve of his ragged cloak, Obba wiped some sweat from his eyes. "Me point is, think about what White Hands said. *On top of the flaming cliffs, you shall find the child.* Them's his exact words. An' then he says to us: *Beware the eagle-mother, who will do anything to protect her young.* Don't that make it clear 'nuf? The child's in a nest."

"Clear as smoke," his brother retorted, waving away another plume. "Even if thar *is* some eaglechild hidin' up thar, it could be the wrong one. Could be any ol' child—or even the Dark child that everyone's jabberin' about!"

Obba reached over and grabbed his sleeve. "Use yer brain, will ye? There ain't hardly any children bein' born this year—not in any realm, remember? An' lots o' those that are born get killed straightaway, fer fear they could really be the Dark one. So if we do finds any child up here, it's more'n likely the right one."

His eyes gleamed savagely, reflecting the flames. "Anyways, we don't really care, do we? If ol' White Hands wants to pay us fer a child, we brings him a child. An' if he wants to believe that the true heir is so young—foolhardy, if ye ask me—that's his own friggin' folly! Besides, didn't his liddle entrails readin' also tell him the child wouldn't come into power fer seventeen years? That's plenty o' time fer us to vanish wid all our coins."

A slow grin creased Ossyn's face. "Maybe yer not such a wood-enbrain after all." Suddenly he yelped, as a clump of hot ash blew into his eye. "Ogres' eyeballs!" he swore. "Whatever we're paid won't be 'nuf." He swung his fist at the smoky air—and smashed his brother hard on the ear.

Obba howled, then punched him back in the gut. "Ye clumsy troll! Any pay's too small wid all yer foolishness." He slumped against a cracked boulder, tugging the hunting bow on his shoulder. "But we won't get paid nothin' if we don't—*ehhhh!*"

He leaped away from the boulder just as three fiery fingers pinched his rear end. Tripping, he sprawled and sent some loose rocks clattering down the cliff. He landed hard—right on his scorched bottom.

"Owww," he cried, flipping back over onto his knees. "Ye fried me friggin' bacon!" Obba clutched his sore rear end with one hand, while shaking a blackened fist at the fire plant that had singed him so badly. And so rudely. "Ye cursed plant! I'll—"

"Shush," hissed Ossyn suddenly, pointing at the nest above.

A rustle—then a pair of enormous wings slapped the air. Spanning nearly three men's height, the wings rose out of the nest, glowing orange from the fires below. Upward on the swells they rose, bearing the feather-covered body of an eaglewoman. As she flew, her feathery legs—and sharp talons—hung low, while her head, which kept its human form, turned toward the cliffs. Beneath streaming locks of silver hair, her fierce eyes flashed.

The eaglewoman raised one wing. Instantly she veered away, following the ridgeline. A screeching cry—part human and part eagle, loud enough to freeze the two men's hearts—struck the cliffs. She sailed behind the rocky rim and vanished into the night.

At last, the brothers breathed again. They traded relieved glances. Then, hit by the same idea, they started scurrying up the cliff toward the nest—although Obba did pause to glare at a certain fire plant. It just sputtered noisily, almost like a wicked chuckle.

Higher and higher the two men climbed. Several minutes later, they reached the top, a long ridge of steep cliffs broken only by a few pinnacles of rock. And by one enormous nest, a mass of broken branches and twisted trunks that the eaglefolk had carried all the way from the lowland forests in their powerful talons. The brothers clambered up the side of the nest. With a wary glance at the sky, they jumped down inside.

Soft, downy feathers broke their fall. Some were as small as their hands; others were longer than their outstretched arms. The feathers lay everywhere—along with heaps of gray droppings and broken bits of shell. Plus hundreds and hundreds of bones, all picked clean by sharp beaks, all gleaming red from the cliff-fires.

And one thing more. There, at the far side of the nest, lay a small, naked boy. Warmed by the smoky fumes from the vents, he needed no covers beyond the pair of large feathers that lay upon his chest. Though he looked like a human child of five or six, he had only just hatched. That was clear from the temporary freckles that covered his entire body below his neck, marking the places where, as an adult, he would be able to sprout feathers at will. Unlike his hooked nose, hairy forearms, and sharply pointed toenails, those freckles would soon disappear.

"Get him!" whispered Obba, seizing his bow. "I'll watch fer danger."

"Ye mean the mother?" Ossyn shoved his brother jokingly. "Or them fire plants?"

"Move it," growled Obba. But just in case, before he looked skyward, he glanced behind himself for any sign of flames.

Meanwhile, his brother untied a cloth sack from around his waist. A plume of smoke blew past, but he stifled his cough. Stealthily, he crept across the nest, until he stood right over the eagleboy. His smirk faded as he gazed down at the child. "Do ye really think he'll pay us all that coin fer jest a scrawny liddle birdboy?"

"Do it, will ye?" Obba whispered urgently. He was watching the billowing plumes of smoke overhead, aiming his arrow at every new movement.

His brother nodded. Swiftly, he grabbed the sleeping child by the ankle, lifted him high, and plunged him into the sack.

But not before the boy awoke. With eagle-fast reflexes, he swung out his arm and caught hold of the sack's rim. Twisting, he freed one leg, let out a shrieking cry, and slashed sharp toenails across his attacker's face.

"Ghaaaa!" Ossyn howled in pain. His hand flew to his cheek, already starting to drip with blood. He dropped the sack.

Almost before he hit the nest, the eagleboy wriggled free. His yellow-rimmed eyes flashed angrily, and he jumped to his feet. His mouth opened to shriek again.

Just then a heavy fist slammed into the eagleboy's head. He reeled, lost his balance, and fell into a heap amid the feathers.

"So thar," spat Obba, rubbing his fist. "He'll sleep plenty good now." He rounded angrily on his younger brother. "Look what ye did, ye clumsy troll! Quick now, stuff him in yer sack. Afore the mother comes flyin' back."

Cursing, Ossyn jammed the unconscious boy into the sack. He slung it over his shoulder, then halted. "Wait, now. What about the stick? White Hands said there'd be some kind o' stick, right here wid the child."

Obba picked up a branch and hurled it at him. "Ye bloody fool! This whole blasted nest is made o' sticks! Hundreds an' hundreds o' sticks. Jest grab one an' shove it in the bag. Afore I shove it in yer ear."

"But what if it's not the right—"

A loud screech sliced through the night. Both men froze.

"She's back!"

"Hush, ye fool. I still got two arrows." Obba crouched down against the wall of the nest. He nocked an arrow, its point of black obsidian gleaming dully in the light of the flame vents. Slowly, he pulled the bowstring taut, waiting for the huge wings to come into range. Sweat dribbled down his brow, stinging his eyes. But still he waited.

"Shoot, will ye?"

He let fly. The arrow whizzed up into the smoky sky and disappeared. The eaglewoman veered, screeched louder than before, and plunged straight at them.

"Bloody dark! Can't see to aim."

"Quick, out o' the nest! Maybe we can—"

A sudden gust of wind blew them backward, as a great shadow darkened the night and talons slashed like daggers above their heads. Ossyn screamed as one talon sliced his arm. He staggered backward, dropping the sack on the downy branches. Blood gushed from his torn limb.

The eaglewoman, eyes ablaze, swooped down upon him. Her wide wings flapped so that she hung just above this man who had dared to try to steal her child. Whimpering, Ossyn looked up into those golden orbs and saw no mercy there. With a wild screech that rattled the very timbers of the nest, she raised her talons and—

Flipped suddenly onto her side, thrown over by the force of the black-tipped arrow that had just slammed into her ribs. Her lower wing dragged across the branches, sweeping up Ossyn's cowering body. Together, they rolled across the nest, burst through the rim, and tumbled down onto the rocks below. Their shrieks echoed, pulsing in the air.

Then . . . silence. Only the hiss and sputter of flame vents rose from the cliffs.

On wobbly legs, Obba dropped his bow and stepped over to the edge. Looking down into the blackness below, he shook his head. "Ye clumsy fool . . ." He stayed there a long moment, resting his chin on a barkless branch. At last he turned toward the sack that held the limp body of the eagleboy. And slowly, he grinned.

"Well, well, me liddle brother. Guess I'll jest have to spend yer share o' the pay."

He bent to pick up the sack, then stopped. Remembering Ossyn's point about the stick, he grabbed a straight, sturdy branch from the floor of the nest and thrust it in with the eagleboy. Then he swung the sack over his shoulder, climbed over the side, and skidded down the wall of interwoven branches. Finally, his boots thudded against solid rock.

Obba stood on top of the cliffs, checking warily for flame vents. And, even more, those pesky fire plants! Then he spied what he wanted—a spiral-shaped tower of rocks on the ridge of cliffs—and off he strode.

Now fer the easy part, he told himself. No more crawling or climbing! All he needed to do was follow the ridgeline to that tower. Why, he could almost just ignore the putrid flame vents . . . and pretend he was out for an evening stroll. Like some village elder, maybe. An elder who would soon be very, very rich.

So why not enjoy himself a bit? He stopped, dropped the sack, and uncorked a small tin flask. Firebrew, the locals called it. With good reason! He took a sizable swig, feeling the burn go right down his gullet. And then another.

Aye, that's better.

He burped and grinned again, this time a bit crookedly. Peering down at the sack on the rocks, he thought it might have stirred a little. One swift kick with his boot took care of that. The boy inside groaned, and the sack lay still as stone.

Again he took up the load. Strange, walking seemed a bit trickier now—as if some little tremors were making the rocks wiggle under his feet. No cause for worry, though. As long as he kept his distance from the steep edge of the cliffs, he'd be fine.

Now he could see the flecks of green flame at the base of the spiral tower. Just like White Hands had said. That old schemer sure did have this whole thing figured—the cliffs, the child, even the eaglewoman. Obba nodded grimly, patting the strap of his empty quiver. And he recalled the final instructions: *Just bring the child through the portal of green flames, say the chant, and let my power guide you home.*

A pair of sizzling fingers sprang out of a crack and clutched at his boot. Obba sidestepped, nearly tripping. Those tremors again! The whole ridge seemed to wobble under his feet. With a glance at the spiral tower, he wondered how it stayed upright in all this swaying.

Ah, but he had other things to think about now. More important things, like his payment. He could almost feel the heft of those coins, hear them clinking in his palm—his share as well as Ossyn's. Ha! *An' he called me woodenbrain.*

All of a sudden he stopped short. There was the tower, all right, just ahead. Looking taller than he'd guessed—as tall as a full-grown oak tree. And it seemed more rickety than ever. But what was that? Moving in front of the green flames?

Obba blinked. Someone else was there!

He stared at the figure, dark as the smoky night, as it moved closer to the spiral tower of rocks. When it approached the flickering green flames at the tower's base, he could see at last what it was.

A woman! Young. Peasant stock, by the looks of her shredded robe and scraggly red hair. Obba smacked his lips. Now things were really looking up! Maybe he'd have a bit of fun before heading back through the portal with his prize.

Quietly, he slunk closer, ducking behind a blackened boulder. He studied his prey. She was facing the green flames, with her back to him. Probably warming her hands. Suddenly he roared and charged straight at the poor woman. Startled, she screamed and whirled around, nearly losing the bundled infant she held in her arms.

Just a few paces away, he halted. With a lopsided leer, he dropped his sack, which hit the ground with a thud. Then, arms open wide, he rasped, "C'mere, me liddle flower." His crooked teeth glowed green. "Time fer gettin' warm on this cold night."

She shook her wild red mane. "Go away!" she cried in the Common Tongue, though with an accent that Obba hadn't heard before. "Before you meet the greater cold of death."

"So yer a bold one, eh? Jest how I likes me flowers."

He moved closer, knowing that she was trapped between him and the tower. Even if she did know that the green fire was really a portal, she wasn't likely to try to escape that way, unless she knew the special chant to protect a baby. By the wizard's beard, this was going to be easy!

She scowled at him savagely. "Come no closer, man! Or I shall . . . I shall . . ."

"Shall what, me blossom?" For the first time, he noticed her eyes: fiery orange, upturned at the corners. Flamelon eyes. *So, she isn't human at all. Jest one o' them fire-people.*

"Now c'mere, afore ye gets me angry." He stooped to grab a rock. "So I don't have to hurt yer liddle one."

"No!" She clutched her bundle more tightly.

Obba advanced on her. "Time fer pickin' flowers, heh heh."

"Go away, I said!" Trembling, she raised her left hand, as her fingertips began to glow like fire coals. Bright orange they turned, sizzling and crackling with growing heat, preparing to hurl a firebolt into the very heart of her attacker. Her arm straightened, her fingers pointed, when—

Obba's rock flew into her forearm, cracking her bones. She cried out in pain as the glow faded from her fingers. Stumbling backward, she fell, dropping her baby on the ground. She crawled toward the shrieking bundle.

But Obba got there first. He lifted the infant high in the air, out of her reach. His eyes burned like flame vents. "Now, now there. Lemme jest quiet yer liddle one."

"Stop!" Still on the ground, she kicked at him. But he just stepped aside, chuckling, as the baby in his hands wailed loudly.

Obba planted his feet, ready to smash this noisy creature against the rocks of the ridge. "Yer goin' to crack right open now, jest like an egg."

"Nooo!"

His arms tensed. He started to throw.

At that instant, something hard rammed into him. Not a rock—but a head. The head of the eagleboy!

Obba staggered backward and fell hard against the tower. The baby slipped from his grasp. Springing, the woman caught her son and rolled aside.

The eagleboy, his cheek swollen and bruised, screeched angrily. Heedless of his much smaller size, all he wanted was to attack this man who had taken him from the nest on this terrible night. He braced himself to pounce—when a sudden rumble from above made him freeze.

The tower of rocks swayed, buckled, and split apart. All at once, the entire top section came tumbling down. Rocks larger than Obba himself fell toward the people below. There was no time to cry out, let alone escape. The eagleboy held his breath; the woman on the ground squeezed her baby for the last time.

Something pricked the eagleboy's shoulder. A talon! It closed on his shoulder, grasping him firmly without slicing his skin. He looked up anxiously, relieved to see his mother's face again.

But it wasn't his mother! In a blur, as the boulders came cascading down, he saw a powerful eagleman swoop just above him. One talon held his shoulder, while the other grabbed the huddled woman and her child. The eagleman's great wings carried them to safety, whooshing like the wind.

With a great, grinding crash, the spiral tower collapsed. Shards of stone and clouds of soot exploded into the sky, merging with the plumes of smoke. The rescued people escaped by the breadth of a single feather. Obba wasn't so fortunate: His dying, anguished thought was of all those precious coins he would never get to see.

The eagleman veered, flapped once, then set them down on a broad, flat stone at the edge of the cliffs. He landed a few paces away. For a moment he just gazed at them, his golden eyes aglow—not from the flickering fires all around, but from a far stranger fire within.

The eagleboy and the woman stared back at him in silence, their faces full of wonder. Even the small baby fell hushed.

All of a sudden the eagleman's body began to shimmer. His huge wings faded, then shrank into arms. The feathers on his chest swiftly melted away. The eagleboy shrieked in surprise, while the woman's astonished eyes opened wide.

Before them now stood a man. Indeed, a very old man. His tangled, white beard fell below his waist; his ancient eyes seemed to be laughing and crying at the same time; his nose seemed almost as hooked as an eagle's beak. He wore a long robe of azure blue, flecked with runes that shimmered like mist in morning light. Upon his head sat a miserable, half-crushed hat, whose pointed tip leaned to one side.

The woman gasped, bringing her hand to her mouth. "I know you," she muttered. "You are—"

Instantly he raised his hand in warning. "Speak no more, my dear. Not here." His dark eyes roamed over the ridge, hovering briefly on the smoking pile of rubble—all that remained of the spiral tower of rocks. "Eyes may be watching, ears may be listening. Even now."

He leaned toward her, one of his hands twirling strands of his beard. "You know me, yes. And you know that I have come all the way here for good reason. To save the life of someone most precious—not just to me, but to the entire world of Avalon."

His eyes, suddenly sorrowful, moved to the eagleboy. "Take care of him, will you, good woman? Protect him even as you will protect your own son. For he has lost his own mother on this dreadful night."

The eagleboy winced at these words. His whole body trembled, but still he tried to stand up straight. Gently, the woman placed her hand on his shoulder. He shook it off, without even turning to look at her. Rather, he kept his yellow-rimmed eyes focused on the old man.

Doffing his misshapen hat, the elder bent down on one knee. His long, hooked nose almost touched the eagleboy's. "Your name is Scree, is it not?"

Stiffly, he nodded.

"You are destined to play a great role in this world, my lad. A very great role. There isn't much I can do to help you, I'm afraid. But at least I can give you this."

Deftly, he plucked a single white hair from his beard. He held it in the palm of his hand, where it fluttered in the night air. Then he cocked his head ever so slightly—and the hair suddenly changed color, darkening to reddish brown. At the same time, it thickened and lengthened until it resembled a stick of wood with a knotted top.

And it kept right on growing. Thicker and longer it grew, right before the amazed eagleboy, until it was a full-size staff, gnarled and twisted along its whole length. Strange runes carved on its sides glowed mysteriously. The old man paused a moment to study the staff, turning it slowly in his hand. Then, with a sigh, he tapped its knotted top. The runes shimmered and vanished completely.

"Your staff." He took the eagleboy's small hand and placed it on the wood below the handle. "It has served me well, over many long years. And now, I hope, it will serve you."

The eagleboy's fingers curled around the staff. Seeing this, the old man's bushy white brows drew together. "Promise me, now, that you will keep this staff safe. It is precious—more precious than you can imagine."

The boy nodded.

"Good. The word of an eagleboy is worth a hundred wizard's spells."

The boy's shoulders straightened. He took the staff, hefted it, then brought it close to his chest.

The elder's expression brightened for an instant, then turned somber again. "Are you too young to have heard of the Dark Prophecy?"

He just frowned.

The old man bent even closer and whispered into his ear. Slowly, the eagleboy's eyebrows arched in amazement. The woman could hear only a few clipped phrases: "For the child . . . terrible, terrible danger . . . when, at last, the wizard's true heir . . ."

At last, his face grave, the old man arose. He placed one hand behind his hip and straightened his creaky back. "Ah, to be an eagle all the time," he said wistfully. "Flying is far more pleasurable than standing or strutting about! And better on the back, too."

Once more he fixed his gaze on the eagleboy. "This is no small task I leave you, my young friend. It will be lonely. And dangerous. And long—as long as seventeen years. But this, at least, I can promise. One day, you shall have great wings of your own. And then you shall fly! High and far, you shall fly."

One last time he ran his finger down the gnarled staff. Then he turned back to the woman. Bending over her baby, he asked, "A boy?"

She nodded.

"And his name?"

Her cheeks flushed. "Tamwyn."

"Hmmmm, yes. Tamwyn." He stroked his beard in thought. "His future is much more clouded, I fear."

At this, the woman stiffened.

"His name means Dark Flame in the language of your people, does it not?"

Hesitantly, she gave a nod.

The old man sighed. "A fitting name for a night such as this. But I wonder, will it fit the boy as well? Will he bring to Avalon the light of flame or the dark of night?"

He reached toward the infant and placed the tip of his bony finger upon the tiny brow. "Unlike your new brother, you will have no wings of your own. And yet, perhaps . . . you might find your own way to fly."

Smiling ever so slightly, he took a step back so that he stood on the very edge of the cliff. In a ringing voice, he said: "Farewell, my good people. I doubt we shall ever meet again." He paused, viewing them with eagle-bright eyes. "Yet I shall still be with you."

Once again the woman put her hand on the eagleboy's shoulder. And this time he let it stay.

"And now I must go. To other worlds, other times." Just to himself, the old man whispered, "Such is the fate of Olo Eopia."

"But . . ." the woman protested. "How will you go?" She waved a hand toward the massive pile of rubble that had buried the vent of green flames. "The portal is gone."

He didn't seem to hear. Shimmering light glowed all about his body, and he transformed again into a great eagle. Wings spread wide, he leaped into the air and surged upward. Higher and higher he climbed—then suddenly veered back toward the cliffs. With a screeching cry that rolled across the ridge, he plunged toward the smoking stack of rubble.

The eagleboy shrieked in fright, as the woman's hand squeezed his shoulder.

Just before hitting the rocks, the eagleman tucked his immense wings behind his back. He shot downward, gaining speed. But he did not crash. Instead, he dissolved straight into the stones, leaving only a whoosh of wind . . . and then silence.

Part

I

1 · Land of Bells

CAREFUL, YOU STUPID SLUG!"

Master Lott planted his fists on his flabby hips, jangling the bells on his belt. He glared up at the young man climbing the ladder. "You'll drop your load again—for the fifth time today. And you'll never get to the rooftop at that pace. You addle-brained ass!"

Tamwyn grunted, the only reply he could manage. His mouth felt as dry as a desert lizard's back. Slowly, he climbed up another rung on the wobbly ladder—hard enough without having to hold a huge bale of thatch on his shoulder. And a hammer and a sack of nails in his hand.

The ladder suddenly shifted, creaking under all the weight. Tamwyn held tight, but glanced down at the worn vine lashings that held the thing together. They looked ready to burst. *Just hold on*, he pleaded silently. *Don't break on me now. This is my last load. My last bale.*

He tried to shake the hair out of his eyes. *And my last day as a roof thatcher. That's a promise.*

What a mistake he'd made agreeing to work for Lott today—

and the unending insults were the least of it. His back ached. His legs throbbed. Countless spears of thatch poked him in the neck and cheek. And those blasted lice . . .

He growled at the thought. Lice. Unlike most other creatures he'd met in his travels, they never listened. Never spoke to him. Never did *anything* but bite. They were just tiny versions of ogres, they were. Why, if another one crawled into his ear, he'd hurl it all the way to the next realm! By the bark of the Great Tree, he would.

"Wake up, you worthless wastrel!" barked Lott from below, his enormous belly quivering. "Finish the job, will you?"

Tamwyn started to climb again. But after just two more rungs he paused, panting. Though lanky and strong for a seventeen-year-old, he felt nearly spent after a whole long day hauling heavy bales up this ladder. Let alone all those ridge beams, support poles, and rolls of twine. Everything needed to put a roof on this half-built stone house.

"Come on, you mindless muddlehead! My five-year-old daughter could've finished this job hours ago." Lott chewed on his chubby lower lip, suddenly curious about something. "Just how old are you, anyway?"

"Oh, er . . . eighteen," lied Tamwyn. He'd learned long ago that revealing he was born in the Year of Darkness got him only fretful looks and suspicion—and, in one village south of here, a dagger thrown at his back. Although the year had long passed, and light had returned at its end, some people, even normally peaceful priestesses and priests from the Society of the Whole, were still scouring Avalon's seven root-realms for any sign of the child of the Dark Prophecy. Why, he'd even heard that the elves in Woodroot had offered a big reward to anyone who found—and killed—the Dark child. So anyone born in that year was at risk.

Tamwyn gulped, despite his dry throat.

"Are you sure about that?" pressed the suspicious roof thatcher. His eyes, sunk deep into the rolls of flab on his cheeks like a pair of almonds in a mound of dough, scrutinized Tamwyn.

"Y-yes, Master Lout. I mean . . . Louse. No, Lott!"

The thatcher's face turned as red as a ripe apple. "However old you are, you're a dim-witted dunce. A rascally rogue! And if you don't finish soon, you won't get paid."

"I mean to finish," grumbled Tamwyn.

"Then do it."

Tamwyn rolled his stiff neck. "Just let me stretch a moment, will you?"

Lott stamped his foot impatiently. But Tamwyn ignored him, trying without success to loosen his neck.

The young man sighed, feeling weighed down by more than the bale on his back. This was about as far away as he could get from his work as a wilderness guide—work that he greatly enjoyed. And not just because it took him to the wildest parts of Stoneroot, a realm so vast that in seven years of walking its rocky hills he'd covered less than half of it. No, there was something else that kept him roaming this realm—something that was, at once, more alluring than the scent of honeygrass sprinkled with dew, and more frightening than the look of an old troll's eye.

Finding Scree. The work of guiding people through uncharted parts of the realm allowed Tamwyn to keep searching for his lost brother. But since the start of the drought, fewer people had been venturing into the wilderness. And so, until he could guide again, he'd been trying out other kinds of work.

Such as weaving thatch. Yesterday, when he'd wandered into this village, he'd assumed that by helping Lott he could learn the work of a thatcher. As it turned out, all he'd done was the work of a freight ox. Except that even a freight ox was smart enough not to climb ladders.

Tamwyn licked his dry lower lip, tasting the bitter mix of salt and soot. He was thirstier now than he'd been even in the hottest days of summer. Hang the drought! Right now, he'd give anything to be drinking from the water gourd that hung from his belt—but that was empty again. Or even better . . . from a clearwater stream, one that tumbled through lush grasses. Or through white lilies, like that stream he'd found last year by the—

"Move!" Lott thundered again from below, making all three of his chins jiggle. "That thatch won't carry itself to the top."

"Right, Master Lott."

"And don't you drop another bale, or you'll lose not just your pay, but your supper." He spoke that last word with something close to reverence; his chins turned up in a triple grin. "The wife promised me grilled rabbit tonight, since I've been working so hard on this roof."

Tamwyn bit his tongue.

"Think I'll just check on her right now," Lott announced. "Could be she's needing some help in the kitchen. Mmmm . . . grilled rabbit." He smacked his lips, then shot his laborer a murderous glance. "And by the time I get back, you'd better be done."

"Right." The very mention of food had reminded Tamwyn that he wasn't just thirsty, but hungry as well.

Oh, for a fistful of fresh moonberries, all plump and juicy! But grilled rabbit . . . he could almost smell it, simmering on the fire, dripping with juices. Like any bear or hawk he'd seen in the wilderness, he didn't mind eating the meat of another creature—just as long as the food had been killed swiftly, prepared without waste, and eaten with the usual words of thanks. He almost grinned, wondering whether a hungry bear ever paused to say the Drumadian Grace.

Before he could eat and drink, though, he'd have to finish. He'd promised Lott that he'd do the job. And if Scree had taught him anything, it was that promises matter. Eaglefolk were nothing if not true to their word! Except that Scree himself had promised, on the day their mother died, that the two brothers would never be separated.

Tamwyn wiped the sleeve of his brown tunic across his brow, brushing away whatever had made his eyes water. He shifted the bale on his shoulder and climbed up another rung. And another. Several flakes of soot settled on his eyelashes, but he ignored them. At least they weren't lice.

Just three more rungs to go. Then I can dump this load for good.

Shaking with the weight, Tamwyn heard the jangle of the sack of nails in his hand. Like the bells, small and large, that chimed and clanged and rattled throughout the villages of Stoneroot, there was something oddly comforting in that sound. Tamwyn couldn't explain why, but he felt grateful that he'd spent so many years—ever since he'd lost Scree—in the land of bells. That was one of Stoneroot's most recognizable qualities: as traditional as the houses made with roofs of thatch and walls of flatrock; as noticeable as the northern mountains that could be seen from almost any part of the realm.

Bells. They hung from the necks of plow horses, and even from the plows themselves. They jangled with the steps of pigs, sheep, and goats. They topped the stone houses, barns, weather vanes, and doors to cellars that held great vats of brewing beer. And they even dangled from the belts of people such as Lott. And Tamwyn himself, who wore a small quartz bell on the hip of his tunic . . . a bell that rang steadily whenever he ran through forests and vales, as free as a feather on a breeze.

Twisting his head slightly against the bale, he peered down at the village. With so many identical houses—all built with the same flatrock walls, all in straight rows—the village resembled a field of big, squarish pumpkins. Even more so because it was now autumn, and like everywhere else in Stoneroot, the rocks were turning their seasonal shades of orange and gold. Even way up north, in the upper reaches of Stoneroot, where the drought seemed to be sapping the colors out of everything, the rocks still changed with the seasons.

Tamwyn bit his lip, wondering. If the rocks of Stoneroot changed colors every autumn, winter, spring, and summer, would the same be true in Avalon's other realms? All seven of those realms were roots of the same Great Tree, to be sure . . . but whether they, too, changed every season was a mystery. Would streams and ponds change color in Waterroot? How about the dark caverns of Shadowroot? And the legendary trees of Woodroot?

He shook his head. Trees! Now *that* was really difficult to imagine. The very idea of a tree changing colors!

With a sigh, he thought of how little he knew about his own realm, let alone the others. Even after seven years of exploring the wildest parts of Stoneroot, looking for Scree, he'd found no sign at all of his brother . . . and no end to the surprises of this realm. Not only in its varied landscape, but in its creatures, too—from the hill-tall giants of the high peaks to the tiny mite faeries whose largest village could fit on his thumbnail.

Just how big Stoneroot really was, he could only guess. All he knew was that he could walk a full month in any direction from most parts of the realm and never reach the sea of mist that hugged its shores. And if it was so enormous, as just one root of the Great Tree . . . think how incredibly vast the Tree itself must be—combining the seven root-realms, the trunk that had barely even been explored, the magical portals inside the heartwood, whatever branches might exist, and the mysterious stars on high. Such size, such scale, was almost beyond imagining.

"Are you dead or alive, you stupid slug? Here you are, just where I left you."

Lott's voice jolted Tamwyn back to his job. He heaved himself up another rung. Only two more to go. *Uuugggh.* Just one left. He lifted his thigh, set his bare foot on the last rung, and—

Oww! A louse bit the back of his ear. Furious, Tamwyn shut his eyes, trying to hold back his temper. *Why'd you do that?* he demanded with his thoughts—the same silent language that helped him talk with almost any creature. *I'm not your next meal.*

The louse responded with another bite, this time on his ear-lobe.

Stop, roared Tamwyn's inner voice. *By the Thousand Groves, stop!* It took all his concentration to keep himself from dropping the bale. He couldn't even reach up to rub his sore ear. All he could think about was climbing that very last step. Then he'd dump this cursed load—and promptly break the Drumadians' first law, the one about never murdering a fellow creature. And enjoy it, every instant.

He straightened his leg. The ladder creaked. Suddenly the rung under his foot snapped in two, pitching Tamwyn forward into the wall. His nose and cheek smashed into the stone. Desperately, he clutched at the ladder, and then at the bale that was slipping off his shoulder.

Too late! The bale plunged to the ground and exploded at Lott's feet in a black cloud of soot.

"Fool of a . . . of a . . . of a *fool!* An acorn has more brains than you." His whole body quivering, Lott glared up at him with eyes that could have set thatch aflame.

"I'm sorry, Master Lott." Tamwyn placed both feet on a lower rung. "I didn't think—"

"Didn't think. That's the truth!"

"No, the ladder . . ." Tamwyn pointed down to the broken rung. But as he moved his arm, the sack of nails hit his knee and knocked loose. Nails flew in every direction, smacking the wall of the house, bouncing off the ladder, and pouring down on Lott's head. Tamwyn grabbed for the sack, and in doing so dropped the hammer. He bobbled it, dropped it again, then barely managed to catch it between his foot and the rung.

Lott tore a handful of nails out of his hair and shook his fist at Tamwyn. "You're a bloody blight! A poisonous plague!"

He hurled the nails straight at Tamwyn. But as the young man ducked, he moved off the hammer. The tool plunged downward—and slammed onto Lott's plump foot.

"Aaaaowww!" bellowed the thatcher, hopping around in pain. He tried to bend over to hold his injured foot, but his prodigious belly kept him from reaching it. All he could do was hop on one foot, curse, sputter, squeal, and groan. Spittle drooled down his triple chin.

Awkwardly, he stumbled off toward his own house at the other end of the village. "I'll be back, you . . . you stupid, sluggish, scramble-brained scalawag! And when I return, you'd just better have that bale back up on top. Or I'll dice you up and feed you to the fleas!"

Tamwyn kicked one foot angrily at the air. But the motion jolted the ladder, and he almost fell off. Cursing to himself, he didn't even hear the gentle ringing of the bell on his hip.

2 · Banished

STILL SEETHING, TAMWYN TOOK A SWIPE at the louse that had bitten his ear. But it had already dropped off. *Curse that beast. And this ladder. And this job!*

Grabbing the upper end of the ladder, he pulled himself up to the wooden platform at the edge of the roof. There he sat, legs dangling, and stared down at the burst bale of thatch on the ground. His fists clenched in anger. Why should he clean up that fat man's mess? And why should he stay around here any longer?

That was the answer: Just leave. If he set off running east, sometime during the night he'd reach the coastal marshes. Though he hadn't been there for a few years, he remembered vividly those flowing pools of watergrain. Despite the drought, there should be at least *some* water there. More than he'd found in weeks. And elf berries, too. A bit overripe, maybe, given the season—but still good eating.

He ran a hand through his straight black hair, the locks so long that they reached almost to his shoulders, and pulled out some clumps of thatch. And he sighed, knowing he wouldn't be eating any elf berries tonight. No, he'd be staying right here until he finished the job. Not because he wanted to. And not because Lott deserved it.

Because he'd given his word.

He gave his knee a slap. If only he'd never stopped in this runty little village. Much as he loved to wander the landscape, finding surprises on the way . . . sometimes those surprises were like stepping into a pit of angry gnomes.

All right then, better get started before it's too dark. He knew well that these days many creatures roamed the lands after starset. Whether they were just homeless spirits walking aimlessly, or gobsken looking for some beer to steal—or some trouble to start— they were usually worth avoiding.

First, though, I'll need to fix this blasted ladder. He reached down to his waist, feeling for the coiled length of vine he always carried on his tunic belt, right beside his dagger. As he unraveled the vine, his hand brushed against the quartz bell on his hip, which sounded its gentle, earthen tone.

Just then, an owl hooted softly from the tall harkenfruit tree just beyond the village. Tamwyn stopped and looked up—right into the starset, that magnificent burst of golden light from the stars that marked the day's end. Bright beams traced the tree, illuminating every branch and twig so that they themselves looked like trees of light. Thin leaves shimmered in the breeze, glowing gold. And beyond the tree, high peaks on the horizon lifted, ridge upon ridge, like rows of waves on a shining sea.

Even the village, its gray stones catching the light, seemed at this moment bejeweled. And something more, Tamwyn realized.

Built from whatever materials the land offered freely—stone and wood and thatch—this village simply belonged here. It was rooted in this place, as much as the harkenfruit tree. As much as the nearby fields of ripened oats and barley, the stacks of summer hay, the barrels of dark brown beer in almost every cellar, the shrine to Elen built by Drumadian followers, and the large piles of compost and dung. As much as the litter of tiny pigs over by the common barn who lay sprawled on top of their enormous mother, using her as a living bed.

The aromas of barley, dung, and pigs wove into the air, mixing with the smell of thatch, for they, too, belonged. Just like the square iron bells set on the ridge beam of every house. The owl hooting from the tree. The rough-hewn stones of the village walls.

Tamwyn cocked his head thoughtfully. Everything around him—this village, this landscape, even this little quartz bell on his hip—all seemed to fit. To belong.

Unlike Tamwyn himself. He wiped some sooty thatch off his brow. Where *did* he belong, after all?

Swinging his legs at the edge of the roof, he looked again at the shining peaks in the distance. Maybe he just belonged out there, in those woods and fields and ridges where he loved to run. Clumsy as he felt in a village like this . . . something *happened* when he ran free, leaping over stones and streams.

Something magical.

Craning his stiff neck, he lifted his gaze to the stars. So many of them—and so beautiful. He traced the outlines of some favorite constellations: There was Pegasus, ears back and eyes ablaze, soaring on high. And the Twisted Tree, reaching its long branches across the shadowed sky.

He smiled, wondering what it would be like to run—really run—among those stars, weaving through the clusters of light as if they were groves of trees. Oh, to stride across those starry fields!

Even as he watched them now, the stars dimmed, bringing on the night. While their brightness faded, their individual positions grew more clear, making it easier to connect them into constellations. Tamwyn wondered, as he'd done so often, what the stars of Avalon really were . . . and whether someone, someday, could find a way to explore them.

He pursed his lips, thinking. Nobody knew why the stars dimmed at the end of every day, after that final flash of golden light. Nor why they swelled bright again every morning. Just as nobody knew why, here in Stoneroot, the stars shone brighter than in any other realm—something he'd learned from wandering bards. How different from Shadowroot, where the stars didn't even shine at all . . . All these questions added up to the great unsolved riddle of the stars' true nature—something that had puzzled people through all the ages of Avalon.

Many a night, as Tamwyn peered up at the stars from a sheltered glade or a mossy rock, he'd pondered such things. The stars always seemed so distant, so mysterious. Frightening somehow, and yet alluring. Almost as if they called to him.

How he'd love to travel there. Yes, and to all the other realms of Avalon. He'd find the right portals and travel through them to other lands, other peoples, other trails that he could run. Perhaps he'd even find some way to explore upper Avalon—the trunk itself, and whatever lay beyond! Why, maybe he'd even discover other kinds of creatures there . . . creatures that no one in the Seven Realms knew existed. He could be a great explorer—just like Krystallus Eopia, the famous son of Merlin.

Ouch! He winced from the louse biting his forearm.

With a scowl, he flicked away the little scoundrel. Some explorer he was! Why, today he'd ventured all the way to the topmost rung of Lott's rickety ladder. And even battled some man-eating lice.

His legs kicked at the air by the roof's edge. Truth was, the life he was leading couldn't have been any more different from that of Krystallus. Or from his own shadowy beginnings. He bit his lip, recalling his very first memory—those vague, confused images of a fiery mountain, an old man with the wings of an eagle . . . and a woman's warm embrace.

He shook his head. How could he even be sure that memory was real? More and more, that night on the fiery mountain seemed just a dream. A twisted dream. He hadn't even dared to talk about it with Scree, not after everything they'd been through, although it hovered between them like a ghoul—always present, yet always invisible.

Not that this unspoken memory had spoiled their time together—no, far from it. Scree and Tam (as his brother called him) had ranged widely, exploring much of Fireroot's volcanic lands. They'd climbed peaks, crawled through lava tunnels, slid down glass-smooth slopes of black obsidian, hurled fistfuls of ash at each other's heads, wrestled among spouting flame vents . . . and so much more. Just as long as the boys avoided any contact with the warlike flamelons, and returned home to their cave by dark, they'd had plenty of freedom. And they'd also had a genuine family, thanks to the woman who was mother to them both: for Scree, by adoption; for Tamwyn, by birth. She had always been there to welcome them home, her orange eyes aglow.

Until the day she died and left them with nothing but each other.

And then, seven years ago, they had lost even that.

Tamwyn blinked at the stars, which seemed suddenly blurry.

What good did it do to think about that? Scree was gone now—maybe even dead. And even if he was still alive, he'd been impossible to find.

Still, Tamwyn couldn't keep himself from wondering . . . or searching. That was why he'd spent most of the last seven years wandering across Stoneroot—over rocky hills, meadows, marshes, forests, and snow fields—looking for any sign of Scree. Though he'd found nothing yet, hope still burned inside him. If he just ran enough trails, however remote or dangerous, maybe somehow he'd—

"Eehee, eehee, look there. A real live man made of charcoal! Darker than a dead torch on a moonless night, he is. Eehee, hoohoohoo, ahahaha."

The raucous laugh cut short Tamwyn's thoughts. He looked down from the roof platform to see someone standing on the broken bale of thatch, peering up at him. It might have been a man—except this person stood only half a man's height and was as thin as a ridgepole. He had very large hands (almost as big as his head), long arms, and circular eyebrows that went all the way around a pair of silver-colored eyes. For clothes, he wore just a sack-shaped tunic, a belt with a slingshot, and a woven red headband.

A hoolah, thought Tamwyn, shaking his head grimly. Just what he didn't need right now. Hoolahs had no sense of decency—and basically no sense at all. Wherever they went, they brought mischief.

Tamwyn moved to the edge of the roof and waved his hand, as if shaking off some lice. "Go away, hoolah. I've got work to do."

The skinny little fellow waved his own oversized hand in return. "What's your work, grimy man? Taking a bath in a tub of soot? Eehee, eehee, just to get yourself cleaner? Eeheeyahahahaha." He slapped his thighs in laughter. "Soot. Cleaner. That's how dirty you are! Eeehee, ha-ha-ha."

Tamwyn growled, his temper rising. "Get out of here, I say." He grabbed Lott's heavy wooden bucket and waved it above the hoolah's head. "Or I'll drop this and more right on top of you."

Before the hoolah could reply, someone else stepped out of the deepening shadows beside the house. It was a girl, very young—and very portly. Round as a boulder she was, with at least two chins and fleshy jowls that spilled over the copper bells sewn onto her collar.

Tamwyn caught his breath. Lott's daughter!

As she waddled over to the base of the ladder, the hoolah jumped off the bale and slipped into the shadows. Not far away, though. Tamwyn could still see the silver gleam of his eyes by the corner of the house.

The girl slapped the broken ladder with her chubby hand. "My papa says to warn you that, that . . ." She stopped to suck her knuckles for a moment. "That he's . . ." Suck, suck. "Comin' back soon. Just as soon as he finishes . . ." Suck, suck. "Eatin' his brambleberry pie."

Tamwyn's eyes narrowed. He was just about to tell her exactly what her papa could do with his pie, when a pair of new voices rasped from below.

"Well, well, now. See here!" *Hic.* "A cutesy li'l girl."

"Aye, an' she's out here," *hic-cic,* "all alone."

Tamwyn's heart pounded. Gobsken! Half drunk, too, from the sound of it—probably from stealing someone's barley beer.

Sure enough, as he watched from the rooftop, two hulking figures with hunched shoulders and very long arms approached the empty house. One of them, the bigger of the two, was rubbing his hands together and making a throaty, cackling sound.

"C'mere, li'l girl." The gobsken stretched his arms out toward her. "Lemme see yer pretty face."

The girl shrieked. She backed up against the stone wall of the house, quivering in fright. "Leave me alone," she whimpered, sucking her knuckles. "Or my papa will . . ." Suck, suck, suck. "Will come."

"Ooh," said the big gobsken in mock fear. "I'm muchly scared." He cackled and took a step closer.

"Meself, I'm just," *hic*, "feelin' hungry," replied his friend. "An' this girl could make us a tasty meal."

Tamwyn leaped up and grasped the top of the ladder. "Back off, you two!" he shouted.

Surprised, the two gobsken froze. Just as they looked up, Tamwyn started to descend. Swiftly, he stepped on the top rung. Except there *was* no top rung. With an agonized cry, he lurched backward, his arms flailing. Off the ladder he fell—

Right on top of the bigger gobsken. They slammed into the ground, sending up a cloud of thatch and soot. Tamwyn rolled off and regained his feet—just as the other gobsken roared and hurled himself at this attacker from the sky.

But as Tamwyn struggled to get his balance, he tripped on the broken bale of thatch. He sprawled sideways. The gobsken flew right past, and crashed headfirst into the stone wall.

Terrified, the girl shrieked again. She kicked at one of the gobsken, but her blow landed smack on Tamwyn's shin. The kick hurt, to be sure . . . but not as much as the hysterical laughter from the hoolah still hiding by the side of the house.

Tamwyn whirled around, just as angry at the hoolah as he was at the two attackers. But as he turned, his shoulder struck the ladder, which slid along the wall and bumped against the wooden bucket sitting on the edge of the roof. The bucket wobbled for an instant, then came tumbling down.

Right on the girl's head! She promptly fell over, unconscious—hitting the dirt, facedown, with the force of a fallen tree. Seeing this, the hoolah laughed harder than ever.

Meanwhile, the two gobsken rose on shaky legs. The bigger one grimaced, clasping a limp arm to his chest. Having found much more of a fight than they'd expected, they traded glances and staggered off into the fields beyond the village. Soon their dark forms faded into the shadows.

"Say, now! What goes on here?"

On hearing Lott's booming voice, Tamwyn's knees felt weak. How was he going to explain this? He knelt beside the unconscious girl, who lay flat on her belly, arms splayed, like a sleeping hog.

Lott rushed over, still limping from the hammer Tamwyn had dropped on his foot. But his look of pain deepened dramatically when he saw his daughter. Angrily, he shoved Tamwyn aside. "What have you done to her, you lame-brained lout?"

"I . . . I, well—"

"He hit her, he did!" called a voice from the shadows beside the house. "Clonked her with a great big bucket."

The voice paused a few seconds, sounding as if it were choking—or stifling laughter. Then it added, "Brutal that was, terribly brutal."

Even in the dim light, Tamwyn could see Lott's flabby face turn pink, then red, then dark purple. His whole massive body shook like an oversized dumpling about to explode. Tamwyn sprang to his feet and backed away.

The girl moaned. Lott turned back to her and pressed his thumb against her wrist, feeling her pulse. At last, satisfied she was alive, he faced Tamwyn again.

"Go!" he bellowed. "Leave this village, you horrible hooligan. And never, ever come back, do you hear? Never!"

Tamwyn swallowed, then stepped slowly away. As he disappeared into the deepening night, he heard himself sigh. And then he heard something else—something like raucous laughter from the shadows.

3 · A Pale Hand Beckons

HIDDEN BY THE SHADOW OF THE GREAT stone tower, a lone figure prowled. His hooded cloak blended so completely into the darkness, he seemed just a layer of black upon black, no more visible than a raven against a starless sky.

Except for his hands.

Pale white, with perfectly clipped fingernails, the hands sometimes rose briefly out of the shadows. Not even a callus, let alone a scar, marred the smooth flesh of the long slender fingers. They grasped the cloak at its neck, holding down the hood, whenever a fierce gust of wind whipped across the land, piercing even the slim cracks in the tower.

Such gusts blew often here in the northernmost reaches of Waterroot—the region the bards called High Brynchilla. For here, in this land where few creatures ever visited, wind and water were the only constants. Both flowed freely, just as they had done since the very birth of Avalon. In the words of the old saying:

Where long wind blows
And water flows,
High Brynchilla
No one goes.

Where currents soar
And torrents roar,
None but wind and
Water knows.

As the cloaked figure looked out from the shadows, he peered down at an enormous, high-walled canyon—and clasped his hands in triumph. For he had now nearly accomplished what no one else in Avalon's history had even dared to try. He had changed forever the face of this remote canyon, and the magical water that it held.

For ages, water had flowed down this redrock canyon at the far northern edge of the realm—so much water that it fed almost all the rest of Waterroot. From the thinnest rill to the widest lake to the lowest depths of the Rainbow Seas, which were so vast that they seemed to have no shore and no bottom, water from this canyon could be found. Some of it even plunged back down into underground rivers that flowed to the neighboring realms of Stoneroot and Woodroot. But whatever the water's ultimate destination, every drop that ran down this canyon first began in one single place: the White Geyser of Crystillia.

Slowly, the cloaked figure turned to face north. There, at the very top of the canyon, was that tower of spray, the legendary White Geyser. So powerful that none but the wind dared to approach its foaming crest, it made a ceaseless rumble that rolled like everlasting thunder down the high cliff walls. And yet, because of its remoteness, almost no one had ever visited the geyser—just as almost no one had ever gazed down into its canyon. People knew about them only through the journals of the explorer Krystallus or through the songs of wandering bards.

Straight up shot the White Geyser, spurting water from unknown depths to the height of a hundred oak trees. Just as it had done day and night, season after season, year after year, through all the ages of Avalon.

"But now," rasped the voice beneath the hooded cloak, "you are mine, mmmyesss. Not Avalon's. Not Waterroot's. Not anyone's but mine."

His pale hands clenched into fists as he thought of all the ballads he'd heard that sang the praises of the Canyon of Crystillia and the White Geyser whose water filled it. Ballads that gushed as much as any fountain, celebrating the eerie glow of this water—a glow that came from *élano*, the magical sap of the Great Tree. Those ballads also celebrated the sheer quantity of water that erupted here; its whiteness that split into the seven colors of the spectrum when the water reached Prism Gorge at the lower end of the canyon; and its destiny to flow southward, carrying colors everywhere in the realm, all the way to the Rainbow Seas. But most of all, they celebrated this water's freedom, its permanence, its unstoppable power.

"No more," said the figure with satisfaction. "For I have stopped you. Mmmyesss. I—the greatest sorcerer of all time."

Gleefully, he rubbed his hands together. From this vantage point, in the shadows of his tower on the canyon rim, he could see the gigantic stone dam that now spanned Prism Gorge. Above the dam, an enormous white lake, still and somber, filled the canyon almost to its rim. And below the dam, no more water flowed, and no more colors danced, down the seven lower canyons to the lands and seas beyond.

He chuckled to himself. In just a few more weeks, the dam would be done, the lake would be full, and his long-awaited moment of triumph would arrive. All he lacked was one more thing—his prize. And now, at last, he knew just where to find it.

Clutching the hood of his cloak against the wind, the sorcerer paced excitedly along the rim. Why, only a few months ago, the fabled Canyon of Crystillia had smelled of fresh water, mixed with élano from deep within the Great Tree. But now this canyon—his canyon—had a different smell. It wafted from the open-pit quarries, from the stumps and shards of trees hacked down in the bordering forest of Woodroot, and from the blood of hundreds of paws, hooves, and wings. The dam reeked of this smell, a smell unlike any other in Avalon.

It was the smell of slavery.

He stirred, seeing someone approach, and drew back into the shadows. It was a man—a warrior who stood as thick as an oak, with a wide slab of a face that looked as hard as the dam itself. Around his waist he wore a wide leather belt that carried a broadsword, a rapier, two daggers, and a spiked club.

The warrior stopped to peer down into a quarry pit beside the tower. "Move!" he shouted at the half-dozen horses and oxen straining to pull a pair of enormous stones, just chiseled loose by a team of somber dwarves in shackles. "We needs them stones afore the end o' time!"

One of the sorcerer's pale hands beckoned—and the big man suddenly straightened, his face tense. He strode briskly over to the tower, stopping just at the edge of the shadow. A trace of fear in his eyes, he asked, "Ye called, Master?"

"Mmmyesss, my Harlech," spat the voice from the darkness. "I need something from you."

A bead of sweat slid down Harlech's brow, rounded his eyebrow, and disappeared in the scar that creased his wide jaw. In a voice barely loud enough to be heard over the sounds of pounding chisels and scraping stones from the quarry, he asked, "What do ye need, Master?"

"A slave. Mmmyesss."

"Sure, sure." Harlech wiped his brow in relief. He waved at the quarry pit—and beyond, at the huge dam that walled off the whole canyon. "We gots plenty o' them. More every bleedin' day. More 'n I kin—"

"Silence," hissed the voice. "Not just any slave."

Nervously, Harlech glanced back at the quarry pit. From its depths he heard the sounds of horses neighing and hooves slammed hard against stone. Then came the raised voice of a man—one of his slavemasters—more neighs, and a shout. Then the sharp crack of a whip, and the painful braying of a wounded horse.

Harlech grimaced, then turned back to the shadows. "Them beasts is gettin' rebellious, Master."

"Do not worry. It shall not be long now."

"What sort o' slave do ye be wantin', then? I got plenty o' four-leggeds, 'specially horses, does, an' stags. Plus a bear er two, an' jest last week I stole us a—"

"Silence, you blithering fool! Right now, mmmyesss. Or I'll see how you sound with no tongue in your empty head."

Harlech swallowed. "Aye, Master."

A shrieking gust of wind swept suddenly over the canyon. The sorcerer's white hands grasped the neck of his cloak, holding tight as the wind tugged at the hood and slapped against the cloth. Higher shrieked the wind, and higher still, swirling the surface of the lake until the canyon seemed like an open mouth, frothing white, that cried out in torment. Only after several minutes did the air fall still, and the canyon grow silent, but for the sounds of forced labor that echoed rim to rim.

The sorcerer lowered his hands at last. "Hear me well, my Harlech. I need a slave unusually smart, mmmyesss. Smarter than my ghoulacas—whom I have bred for obedience and ferocity, not cleverness."

Seasoned warrior though he was, the mention of those killer birds made Harlech wince. Two ghoulacas had attacked him once, just for sport, and he had scars on his jaw and both arms to prove it. With their nearly transparent wings and bodies, and their enormous bloodred talons and beaks, it had taken all his fighting skills—and all his weapons—just to escape alive.

"Ah, I see you remember them, my Harlech. Then you might also recall that, for years, I have made them search the Seven Realms for something I want—the only thing I still need. But they have failed me time and again. Just as they have failed to kill my one great enemy . . . or to find my one great ally, the one I've been waiting for since I first heard the Prophecy. But none of that matters now. All that matters is what I want—my prize. And this time . . . there shall be no failure. Do you understand?"

"Aye, Master."

"I could send you to do this task, couldn't I, Harlech?"

"Aye, Master." Anxiously, he touched the scar on his jaw.

"But no, I need you and all your men here to keep the slaves under control. We haven't any time now for rebellion. But the slaves' work is almost done. And when the dam is all finished— they will be finished, too."

Harlech allowed himself a slight grin. He understood perfectly.

The white hands slashed the air. "So bring what I require! A slave who is smart enough to do my bidding. Who has some family or loved ones—so I can secure its loyalty. And who has some fight left, enough to survive a long journey, mmmyesss."

Harlech frowned. "Some fight left, eh? Not many o' those, Master." He fingered the hilt of his rapier. "Iffen a slave gits too, ah, feisty, I uses him fer sword practice, ye see? An' then they can't walk none too good. Er run. No escaped slaves, though, this past three months . . . at least none that's alive."

The voice in the shadows merely grunted. "So long as most of them can still work, I don't care what you do. But now, my Harlech, I need that slave."

The man shifted his weight, his broadsword clinking against one of the daggers. "Can ye tell me anythin' more about this task, Master?"

From the darkness came a low, mirthless laugh. "To bring me the prize. Mmmyesss! It is something very special, my Harlech. Something I once found, then lost—and have finally found again."

"What, Master?"

Again came the laugh, merging with the swelling wind that battered against the stone tower. "Something that holds the power . . . ." The pale hands squeezed the air as if they were strangling someone. "Of Merlin himself."

4 · Hot Wax

CLAAAANG!

The great iron bell rang out, echoing all across the Drumadians' compound. This was no small feat, since the compound covered several leagues of gardens, tree-lined walkways, monuments, meeting halls, dormitories, craft centers, shrines, and other facilities of the Society of the Whole. Sometimes, when the wind blew strong, the bell's clanging could even be heard beyond the outer walls, in the countryside of Stoneroot.

Many a bard had sung the story of this bell. Made from the belt buckle of a giant, melted down by the breath of a fire dragon, molded into shape by the hands of dwarves, and exquisitely decorated by faery artisans, it symbolized the Drumadians' most basic ideal: unity and cooperation among all creatures. Some believed that the Buckle Bell, as it was fondly known, had been the idea of Elen the Founder. That would make it almost as old as the circle of stones that formed the compound's Great Temple . . . and nearly as old as Avalon itself.

The elderly priestess who stood beside the bell right now, wearing woolen earmuffs to protect what little hearing she had

47

left, didn't look much younger. Priestess Hywel's few remaining strands of white hair bounced with each new clang. They also bounced with every wave of her hand, which was her signal to the team of eight obedient dog faeries—all with walnut brown fur, white wings, and dangling pink tongues—who pulled the bell rope on command.

Hywel had lived in the compound longer than anyone—including High Priestess Coerria, now almost two hundred years old—and had been an Elder since before some of the other Elders were even born. And yet, though she bent low to the ground, her sharp eyes scanned everything nearby for any signs of disarray. For she took very seriously her title, Dean of Timeliness and Decorum—especially where young apprentices were concerned.

As the bell's final note faded away, over two dozen apprentices came running from different directions. For it was time to stop their classes, memorization work, craft projects, or service to their mentors: Formal Prayers were about to begin. And no one ever, *ever* missed Formal Prayers.

Hywel watched closely as the apprentices approached the Buckle Bell. Her back straightened ever so slightly, as she felt a surge of pride at seeing the new generation of her beloved Order. Of course, she'd never reveal that pride to any of *them*. But as she watched, her old eyes glowed like the candle that burned in the holder by her feet—a candle that every senior priestess or priest carried today, the Flame of Faith holy day.

All the apprentices, young women and men alike, wore the traditional garb of Drumadians: greenish brown robe, leather sandals, and a wooden clasp at the throat, carved in the shape of an oak tree. And all of them were joined by their *maryths*—distinctive companions whose loyalty would last as long as their lives as Drumadians. Hywel's own maryth, a rather ancient grass snake wound around her forearm, also watched the approaching crowd.

And what a crowd it was! Since, by Drumadian law, maryths could be any kind of creature but human, the young priestesses and priests were joined by a complete menagerie of does, stags, birds, beetles, dogs, cats, lizards, sprites, dwarves, faeries, and even a couple of tree spirits. These maryths, like the many who had bonded with Drumadians in the past, were as varied as all the creatures of Avalon. In fact, it was often said that maryths had just one quality in common: absolute devotion.

The apprentices, in turn, bowed respectfully to the Elder. One teenage boy, who had shoved his friend jokingly a few seconds before, got shoved back just as he bowed. His foot kicked Hywel's candle, splattering hot beeswax on his shin. He winced—but his pain was less from the burning wax than from the burning look he got from the old priestess.

Slowly, the crowd dwindled as apprentices and maryths shuffled down the intricately carved wooden steps that led to a small, open-air theater: the Shrine of Elen. Here, they knelt before a statue, carved from the trunk of an oak tree, of Elen binding the leg of a wounded troll child. Just as the last person arrived, the whole group started to chant—the very first of a long litany of prayers to the Founder that would last all morning.

Everyone spoke in perfect unison. Listening from her post up by the bell, old Hywel almost smiled. For no one lagged. No one forgot a phrase. And, of course, no one was absent.

Except for Elli.

Even as the bell began to toll, the young priestess, a newly admitted apprentice third class, had slipped out of sight. Ducking behind the apprentices' dormitory, she had hidden among the burly roots of an ancient elm until the clanging finally ceased. Then a strange light came into her hazel green eyes. She ran a hand through her mass of brown curls—as thick as a faery's garden—and darted off. As quietly as a wood elf she moved, making no sound but the soft jangle of the handmade harp slung over her back.

And one more sound: the gruff *hmmmpff* that came now and then from the small pinnacle sprite who rode on her shoulder. At this moment, Nuic's whole body—perfectly round but for his tiny arms and legs—darkened to brown, so that he looked almost like a second head upon her shoulders.

"Hmmmpff. Skipping out of prayers again, are we?"

"Sure," answered Elli with a soft, melodic laugh. She padded past the Temple of Seven Fountains—now just seven trickles of water—before saying more. "No one will miss me, with everybody crowded into that little shrine. Not even that old goat who loves to yell at apprentices."

"Now, now," chortled Nuic, his color brightening a shade. "No disrespect to your elders! Just because Hywel caught you out picking raspberries the other day, when you were supposed to be in recitation class, there's no reason to get rude."

Elli suddenly swerved, hiding behind a cart full of squashes, carrots, and tomatoes—just in time to avoid a stern-faced priest carrying a tall candle. Right beside him trotted his maryth, a deep blue unicorn whose horn glowed dimly.

Turning toward Nuic, she whispered, "You were right there with me, as I recall, soaking yourself in the stream while I got those berries."

Nuic's color went misty blue, as if his round body was still immersed.

"Right you are. I deserved that little bath, after two weeks of being your maryth! Why, I've never worked so hard—teaching you about herbs, reminding you where you're supposed to be, and most of all, trying to keep you from getting expelled from the Order. Though I don't know why! It's bound to happen anyway, at this rate."

Again, his color darkened to brown. "Hmmmpff. I should have stayed in that pitiful little stream, even after that old goat told me to get out and do more to keep you out of trouble."

Elli's eyes narrowed. "How come you can call her an old goat, and I can't?" In a mischievous tone she added, "Aren't you being disrespectful to your elders?"

"For one thing," grumbled the sprite, "I'm at least six or seven centuries older than she is. So she *isn't* my elder. Not even close! And you, who are just sixteen, should appreciate that. And there's another thing."

He lowered his voice to a whisper. "That old goat really *is* an old goat."

Elli started to laugh, when a pair of priestesses, deep in conversation, walked by the cart of vegetables. Each of them carried a beeswax candle, shielding it from breezes with an open hand. Behind one priestess glided an owl, gray wings fluttering with every swoop; behind the other shambled a medium-size brown bear. As they passed the cart, the bear grabbed a carrot and started munching—but not before giving a sly wink to the two fugitives behind the cart.

"Let's get moving," said Elli with a shake of her abundant curls. "Before someone else sees us."

"Right. Maybe even someone with enough rank to expel you—and send me back to the mountains once and for all. Someone like

High Priestess Coerria herself! Or that young twit who's trying so hard to become the *next* High Priestess."

This time it was Elli's skin that darkened, going from its usual ruddy complexion to something more like beet red. "Llynia. No one—not even the Chosen One to succeed Coerria—should be that stuck on herself."

Nuic reached up, grabbed a small tomato in his hand, and chewed it thoughtfully. "They say Llynia's the youngest Chosen One in ages—since Elen's own daughter, Rhia, almost a thousand years ago."

"She's the *stupidest* one in ages," muttered Elli. "The day before you came to the compound, she made me wash all the floors and windows of the woodworking lodge. Twice! And do you know why? Because I dared to speak to her maryth, a tree spirit, without asking Llynia's permission first!"

"Hmmmpff. I guess if Hywel's an old goat, then Llynia's a young ass."

Elli grinned. Nuic might be as rough as a mountain boulder sometimes—and as hard to make smile—but she really did enjoy him. Even like him.

"So tell me something, Nuic. What made you come here, anyway? Why did you ever leave your home way up there in the hills to become a maryth?"

"Boredom, that's all."

Elli frowned, not believing that for an instant. But she knew that Nuic wasn't about to tell her more. Why he came to the Society of the Whole was a secret known only to him—and perhaps to High Priestess Coerria, who for some reason had assigned him to Elli.

She sighed glumly. *We both have our secrets, don't we?* At least nobody knew hers—just where she'd spent the past nine years. And with whom! Until, at last, she'd escaped. No, not even the High Priestess knew about all that. For if she did, she never would have allowed Elli to join the Order. That was certain.

After glancing around to make sure that nobody was near, Elli darted out from behind the cart. She sped over to the millhouse, its enormous waterwheel barely turning in the low river that flowed through this part of the compound. She hopped across the bank, and started to run into some nearby trees—when she stopped, turned around, and loped back to the river. In one swift motion, she jumped down into the muddy channel, scooped up some water in her hands, and splashed Nuic in the face.

"Wha-what was that for?" he sputtered.

"You said you wanted a bath, didn't you?"

Elli didn't notice, but as she climbed back up the bank, the sprite on her shoulder turned a pleasant shade of bluish green.

Onward she ran, right through the moss garden that covered a whole hillside. Nuic had told her (with seriousness bordering on reverence) that this garden contained more than five thousand different kinds of moss from all the root-realms. Mosses of every conceivable shade of green covered stones, tree trunks, footpaths, and benches; still more hung like beards from branches, filled the creases of boulders, and made shin-deep cushions for weary walkers. Hundreds of moss faeries, looking like tiny green humans with translucent wings, zipped across the hillside—tending, trimming, and carrying hollowed-out acorns filled with water. Thanks to the faeries' hard work, the drought hadn't yet harmed the lushest growth, although patches of brown were starting to spread across the hillside.

Elli slowed down, looking cautiously from side to side, as she approached a wide walkway of gleaming white stones—the dividing line between the compound's second and third Rings. Seeing no one, she leaped across the walkway. The stones flashed beneath her, reminding her of how they glowed at night under the dimmed stars, thanks to their coatings of élano.

As she ran on, passing the entrance to a cavern of pink and violet crystals, she marveled at the sheer beauty of this place. Its overall design—from the seven concentric Rings that represented the seven sacred Elements of Avalon, to the remarkable trees chosen from every root-realm, to the majestic circle of stones that was both the compound's Inner Ring and the Great Temple at its heart—made this the most inspiring place she'd ever seen. And that, of course, had been the goal of Elen and Rhiannon when they designed these grounds so long ago.

Even as she ran, Elli couldn't help but grin. She understood now why her father had loved this place so much during his years as a Drumadian priest . . . even if he, like Elli, had broken the rules now and then. She bit her lip. *I wish I'd known him better. Him and Mama both.*

She kept on running, occasionally ducking behind trees, boulders, and wooden signs carved with prayer runes, to avoid being seen. At one point, she veered sharply, almost throwing Nuic off her shoulder. The sprite's tiny feet pinched her skin, and he demanded, "Why do you have to go so far, if all you want to do is meditate?"

Without slowing her stride, she answered, "I've told you before, the Great Temple is totally empty in the mornings. No one goes there, so no one disturbs me. And this is my best chance, when everyone else is at Prayers."

"Hmmmpff. There's no difference, anyway, between a prayer and a meditation."

"But there *is*."

"What? Tell me, O High Hostess."

Elli slowed to a trot, then stopped by the edge of a circular mud pit that had once been a lily pond. Picking up a stone, she hefted it in her hand before hurling it out into the middle. It splatted on the damp mud.

"All right," she declared. "Try this. Prayer feels mostly like telling. Saying things to the gods—Dagda, Lorilanda, whoever. But meditation . . . that's different. Meditation feels less like telling, and more like, well, *listening*."

Nuic shook himself, swinging his tiny arms. "Sounds pretty much the same to me."

"Know what, my little friend? You're hopeless."

"We've been together for over two weeks, and you've just now figured that out? Hmmmpff, you're dimmer than an ogre's eyeball."

Starting off again, Elli jogged past the long flatrock building that held the pottery kilns. Trails of smoke drifted out of several chimneys. Then she sped through a grove of white birch trees, brought here all the way from Woodroot. She wasn't completely sure, but it looked as if their leaves were actually turning color— golden yellow with hints of orange—just like local stones. Strange.

She veered sharply to cut behind the high wooden fence that surrounded the residence of the High Priestess. This, she knew well, was the most dangerous part of her journey. Elders and others often visited the residence, striding through a simple oaken gateway in the fence. As she neared the gateway, she stopped abruptly. Hidden behind a hawthorn tree with branches as thick as her own hair, she crouched in silence, watching for any signs of trouble.

All clear. Elli stood up and dashed past the opening.

Just at that instant, someone stepped through the gateway— a priestess carrying a large red candle in an ornate holder. Elli smashed right into her. Hot wax sprayed everywhere, the senior priestess screamed, and both of them tumbled to the ground. Nuic went rolling into a thorny shrub.

"Idiot girl! Idiot!" raged the priestess, her arms flailing wildly. Candle wax splattered her face, neck, and hair—but even so, Elli recognized her instantly.

"Er, um . . . sorry about that, Priestess Llynia."

"You'll be sorrier once I've—owww!" Llynia tore a big chunk of wax out of her straight blonde hair. "Once I've had you boiled to death. Beaten to death. And then expelled!"

Elli glanced over at Nuic, now a mirthful shade of pink. Despite the trouble she was in, it was hard not to laugh out loud. Especially since Llynia didn't exactly look like the second-highest-ranking priestess in the Society of the Whole. She looked a lot more like a country jester who'd just been splattered with cherry pies.

"Oooh, I'll get you for this," Llynia declared in a malicious voice. She yanked at another glob of wax on her head, pulling out some hair by the roots. "Aaaghh! By the breath of Elen the Founder, I will. Death by drowning. Then torture. Then . . . more torture. Just count yourself lucky that Fairlyn, my maryth, isn't here, or she'd have murdered you already."

Innocently, Elli said, "I thought the first Drumadian law forbids that."

Llynia scowled at her. She shook her head, making a big piece of wax flap against her nose. "Every rule has exceptions. For idiots. And assassins!"

"What in Avalon's name happened here?"

A tall, lanky priest strode up, peering at them with eyes as keen as the silver-winged falcon perched on his shoulder. He set down his candle, and helped Llynia to her feet. She shook herself free of his grip and started to sputter so angrily that saliva dribbled down her chin. Just then another priestess, with a sallow face, joined them. Seeing Llynia, she gasped—almost dropping the ginger cat in her arms, as well as her own candle.

Llynia's wax-covered hand pointed at Elli's face. "This girl . . . attacked me. Me! The Chosen One."

The sallow priestess gasped again, while the cat she held snarled and clawed at the air.

Elli waved her hands in protest. "No, I didn't! It was just an accident."

"A nearly *fatal* accident," hissed Llynia. "Why you . . . you . . ." She grabbed a clump of red wax that was dangling from her eyebrow, swinging like a pendulum, and threw it at the ground. "What's your name, girl? I've tried to forget, since the last time we met."

With a gulp, Elli answered. "Elliryanna Lailoken."

At this, the tall priest stiffened. He turned toward Elli, studying her strangely.

"Is something wrong here?" asked a quiet voice, just above a whisper, from the gateway.

"Wrong?" shrieked Llynia, whirling around. "Wrong? Let me tell you how—"

She stopped herself abruptly, seeing who had joined them. Everyone else, including Elli, fell silent as well.

There by the wooden gate stood an elderly priestess—almost as old as Hywel, perhaps. Yet she seemed much more spry. And, to Elli's mind, much more beautiful. She carried no maryth, at least none that could be seen, although Elli suspected that her maryth would be as remarkable as the priestess herself.

The woman's long white hair fell to the middle of her back, and her crystal blue eyes were like prisms that caught light, bent it, and set it free again. She stepped toward the others, moving with striking grace and beauty—the sort of grace that is only earned by struggle, and the sort of beauty that is only deepened by time.

"High Priestess Coerria," said Llynia, controlling her voice so she no longer ranted. She bowed her head in greeting, which sent flecks of wax falling like hailstones.

"Llynia," said the elder woman softly, bowing her own head.

Her long white locks rippled as she moved. So did her gown, the formal dress of the High Priestess—said to be the very same one that Elen herself had worn. Woven of pure spider's silk, it had been a gift to Elen from the great white spider of Druma Wood, the magical forest in Lost Fincayra that had sheltered Elen's daughter, Rhia, for many years. So often did Elen refer to that beautiful forest—and wear that dress—that her followers came to be called *Drumadians*.

The High Priestess gave a similar bow to the tall priest. "Lleu, always a pleasure to see you. And your friend Catha."

He smiled, as the falcon on his shoulder ruffled both wings proudly. "The pleasure is ours, High Priestess."

"And you, Imbolca?" she asked the other priestess. "I hope you and Mebd are well."

"We were, High Priestess, until we came across this . . . this wretch of an apprentice." She pointed accusingly at Elli. "She attacked the Chosen One!"

The cat gave a fierce snarl.

One of Coerria's white eyebrows lifted. "Did she, now?" She faced the young woman. "It's Elliryanna, isn't it?"

"Y-y-yes, High Priestess," said Elli. She clasped her hands behind her back, working them nervously. "But I didn't attack her. It was just . . . just an accident."

"Tell the truth!" yelled Llynia, tearing a thick glob of wax out of her ear. "You tried to humiliate me. Or worse! Tell the truth now, you—"

Coerria lifted her hand for silence. She took a step toward Elli and scrutinized her with those deep blue eyes. For a long moment, there was no sound but the cat's loud purring.

"No," Coerria whispered at last. "I don't think you meant any harm. And if you were going to bump into anyone," she added wryly, "it's fortunate that you picked someone with such grace and good humor."

Llynia was quaking, beside herself with anger. Her eyes, almost as red as the spilled wax, bulged in their sockets. "Aren't you going to punish her?"

Coerria shook her head, brushing her white hair across her shoulders. "Not for that, no. Why, I've bumped into several people myself at this very spot."

"Bu . . . bu . . . but," sputtered Llynia, "she could have harmed me."

"Or killed her," insisted Imbolca. Her skin tone changed from its usual sallowness to something darker. "It would be an outrage if she weren't expelled."

The High Priestess stroked her chin. "You know, if I expelled everyone who did something clumsy, there would soon be nobody left in this compound." Her bright eyes darted to the small, round creature who was standing by the shrub at the edge of the walkway. "Except possibly you, Nuic."

The old sprite said nothing, but gave a watery sort of chuckle.

Coerria's eyes moved back to Elli. "Now, being clumsy is one thing." Her tone grew more serious. "But skipping Formal Prayers is another."

Llynia and Imbolca traded glances, and a new look of satisfaction crept over their faces.

Elli lowered her eyes, staring at her sandals.

The High Priestess observed her for another moment, then said simply, "Just try to do better, my child. And you, too, Nuic."

Elli looked up, surprised. "That's . . . all?"

The High Priestess nodded. "That's all." Then she added gently, "I've noticed you more than once in the Great Temple, just you and your maryth in that immense circle of stones."

"You have?"

"Yes, my child. And I know what you were doing."

Elli swallowed. "You do?"

"I do. And while prayers are good for the soul . . . so is meditation."

The two of them simply looked at each other, speaking without words.

"But that's outrageous," spat Imbolca. She started to say more, but was silenced by a wave from Llynia.

The Chosen One slid closer to her superior—though her stance was anything but respectful. She glared at Coerria, practically putting her nose in the Elder's face. "I know you have many important things to deal with, High One. So I've not troubled you with the minor difficulties that I've been having with this particular apprentice."

Elli stirred nervously. Was Llynia going to make something terrible out of that incident at the woodworking lodge?

"But you may not know," Llynia went on with a malevolent curl of her lip, "about this girl's history. *Before* she came to the compound."

Elli froze. She couldn't breathe. Did Llynia really know? And if she did, would she actually reveal it to the High Priestess? That would ruin everything. Everything!

Coerria gazed at Llynia with such steady ferocity that the younger priestess took a step backward. "I know enough to give her a second chance."

Elli's heart swelled with gratitude. She would have kissed the High Priestess if it wouldn't have been utterly improper.

Llynia's blue eyes narrowed. "Are you aware that she was a slave, for several years? To gnomes! Murderous, thieving gnomes, who kill humans in their sleep." She glanced at Elli. "No doubt that's where she learned her manners. And are you prepared to ignore that, High Priestess? Are you prepared to put all the rest of us at risk?"

Elli's whole body shook—not so much with anguish that her only chance to be a priestess was now lost, as with rage. Rage at Llynia, at Imbolca—and at those miserable, violent creatures who had kept her captive for nine long years.

"Those gnomes," she said in a voice shaking with fury, "killed my parents. Both of them. Then carried me away, to their holes underground." She looked squarely at Llynia. "They took everything from me. My home, my family. Everything but this."

She whipped off the harp that had been slung over her back. Holding it in one hand, she stroked the side of the maple burl that formed its sound chamber. Through her choked throat, she repeated, "Everything but this."

Llynia shook her waxen head. Feigning a tone of sympathy, she said, "I am sorry for your misfortune, my dear. Truly I am. But given your background, not to mention your own violent tendencies, you simply don't belong here. This Society is based on reverence for life, respect for all creatures—just the opposite of where you've learned all your values. And I don't see how this pitiful little harp of yours changes anything."

Elli's eyes flashed. "This harp was made by my father. A Drumadian priest."

At this, Llynia blinked. "A priest of our Order?"

"And a fine one," declared Lleu. Bending his lanky frame, he put his hand on Elli's shoulder. "I knew your father, knew him well."

"You . . . did?" Elli tried to blink the mist from her eyes.

"He was a good man." With a sharp glance at Llynia, he added, "The sort of man who would have raised his daughter with true and lasting values." He frowned, then turned back to Elli. "While he could, at any rate. I'm sorry to hear such terrible news. We were good friends, but we lost track of each other after he left for Malóch."

Elli's chin quivered. She could only say, "But you knew him."

The tall man nodded. "Yes, Elli. Well enough to tell you that even my great-grandfather, Lleu of the One Ear, would have thought highly of him."

"You're . . . you're descended from *that* Lleu? The one who was a friend of Merlin? And Elen the Founder? The one who wrote that book that everyone here carries around?"

"Cyclo Avalon," he said, grinning. "He wasn't very ambitious, nor skilled in politics, like some." He shot another glance at Llynia. "But he did listen well. So the *Cyclo Avalon* holds everything he ever learned about the seven sacred Elements, about the powers of élano, about portalseeking, and even—"

"Fascinating," interrupted Llynia with a sneer. "But we have more serious matters to deal with."

"Yes," declared Coerria, "like a drought. And a Council of Elders, called to discuss that—and more. Need I remind you, Llynia, that it's scheduled for tomorrow? We have Elders from all Seven Realms arriving, even now."

The younger priestess bridled. "And need I remind *you,* High Priestess, of what you have heard? Are you going to override all our years of suffering at the hands of gnomes—the murders, the thievery, the sacking of Drumadian consulates in so many realms— just because of the sentimental views of one priest? Are you just going to ignore this troublesome girl in our midst?"

All of them turned to the Elder. She gazed back at them, her face troubled. "No," she said quietly. "I shan't ignore her."

Llynia's eyes gleamed with triumph. She winked slyly at Imbolca.

Coerria straightened, tossing her hair behind her shoulders. Looking directly at Elli, she said, "I'm afraid that I have changed my mind. Forgive me, child, but . . ."

Elli cleared her throat. "But what?"

"I have decided that, given all this, I must change your situation."

Llynia gave a confident cackle.

"Change?" asked Elli. "How?"

"I have decided that you need," declared the High Priestess, "a mentor."

Llynia's jaw went slack.

"A mentor?" Elli stole a quick look at Lleu, who beamed down at her. "To help me learn the ways of the Order, you mean."

"Exactly, my child." Coerria's eyes suddenly brightened. "Which is why I've chosen the best possible person to teach you— and, I dare say, to learn from you."

Lleu bowed his head. "I'd be honored."

But Coerria shook her head. "Not you, my son. The person I choose for Elliryanna's mentor is . . ." She spun to face the wax-splattered priestess. "You, Llynia."

5 · Green with Envy

OUT OF MY SIGHT, YOU WORTHLESS WRETCH!"
Llynia shoved Elli through the wooden gate in the
fence surrounding the Baths, three natural hot-spring
pools whose waters had been restored by orders of the Elders. Just
for today. And just for Llynia.

She took a kick at Elli's backside for good measure. And though
her kick missed its target, her words did not: "Think you had it
rough before, do you? Just wait until I'm done. Ha! Then you'll
really know what it's like to be a slave."

Elli bit her tongue as she walked across the Baths, the harp on
her back jangling roughly. She strode right past the three steaming
pools, the rising clouds of lavender-scented mist, the fragrant candles burning everywhere, the lush ferns and flowering vines. But
she didn't notice any of it, nor even the glittering stars above—all
the brighter now that starset had happened. Only when she neared
the waterfall at the far end did she stop to take in her surroundings.

For at the very top of the waterfall, seated in a cloud of spray,
was Nuic. He looked almost like a cloud of spray himself, but for
the deep purple eyes that were watching her.

"Hmmmpff. Took you long enough to get here."

Elli scowled, but not at his typical gruffness. "She made me fold all her clothes—piles and piles of them, the ones she'll be taking on her big journey. Then she came over, dumped everything on the ground, and made me do it all over again."

Her fists clenched. "It's been just two days since she became my so-called mentor, and it feels more like two years. By the elbows of the Elders, Nuic! I can't take this much longer." She swung at a lavender-tinted curl of mist that was floating by. "Why did Coerria ever do this to me? I thought she liked me."

"Hmmmpff." Nuic's colors shifted through his vaporous form, leaving unchanged only his purple eyes and the tuft of green hair common to all pinnacle sprites. "Maybe she has her reasons."

"And maybe I'll turn into a pink-eyed giant!" she yelled in exasperation.

"Hush, you wretch!" rang Llynia's command. "Stay back there by the waterfall. And stay silent. I'll call you when I need you for my facial."

Elli just nodded. But her hazel green eyes narrowed, as if she'd just made up her mind about something. Nuic noticed her expression . . . but decided not to ask what it meant.

Meanwhile, a large cloud of steam billowed up from the first pool. Llynia had just climbed into the hot, steaming water—and for her, right now, Stoneroot's months-long drought seemed just a misty memory.

"Ahhhhh," she sighed, as she sank down into the hot water. This was the first bath she'd taken since before last summer—and the first triple-pool herbal bath she'd taken in her life. First would come the cleansing pool, where she was now; then the water-massage pool; then, finally, the relaxation pool. And all this was thanks to what had happened yesterday at the Council of the Elders. In all her scheming and plotting in advance of the meeting, she'd never dreamed that things would have worked out so well.

But now . . . time to enjoy the bath. She'd felt better right away, as soon as she had removed her greenish brown robe—far too simple a garb for the Chosen One, but just another one of Coerria's insults that Llynia was forced to endure.

For a while, at least. Her time of triumph was swiftly approaching.

"Open those spigots! All of them!" she commanded the pair of winged faeries at the edge of the pool. Both little men, no bigger than ripe pears, buzzed into the steamy air. They waved their arms frantically, fluffing up the sleeves of their ruffled white shirts.

"Forget about the drought," Llynia barked. "Haven't you heard? I am the Chosen One—the next High Priestess. And I have an important journey tomorrow. So do as you're told."

The faeries retreated, hovering over the spigots. As they twisted each spigot all the way open, Llynia smiled in satisfaction. Yes, *the next High Priestess.* She dearly loved the sound of that! Think of all the good she could do for the Order and those loyal to her . . . and all the justice she could bring to her enemies.

She sank deeper and smiled broader. As her lower back submerged in the healing warmth, then her spine, then her shoulders, then at last her neck, she gazed all around. Candlelight, reflected dimly on the spirals of lavender-scented steam, softened her surroundings. She could barely see the glint of stars above, barely hear the gentle rustling of vine leaves, dripping with dew, just above her head.

Why, with all this steam, she almost couldn't count the number of steps in the cascade that emptied into her pool. But she knew well there were seven, carefully designed and engraved to represent the seven Elements of Avalon: Earth, Air, Fire, Water, Life, LightDark, and last of all, Mystery—what Elen had once called "the seven sacred parts that together make the Whole."

Down that winding stairway of stones, the cascade flowed, pouring into her pool water from the glaciers of Stoneroot's high peaks. That cool water mixed with hot water from the spigots, drawn from simmering springs that bubbled up from the depths of the Great Tree. And her pool also held a third, very precious kind of water: Through a tiny silver faucet near her head came a thin trickle, glowing with élano, from the fabled White Geyser of Crystillia. Together, these waters produced the perfect balance of temperatures, powers, auras, and nutrients.

The perfect bath.

Llynia stretched out her hand, pressing her fingers into the thick, luxuriant moss that lined every edge of the pool. This moss, she knew, had been specially bred, over long centuries, to maximize its healing oils—which could strengthen sore muscles, mend bruised skin, and ward off fatigue.

Dozens of faeries lifted off from the shelves lining the walls and buzzed about the pool, carrying pouches of scented soap, herbal creams, and magical bubble mixtures. Their translucent wings—tinted silvery green, like most faeries—made that melodious hum that only faery wings could produce. Llynia couldn't imagine any sound more lovely, rising and falling against the continuous thrum of the cascade.

No, she thought, *not even the song of a museo could better this. Besides, no one ever hears museos anymore.*

A female faery, wearing a yellow robe that reached down to her ankles, landed on Llynia's brow. The creature plunged her tiny hands into her leather pouch and pulled out a heap of light brown cream. It smelled faintly of cocoa and cinnamon.

"Ear wash, m'lady," the faery sang out. As Llynia leaned one side of her head on the moss, the faery began to rub the cream into every part of her ear, inside and out, pushing aside the hair still wet from her latest shampoo. The cream, as Llynia knew, was meant to improve her hearing. But right now she just enjoyed the cool feel of it on her ears, and the gentle massage of the faery's hands.

Meanwhile, other faeries zipped to and fro through the clouds of steam. Several carried colorful powders to go into the bath—powders meant to prevent muscle cramps and promote flexibility. Two faeries had almost finished the final scrub of Llynia's toes, while another pair (with unusually large wings) carried a satchel of herbs to the base of the cascade and dumped them into the pool, causing a sudden foaming of pink bubbles. Yet another faery, a husky little male wearing a bright red vest, landed on the edge of the pool and began stirring a clay pot that contained the facial mud preparation.

Beyond all the bustling faeries, of course, Llynia could see Fairlyn, her maryth. With all her dozen arms, Fairlyn was busily directing every aspect of the faeries' work. She could be seen everywhere around the pool—and smelled everywhere, too. For while Fairlyn was a tree spirit, she was no ordinary one: She was the spirit of a lilac elm from the legendary groves of the Forest Fairlyn in Woodroot, where the fruited groves and fragrant pathways could be smelled from many leagues away. Many a visitor to that forest returned home convinced that it held the richest trove of smells of any forest in any realm . . . and that the most spectacular smells of all belonged to the lilac elms.

Llynia smiled as Fairlyn reached down a pair of arms and gently swept the pink bubbles over to surround her head and neck. *All this,* she told herself, *is Fairlyn's way of saying she loves me.* And so it was, because the tree spirit had no voice. Instead, Fairlyn spoke through her long, leafless arms studded with purple buds. And through her large brown eyes. And most of all, through her aromas.

Right now, Fairlyn smelled distinctly of wild alpine roses, a sweet and joyous scent if ever there was one. That was good for the faeries, since that showed the tree spirit approved of their work. For the moment, at least. If they ever caught the smell of burning wood (or worse, crushed faery wings), big trouble was brewing.

Llynia sighed dreamily, having placed herself completely in Fairlyn's care. For like every maryth, Fairlyn had certain special skills. And in her case, those skills happened to make for an astonishingly sensuous bath.

At that moment, Fairlyn dipped one of her thinnest boughs into the pot with the facial mud. The smell of roses intensified. The preparation was almost ready. Just a few more minutes. And then—the facial, what Llynia felt sure would be her favorite part of her experience in the Baths. Not even the clumsy hands of that young wretch could botch a facial! And just to make sure, Fairlyn would be watching.

Llynia raised herself a bit higher in the pool and laid her head back against the pillow of moss. Her feet sloshed in the warm water, splashing the departing toe-scrub faeries. And she thought back dreamily to yesterday's Council of Elders, and what had happened there.

She recalled how impressive the Great Temple had seemed when she entered, striding into the circle of stones. Surely those stones hadn't looked so magnificent, so regal, since the earliest days of Avalon—when they were first set in place by Elen and her followers after being carried all the way from Lost Fincayra. The entire circle fairly glowed with midday starlight. And the Elders who gathered there, from all Seven Realms, gave an air of profound importance—and expectation—to the meeting.

Just as Llynia had expected, the session began with many of those Elders, joined by their maryths, describing the worsening drought. Upper Waterroot (called High Brynchilla by most), as well as parts of Stoneroot and Woodroot, had been hardest hit. Frighteningly, those places weren't just withering, but also graying: Even their colors seemed to be drying up. Could something have caused a change in weather patterns? Or could something have altered the waters of High Brynchilla, believed to flow through deep underground channels into the neighboring realms? No one could say.

Then, with growing anxiety, Llynia had listened as more voices—and more troubles—seized the Council's attention. From every realm, Elders told strange and shocking tales. A new breed of flying beast, with transparent body and deadly talons, had been attacking people in even the remotest villages. These creatures traveled through the portals, so it was impossible to say just where they came from—or would next appear. In addition, one clan of eaglefolk in Fireroot had broken off from the rest of its noble kind, and was ruthlessly slaying and robbing. Angry flamelons were threatening all-out war against them, and other eaglefolk as well.

On top of that, the gnomes' bloody raids were growing worse, especially in Mudroot. Many humans, including priestesses and priests, had been murdered in their sleep. And most disturbing of all, perhaps, came the news that some groups of humans, angry and scared by all these attacks, were banding together to slay non-human creatures—a direct violation of the basic Drumadian laws that governed every realm.

By this point, fear was palpable in the Great Temple. So was confusion. Cries of woe and calls for justice drowned out any discussion. When one Elder tried to urge compassion for the gnomes, she was rudely shouted down. Only when High Priestess Coerria herself rose to speak, and read aloud a soothing letter from Hanwan Belamir, the famous teacher from Woodroot, had the group quieted—though just briefly.

For everyone there had known the darkest truth of all: that this was the seventeenth year since the Year of Darkness. And that, if the Lady of the Lake's prophecy was correct, a child had been born in that year. A child who would ultimately destroy Avalon. A child who, like most wizards and sorcerers, would come into his or her full powers at age seventeen—this very year.

Llynia sank deeper into the bathing pool, sloshing warm water over her toes, smiling broadly. For now she recalled, with delight, her favorite moment of the meeting, the moment when everything had changed.

She had stepped forward and raised her hands, calling for attention. It amazed her even now that she had acted so boldly, and spoken so confidently. She had declared for all to hear that she'd had a vision the night before, after evening prayers—a vision of the Lady of the Lake herself. Merely uttering the name of this great enchantress, who was both revered and dreaded across the realms, was enough to bring silence to the meeting. A hush fell over the Elders and their maryths; even the massive pillars of the stone circle seemed to lean toward Llynia, listening.

For the Lady of the Lake was shrouded in mystery, as thick

as the mists that swirled around her magical lair somewhere in Woodroot. No one knew where she had come from, nor how she had gained her powers. Even her precise location was a mystery: Many had tried to find her, but all had failed—and some had never returned.

But two facts about her were known for certain. First, she was very old—old enough to have known the great wizard Merlin during his last days in Avalon. Together, they had finally ended the terrible War of Storms and crafted the famous Treaty of the Swaying Sea that all creatures had signed (except gnomes, gobsken, ogres, trolls, changelings, and death dreamers). And second, she had always shown a special interest in the Society of the Whole. Just why this was, nobody could explain, but the Lady seemed to hold Drumadians with some esteem.

And so, down through the centuries, she had appeared occasionally in visions—but only to the High Priestess. Or to someone soon to become High Priestess. These visions were events of enormous importance—although none had occurred for well over a hundred years, just after Coerria herself had become leader of the Drumadians. It was also said that, one day, the Lady of the Lake would do more than appear in a vision, that she would actually welcome a priestess into her lair—and that this priestess could transform the Society of the Whole, becoming its greatest leader since Elen.

Of course, no priestess had ever actually been welcomed into the Lady's enchanted lair. Nor had any priestess ever had a vision that invited her to come.

Until now.

Llynia cackled softly, blowing some pink bubbles off her chin, remembering the hushed excitement of everyone in the Great

Temple. And, best of all, the look of surprise—no, shock—on Coerria's face. For not only had the vision of the Lady come to Llynia, thus ensuring that she'd soon be High Priestess, the vision had *not* come to Coerria. So Coerria's time, at last, was coming to an end.

Oh, but that wasn't all! Llynia swept her hands along the mossy edges of the pool, combing the thick strands with her fingers, feeling their luxuriant softness. And she nodded, remembering how much she'd savored announcing her final news to the Council of Elders: In her vision, the Lady of the Lake had taken her into the lair!

After that announcement, the full Council had broken into cheers. All except Coerria, of course, and a few of her most loyal dunces, such as Lleu. But the Council had then moved swiftly to authorize Llynia to take a journey to Woodroot—to find the Lady of the Lake, and to seek her wise counsel in this time of such grave difficulties.

But first . . . to take a bath, as only the Drumadians can prepare. Llynia worked her fingers in the warm water, fingers that would before long touch the very hand of Avalon's greatest enchantress. Then she bit her lip—not in doubt, exactly, but with a trace of uncertainty.

What was it, really, that she had seen in her vision? It was just a flash—a brief, distorted image. She had seen the Lady stepping toward her, on the waters of a magical lake surrounded by mist. The Lady raised her hand in greeting . . . and then suddenly vanished.

That was all. Was it really what she'd thought it was, the long-awaited welcome? Or not?

And something else troubled her, as well. Something more

fundamental. For some time now, she'd been worried about her very gifts as a seer, gifts that had allowed her to claim remarkable rank and power at a very young age. Visions had come to her often since childhood—the first when she was no more than three, warning her about a fierce hailstorm. But more recently, her powers seemed to be fading. Nobody else knew the truth . . . but until that vision of the Lady, she'd had none at all for almost a year. More than anything, she hoped that this new vision was a sign that her powers were, at last, returning.

Llynia's hands curled into fists, and her jaw clenched. Seeing this, the ever-attentive Fairlyn started wafting smells of lilac blossoms, to bring peace of mind, and of thyme, to soothe worries.

Slowly, a sense of peace returned to Llynia. Her thoughts came back to her facial, which should be ready by now. She could almost feel the tingle of that specially prepared mud on her cheeks and chin, nose and brow. And the penetrating warmth that would protect her face from even the harshest starlight.

Then, to her delight, Fairlyn lifted up the clay pot holding the mud. It was time.

But where was that apprentice? "Get over here, girl!" Llynia's cry was so loud that several hovering faeries jolted in fright and zipped off to hide by the waterfall. "Right now, I say! Before my facial goes stale."

Llynia growled to herself. She'd only allowed that poisonous girl into the Baths at all because of the facial. Since it had to be applied very quickly, it needed hands much larger than faeries' to do the job. Human hands, if possible. But what was the point if Elli ruined everything by being so slow?

Then a comforting thought came to her, one that made her feel more content than all of Fairlyn's wondrous aromas. The first thing she'd do as High Priestess—the absolute very first—would be to toss that little wretch out of the Society. And into the nearest ditch.

Elli jogged over. "Here I am, priestess."

"Good," snapped Llynia. And then, chuckling to herself as she feigned a tone of concern, she said, "I was starting to worry about you."

Elli's face hardened. "No you weren't. You were just worrying about yourself, as usual."

Llynia gasped in surprise, inhaling a mouthful of pink bubbles. She coughed—and splattered bubbles all over Fairlyn's trunk. The tree spirit started to smell a bit like rotten eggs.

"Get on with your job, girl. Now! I'll take care of your insolence later."

With that, Llynia leaned back against the moss and closed her eyes. "Remember, now, be quick as you can. And don't miss any spots."

"Don't worry," grumbled Elli.

She dug some mud out of the pot and started to apply the facial. Spreading it over Llynia's face, she glanced up at Fairlyn, whose large eyes were watching her suspiciously. Elli smiled sweetly, hoping to lull the tree spirit into leaving them alone. But Fairlyn never moved, observing Elli's hands as they moved across Llynia's cheeks, temples, and forehead. Elli bit her lip, afraid her plan wasn't going to work.

Then came a ruckus from over by the gate. And a crash. Two faeries, squabbling over a bottle of oil, had dropped it, shattering glass on the ground. Fairlyn stepped away for just a few seconds to clean up the mess, swatting her arms at the faeries and smelling like moldy worms.

That was all the time Elli needed. With a furtive glance over at Nuic, still soaking in the spray of the waterfall, she pulled out of her robe a small leather satchel. Quickly, she dumped its contents—some sparkling green powder—into the pot, then stirred it all in.

By the time Fairlyn returned, Elli was gently applying more mud to the priestess's brow. She continued, filling in the gaps on Llynia's nose, massaging her temples, and coating her eyelids. As she worked, she kept herself from laughing, or doing anything else that might arouse suspicion, by reciting to herself the Drumadians' first prayer—composed, it was said, by Elen herself. It was called the Humble Primary:

> *O Goddess, God, and all there is—*
> *Keep me*
> *Humble as the lowest roots,*
> *Grateful for the living seed,*
> *Mindful of the farthest branch,*
> *Joyful for the distant stars.*

"There," Elli declared at last. "All done."

"Goob," snarled the priestess, unable to open her mouth with the mask of mud. "Now ged oub! Leab me alobe."

"Whatever you say." Elli rose to her feet and walked briskly back to the waterfall at the far end of the Baths.

When she arrived, she peered into the spray at the top. There was Nuic, wiggling his tiny toes, as waves of turquoise and violet flowed through his body. She could easily imagine him spending much of his life just like this, soaking contentedly in alpine streams.

"I'm done," she announced.

Nuic opened his eyes. "Did she drown?"

"No. Afraid not."

"Hmmmpff, too bad. Would have made her better company."

Elli covered her mouth to stifle a laugh. "She's over there now, resting after the facial."

"Hope she gets a good rest. About twenty thousand years, maybe."

Then, noticing Elli's grin, the sprite's round face wrinkled. "You did something, didn't you? Tell me, you minx. What have you done?"

"Well," she whispered, "let's just say I did my best to make this facial . . . unforgettable. I, um, added a little ingredient of my own."

Nuic's purple eyes swelled larger. "Oh, did you now? *Not*, by some remote chance, my last satchel of deepergreen powder? I couldn't find it this morning. Been using it to perk up the ferns in Coerria's garden."

Elli reached into her robe, pulled out the empty satchel, and tossed it over to Nuic's feet on the wet stone.

The sprite tried to look angry, but Elli could see he was more amazed than anything. "You didn't really?"

She nodded cheerily. "Let's just say that after this facial, Llynia's going to be the envy of everyone."

"Especially the ferns!" Nuic released a splashy-sounding laugh. "Why, they'll be just *green* with envy."

Elli, too, burst out laughing. "But nobody will be greener than Llynia."

"You wicked, wicked child," scolded Nuic. "That was a dreadful, terrible, cruel, utterly *horrible* thing to do." His eyes positively sparkled. "Well done, Elliryanna. Well done."

Elli beamed. "Couldn't have done it without you. That's one advantage of having a maryth who's also an expert herbalist."

"Don't try to pin this on me," he answered gruffly. "If Mistress Greenface over there finds out how it happened—"

"She won't," assured Elli. "She'll just think it was some mislabeled bath ingredient. Happens all the time, the faeries told me so."

"Hmmmpff." He shook himself in the spray. "I tell you, if she ever does find out, she'll curse the teeth right out of your head! And that's only the beginning."

Elli looked over at Llynia, lying quietly in the swirling waters of the pool. Pink bubbles ringed her face like a frilled collar . . . and the slightest hint of green was starting to show in the mud beneath her eyes.

The rim of the pool, all the way around, was lined with faery people. They were, for a change, at rest—chatting and drying their translucent wings. And waiting for their next task from Fairlyn, whose arms were busily putting dozens of soaps, powders, and herbs back on the shelves. As Fairlyn's eyes glowed in satisfaction, the Baths smelled of chestnuts warmed by mid-day stars.

What smell, Elli wondered, would Fairlyn produce once she noticed the changing color of the mask? Not to mention what lay *beneath* the mask.

No doubt about it, Elli told herself. This was one facial that Llynia wouldn't ever forget.

Suddenly, the Baths' wooden gate flew open. Someone entered, along with a gust of cold air that shredded the clouds of steam.

6 · A Dead Torch and a Heap of Dung

TAMWYN STRODE OFF INTO THE NIGHT, ANXious to get away from Lott's village and that blasted hoolah. To find some food and water. And to move his limbs—so cold and stiff under his sweat-drenched tunic and leggings.

He clenched both fists, recalling the hoolah's taunts and coarse laughter. How he'd like to shake some sense into that rascal. Or even better, to wring his scrawny little neck! Just the thought made Tamwyn feel a bit warmer. Someday, maybe, he'd have that pleasure.

Most nights, when Tamwyn walked anywhere, he looked up at the stars, so mysterious and inviting. Sure, he crashed into branches or stubbed his toes now and then, but he didn't really mind. He just loved watching the stars, reading them as if they were blazing words on a blackened page. A page from a book that great powers had been writing for ages and ages—starting even before Merlin planted the magical seed that became the Great Tree of Avalon.

Tonight, though, he only looked down. At his bare feet, smudged with soot. They slapped against the packed dirt of the village path—dirt that Tamwyn knew would be white with frost by dawn, when the stars would brighten for another day.

He plodded on, nearing the communal stable at the edge of the village. Built from local flatrock, it had lasted several centuries—though from the way it was crumbling, it looked as if it wouldn't last another one. Tamwyn looked closer, especially at the withered patches of moss in the cracks. Was he imagining it, or was this rock—normally a deep orange by this time of year—losing its color? Just like so much of the landscape he'd seen this summer up in the north, the rock seemed bland, washed out. What kind of drought was this, anyway, that took both water and color from the land?

He shook his head. Maybe the colors weren't fading, at least not this far south. Maybe it was just a trick of the dim light. Or maybe he was just too tired to see clearly. As he approached the stable, a pair of starflower faeries took off from the wall, their buttery wings gleaming yellow in the starlight.

Tamwyn slapped his arms against his chest, sending up a puff of soot and broken thatch. By the wizard's beard, it was cold tonight! He blew a misty breath. Then he leaned over to stretch his stiff back. He felt as if he'd been hauling whole trees up Lott's ladder all day. Hungry and thirsty though he was, what he wanted now more than anything was someplace soft and warm, someplace to rest his weary bones. Perhaps even sleep.

His eye caught that of the nearest goat, standing off to one side of the other half dozen goats inside the stable pen. He was a black, short-eared fellow, with shaggy fur and a head so thin that his eyes looked pinched, ready to pop right out of his head. *Hello there, my friend. You cold as I am?*

The thin-faced goat shook himself, even his little nub of a tail. *Mmm-a-a-a-a-a.*

Tamwyn grinned. *Even colder, you say? Well then, why don't you get in there close with the others? They'll warm you up.*

The goat gave a sharp snort. Or a sneeze. It was hard to tell which.

Tamwyn's grin broadened. *Family feud, eh? Well look here, there are lots of other places you could go, you know. The gate's wide open.*

He pointed to the pen's wooden gate, left open in keeping with the Drumadians' law that no creature, unless it had intentionally wrought harm, could ever be confined against its own will. So the goats and geese and pigs, and even the plow horses, stayed in this human village purely by choice. In exchange for plenty of food and protection against marauding gobsken or trolls, they gave humans milk, eggs, and occasional meat (and, in the case of this shaggy fellow, lots of good knitting yarn).

Mmm-a-a-a-a-a.

Tamwyn raised an eyebrow. *Is that so? Well, they probably feel the same way about you! They'd butt you into that smelly old dung heap if they could.* He paused. *Say, there's an idea. Dung heaps are warm, you know. Why don't you just go over there and crawl in?*

Another sharp snort.

Ah yes, your dignity. What you really mean is your stubborn pride! Who cares how bad you smell? If you really want to get warm . . .

Tamwyn caught himself, midthought. Then he finished—not to the goat, but to himself: If you really want to get warm, you should just climb into the heap.

He turned to the heap of goat droppings, garbage, and who knows what else, piled against the side wall of the stable. And yes, it did smell awful. Truly awful! But then, after his long day's labor, Tamwyn hardly smelled much better. And no matter how wretched a dung heap smelled . . .

It was warm. Really warm.

Wearily, he checked over his shoulder to be sure no villagers—or that miserable hoolah—were watching. Seeing no one, he gave the goat a broad wink (and got a rude snort in return). Then he strode over to the heap. It steamed invitingly.

He crawled onto it, sinking his legs into the warm muck. A wave of horrific, rotten smells washed over him, and for an instant he felt nauseous. He almost pulled himself back out into the cold night air.

The nausea passed swiftly, though. And the warmth against his bare feet made his toes tingle. With a squirm, he plunged in deeper. And so . . . at the very same moment that the priestess Llynia, in another part of Stoneroot, sank into her herbal bath, Tamwyn sank into something entirely different.

Shoving aside some rotten ears of corn, he slid down into the muck until his whole chest was buried to his armpits. As he stretched his arms out on the dung, his long hair brushed the top of the heap. Tamwyn's back felt supported, comfortable at last; his nose grew used to the smell. He sighed, imagining himself lying in those knee-deep beds of foxtail fern near the Angenou hot springs, one of his favorite places to camp.

Suddenly he sneezed. Some lice had crawled up his nostril! Tamwyn rubbed his nose very hard. And did his best to ignore the goat who stood watching him with laughing eyes.

Tamwyn grimaced. There wasn't any doubt about where he was really camped.

In a dung heap. A pile of rotten vegetables and goat droppings.

And lice.

Maybe that old hoolah, worthless scum that he was, had been

right about one thing. *Darker than a dead torch on a moonless night.* Those were the words he'd used. But the hoolah didn't understand Tamwyn's real darkness, not at all. For it had nothing to do with all the soot on his face and feet and everywhere between. Nor with his coal black hair and eyes.

No, Tamwyn's real darkness couldn't be seen. Only felt. It sprang from the mother he barely remembered, the brother he sorely missed, and the future he couldn't imagine. And at times it felt dark, indeed. Dark as a dead torch.

Tamwyn shivered, despite all the warm muck surrounding him. His name, after all, meant Dark Flame in the tongue of his mother's people, the flamelons. He kept it, because it was the only thing she'd given him that he still possessed. Yet sometimes he wished she'd given him another name. A brighter name—something more befitting an explorer of the stars, instead of a homeless wanderer.

He closed his eyes, seeing in his memory the bright fires of the distant land where he'd been born. Fireroot—the place his mother called Rahnawyn—seemed so far away now that it was almost imaginary, like his confusing dream of that night on the fiery mountain. And yet, he knew in his heart that Fireroot was real—as real as the brother he longed to find.

Even now, in his mind, he could see the fires burning all along the rim of that crater, with towers like crooked teeth, where he and Scree used to play. Or, just as often, to fight. He flinched, remembering the big fight they'd had on their final day, seven years ago, right before the attack—and right before Scree had made his sudden, bold choice. The choice that had saved Tamwyn's life, and sent him hurtling into a new realm.

That day, and that choice, had changed everything. Absolutely everything. And left Tamwyn struggling with a host of unanswered questions.

Was Scree still alive? And if so, where? Somewhere here in Stoneroot, or in another realm? Was he still the strong young man that Tamwyn had known seven years ago—who was the same age as Tamwyn, but bigger and more muscular due to his eagleman's heritage?

And what about that walking stick of his? Scree had carried it everywhere he went, even when he took flight as an eagleman, refusing to let anyone else even touch it. There was something odd about that gnarled piece of wood . . . something Tamwyn could never quite put into words. It had always intrigued him.

He opened his eyes and plunged his hand into the muck. As he drew the dagger from his belt sheath, he thought of the old farmer who had given it to him years before. Tamwyn had been helping with some plowing when, right in the middle of a cornfield, he'd plowed up the dagger, which the farmer had called "a gift from the land." The blade was battered even then, and rusty at the hilt. But it worked well enough in his young hands, and it was all he needed for cutting fresh stalks of eelgrass, slicing open a fistnut, or carving his own water gourd.

Or just for whittling.

He spied a shard of wood, part of a broken branch, on the heap. In the stars' dim light it looked blacker than the dung, and just within reach. A squirm, a stretch—and he grabbed it.

Just why he always felt better when he whittled, he couldn't say. But it never failed to help. Even when he sliced his poor thumb, which he'd done too many times to count, he found this work somehow soothing.

He turned the wood in his hand, feeling its contours, then

started shaving the bark. Thin, twisting curls fell away. Tamwyn gripped harder and cut a few deep notches at the base of the shard. Were it not for the stench of the dung heap, he could have told what sort of wood it was by its scent. Or, if it hadn't been night-time, by the color and grain.

Probably ash, he thought. *Or some of that thorny spikewood, the sort that always rips my tunic.* He grinned. Already he was feeling better.

A sound by the stable made him stop whittling and look up. There, beyond the far side of the goat pen, five or six shadowy figures were passing by.

Tamwyn squinted, peering into the darkness. They weren't humans. Nor elves. Nor gobsken. These figures didn't move with the sway or bounce of two-legged creatures. And not four-leggeds, either. No stag or doe would stand so upright.

A clutch of young ogres, perhaps? No—these people, whatever they were, moved far too smoothly. Silently. As if they were not walking at all . . . but rolling. Or floating upon a breath of magic.

Tree spirits.

Tamwyn watched, his heart thumping in wonder. The spir-its, though varying heights, all had the same lush hair that swept down their sides and swished from side to side as they floated along. That, plus their lithe forms—and the sheer grace of their movements—made him guess that they had once been willows.

As a regular wanderer in the wilderness, Tamwyn knew that it was rare indeed to see tree spirits moving about freely. In all his time trekking through Stoneroot, he'd seen only one: a maple spirit who was the maryth of a Drumadian priest. And to see so many at once—this was truly extraordinary. For tree spirits only traveled freely when their host trees died or were gravely ill. Even then, they often stayed very near the spot where they had so long been rooted, hiding themselves away in hollow trunks or abandoned burrows.

Something else struck him, as well. If tree spirits ever did travel far from home, it was usually because their host tree and all of its surroundings had been so badly damaged, or made so unlivable, that they just couldn't remain there any longer. Maybe that was why these willows seemed, beneath their grace, so very sad.

Tamwyn swallowed. These creatures were beautiful, to be sure. But they were also a sign. Of what, he couldn't guess . . . though he felt sure it wasn't good.

At that moment a new figure appeared, striding in the opposite direction. A man—and a strange one from the look of his silhouette. He walked in a jaunty, carefree way, like a young fellow just come of age. Yet he wore a thick beard that looked wider than it was long. Its pointed tips glowed silver in the starlight. Was he young or old? Tamwyn leaned forward in the dung heap, trying to see better, but he just couldn't tell.

Then there was his hat. If it really was a hat! Wide-brimmed, with a crown that curled like one of Tamwyn's wood shavings, it hung down over one ear, as lopsided as any hat could be.

To Tamwyn's surprise, the tree spirits didn't scatter and hide. They simply flowed around the man, moving as smoothly as honey poured from a bowl. All at once they joined their long arms, enclosing him in a circle. There they stood, swaying expectantly under the nighttime stars, as if waiting for him to perform.

Of course! A bard.

Sure enough, the man pulled a small lute from his cloak and plucked a single resonant chord. Then, his face grave but respectful, he gave the willowy figures a deep bow.

As he bent forward, his hat fell off. Tamwyn started to chuckle, then caught his breath. For sitting on top of the bard's bald head was a small, teardrop-shaped creature with bluish skin, flecked with gold. It wore nothing but a long translucent robe that shimmered in the starlight. And though the features of its narrow face were delicate, they seemed also very flexible—and very expressive. Right now, the creature's wide mouth was curled downward, in a mixture of impatience and boredom. Or maybe lack of air from being too long under the hat.

Just then, the creature started to hum—a rolling, layered hum that was both far deeper and much higher than any sound Tamwyn had ever heard. It vibrated in his ears, and even more, in his bones. He felt slightly giddy, as if he'd drunk too much mead, caught up in a swirl of emotions too strange to name. And he knew, without doubt, just what sort of creature this was.

A museo, he thought, feeling a new surge of awe. He knew about them, of course—who in Avalon didn't?—but he'd never seen one before. Or heard one hum, in that amazing voice. Now he truly understood the old saying *As rare as the note from a museo's throat*.

And besides, as Tamwyn knew well, museos themselves were rare, even in their native realm of Shadowroot. People disagreed about whether they had always been so few in number, or whether they had been hunted down by the dark elves, death dreamers, and other savage creatures in Shadowroot who had no use for songs of any kind. Some people believed that the museos had been driven out of Shadowroot altogether, centuries ago, after some of them had sided with the humans, wood elves, and eaglefolk in the bloody fighting of the Age of Storms.

Whatever the truth, this much was agreed: What few museos

existed no longer lived in Shadowroot. Over the centuries, they'd been reported in most of the other realms of Avalon—even, it was said, in faraway Woodroot. They usually traveled with a bard, but not just any one would do. Only the wisest and most skillful bard could hope to win the loyalty of a museo.

Tamwyn shifted in the dung heap, suddenly puzzled. Could that silly old man with the sideways-growing beard really be enough of a bard to carry a museo?

As if in answer, the bard strummed a new chord on his lute. He swayed jauntily, though his face remained serious. Starlight glinted off his horizontal whiskers. And he began to sing, more clearly than a meadowlark on a summer morn.

> *The oldest song I sing ye now*
> *Of dreams that yet survive,*
> *Of yearning, suff'ring, hopes long lost—*
> *And spirit still alive.*

So that's what they've chosen, thought Tamwyn. It was "The Ballad of Avalon's Birth"—his world's oldest and most cherished song. He'd heard it many times before, to be sure. But never like this.

He leaned farther forward. And opened himself to the song, at once so old and so new.

7 · The Ballad of Avalon's Birth

TAMWYN STRETCHED FORWARD, LISTENING. The night air remained cold, but he felt warmer than before. Not just from the heat of the dung surrounding him, nor from the pleasing sight of all those thousands of stars above. Instead, this new warmth came from the music itself—music made from the voice of a bard, the hum of a museo, and the pluck of a lute. And from something else . . . something more magical still.

> *The oldest song I sing ye now*
> *Of dreams that yet survive,*
> *Of yearning, suff'ring, hopes long lost—*
> *And spirit still alive.*

> *The mythic birth of Avalon,*
> *A world begun a seed,*
> *Embraces all we might become*
> *And lo, what all we need.*

Yet in the seed is found as well
The greed and rage and fears
That make the freely flowing rill
Become a trail of tears.

What shall become of Avalon,
Our dream, our deepest need?
What glory or despair shall sprout
From Merlin's magic seed?

The seed that beat just like a heart
Was won by Merlin's hand
When he the magic Mirror saved
And found a distant land.

The wizard Merlin lost his home,
Fincayra wrapped in mist—
But gained the seed, a simple sphere,
By endless wonders kissed.

So even as Fincayra fell,
And heard his parting speech,
The Isle Forgotten joined the shore
Impossible to reach.

A day of miracles emerged
From winter's longest night—
A day of wings, and children brave,
And dazzling dreams so bright.

Yet none of these could e'er outshine
The secret of the seed.
It held a Tree of boundless size
And lo, a whole new creed:

That creatures all might live in peace,
With Nature's bounty theirs;
That here between the other worlds
Exists a world that dares

To celebrate the sweep of life
That walks or swims or flies,
To honor ev'ry living thing
That breathes and grows and dies.

Fair Avalon, the Tree of Life
That ev'ry creature knows—
A world part Heaven and part Earth
And part what wind that blows.

The bard paused, allowing his words to echo through the night: *And part what wind that blows . . . what wind . . . that blows . . . that blows . . . that blows.*

His eyes glistened darkly. Then he turned just a bit so that he almost faced the stable and the dung heap. Tamwyn couldn't be sure, but he felt that maybe the bard had seen him. And was watching him from the edge of those dark eyes.

Tamwyn sat utterly still, hardly daring to breathe. Please, he thought. Please don't leave. *Let me hear more!*

Just then, the tree spirits surrounding the bard began to dance.

Their willowy shapes spun in slow, graceful circles; their long hair flowed outward, gleaming in the light of the stars. All at once, they kicked their rootlike legs, arching their backs like saplings bent with snow. Yet their faces, still and somber, never changed. Around and around the bard they spun, their slender feet never touching the ground.

The museo, meanwhile, leaned back a bit on the bard's bald head so that its narrow face turned toward the stars. It started to hum louder than before. Just one note—a single note that rolled right underneath the bard's echoing words, carrying them farther and farther, like a swelling wave on a boundless sea.

The note pierced Tamwyn's heart, emptied it out, then filled it up completely. Feelings swept through him, one after another. First loneliness, then hope, then yearning for something powerful—something he couldn't quite grasp, nor even name. Yet he wanted it, longed for it, ached for it dearly.

At last, the bard strummed again upon his lute. The museo's hum grew quieter; the tree spirits stopped their dance. Then the bard tilted his head slightly, half of his beard shining with starlight, and began to sing:

> *Now mist surrounds another world—*
> *The world of Avalon.*
> *Its roots enormous are the realms*
> *That all may live upon.*

> *Above the root-realms stands the trunk,*
> *A bridge that binds us all:*
> *Between the Earth and Otherworld,*
> *Our Avalon stands tall.*

And so the Tree's foundation is
The Seven Realms of lore:
First Mudroot, where new life begins,
Malóch its name of yore.

Then Shadowroot, so dark and cold,
Lastrael was its name;
And Stoneroot with its mountains high
Olanabram became.

Now Waterroot, so wide and deep,
Brynchilla called at first;
And Fireroot, fair Rahnawyn,
By foes too often cursed.

Next Airroot, home to sylphs afloat
In Y Swylarna's skies;
And Woodroot, most remote of all,
El Urien so wise.

I ask again and asked afore
The question ages old—
The question clear whose answer still
Has never been foretold:

What shall become of Avalon,
Our dream, our deepest need?
What glory or despair shall sprout
From Merlin's magic seed?

At this point, Tamwyn caught another glance from the bard. This time he felt sure that the fellow had seen him. But the bard went right on singing, as if nothing mattered but the song itself.

> *The Age of Flowering began,*
> *The first of Avalon.*
> *So came the founders of the creed:*
> *Elen and Rhiannon.*

> *As creatures thrived, they filled the lands*
> *So wondrous and diverse.*
> *The stars shone bright on Avalon,*
> *And sang elusive verse.*

> *Enchanted portals linked the realms:*
> *Serella led the way.*
> *And Merlin left, though prayed he might*
> *Return another day.*

> *Then stars aligned in strange new ways,*
> *Destroying cherished forms—*
> *And soon across the Seven Realms*
> *Began the Age of Storms.*

> *The winds of greed and arrogance*
> *Blew now relentlessly,*
> *And sucked the precious sap of life*
> *From deep inside the Tree.*

At last, long last, through Merlin's aid,
The storms of war fell still.
Yet now the winds of Avalon
Contained a subtle chill.

And so the agonies that birthed
The Age of Ripening—
A time when all through Avalon
The highest hopes took wing—

Gave birth, as well, to prophecy.
Our Lady of the Lake
Arose and did for all to hear
A Dark prediction make:

"A year shall come when stars go dark,
And faith will fail anon—
For born shall be a child who spells
The end of Avalon.

"The only hope beneath the stars
To save that world so fair
Will be the Merlin then alive:
The wizard's own true heir."

What shall become of Avalon,
Our dream, our deepest need?
What glory or despair shall sprout
From Merlin's magic seed?

The bard fell silent, as did the museo. A gentle breeze arose, rustling the hair of the encircling tree spirits, and the fields of barley beyond the village. But other than the soothing whisper of night air, no sound could be heard.

In Tamwyn's mind a certain phrase stuck, clinging to his thoughts like a burr to his leggings: *the wizard's true heir*. He felt sure that he'd heard that phrase a long time ago—before he'd ever heard it in the ballads of wandering bards.

He closed his eyes, trying to remember. Was it from a dream? From *the* dream? He could almost hear it, spoken aloud, with reverence and a touch of fear. *The wizard's true heir*. But who had said it? And why?

He shook his head, unable to remember. And yet . . .

Hearing some movement, Tamwyn opened his eyes. They were leaving! As the tree spirits bowed low and floated away into the night, the bard replaced the lopsided hat on his head, covering the museo. And then, with a twirl of his sideways-growing beard, he strode off.

Tamwyn swallowed, for he knew that his moment of peace—as well as his vague memories—had disappeared, as well. Now he was back in the dung. By himself, as usual.

No, wait—not quite by himself. He lifted his gaze to the stars. They were still here, still his companions! Amidst the vastness of the night, so many lights shone—thousands upon thousands of them. There were the constellations he knew so well: Pegasus, the Golden Bough, Twisted Tree, and White Dragon.

And there, just above the hills on the horizon, the Wizard's Staff. Not the most beautiful constellation—just seven stars: a line of five crowned by two at the top, so close, they nearly touched.

But those stars were probably the most storied ones in Avalon. For those stars had gone dark, one by one, several centuries ago— right before the dreadful Age of Storms.

Up to that time, no celestial event in the history of Avalon had caused so much turmoil. When the Wizard's Staff vanished, there had been riots among the dwarves in Fireroot, and mass marches on the great temple of the Society of the Whole, right here in Stoneroot. For many people, the War of Storms didn't end when the peace treaty was signed at last—but when Merlin, through some powerful magic, finally rekindled the seven stars.

Tamwyn chewed his lip. The only other time Avalon's stars had ever gone dark was the stellar eclipse in the Year of Avalon 985. That was the Year of Darkness—the year of Tamwyn's birth. And also, if the stories were true, the year of someone else's birth, someone who would bring about the end of Avalon.

Who was the child of the Dark Prophecy? And who was that child's greatest foe, the true heir of Merlin? Tamwyn had heard many debates over the years, in taverns and farm fields, about whether such an heir even existed. Or, if he or she did exist, who it might be. Some believed it was the Lady of the Lake herself: She had, after all, helped Merlin end the War of Storms. But more and more people were claiming that a humble teacher somewhere in Woodroot, a fellow named Hanwan Belamir, was really Merlin's heir.

Tamwyn lowered his gaze. Those were exactly the kinds of questions that Scree had always liked to debate. All through the night, until the stars brightened again the next morning. He just loved a good argument, waving his arms—or his precious walking stick—to make his points. *I miss that stubborn old scrap of bark. Even if he was just as gnome-headed as, well, as . . .*

Tamwyn swallowed hard. *As a brother.*

Once again he looked up at the stars, blinking to clear his vision. At first he didn't notice what was happening to the Wizard's Staff. Then something struck him as odd.

He blinked again—and caught his breath. For the constellation had, indeed, changed. Right before his eyes. Where just a moment ago there had been seven stars, there were now only six. A star had gone dark!

What that meant, he could only guess.

8 · Out of the Shadows

WITH SURPRISING SPEED FOR SUCH A bulky warrior, Harlech took a step backward. He moved away from the base of the stone tower that rose from the rim of Waterroot's deepest canyon, the Canyon of Crystillia. Away from the shadows that were darker than the darkest pit. And away from the cloaked figure skulking there.

"Merlin hisself?" he sputtered. "Yer goin' to steal somethin' from the wizard Merlin?"

"No, you fool. Merlin is gone, long gone! I shall take it from the person the prophecies call *the true heir of Merlin*. But the effect, my Harlech, will be the same. Mmmyesss." He gave a low, throaty laugh. "You see, he carries with him a staff—the staff of his master! It looks like just a simple walking stick, my Harlech, which is why I've had to search so many years to find it. But this walking stick has great powers, mmmyesss. Powers I shall soon possess."

The white hand of the cloaked figure stabbed at the air, pointing to the great stone dam that spanned the canyon below them, to the enormous white lake it contained, and to the teams of enslaved horses, deer, mules, dwarves, wolves, and oxen. They were dragging new stones from the open-pit mines, hauling more freshly cut trees for scaffolding, pulling heavy barges across the lake, and making repairs to the narrow road that ran across the top of the dam—all at the insistent cracking of men's whips. In the distance, the White Geyser of Crystillia rumbled and threw its water high into the air, just as it had done since the birth of Avalon from Merlin's magical seed.

Only now the geyser's white water did not flow down into Waterroot and its neighboring realms—but stopped here, trapped behind the dam. To the very few explorers who had ever reached this remote place, the sight of the dam, the lake, and the dry canyons below Prism Gorge would have been shocking. And the sight of slaves—even more so.

"I shall use that staff, mmmyesss, my Harlech. For something most special. Most special, indeed. And then . . . I shall destroy it! And at the same time, I shall destroy forever Merlin's hold on this world."

Harlech tilted his head and scratched the jagged scar that ran across his jaw. "The wizard ain't goin' to like that, Master. Nor, I 'spect, his true heir."

"You think that matters?" The sorcerer released a high, whistling laugh, like the hiss of a satisfied snake. "The lost staff will soon be the least of their problems. For I will use it, my Harlech, to gain something far greater: the control of Avalon."

"Jest how, Master?" Harlech edged closer to the shadows. "Can ye tell me?"

The white hands rubbed together. "This much I will say, all your feeble mind can hold. With the help of that staff, I will make something powerful—so powerful that, before long, I will control all Seven Realms, the very roots of the Great Tree . . . roots that support the entire Tree, give it strength, and produce the élano that runs through its veins. And as the roots go, my Harlech, so shall the Tree. All of Avalon, to its remotest branches, will then be in my grasp! Mmmyesss, as surely as the spirit lord Rhita Gawr rules on high."

Harlech brushed a bead of sweat off his temple. "But Master, won't yer enemies try some tricks to stop ye?"

"Tricks, mmmyesss. But I have something better than tricks. I have knowledge! Just as no one else in Avalon knows what I have built here, at the wellspring of High Brynchilla, no one else knows that Merlin's staff is still in Avalon."

"The true heir—"

"All right, he himself probably knows! But no one else. Not even the child of the Dark Prophecy, whose help I have long awaited . . . not even he knows about the staff. Unless, of course, he can read entrails as well as I can."

The mirthless laugh came again. "For you see, my Harlech, I have learned something just this morning, from a wild boar that one of my ghoulacas found in Fireroot. A boar whose bloody entrails told me what I have been seeking to learn for seventeen years."

He cracked his white knuckles in delight. "I know where it is, my Harlech. *I know where the staff is hidden.*"

A wild wind rose out of the canyons, shrieking as it passed, hurling sand and shards of stone from the quarries. Harlech winced as the gust blew over him—whether from the biting shards, or his master's words, or both.

As the wind died down again, the voice from the shadows

clucked with amusement. "You needn't worry, though, my Harlech. Just do as your master says, and your own entrails will be safe."

Looking unconvinced, Harlech's hands played nervously with the handles of the daggers, club, rapier, and broadsword dangling from his leather belt. "As ye wish, Master."

Just then a mother nuthatch, blown so hard by the wind that she almost hit the tower, flew over them. In her beak she held a writhing slug, food needed by her three fledglings, who were now peeping hungrily from their nest in the boughs of a cedar on the nearest edge of Woodroot. But the sight of the sorcerer in the shadows—and the teams of slaves working on the dam—made her flap her wings in sudden fright. She shrieked, dropping the slug.

In one swift motion, Harlech whipped out his broadsword and sliced through the air. The bird's shriek ended abruptly as her headless body spun into the shadows, followed by a pair of drifting feathers. The head itself struck the side of the redrock tower and bounced to the ground.

Harlech glanced down at the head, its eyes frozen wide with terror. He gave a sharp kick with his boot. The head took a final, brief flight, then rolled across the rocky ground and fell into the quarry pit.

"Swift work, my Harlech. I have relied on our remoteness to keep us safe. That, and a spell to ward off any small beasts that might stray too close to this canyon—and our little project. Even so, the cursed wind still tries to thwart me. And yet we simply can't have any spies discovering our plans, can we?"

Harlech's upper lip curled in satisfaction. He blew a bloody feather off the blade and sheathed his sword. "No, Master."

"So now . . . do you have the slave I need?"

The man tensed again. He fidgeted, thinking hard. "Er, I'm not sure, Master. Ye needs one wid fight, ye say. An' what else?"

The sorcerer's voice lowered ominously. "With a brain— bigger than yours! Mmmyesss, so it can understand language."

"Language, Master? What kind do ye mean? The oxen'll speak theirs, the bears'll do theirs, and those damn wolves'll go a-howlin' theirs, 'specially when they're feelin'—"

"Silence!" spat the voice. "I mean the only language that matters, the only language that truly deserves that name."

"Aye, ye mean *human*."

"Yes, and there will soon be one human who speaks no more, if he doesn't work faster."

Harlech gulped. "Me pardons, Master, but . . . er, we don't have any human slaves, as ye know. As ye commanded, these many years ago. Only dumb beasts."

The pale fingers stretched out and clutched at the air, as if they were squeezing someone's neck. "Dumb beasts is right! I didn't say the slave should *be* a human. Just that it should *understand* a human. To grasp my instructions!"

Harlech started to edge away. "The-there's them dwarves, they kin speak human tongue. B-but no, they never foller orders. Stubborn as blind one-eyed jackasses! Jest this mornin' I cut the ears off o' that—"

"Harlech!"

"W-well . . . there's a wild horse, Master, a right smart mare indeed. M-m-mebbe she'd do. But," he added nervously, "fer them two lame legs."

One of the white hands flashed out from the shadowed wall and grabbed his wrist. "Something better, Harlech. Think fast."

"Aaaargh!" The big man's face twisted as waves of pain surged through his arm. Sweat poured off his brow, stinging his eyes. "I, I . . . don't know, M-M-Master."

The white hand flexed ever so slightly. Harlech yowled again and fell to his knees. The sword blades clanged against the ground as he writhed.

"Elves!" he blurted, twisting to free himself.

The white hand released him. "Elves? I don't recall seeing any such creatures here. When did you capture them?"

"Only a few days ago, Master." Harlech rubbed his wrist under the burned sleeve of his shirt. "Two o' them, an ol' geezer an' a she-elf. His kin, mebbe. Useless in the quarries, too thin an' weak. An' that she-elf, too damn sassy. So I been puttin' them to use haulin' ropes for the barges." He grinned maliciously. "They don't seem to likes followin' orders."

"How did you come by these elves?"

"Garr, I done snared their horses o'er in Woodroot. Then they tracked me, an' tried to waylay me wid their bows an' arrers. I bested them, but lost two o' me best men. After all they'd seen, me first thought was to kill them quick. But then I thinks—no, Harlech, here's a better idea. Jest bring them back fer slaves."

"Mmmyesss, well done. Elves are haughty creatures, thinking themselves the equals of humans. But they should be intelligent enough for the task. And from what you say, they should be . . . persuadable. Bring them to me at the Overlook."

The dark figure left the shadow of the tower, drew the hood of his gray cloak tight, and slunk away along the rim. Harlech watched the sorcerer leave. After a few seconds, he cursed silently and wrenched himself to his feet, still rubbing his sore arm through the hole in his sleeve.

Harlech glanced down into the quarry pit, where two of his men were whipping an unruly mare. He nodded in approval, then started down the road that led to the top of the dam. That was where most of the work was happening now, as the final layers of stone were being moved into place. And that was where he'd find those elves, slacking off, no doubt.

His heavy boots pounded on the road, sending up clouds of red dirt. Though made by slaves only a few months before, this road already showed many ruts and holes from all the tree trunks and blocks of stone that had been dragged along its length. The whole project was nearly done, but he made a mental note to get some slaves up here to make repairs on the road. Slaves were best off staying busy, right up until the moment the master had no more use for them. And then . . . Harlech smiled savagely.

Just as he rounded the final bend beneath the hill, a slim figure came hurtling around the curve from the other side and smashed right into him. Both tumbled over on the dirt. Harlech, though surprised, drew both his daggers at once. He rolled on top of whoever it was and pointed his blades at the angry face. A face with deep green eyes, pointed ears, and an extremely sharp tongue.

"Get off me, you giant turd! Before I . . ."

"Why, if it ain't the she-elf," Harlech said with a savage grin. "Saved me the trouble o' fetchin' ye wid forcible means, ye did."

"I'll save you nothing," declared the young elf. She tried to twist free, but he grabbed her by her long braid of honey-colored hair and yanked her back. She glared up at him—then spat right in his eye.

Harlech growled with rage and pressed his daggerpoints against her throat. "Slipped outa yer chains, did ye? Tryin' to run away? Lucky I ain't free to slice off yer pointy ears, ye liddle snake. Cuz iffen I could, ye'd be bathin' in yer own blood right now."

"Snakes don't have pointy ears, you dolt." She started to say more, then froze, as her eyes shifted to something behind the warrior. "No, Granda!" she shrieked. "Just get away!"

In an instant, Harlech turned, dodged the swipe of a wooden cane, and threw out an arm that tripped the old, white-bearded elf who had tried to strike him. Before the elf could rise again, Harlech sheathed his daggers and grabbed both of the elves around their necks. His fingers squeezed so tight, they both coughed, barely able to breathe.

All the way back up the road he dragged them, battering their bodies against jagged rocks and deep ruts. His grip around their necks never slackened. When he reached the stone tower, he turned roughly and hauled them along the rim for quite some distance until he reached a ledge that overlooked the steepest wall of the canyon. By the time he dropped them at the ledge, the elves' once-green robes of sturdy barkthread were torn and splattered with blood. Both elves lay motionless.

A low cackle sounded from the shadows under a huge, rectangular stone at one side of the ledge. The monolith's face had been carved with intricate runes useful in the dark magic of disemboweling creatures while they were still alive: spells to keep their writhing to a minimum; chants to cast their heart or intestines or stomach in just the right way so that hidden truths could be revealed from organs and blood; and, of course, incantations to keep the sensation of pain as strong as possible—since pain often prolonged the victim's life. Beneath the monolith, the remains of a freshly killed wild boar lay scattered on the ground.

"Excellent work, my Harlech. Excellent."

As Harlech stood watch over the limp bodies of the slaves, the cloaked figure turned and stepped closer to the very edge of the canyon, now nearly full of white water. Here he stood, pale hands outstretched to the view before him. The vast dam, built of stone and magically strengthened mortar made from the white water itself, spanned the gorge, binding together its red rock walls. One face of the dam was covered with scaffolding, sliced from trees that once grew on the rim closest to Woodroot. The other face held back the lake full of water from the White Geyser of Crystallia. Wind whipped the lake's surface, making waves that slammed against the barrier of stone. Far in its depths, phosphorescent flecks sparkled in the whiteness. Like a beast caged against its will, the great lake heaved and frothed, trying to break free.

Below the dam, Prism Gorge looked as dry as a fire dragon's throat. Only a year ago, before construction began, white water tumbled through this place, sparkling day and night with a phosphorescent glow, before separating into seven rushing rivers of different colors. But now only the dark shadow of the dam towered over the gorge. No more water, not even a trickle, ran down the seven smaller canyons. The only motion came from the many enslaved creatures who were still toiling at the base of the dam.

Hundreds more slaves could be seen on the scaffolding, the canyon walls, and the top of dam. Horses, deer, oxen, goats, and dwarves, their legs and necks chained, hauled blocks of stone from the quarries to the barges. Ropes, boards, tools, and other lighter materials were carried by teams of haggard owls, cranes, crows, and condors. And flocks of tiny light flyers hovered in shadowy places, giving enough light for the masons to fit their stones—and the slave drivers to crack their whips. Whatever task these slaves performed, they didn't understand the purpose of their labors. All they understood was that they had lost forever their freedom. And that their only escape from this torment of labor, hunger, and cruelty would be death.

Beneath his hood, the cloaked figure clucked in satisfaction. The monstrous project was nearly done. Only two weeks left—three perhaps, given the sluggishness of these slaves. And then, after tapping the power of Merlin's staff, his life's greatest dream would become reality. With the help of Rhita Gawr, he would control Avalon, destroy his enemies, and eliminate forever the influence of Merlin. Then he would remake this world in another design—a design befitting the greatest sorcerer of all times.

Suddenly the young elf woman coughed and rolled onto her side. Though her braid was coated with dirt and blood, it still shone with light. The cloaked figure lowered his hands and moved closer, watching her from the shadows. After more spasms of coughing, she opened her eyes.

What she saw first nearly made her retch. Intestines, a bladder, and a shredded liver, all still bloody, were strewn across the rock ledge. Just beyond them lay the disemboweled body of a young boar—killed not for its meat, nor even for its fiery orange tusks, but for a purpose far more despicable. Entrail reading! She had heard stories of evil sorcerers on mortal Earth who practiced that art. But here in Avalon?

Clenching her teeth, she rolled over. There lay her grandfather! As still as stone. She crawled weakly to his side and lay her head on his chest, just below his ragged white beard. "Breathe, Granda. Breathe!"

Nothing.

She planted her hands upon his ribs and pushed—once, twice, three times. "Breathe! Oh, please . . . breathe."

Still nothing.

"Here now," bellowed Harlech. "Yer not pushin' hard 'nuf. Try this!"

He kicked his heavy boot into the side of the old elf's chest. With a sickening crack, several ribs snapped. The elf's slim body lifted right off the ground, rolled in the air, and landed hard.

"No! Stop!" shrieked the elf maiden, diving to catch hold of Harlech's leg.

Easily sidestepping her, he moved closer to the limp form of her grandfather. "Once more jest might do it."

Drawing back his leg, he slammed his boot again into the elf's side. Again the old elf flew into the air, releasing a painful groan when he fell back on the ledge. A trickle of blood ran down from his mouth.

"Stop! Stop!" his granddaughter cried, cradling his broken body in her own.

"Jest a few more times, dearie." Harlech stood over her, his hand on the hilt of his rapier. "Or mebbe you'd rather I try pokin' around wid me liddle blade here."

"No, no, please."

Harlech drew his sword. His heart raced, fed by the fear he could see in her green eyes. The blade lifted, catching sparks of light from Waterroot's stars.

"No!" she cried.

Harlech's sword plunged, straight for the old elf's ribs—

And suddenly froze. The tip halted just above the elder's chest. Harlech tried to move his arm—without success. He swore, twisted, and grunted with effort, but he seemed held by invisible bonds.

A voice rasped from the shadows by the stone monolith. "There, there now, my Harlech. That's quite enough." A white hand waved, and the big man fell over backward, dropping his sword on the ledge. "One might think you were trying to *harm* the poor fellow."

The elf maiden, cheeks glazed with tears, turned to the cloaked figure. "Who are you?"

"I am someone who can help you," came the reply. "Mmm-yesss."

She glanced back at Harlech, who was cursing under his breath as he retrieved his sword. Then she eyed the shadowed form suspiciously. "Why don't you show yourself?"

"I have my reasons." His voice lowered grimly. "Once, long ago, I walked freely under the stars. And one day soon, I will again."

The cloaked head turned upward, as if it were scanning the sky. Then, under his breath, the figure muttered, "Where *are* those ghoulacas? They are late . . . though not so late as the child of the Prophecy."

Something about that voice, let alone his words, made the elf maiden shudder. Yet if there was any chance at all he could save her grandfather—she had to find out. "You said you could help."

"Indeed I can, mmmyesss."

"And not the way you helped that boar over there."

The cloaked figure clucked his tongue. "Now, now, elf maiden. You are a pretty one . . . but a bit more respect would serve you well. That little boar has helped me much today. So much that I told my ghoulaca who brought it to go find the rest of its flock and bring them back to me. For now, with what I know, I do not need to wait any longer—not for the child, nor for anything else." He made a throaty laugh. "Mmmyess, so you would like the old elf to live?"

She pressed her cheek against Granda's forehead. "You . . . can really save him? You have that power?"

A sharp gust of wind wailed across the rim of the canyon. A fragment from the monolith, high above the sorcerer's head, broke loose and fell to the ground. Then the wind suddenly shifted, blowing a great sheet of spray off the lake. A shower of water rained down on the ledge, making him clutch tight to his hood.

When the spray finally stopped, the voice came again, now with an edge of anger. "I have that power, mmmyesss. And soon, I assure you, I will have more. Much more. Enough to turn aside the wind!"

The voice paused for several seconds, then spoke more calmly. "That is why I have built this dam, which holds so much precious water, as well as . . . well, you needn't hear more. All you need to know is—"

"That you *didn't* build the dam," she interrupted, unable to hold back her temper. "Slaves built it! Free creatures—chained and whipped and beaten to do your work! Whatever you plan to do with all that water you've stolen, it isn't worth that."

Another laugh came from the shadows. "Is it worth your grandfather's life?"

Her back straightened. As an elf, she'd been taught from birth to value all life—from the unfathomably huge, all-embracing boughs of the Great Tree to the tiniest little insect. And yet there was one life, one person, she valued above all others. "Yes," she whispered hoarsely. "It is."

"Good. Then tell me your name."

"Brionna." She stroked Granda's bloody lip. Only the faintest breath, warm against her hand, told her he was still alive. "Please, whoever you are. Please save him!"

"Certainly, Brionna. I will save him, mmmyesss. All I need, my pretty one, is a small service from you."

She swallowed. "What service?"

"I need you to fetch something. Something, mmmyesss, I have long desired."

9 · A Dangerous Journey

THE BATHS' WOODEN GATE FLEW OPEN, slamming against a tall set of shelves. Vials of oils and herbs tottered and fell—some into a thick clump of ferns, and others onto the ground with a smash of broken glass. Faeries flew up in fright, wings all abuzz, zipping through the thick clouds of steam. Fairlyn swung around, all her arms waving, her aroma now a mixture of rotten rat carcass and crushed condor egg.

Llynia sat up sharply, spraying water and bubbles and chunks of mud paste everywhere. Some mud fell into the swirling pool, whose waters turned dark green for an instant before returning to pink. Her exposed cheek and brow (along with some of her once-blond hair) shone a pale green color, which seemed to deepen by the second. And though she didn't know about her new skin tone, she *did* know that someone had rudely disturbed her bath.

"In the name of Elen the Founder!" she thundered, the veins in her greenish temples pounding with rage. "Who dares to interrupt the bath of the next High Priestess?"

"Merely one of Elen's disciples," answered a quiet voice from the billowing mist.

Llynia, recognizing the voice, gasped in surprise. She lurched backward, splashing more water over the lush moss of the rim. More of her mud mask broke off, so that now she had only splotches left, including one large chunk that clung to her chin like a scrawny beard.

"High Priestess Coerria," she said apologetically.

"That's right," declared the elderly woman, her long white hair falling over her shoulders. "The *current* High Priestess."

Hastily, Llynia tried to stand, but slipped and fell into the pool with a resounding splat. Again she stood, aided this time by one of Fairlyn's outstretched arms. Then she grabbed a wet towel, shook off the frightened faeries who had landed there, and wrapped it around herself as a robe.

"I . . . I'm sorry," she said, trying to speak calmly. "I wasn't . . . er, expecting you."

"No," replied Coerria, "I suppose you weren't."

From the waterfall on the far side of the Baths, Elli leaned forward to see better. She watched Coerria step out of the steam to the edge of the pool, her silken gown rippling gracefully. Then, as the Elder turned, Elli noticed something new: Just behind her head hovered a small, flying creature that resembled a bumblebee—and was busily braiding her hair, strand by strand.

Elli smiled. Was that tiny little creature her maryth? No wonder Elli hadn't noticed before.

The old woman's eyes, as blue as an alpine tarn, studied Llynia. "I hadn't planned to disturb you, my child. But . . ." She paused, her expression concerned. "Are you feeling all right? You look a bit . . . green."

Within the spray of the waterfall, Nuic made a sound like a pig snorting.

Meanwhile, Fairlyn bent closer to Llynia and swept a blossom-rimmed arm across her cheek. The smell of rat carcass grew suddenly stronger. What few faeries remained near the pool buzzed off to the far corners of the Baths, or out into the night.

Still disoriented, Llynia blustered, "No, no, I'm fine. Fine." Then she brushed aside Fairlyn's arm and snapped, "Foolish maryth! Stop smelling like that, will you? Or you *will* make me sick."

Fairlyn withdrew, as a new scent—something akin to bruised melons—wafted through the steam.

The Elder seemed, for an instant, thoughtful. Then her face turned gravely serious. "As I said, I hadn't planned to disturb you. But something has happened."

"What?" demanded Llynia, her old haughtiness returning. "What could possibly be important enough to make you barge in here like this?"

"That." Coerria raised her thin arm toward the night sky. Countless stars, shimmering through the rising mist, shone overhead. It was one of those nights that inspired poetry and songs about the vastness—and mystery—of Avalon's stars.

But Coerria was pointing to one particular constellation—a line of seven stars. Only now, one of those stars had gone dark.

Llynia sucked in her breath. "The Wizard's Staff . . ."

"That's right," said the High Priestess somberly. "It's lost a star." Under her breath, she added, "Now, in the seventeenth year of the Dark child."

At those words, the remaining faeries, wherever they were hiding, panicked. All at once they flew into the misty air and buzzed around, shrieking, swooping, and bumping into each other in their frenzy. It took all of Fairlyn's many arms to shoo them over the wooden fence surrounding the Baths.

Elli, for her part, was so stunned, she stepped backward—right into the waterfall. The harp on her back banged against a stone and jangled loudly, while Nuic cried out in surprise.

Llynia spun around, the muddy beard on her chin quaking with rage. "Get out of here, you little—" Catching a reproachful look from the High Priestess, she abruptly changed her tone. "Little . . . little one."

Llynia swept an arm toward the gate, clipping the wing of a red-suited faery who was flying past. As the faery plunged into the pink bubbles of the pool, Llynia kept her eyes fixed on Elli. "Now go!"

Frowning, Elli glanced at Nuic, who had hidden himself in the spray of the waterfall. She shook the water off her arms, making the strings of her harp twang. Then, head down, she strode past the two priestesses—although she did peek up at Llynia's face, which was looking decidedly green.

Just as she reached the wooden gate, however, she hesitated by the tall set of shelves. With a swift step to the side, she ducked behind them. Llynia, who was looking again at the night sky, didn't notice. Nor did Fairlyn, who was helping the poor faery who had nearly drowned in the bubbles. But High Priestess Coerria, whose old eyes missed very little, gave a flicker of a grin.

Llynia shook her wet head in disbelief. "When did it happen?"

"Just now, only minutes ago." Coerria sat down on an oaken stool and motioned for Llynia to sit as well. "The seven stars—symbols of the glowing runes on Merlin's own staff, which stood for the Seven Songs of his youth—are now only six."

Llynia, who had seated herself on the mossy edge of her pool, moved her feet through the water. "That's what happened before."

"Yes, in the Year of Avalon 284—the onset of the Age of Storms. First one star in the Wizard's Staff went dark, then another, and another . . . until all of them were gone. The whole thing took just three weeks. Three weeks! And then all sorts of wickedness erupted."

"Which didn't stop," Llynia added, "until centuries later, when Merlin came back to Avalon."

"And restored the peace that began the Age of Ripening." Coerria sighed, gazing at a flickering candle that was set in the hollow of a stone. The beelike creature that had been braiding her white hair stopped, buzzed over to her cheek, and stroked her skin with long, feathery antennae. But the Elder didn't seem to notice. It was a long moment before she spoke again.

"Before Merlin left Avalon again, this time for good, he magically rekindled those stars—all seven of them, somehow. And so, for over three hundred years, with the sole exception of the Year of Darkness, the Staff has burned bright in our sky, and Drumadian peace has flourished in the realms."

She looked straight at Llynia. "What this means, no one knows. Not I. Not Hywel. Not even Ruthyn, who studies the stars day and night." She peered closely at the Chosen One. "Not you . . . unless you've had another vision."

Llynia bridled. Did Coerria suspect the truth? Could she know how rare—and unreliable—her visions had become? *No*, she told herself. *More likely the old twig just wants to make me stumble. Humiliate myself somehow. Well, it won't happen.*

She shook her head, dripping water and flecks of mud on the moss. "No. Not since the vision I described to the Council."

"Then the only person who might know what this means is . . ."

Llynia cut her off. "The Lady of the Lake." The name seemed to hover, mothlike, in the steamy air. Then a look of pride touched Llynia's face, and she added, "So now my quest to find her is all the more important."

Coerria watched her grimly. "No. It's now *less* important."

The younger priestess stiffened. "What do you mean, High One?"

Over at the waterfall, Nuic stepped out of the spray to hear better. Elli, crouching behind the shelves, couldn't resist peeking around the side to watch.

"I mean," replied the Elder, "that your quest has changed."

"Changed?" Llynia leaned forward on the edge of the pool. "What then is my quest?"

The old woman didn't answer. Instead, she opened her hand, palm up, and the small creature hovering by her cheek settled there. Its tiny wings, tinted purple, folded against its back. Coerria smiled gently. "Take some rest now, Uzzzula, my faithful maryth. Even a busy hive spirit needs to pause now and then."

At this, the little creature gave an insulted shake and buzzed off to start braiding her hair again. Taking one strand in her small arms, she laid it over another, then reached for a third, which she carefully placed over the middle strand. Flying just behind the priestess's head, she continued to wrap the strands together, joining them in a thin, delicate braid.

Coerria nodded. "Your work, my small friend, is your life. Your all."

Just like you, High Priestess, thought Elli as she watched.

Llynia shifted her feet impatiently in the pool, splashing some water over the rim. "Will you not answer my question? What exactly is my quest?"

The Elder's eyes widened. "To find, if you can, the true heir of Merlin. And the stars are saying that you have just three weeks to do it."

Llynia's cheeks, even under the green tint, went pale. "But . . . but how can I do that? No one even knows if such a person exists!"

"Quite true, my child." The voice of the High Priestess turned raspy. "And so if you cannot find Merlin's heir, you have but one choice left. To find Merlin himself, if he still lives."

Fairlyn's many arms, even the ones shooing stray faeries over the fence, froze. She released a strange, uncertain smell, like the wet wings of a fledgling about to fly from the nest—or fall to the ground.

"But—" began Llynia.

Coerria silenced her with a hand. "There is no other way to save our world, I fear. You heard the Elders yourself. Avalon's troubles are growing like mushrooms after a rain! And the true storm has only just begun."

"The true storm?"

"This will be a dangerous journey, Llynia. Dark days—and dark foes—await you. Even, perhaps, the child of the Prophecy. Those enemies will do anything, even commit murder, to stop you. I can only hope that your gift of Sight will help you, as well as your . . . your invitation from the Lady. But as much as I want you to go, and as much as we need you to succeed—I fear for you. And so I cannot command you to take this larger quest. I can only ask."

Llynia swallowed. *Dark foes . . . murder . . .* She hadn't been counting on all this.

Then, all of a sudden, her eyes narrowed. "I know what you're doing. You're just trying to scare me! To frighten me off! You don't want me to go—and certainly not succeed." Venomously, she added, "You know exactly what it means for you if I do."

Coerria's eyes flashed, but her face seemed more sorrowful than angry. "Is that what you really believe?"

"You never wanted me to be your successor. Never! You only supported my selection as Chosen One at the end, because you knew my victory was assured."

"No, my child. I supported you at the end because I came to believe that, with enough time, you would grow into a mature leader, with wisdom to match your gifts." She shook her white head. "Instead, you have grown into—"

"An absolute ass," called a gruff voice from the waterfall.

All eyes turned toward Nuic. The round little sprite, standing in the foaming water at the top of the falls, glared right back at them.

Llynia, her face a dark reddish green, growled angrily. "What are you doing there? I told you and your apprentice to leave!"

Nuic's own color darkened so that it almost matched hers. "Well, I disobeyed."

Behind the shelves, Elli cringed. *No, Nuic, please. Please don't tell them . . .*

The sprite pointed a tiny hand toward the spot where she was hiding. "And so did she."

Elli emerged, biting her lip.

"You wretch!" shrieked Llynia, stomping her feet and splashing herself with water. "I should have known you were eavesdropping. Just you wait until—"

"Be still, now." There was a new tone in the Elder's voice, a sternness that even Llynia couldn't ignore.

Shaking with fury, the younger priestess obeyed—though not before she gave Elli a last withering look. She turned back to Coerria, wishing with all her heart that this old woman weren't still her superior. No wonder the Order was struggling, with such a leader! Still, with great effort, she tried to appear calm. "But she heard . . ." She fumbled, trying to find suitable words. "But she heard about the quest."

"So she did." The High Priestess nodded, so that her white hair shimmered almost as much as her spider's-silk gown. "But that's only appropriate, since she, too, has a choice. The choice of joining you."

Llynia nearly choked. "Her? Joining me? Why, why, I wouldn't think of such a thing!"

"True." The old woman's eyes blazed. "Which is why I am commanding it. If you go, then she goes, as well—if she so chooses."

She turned toward the apprentice. "Well, Elliryanna, my child, what do you say? This journey will be very dangerous. No one would think less of you if you don't want to go."

Elli licked her lips, which had gone suddenly dry. "If . . . if it would help Avalon, High Priestess, then I . . . will go."

The Elder nodded. "So be it."

"But I don't . . ." continued Elli. "I don't know how to help."

"You *can't* help," grumbled Llynia, picking some mud off her nose. "You will only get in the way."

"Perhaps," said Coerria softly, "she will be more help than you expect."

Llynia roared with rage. "And perhaps you are a mad old buffoon!"

Everyone at the Baths fell silent. But for the continuous splatter of the waterfall, the swirl of water in the pools, and the quiet buzz of Uzzzula's wings, no sound could be heard. Not even a breath.

Finally, Coerria spoke again. "May I remind you, Llynia, that you are not yet High Priestess." She stared straight at her until Llynia finally lowered her eyes. "And I dearly hope, if you take on this quest, that you will find something as precious as a wizard: a touch of humility."

Llynia forced herself to nod, though her fists were clenched. "Yes, High Priestess. I . . . er, apologize. And, by your leave, I accept this quest."

"Don't try to fool me with your niceties, child." The wrinkled face hardened. "It is time we spoke candidly, you and I. For we may not have that chance again."

Sparks kindled in Llynia's eyes. "Just what do you mean, niceties? I have always been truthful with you. As truthful as . . ."

"As a changeling! Do you really think I am so feebleminded that I haven't seen all your schemes, all your true desires?"

The younger priestess just stared at her, temples pounding. At her side, Fairlyn quivered, as the Baths smelled of something burning.

"Hear me now, my child." The white-haired woman's voice grew quieter, but no less intense. "You have great gifts, indeed. But your greatest gift is also your greatest flaw."

Llynia bristled. "If you're going to speak candidly, as you put it, then don't speak in riddles." She wiped her face, and the clump of mud finally fell off her chin—leaving a dark green splotch in its place. "Say what you really mean."

"All right, then. Your special skill may allow you to see the future. But you still lack the wisdom to understand what you see.

That's right! You are too sure. Too arrogant." She bent closer to the priestess. "You still mistake truth, which is rarely pure, for purity, which is rarely true."

Llynia kicked at the water in the pool. "More riddles! I can't understand anything you're saying."

"Alas, my child, I had hoped you would."

"Don't call me child!"

Coerria gazed at her with an unreadable expression. Wistfully, she said, "Perhaps in time."

"Time! The one thing we don't have." Llynia stood up, sloshing more water on the ground. Pushing Fairlyn's outstretched arm away, she tightened the dripping towel around her body. "Well, I want you to know something, High Priestess. I'll take this perilous journey, wherever it may lead. But not for *you*."

She sucked in her breath. "No, I do this for our sacred Order. That's the one thing that matters to me. The only thing!"

She stalked out of the Baths, ignoring the robe that Fairlyn held out to her. As she yanked open the door, however, she happened to catch sight of herself in a mirror that hung from a birch tree. Her entire body went suddenly rigid.

"What . . . what could . . . did, but—how . . ." she babbled. Then, after a long pause, she bellowed, *"Aaaaaaarrggghh!"*

Eyes ablaze, she whirled around to face Fairlyn. "Those cursed faeries! Look what they did to me! If I ever catch one of them, I'll . . . I'll . . ." She sputtered incoherently for a few seconds, then shouted, "By the crooked teeth of Babd Catha, I will!"

Out through the gate she stomped. Fairlyn hesitated, smelling like a mound of spoiled cabbage. With sad eyes, she glanced over at the High Priestess, then hurried through the gate after Llynia.

10 · The Staff of Merlin

THE HIGH PRIESTESS, SEATED ON THE OAKEN stool, turned slowly, scanning the Baths. She took in the steaming pools, the shelves of bathing powders and oils, and the tumbling waterfall where Nuic's bluish gray form stood amidst the spray. Last of all, she faced Elli, whose curly brown hair was thicker than the ferns surrounding the pools.

"And what of you, my child? I fear that, as difficult as Llynia's journey will be, your own will be more so."

The young apprentice straightened her back and pushed a tangle of curls off her brow. "I'll do my best, High Priestess."

Coerria looked at her warmly. She tilted her head, making her flowing white hair glisten with mist. "I know you will."

"But . . . but . . ."

"Yes, my child?"

"I, well . . . I really don't know why you asked me to go."

"Because, my dear, I have faith in you."

Those simple words filled Elli's heart as springwater fills a flask. Then, all at once, her doubts returned. "You say that, even after knowing where I came from? Before joining the Order?"

The white head nodded. "Tell me now, do you think it's somehow your fault that you grew up in Mudroot? That your parents were killed? That you were stolen away into slavery?"

Elli's lip quivered. "Everything about those years was wrong! Everything . . . until I escaped from the gnomes."

Coerria frowned. "But the wrongs weren't yours, my child."

The Elder opened her arms. Awkwardly, Elli knelt beside the oaken stool and rested her brow on Coerria's shoulder, feeling the smoothness of the silken gown against her skin. As gently as thistledown landing on grass, Coerria's thin arms embraced her. But to Elli, they felt large and strong, full of love and warmth and . . . She blinked, trying to think of the words to describe it. *Like Mama's arms, and Papa's.*

Finally, she pulled away. She found herself gazing into the old woman's richly blue eyes—eyes as much like sapphires as Elen's were said to have been long ago.

At last, she said, "I've got to go." With a twinkle, she added, "Can't have Llynia leaving without me, can I?"

Coerria smiled at her. "No, can't have that." But as Elli started to rise, the white-haired priestess commanded, "Wait. There is something I must tell you." Her voice dropped to a whisper. "A secret."

Elli raised her eyebrows. "Tell me."

A strange gleam came into the High Priestess's eyes. "In just a moment. But first, Elliryanna, I'd like you to tell *me* something. Just why, after you escaped, did you come here?"

Elli blushed and turned aside. But as she moved, her little harp struck Coerria's knee. It made a soft, ringing note that swelled in the misty air.

"Ah," said the Elder. "I should have guessed. It was because of your father, wasn't it?"

Slowly, Elli nodded. "He always said he loved it here."

Coerria stroked the side of the harp. "Did he really make this himself?"

"When I was five. From a maple burl. And he made the strings from sea kelp from the southern shores of Malóch."

"And the gnomes let you keep it?"

Elli's expression darkened. "Only because I played it for them whenever they commanded." She swallowed. "But what they didn't know was that playing it kept my heart—my memories, and my hopes—alive all those years."

"I see." The old woman brushed a finger across Elli's cheek. "You know, I knew your father."

"Really?"

"Only a little, I'm afraid. He traveled about quite a bit, usually with Lleu. And when he was here in the compound," she added with a grin, "he often skipped Formal Prayers. And yet I did see enough of him to know that he was a very good man."

She nodded—which made Uzzzula, who had been busily braiding her hair, lose track of several white strands. The tiny maryth zipped around Coerria's head, buzzing angrily, her purple-tinted wings flashing through the steam.

But Elli hadn't noticed. Looking up at the night sky, she said, "I wish . . . that we'd had more time together. Just to live." Then she clenched a fist and swung at the air. "Curse those gnomes! They've no right to be in Avalon."

Coerria drew a long, slow breath. "May I tell you something? Something about Avalon?"

Elli cocked her head. "Your secret?"

"No, not quite yet. But if you are going to understand the secret—and use it on your quest—you must first understand this."

She leaned back on the wooden stool. "Avalon, as you know, has all sorts of creatures. Why, even the seven vast root-realms hold more kinds than anyone can name! And though no one has yet explored the higher trunk or branches of the Great Tree, there could be even more creatures up there. But right here, in the Seven Realms, we have plenty: Besides humans like you and me, all the animals and birds and insects of mortal Earth are here. Plus many other mortal creatures that are found nowhere else but Avalon— museos, light flyers, water dragons, wood elves, living stones . . . the list is endless. Some, like the bubblefish, live no longer than a heartbeat. And others may live to be as old as the world itself."

Over by the waterfall, Nuic cleared his throat.

The corner of Coerria's mouth turned up ever so slightly. "My goodness, those pinnacle sprites are long-lived!" She bent her head toward Elli and whispered, "As well as sassy."

Again Nuic cleared his throat, louder this time.

"Let me see," continued the Elder, "who else lives for ages? The giants. And, of course, the wizards and their descendants— who may be human, but whose magical blood keeps them alive far longer than the rest of us. And then, on top of all these mortal creatures, we have immortal ones, too. Creatures who came not from the mud and air and water of Avalon—but from the Other-world of the Spirits."

She studied Elli's face. "Yet with all that diversity, all that vari-ety, I think the rarest being of all is someone who can really com-municate, really *connect,* with a different kind of creature. Who can bridge the gulf between species, or between mortals and immortals. And alas, that skill is especially hard to find in humans. That was why, after all, our founders Elen and Rhia began the practice of pairing every priestess and priest with a maryth. So that none of us would ever forget to open our ears to other songs—no matter how different the melody, or how strange the rhythm."

Elli shook her head, and her curls bounced. "What does all this have to do with me?"

Coerria smiled. "You, my child, have suffered greatly. But those gnomes, unwittingly, also gave you a gift."

Elli's back stiffened. "Gift?"

The High Priestess nodded, making hundreds of delicate braids slide across the shoulder of her gown. "The gift of understanding another people, very different from your own. I cannot say how or when, but I do believe that someday you'll be grateful for that."

"Nothing about gnomes will ever make me grateful."

"Perhaps not. In time, you'll know."

For a long moment, neither of them spoke. Then the High Priestess shifted on her stool, making her gown ripple like star-light on the sea. Seeing this, Elli's face brightened. Gingerly, she ran her hand along the hem of the gown.

"It's beautiful," she said with wonder. "The most beautiful thing in Avalon."

"That it's not, my child. It's no more than a dead leaf com-pared to the miracle of élano, which flows from the depths of Avalon's roots and gives life to us all. Still, it is a remarkable bit of clothing. Woven for Elen herself long ago . . . by the great white spider of Lost Fincayra." She peered at Elli, a curious light in her eyes. "And it's truly wondrous to wear."

"For Avalon's sake!" declared Nuic, pacing on the top step of the waterfall. "Aren't you ever going to tell her your secret?"

"Why, yes, Ancient One," said Coerria good-humoredly. "It's time."

"Finally," grumbled the pinnacle sprite. "Lots is happening out there, you know! Stars dying, droughts worsening, Elders panicking . . ." He paused, savoring a thought. "Even some priestesses turning green. With a bit of expert help, of course."

Elli's hazel green eyes widened. She waved at Nuic to shush, before glancing fearfully at the High Priestess. To her amazement, the old woman showed no outrage, or even concern. In fact, her face seemed almost mirthful.

Before Elli could speak, Coerria raised her hand. "The less I hear about that, the better."

Elli nodded. "And so . . . the secret?"

The old woman's expression turned serious, and she drew a deep breath. "Llynia is not the first priestess, you know, to have a vision."

"You?"

"Yes, my child, just after I became High Priestess. It was the only vision I've ever had. And, like Llynia's, it was of the Lady of the Lake."

Elli frowned. "Do you think she really saw the Lady? Welcoming her into the lair? That's what people say she told the Council of Elders."

Coerria shook her head slowly—until Uzzzula's reproachful buzzing made her stop. "I don't know, child, I really don't. But I do hope she has—not for her sake, but for Avalon's. Because as remote and mysterious as the Lady is, she has always shown a special concern for our Society, and our world. And right now we need her help more than ever."

Rubbing her chin, Elli asked, "But who, really, is the Lady of the Lake?"

"All anyone knows is that she is an enchantress, very old and very wise. And terribly difficult to find! Many have tried; none have succeeded. People say she lives in the eastern part of Wood-root, what the elves call El Urien, where the forest is deepest. But no one is certain—not even Belamir, whose school is in that region."

Coerria's eyes brightened like prisms. "When the Lady came to me, she glowed with light—blue light. And she began by re-minding me of the Dark Prophecy that she'd uttered so long ago:

> *"A year shall come when stars go dark,*
> *And faith will fail anon—*
> *For born shall be a child who spells*
> *The end of Avalon.*
>
> *"The only hope beneath the stars*
> *To save that world so fair*
> *Will be the Merlin then alive:*
> *The wizard's own true heir."*

Elli swallowed, then asked, "And the secret?"

The Elder's voice grew softer than the splash of the waterfall. "That when Merlin finally departed Avalon, at the end of the Age of Storms, he left something behind. Something precious."

"What?"

"A way to find the true heir of Merlin."

"Really?"

Coerria pursed her lips thoughtfully. "You see, when the Lady finished reciting the Prophecy, she added these words:

"So find the staff of Merlin true
And you shall find the heir:
Like a brother to the darkened child,
The light of stars shall bear."

Elli's brow furrowed. "That's it? That's all?"

"It isn't much, child. Just an idea. But a whole world could change because of one idea." The wrinkles around her eyes deepened. "Or one person."

The young priestess twirled one of her curls with her finger, coiling it like a bit of twine. "What do you make of that line about the brother? I mean, the true heir couldn't be the brother of the child of the Dark Prophecy. They're enemies, aren't they?"

"The word *brother* could mean more than one thing."

"All of them confusing!" exclaimed Elli. "And what does *the light of stars* have to do with anything? By the elbows of the Elders! What good is this secret if we can't understand it?"

"Patience, child." Coerria leaned a bit closer. "Like you, I have no idea what the last part means. But the beginning couldn't be more clear. *Find the staff of Merlin true.* Merlin's original staff must be somewhere in Avalon! If you can find it, you'll find Merlin's heir."

Elli wagged her head. "But where do we look? Or even begin? It could be anywhere in the Great Tree!"

"Anywhere," agreed the Elder. "But I can tell you this, from my studies of Merlin's years in Avalon. If he really did leave his staff behind, it was no idle gesture. That staff, you see, is more than just an object. Much more. Its magic—some would say its wisdom—is beyond our knowing. Merlin even gave it a name of its own: Ohnyalei, which means *spirit of grace* in the Fincayran Old Tongue."

She squeezed Elli's hand. "And I can tell you this, too. If he wanted to hide the staff, he would have made the sacred runes on its shaft disappear—as he did once before, when he had to hide it from Rhita Gawr. Those runes, you see, are the staff's essential markings. Hide them, and you have just an ordinary-looking walking stick. The runes glowed blue during the years the staff was in Lost Fincayra, but turned green when Merlin brought it to Avalon. So, to keep the staff safe, he made them vanish completely. And they didn't reappear until Merlin himself held the staff again—and said the words *I am Merlin.*"

Elli twisted another of her curls. "So if the runes are hidden the same way, they might also reappear the same way."

"Exactly."

"Then if the right person holds the staff and says, *I am the true heir of Merlin,* the runes could return." Elli paused, her mind racing. "That gives us a way to tell an impostor—say, the child of the Dark Prophecy—from the real heir."

"That's right, my dear. And that could be especially useful if they seem a lot alike."

Elli nodded slowly. "Enough, maybe, to be brothers."

The High Priestess gave a hint of a smile. "I don't think you've missed much by skipping Formal Prayers."

Suddenly her face turned grim. "You must remember, Elliryanna, that our troubles have all deepened in the seventeenth year after the Year of Darkness—the seventeenth year of the prophesied child. If he or she lives, this would be the year of coming into power."

"It doesn't seem like an accident."

"No, my dear, it doesn't." The old woman squeezed her hand again. "Now, you must promise me something."

"Anything, High Priestess."

"You must beware of the child of the Dark Prophecy. And more than that. If you should ever meet him or her . . . *you must break the Drumadians' first law.*"

Elli's jaw went slack. "You mean . . . kill the Dark one?"

"That's right," answered Coerria. "Kill the Dark one." She peered at the young apprentice. "Now promise."

Though her throat felt like a dry riverbed, Elli said, "I promise." Then her expression darkened further. "I'm worried, High Priestess."

"As am I."

"It won't be easy to find the Lady. Or Merlin's true heir."

"That's right."

"And . . . well, there's something else. I'm still not . . ." She licked her lips. "I'm still not sure why you asked me to go."

"Ah, then perhaps you will discover that, as well." She studied Elli thoughtfully. "But I think it would be fair to tell you . . . that I have an instinct about you. That someday, somehow, you will make a difference to the Society of the Whole. Perhaps a lasting difference."

The young woman stared at her in disbelief.

"And you should also know," Coerria went on, "that you remind me of myself, a very long time ago."

Elli blushed.

The old woman stood, her gown shimmering. Elli rose and offered her arm. But at that moment, they heard a loud "Hmmmpff" from over by the waterfall.

As they turned to Nuic, he demanded, "Aren't you going to ask my opinion? After all, it looks like I'm going to be part of this madness."

The High Priestess bent her head in assent. "But of course, Nuic. So tell us, what do you think?"

Nuic's colors brightened slightly. "I think . . . if you're giving Elliryanna here permission to kill the Dark child, I'd like permission to do the same thing to Llynia."

11 · Tracks

TAMWYN FOUND THE HOOLAH'S TRACKS easily. No mistaking those flat, four-toed feet, even in the dry soil of the fields outside the village.

And no mistaking what the hoolah had done after he'd finished heckling—and making sure that Tamwyn was banished in disgrace. No, even a much less experienced tracker could have followed the hoolah's path from the side of the partly thatched house, to the nearest cornfield, to a corn row where he'd stolen some husks. (He'd even left a row of broken stalks, like trampled signposts, to show beyond any doubt that he'd been there.)

Tamwyn looked at the cornstalks and shook his head. *By the time Lott's finished telling the whole village how I wrecked his house, smashed his foot, broke his ladder, and then klonked his sweet little girl with a bucket . . . they'll probably blame this on me, too.*

He stamped his bare foot on the hoolah's print. *Which, I'll wager, that little menace also planned.*

With that, he started following the tracks northward, toward the foothills that rose—after many, many leagues—into the high peaks of Stoneroot. *I'll find that blasted pest, even if I have to track him over the Dun Tara snowfields. Or to the top of Hallia's Peak!*

As he hiked along, he thought back over the past hour. He'd woken an instant before dawn, at the very moment when the stars began to brighten—a habit he'd learned over years of sleeping outside. Bells on the weather vanes of the village's stone houses, struck by the first breeze of the new day, had just begun to chime. Their slow, sleepy voices called to the bells around the necks of goats, cows, horses, and geese, rousing them also to sound. The jangling bells of a farmer's old wheelbarrow joined in, as did the deep-bonging iron bell on the door of the communal barn. Soon the very air of the village vibrated with clinks, dongs, rattles, and rings.

Right then the hoolah wasn't on Tamwyn's mind. Nor even the dung heap where he'd spent the night. Instead, as he first opened his eyes, he heard again in his mind the magical voices of the museo and the bard with the sideways-growing beard. And saw again the graceful dance of the tree spirits.

And then, with a pang, he'd remembered what had happened to the Wizard's Staff. And how the hoolah had humiliated him— and laughed uncontrollably as Tamwyn was driven from the village.

Now, as he tracked the hoolah, he took a whiff of his own sleeve, streaked with goat droppings and rotten fruit. He scrunched his nose in dismay. "After I finish with that hoolah," he proclaimed out loud, "I'll get myself a bath. Clothes, hair, everything." Under his breath, he added, "If I can find a stream with enough water."

Northward he hiked, following the four-toed tracks. Before

long he left behind the last, distant chimes of the village bells. As he crossed a sloping field choked with gorse, whose yellow flowers seemed paler than usual, Tamwyn felt glad that the hoolah—like himself—preferred to make his own trails. There were too many other tracks and wheel ruts in the hard dirt of the established roads, making it harder to follow someone. And besides, the prettiest countryside began where the roads, and even the ancient footpaths that few people used any more, ended.

He hopped over a fallen spruce tree, and strode through a meadow whose grass had been chewed down by a flock of woolly brown sheep. He glanced up at the sky, and the morning-bright stars. Still no seventh star in the Staff! It had just vanished, like a doused coal in a campfire.

What in the name of Avalon happened? The problem gnawed at his mind as he left the meadow and passed through a stand of alders and maples. *Whatever, it can't be good.*

He picked a long stem of grass and chewed it thoughtfully. There was nothing that he—or anyone else, for that matter—could do about the stars. Why, no one even knew what they really were, let alone how to reach them! And yet . . .

He bit through the stem. *I'd really like to do something. If only I knew what.*

Spying a broken stick on the ground, he bent down to study it. Sure enough, he found the depression left by a hoolah's foot. He nodded grimly. Maybe he couldn't do anything about the stars. But that hoolah . . . *that* he could do something about.

He pulled a pair of plump tubers from the soil and ate them quickly. They were at least juicy, if not very filling. That was all he'd have for breakfast this day. But for dinner, he'd dine on revenge.

Tamwyn started to run, with an easy, loping stride. He kept

his eyes trained on the footprints—or, since the dirt was often too dry to hold a print, to broken blades of grass, bruised leaves, or disturbed pebbles that revealed the hoolah's path. With every stride, the tiny bell at his hip chimed rhythmically. He ran with ease, moving as lightly as a fawn.

How he loved to run, just run! To feel the wind blowing back his hair, the ground compressing ever so slightly under the weight of his feet, the tension building in his thighs before every stride. And the rhythm, most of all: He loved the endless, constant rhythm of his feet pounding the turf, his lungs drawing new air, and his arms slicing up and down, up and down, up and down.

On and on Tamwyn ran. He leaped across several dry gullies that had once been streams. He loped past a circle of still-sleeping daffodil fairies, whose golden wings he glimpsed through a hole in the trunk of a beech tree. And once, in midstride, he swerved to avoid a huge, triangular stone that he recognized. A few years before, hidden by a bramble bush, he had watched a band of black-bearded dwarves move that stone to open a secret passage to their underground home.

As he ran, he couldn't help but notice that the farther north he went, the dryer the landscape grew. This drought had been going on for months now, since early summer. And it was only getting worse, especially here in the hills of upper Stoneroot.

But that didn't make sense! He'd seen dry spells before, but always in the southern parts of the realm. Up here, in the foothills of the high peaks, rivers ran full all summer long. In addition to melting snow, they carried water all the way from High Bryn-chilla, part of Waterroot—through deep underground channels. At least that's what he'd been told by a bard he'd once met, who had studied at the Eopia College of Mapmakers. The bard had even said that some of that water might actually come from the legendary White Geyser of Crystillia.

He ran across a bed of moss, so brittle that it crackled under his bare feet. *What's going on here? And could it be related somehow to that star going out?*

Whatever was going on, this much was certain: Water was scarce. More scarce than he'd ever seen in his years of wandering through the wilds of this realm. Why, even the lakes at Footsteps of the Giants were almost dry. He hated seeing such drought, hated hearing the snap of dry grass and dead leaves underfoot. As thirsty as he was, and had been for weeks, he knew that he was still faring better than the land itself. For he, at least, could run freely, seek out water, and move on. The land, and the trees that were rooted there, didn't have that choice.

Tamwyn slowed his running pace to look at an old rowan tree whose berries should have been bright red at this time of year, but were a faded pink instead. Even the stones like keljade and mica, which changed to bright gold in the autumn, were just dingy yellow. These lands weren't just dryer, but they were also grayer. *Blander,* as if their colors were being slowly sapped right out of them.

Through a once-green valley, now brown and brittle, and past a string of dried-up ponds, he followed the tracks. The footprints, running right through the middle of a muddy stretch between what was left of the ponds, couldn't have been more obvious. It was almost as if this hoolah *wanted* to get caught.

But Tamwyn knew better. This hoolah—like every other hoolah—just didn't care.

Foolish beasts! No matter what their age, their sex, or the

color of their circular eyebrows, hoolahs all shared one quality. They treated life as nothing more than a game, a chance to make mischief—as much mischief as possible.

Truth? Honor? Purpose? Those ideas held no meaning for hoolahs. They just loved to spit in the face of danger, which was why they were so often in trouble. Who cared, if they lived to laugh about it afterward? And they really couldn't understand why other people, especially humans, got so worked up about little things like droughts, plagues, and wars. To hoolahs, these just added to the fun.

All of which made them probably the least loved creatures in the whole of Avalon. Right down there with gnomes, ogres, and trolls. A wandering hoolah had about as many friends as a double-jawed dragon with a toothache.

Tamwyn loped along, climbing through steep-sided hills ribbed with high cliffs. Even as he passed through a tall grove of balloonberry trees, his fists clenched. *Pretty soon there'll be one hoolah who won't cause any more trouble.*

Suddenly he stopped. The hoolah's tracks had disappeared!

He bent down, examining the last footprint. Set in the dry soil between the tree roots, it seemed perfectly normal. All the toes, all the edges, were clear. No sign of a scuffle. Then he noticed a slight depression, deeper than usual, just behind the toes. As if the hoolah had jumped on that final step.

Jumped. But where? He turned his face upward to scan the boughs of the trees.

Splaaat!

A balloonberry, very large and very juicy, exploded right on his forehead. The force of the berry—the size of a man's fist—

knocked him over onto his back. Juice, a lighter shade than usual but still quite purple, oozed into his eyes and hair, sticking like sap. He opened his mouth to shout when—

Splaaat. Right into his mouth!

Splaaat. Splaaat. Balloonberries splattered on his chest and thigh.

"Hungry now, clumsy man?" called a voice from the branches. "Missed your supper, did you? Eehee, eehee, hoohooya-ha-ha! Here. Have some more berries!"

Whizzz, splaaat.

Just in time, Tamwyn rolled to the side. The berry smacked into a tree trunk, spraying purple juice everywhere.

"You, you . . . *blaaaghh!"* Tamwyn spat out the berry skin that was sticking to his tongue. "You pail of spit! You underaged, undersized, underbrained worm!"

He leaped up, caught the lowest branch of the hoolah's tree, and started to climb. Just as he reached for the next branch, he ducked to avoid another whizzing berry. Despite all the purple goo on his hands, tunic, and leggings that made him stick to the bark of the tree, he moved up rapidly. Years of living in the wilderness had made him a skilled tree-climber.

But the hoolah was just as skilled. His large hands gave him strong holds, while his long arms gave him extra reach. For every branch Tamwyn scaled, the hoolah did the same.

"Better be careful, clumsy man! Eehee, eehee oohoohooha. Might fall and break yourself like that bale of thatch!"

Tamwyn peered upward, forced to squint because of the berry juice that had clotted over one eye. "I'll break *you,* you bag of dung! Just wait!"

"Hoohooheehee," laughed the hoolah over his shoulder. "Smells to me like *you're* the one who's full of dung."

Up, up, they raced, until Tamwyn saw the hoolah reach the tree's uppermost limb. He slowed down, knowing that now the hoolah was trapped. Finally, his moment of revenge had come.

But the hoolah merely glanced down at him and cracked a wide smile. "Bye-bye, clumsy man!"

To Tamwyn's amazement, the hoolah stepped out onto the limb, steadied himself, then started to walk away from the trunk. The branch sagged dangerously under his weight, but he didn't seem to care. Chuckling to himself, the hoolah stuffed his slingshot securely into his belt, bounced hard on the branch—then leaped right into the air.

"Yeeheeeee!" cried the flying hoolah. He sailed across the grove, then flung out his arms and grabbed onto the branch of another tree. Pulling himself up onto the new branch, he looked back at Tamwyn. "Guess you'll have to try harder, clumsy man! Hoohoohahahahaha, eehee, hoho."

Tamwyn's eyes blazed with fury. Without even checking the strength of his branch, he jumped straight up, came down hard, then felt the branch spring upward beneath him. At the highest point, he pushed off with all the strength of his legs.

"Aaaooaahhh!" Tamwyn soared into the air, right at his tormentor in the other tree.

Caught by surprise, the hoolah froze. He saw only Tamwyn's wrathful face bearing down on him—and fast.

Then suddenly the hoolah's silver eyes brightened. Tamwyn's greater weight was carrying him down to a lower branch! The hoolah grinned again, knowing he'd escaped.

Just as Tamwyn reached the tree, though, he did something else the hoolah hadn't expected. He stretched up a hand, catching the beast by the ankle. As Tamwyn smashed into limbs laden with balloonberries, he dragged the shrieking hoolah right along with him.

Pounding downward through the branches, cracking wood and exploding berries, the pair tumbled. Leaves, bark, broken twigs, purple juice, and the nest of an unfortunate bird all fell with them. More like a whirling purple tornado than a pair of bodies, they smashed through the bottom branches, hit the ground, rolled down a steep slope, and hurtled over a stone ledge.

12 · Song of the Voyager

STOP OVER THERE!" COMMANDED LLYNIA,
pointing to a slab of flatrock under a cliff. The sheer
stone face, rising high above them, looked more dull
gray than its usual autumn golden brown. "We'll rest a few
minutes—no more, we don't have time. Though my feet could
use about a week."

She turned around only long enough to frown at Fairlyn. The
tree spirit's slender arms held the reins of two pack horses, loaded
down with cooking gear, dried food, and enough flasks of water to last several days. Not to mention Llynia's bundles of spare
clothing, personal effects, and her old, leather-bound volume of
Cyclo Avalon that contained some handwritten notes in the mar-
gins by Lleu of the One Ear himself.

"And don't forget, Fairlyn, to tie up the horses! Can't have
them wandering off with all our supplies just because you were
careless. The way you were yesterday at the Baths."

Fairlyn's eyes narrowed, and her scent changed to something
like burning hair. But she said nothing, and led the horses over

to a young rowan tree at the base of the cliff. A few steps behind came Elli, with Nuic's misty shape on her left shoulder.

Llynia reached the slab of flatrock and sat down with a loud groan. She pulled off her leather shoes, then started rubbing her feet, scowling all the while.

"Out of my sight, you useless wastrel," she barked at Elli. "I should make you carry all the horses' loads, for your impertinence. You're nothing but a millstone around my neck."

Elli's hazel green eyes narrowed. But before she could speak, Nuic gave her some advice.

"Don't mind her," he counseled. "She's just feeling a bit *off-color* today."

Llynia lifted her face, her anger darkening the green tones of her skin. "If that's more of your sassiness, Nuic . . ."

"No, no, not at all." The pinnacle sprite turned himself a sympathetic shade of green. "Just concern for your welfare."

Llynia studied him, scratching her chin—where a triangular patch of green had deepened, looking much like a beard. "If that's the case, then, why don't you and that useless apprentice third class go find me some more of that herb—the one for restoring skin color. I've eaten what you gave me this morning."

"With pleasure." Nuic bowed slightly, then whispered to Elli from the side of his mouth, "Especially since dissimint doesn't really *restore* skin color so much as rearrange it."

Elli's eyebrows lifted. "You don't mean . . . ?"

Her maryth gave a soft, splashy chuckle. "Right. It pulls the new pigments to the darkest place. Which means that while most of her face is getting less green, just as old Nuic promised, her little beard is getting darker. Much darker."

Elli, who was helping Fairlyn tie the horses to the rowan tree, bit her lip to keep from laughing out loud. "I think her mood is getting darker, too."

Fairlyn, who had overheard this last remark, waved one of her long arms, studded with purple buds, in front of Elli's face. But as stern as she appeared to be, rising to the defense of her human charge, her scent had changed to popping corn—an amused smell if ever there was one.

As Elli bent low so that Nuic could slide off easily, the old sprite met her gaze. "Don't waste your time coming with me," he told her. "You don't know dissimint from dysentery! Besides, I saw some by those bramble bushes over there."

"But . . ." she protested.

He dismissed her with a wave of a misty hand. "Go find something else to do, Elliryanna."

She couldn't help but smile. Partly at his unending gruffness, and partly at his use of her full name. His way of saying it always sounded like the splatter of a mountain stream.

But what to do? Glancing at Llynia, who was massaging her feet in the shadow of the cliff, she walked over to the far side of flatrock slab and sat down. Her harp bumped the rock, sounding some discordant notes.

That's it. I'll play something. Elli cradled the rough-hewn harp in her lap, feeling as always the subtle shaping of the maple wood by her father's hands. With all that had happened in the last few days—even before this long day of walking behind Llynia—she hadn't plucked a single note.

She tapped the knotty base of the harp. Less than a month ago, she'd walked through the great oaken gates of the Drumadian compound, having come all the way from Malóch. She'd arrived just as the Buckle Bell was chiming, thinking she could stay at the compound forever, and here she was now, already off on an expedition. And with precious little idea where she was going—or whether she'd ever return. By the elbows of the Elders, this wasn't what she'd expected!

But I never expected to meet Nuic, either. Or High Priestess Coerria. She gave the hawthorn pegs a twist, plucking each string in turn. Then, when the harp sounded in tune, she stole a quick look at Llynia, who was still grumbling at her sore feet. *Or her.*

As she slid her finger down a kelp string, she thought about Papa: how he had loved to play songs of his own making; and how the memory of his hands on this harp had given her strength to survive the touch of those grimy, three-fingered hands that held her captive for so long.

She looked up into the boughs of the rowan tree under the cliff, whose leaves had started to whisper in the wandering breeze. And she began to pluck the strings, so softly that their notes seemed sung by the breeze itself. In time, she put words to the notes, words from one of her father's favorite songs.

"Song of the Voyager," he had called it. And although she'd heard it many times before, today it held new meaning:

> *Over the fathomless seas have I flown,*
> *Searching for what I have missed:*
> *Land of my longing, sought yet unknown,*
> *Alluring so none can resist.*
> *Avalon . . . does it exist?*
> *Avalon . . . does it exist?*
>
> *Dark now the air, and also my heart;*
> *Low does my candle wick burn.*

Seeking the Mystery—whole, not in part—
World of most sacred concern.
Frail though my hope, how I yearn.
Frail though my hope, how I yearn.

Mist swirls about me, darkness abounds;
Nothing can save me, it seems.
Suddenly starlight! Green all around—
Life beyond marvelment teems:
The tree, and the world, of my dreams.
The tree, and the world, of my dreams.

All of this world did a single seed start,
Planted in wonder and whist.
It throbbed as alive, and beat like a heart,
Ready the Fates to assist,
Merlin's own ultimate tryst.
Merlin's own ultimate tryst.

Bursting with power, it sprang into life.
Out of its deepest core came
Avalon great, with mysteries rife,
Wildness no people could tame,
And wonders too many to name.
And wonders too many to name.

Mighty now rises the world-tree so tall:
Part spirit, part body . . . and partly between.
So vast, so enormous, its fibers hold all—
Including the realms of my dream,

Embraced by the magical green.
Embraced by the magical green.

Avalon lives! The last place to keep
All the songs of Creation alive.
Sing every note—sing high and deep:
Voices uplifted shall thrive;
Singers themselves shall survive.
Singers themselves shall survive.

What riddles, what puzzlements, does this world hold?
Answers elusive as mist . . .
A world ever new and still utterly old,
A landscape by destiny kissed.
Avalon does yet exist.
Avalon does yet exist.

The last notes lifted into the air, joining with the whispering boughs. Elli looked up from her harp and saw, with surprise, that Llynia was gazing at her—and not in anger. The expression on her green-stained face was restful, if not exactly peaceful.

Even as the notes faded away, though, Llynia's expression changed. Her gaze hardened. "Why don't you ever do something useful? Instead of just sitting there, plucking your—"

A frightful crashing from somewhere above the cliff, combined with some creature's shrieking wail, made her halt. And look up.

A whirling mass of broken branches, leaves, twigs, smashed berries, two writhing bodies, and the remains of a bird's nest tumbled over the ledge at the top of the cliff. Bits of bark, dirt, hair, rock, and torn clothing plunged down, too. Plus a shower of sticky purple sap.

All this landed with a howling thud—right on top of the travelers. Llynia screamed as someone's foot smacked her in the head. Elli leaped backward, barely snatching her precious harp out of the way before a falling branch could smash it. The pack horses reared, snapping their tethers and scattering supplies everywhere, before they bolted off into the forest.

Nuic, who had just returned with a fistful of herbs, jumped backward to dodge the flying debris. And then watched in undisguised amusement as Llynia tried to remove a sticky chunk of bird's nest from her hair. Fairlyn, her long arms outstretched, ran after the panicked horses.

Meanwhile, the pair of flying bodies had landed—and continued to wrestle in earnest. Across the ground they rolled, throwing up clods of dirt and leaves and shredded cloth. Finally, one of them—a filthy young man with long hair streaked with purple juice—prevailed. He held down the other: a short, thin person with the large hands and sassy face of a hoolah.

Tamwyn twisted the hoolah's arm behind his back, ignoring the creature's howling protests. "You . . . you . . . maggot! No, a maggot's too good for you. You're just the rotten carcass a maggot eats!"

"*Aaawwooo!*" cried the hoolah as it tried in vain to wriggle free. "Clumsy man is killing me!"

"Damn right I am." Tamwyn shook a leafy twig, caught in his hair, away from his face. "And you'll wish you never—"

"Stop!" bellowed Llynia, standing over them with clenched fists on her hips. "There will be no killing. And no more fighting."

Before Tamwyn could protest, a pair of powerful, branchlike arms lifted him off the ground. At the same time, two more arms lifted up the hoolah. Fairlyn, who had just returned from the forest—without the horses—held them both in her sturdy grip. Her large eyes were rimmed in red, and she smelled like whatever part of a carcass even a maggot wouldn't touch.

Catching her scent, the hoolah wrinkled up his nose. "*Hooeee* there, tree! You've got a smell even worse than clumsy man here."

Fairlyn gave him a rough shake, as her odor grew even more rancid.

Tamwyn, swinging his legs in the air, demanded, "Let me down! You've no right to do this."

Elli stepped in front of him. "And you've no right to come crashing down on top of us! You've scared off the horses, for one thing."

"And smacked me in the head, for another." Llynia touched her tender cheekbone. "You could have killed me."

Nuic grumbled, just loud enough to be heard, "Maybe next time they'll aim better."

Llynia spun on him, but before she could say anything, the hoolah called out to her, "You got hit harder than you think, woman. You look sick, you do. Greener than a gullyful of frogs! Ee, ee, hoohoohoo hahaha."

Now Llynia, her eyes ablaze, turned to face both the hoolah and Tamwyn. "You two are very lucky that I am a priestess of the holy Order. One who has never been tempted to bring pain to another creature . . . until now." She sucked in her breath and chanted, "O Lorilanda, dear goddess, give me strength. And Dagda, fount of wisdom, give me patience."

She turned to Fairlyn. "Did you see any sign of the horses?"

The trunk of the lilac elm spirit twisted to one side, then the other, Fairlyn's way of shaking her head.

Llynia glared again at the two vagabonds who had tumbled out of the sky. "You have no idea what damage you've done! By the crooked teeth of Babd Catha . . . you've ruined everything! Without our horses, we can't carry our supplies. And without our supplies, we can't complete our que—" A sharp look from Fairlyn cut her off. "Our journey," she said more cautiously.

Tamwyn, whose temper had only slightly cooled, spoke up. "Look, I'm sorry about the horses. It was an accident, believe me. But if it would help you out, I've worked as a porter before. And more often, a guide. My name is Tamwyn."

Elli tapped the back of her harp in approval and turned to Llynia. "That would help, wouldn't it?"

Over by the bramble bushes, Nuic snorted. "It'll take more than one man to carry just her clothes."

Llynia scowled, but said nothing.

Tamwyn glanced spitefully at the hoolah. "Don't expect any help from *him*, though. Helping's not in his nature."

To the surprise of everyone—most of all Tamwyn—the hoolah thrust out his chin as if he'd been insulted. Light from the midday stars glowed on his circular eyebrows. He straightened the woven red band on his forehead and declared, "Whatever the clumsy man can do, so can I! My name is Henniwashinachtifig Hoolah. And I'm just as good as he is."

"Henni . . . what?" asked Elli.

"Call me Henni Hoolah if you want. Your new porter."

"Don't believe him!" warned Tamwyn. "It's just one of his tricks. He'll take your things and dump them in the first pit he finds, then run off laughing."

"Will not!"

"Will so!"

"Will not!"

Llynia waved her hand for silence. "A pair of porters, is it? The most ragtag, filthy porters anyone could imagine." Her scowl lessened just a bit. "Well, I'd prefer our pack horses . . . but if you can carry our things, then we can keep going."

"You'll regret this," muttered Tamwyn.

"Only because of *you*, clumsy man."

"Is that so? Why, I've guided people halfway to Woodroot and back!"

Llynia interrupted them with another wave. She gazed scornfully at Tamwyn and said, "You're my porter now, nothing else. Don't even *think* about trying to guide. I am our leader . . . and even if I didn't have the Sight, I'd need no help from the likes of you."

Henni nodded vigorously. "Smart move, Lady Greenbeard. Clumsy man there isn't old and wise like me. He'd just lead you into a swamp or a dragon's lair."

"Stop calling me clumsy man!" roared Tamwyn. "Or however old you are, you won't get any older."

Llynia squinted at him. "And just how old are *you*, porter?"

Tamwyn swallowed. "Er, eighteen."

The priestess nodded, but over by the brambles, old Nuic turned a suspicious shade of rusty red.

Just then Henni spat a shred of balloonberry out of his mouth—which just happened to smack Tamwyn right between the eyes.

Angrily, Tamwyn swung his fist at the hoolah. Although he

couldn't reach his target, the force of his swing twisted him free from Fairlyn's grasp. He dropped to the ground, stumbled to stay on his feet, and fell against Elli.

Elli cried out as the harp slipped from her hand. It fell to the ground with a loud *twang*. Tamwyn, meanwhile, finally regained his balance—and planted his foot squarely on the harp. There was a splintering crunch of wood, a gasp of horror from Elli, and a groan from Tamwyn.

And a chuckle from the hoolah.

Then everyone fell silent. Elli stared wordlessly at the shattered remains of her harp. Tamwyn stood frozen, aghast at what he'd done. Even the rowan tree's boughs ceased their whispers.

In a single, swift motion, Elli whirled around and slammed her fist right into Tamwyn's nose. He howled in pain, even as his knees buckled beneath him. He collapsed on the dirt, seeing more stars than in any Avalon sky.

"Elli!" scolded Llynia. "That was totally un-priestesslike."

"And totally deserved." She glared at Tamwyn, fuming. "You *are* a clumsy man. The clumsiest man alive! Or dead! Did your mother never teach you to walk? Or was she just as stupid and clumsy as you?"

Tamwyn glared right back at her, dropping his hand from his rapidly swelling nose . . . and the dark bruise forming under his eye. But just as he was about to hurl a few insults of his own, Nuic interrupted with a shout.

"Don't mind her, good fellow! Nothing for you to worry about, really. You just destroyed her only possession, the last gift from her father before he died. And, oh yes, the one thing that kept her sane through six years of slavery."

The sprite shrugged his round shoulders. "Don't know why she got so upset at you."

Tamwyn, suddenly looking as crushed as the harp itself, turned slowly back to Elli.

She just stared at him, almost tearful but with eyes ablaze. Then she turned and strode off.

13 · Hands of Blood

BRIONNA CLUTCHED A JUTTING EDGE OF rock and pulled herself higher on the canyon wall. Reddish brown dust sprinkled her long, honey-colored braid and stung her eyes. Even so, she didn't stop climbing—just as she hadn't stopped moving since that moment, two hours ago, when the shadowed sorcerer had released her. The life of her grandfather hung in the balance . . . and whether he lived or died depended on her.

On her alone.

Like an oversized spider, she scaled the rock wall. As she hauled herself over a steep outcropping, she groaned with the strain—but a sudden gust of wind forced the sound back down her throat, as it pelted her with pebbles and dirt. A rough edge jammed into her thigh, slicing her skin. A new bloodstain seeped into her loose-fitting elvish robe, once as green as Woodroot's forests, but now so smeared with red and brown that the new stain hardly showed.

As she pulled her body onto the top of the ledge, panting, she looked down at her hands. Dark red dust coated them, rimming her fingernails like blood. Was this a sign? Of Granda's blood . . . forever on her hands if she failed him?

She turned her hands, watching the red dust blow off her palms with the whistling wind. *Or perhaps the blood of that young man whose staff I'm supposed to steal? Will this mean his death, or the death of others?*

No. She couldn't think about that. She had to keep her mind on her task: Find the staff and bring it back here, to this wretched part of High Brynchilla. To this place of violation—of living creatures as well as the living land. To that sorcerer who kept himself hidden, except for his pale hands.

That was her task—her only chance to save the person everyone knew as Tressimir, the revered historian of the wood elves. Everyone but her. To her, he was Granda, the one person she could always count on. The person who had raised her from childhood, helped her through illness, and taught her practically everything she knew about the elves' rich traditions, as well as those of Avalon's other peoples. But most important of all, he'd taught her the meaning of family.

The wind gusted with sudden ferocity, smiting her with dirt and sand, kicking up spirals of swirling red dust all along the undulating rim of the canyon. Hard it blew, and cold. So cold, it made her shiver.

At last the wind died away. Brionna glanced upward. Just a few more minutes and she would reach the top of the rim—and see again the eastern edge of her beloved Woodroot, the forest realm where she longed to live again in peace. But she knew that there would be no peace for her soon. Not until Granda was safe.

She turned, gazing back over the canyon that she had nearly scaled. She could see, on the other side, the stone tower that lifted itself like the head of a bloody serpent. She could also see the ledge where the sorcerer had disemboweled that poor beast, and then given his commands. Beneath the canyon rim lay the white lake, glinting strangely, as deep as a small ocean. And then, last of all, her green eyes fell on that accursed dam, built by hundreds of slaves who had carved, hauled, and fitted its heavy blocks of stone. At the cost of their limbs—and lives.

Brionna shivered again, this time not from cold. She had worked only three days as a slave, pulling ropes for the barges that brought stones to the top of the dam. But that was long enough to get a cut from a man's whip that would give her a permanent scar across her back. And long enough to get other scars, too, less visible but no less permanent.

Why was that sorcerer trapping so much water? That's what she couldn't stop wondering. Just to hold sway over all the lands and peoples who needed it? And who would die of thirst without it? That would give him power, to be sure. Not just here in Waterroot, but in neighboring realms, as well: Granda had once told her that their homeland in Woodroot took much of its water from this region. Could the dam have something to do with the summer-long drought? With the dryness—and blandness—of her favorite forest paths? Why, even the River Relentless was down to half its normal flow.

And yet, water didn't seem to be what the sorcerer was really after. If that was his goal, why would he go through so much trouble to find this staff? Even if it really was the staff of a wizard, it had nothing to do with water. Or did it? The questions echoed inside her mind.

She closed her eyes, seeing once again Granda's face—still and gray, a dribble of blood at the corner of his mouth, flecks of dirt in his ragged white beard. And yet his heart still beat, just enough to keep him alive.

Not for long, though. She thought of the last moment, there on the ledge, when she'd held his hand inside her own. How warm it felt, even then, though she knew that the warmth would soon slip away.

And then, in her mind's eye, his hand started to change. To lengthen, to grow clean and smooth. To whiten—until it was the hand of the sorcerer.

"See that you bring back the staff," he had commanded, slicing the shadows under the stone wall with a sweep of his hand. "And soon! You have just under three weeks, mmmyesss, my pretty one. For only yesterday, the stars of the Staff on high started to go dark, the sign I have long awaited. Mmmyesss, from my lord Rhita Gawr. Ah, that surprises you? That name? Rhita Gawr . . . It is a name you will soon hear much more, my little elf."

His white hand pointed at the dam. "I need just three weeks, no more, to finish my grand creation, just what the stars will take to vanish. And on that day the last star goes out, I shall use the staff you'll have brought me. Use it, and then destroy it! Poetic, mmmyesss? On that day, both the staff on the ground and the staff in the sky will disappear forever."

The voice in the shadows had made a high, hissing laugh. "Succeed, Brionna, and your grandfather shall live. But fail, and he shall die—mmmyesss, most painfully."

The sorcerer's hand had shot out from the dark wall and gripped her forearm. "For seventeen years I have sought that staff, and for all that time I have been thwarted. Mmmyesss, by fools as well as foes! First, by those two bunglers, who could have brought me both Merlin's staff and the boy who would be his true heir—

but missed their chance. And by my ghoulacas, who have searched the Seven Realms for years without success. And also by other forces that have tried to hinder me, no matter how many entrails I've read. But now I have found it! Mmmyesss, with the help of a wretched little beast from Fireroot. How ironic."

Wheezing, he had laughed again. "So now, my helpful maiden, you shall bring the staff to me."

"Why," she had asked, "don't you go yourself?"

"I must oversee the final stages of my creation, mmmyesss. And I have other reasons, as well. Excellent reasons."

He had squeezed her, sending arrows of fire up her arm. "Find me the wizard's staff kept by the true heir of Merlin. The entrails tell me that he is only a young man—but beware, for his powers may be starting to grow. Kill him if he tries to stop you. He is no less my enemy than was his predecessor! And tell no one of your mission. No one! Unless . . ."

He had hesitated for a moment. "Unless, perhaps, you should meet the child of the—but no, I doubt that will happen now."

"But where do I find the staff?"

"Seek it in Fireroot, near a crater with towers like crooked teeth. And bring it to me, mmmyesss, before the last star fades. Or the old elf will die."

Brionna opened her eyes. Though before her stretched the rocky canyon raked by howling winds, she could still see the shape of that ghostly hand. And still feel the pain of that final phrase.

She turned, wiped some dirt from her eyes, and started again to climb.

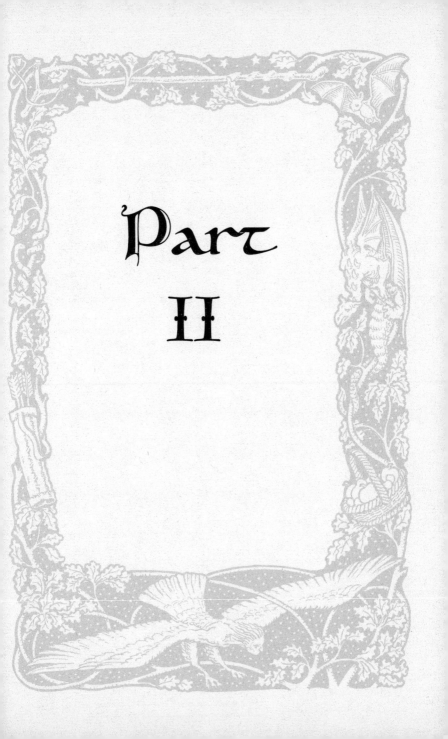

Part

II

14 · Baby Brother

TENDRILS OF FIRE SPOUTED FROM THE
flame vent in the cavern floor. All around, rough rock
walls pulsed with orange light. So did the stalactites
that hung down from the ceiling like the fangs of a great underground serpent, and the chunks of cinder on the cavern floor.
Even the air, which reeked of sulfur, glowed orange.

A lone figure sat beside the vent, wearing only leggings and no
shirt, in the manner of all eaglemen who assumed human form.
Half his face was lit, revealing a strong jaw and sharply hooked
nose. His shoulders, broad and muscular, flexed as he tried to
break a shard of wood—for no reason except to test his strength.
This shard was thicker than usual, and his hands gripped its sides,
digging into the fiber. His whole powerful body shook with the
strain.

Snap! The shard split in half, sending chips flying across the
cavern.

With a satisfied grunt, the figure tossed the wood aside and
stretched out one leg. Using his toes, which sported long nails
that could change into talons at will, he turned a spit over the

flames. The meat of the cliff hare that he'd nabbed just before dawn started to sizzle.

But he didn't seem to notice. With sudden fury, he grabbed a small rock and threw it hard against the cavern wall. It burst into hundreds of cinder bits and a wisp of dust.

"How much longer do I have to wait?" he growled, so used to living alone that he'd grown accustomed to talking to himself. "Since that night on the cliffs . . . I've kept my promise! Done everything just the way the old man would have wanted."

A shadow seemed to cross his face, darkening his large, yellow-rimmed eyes. "Well, *almost* everything."

He turned the spit. "But for that one mistake, I've done just what he asked me to do. And more."

Scree's gaze strayed to the gnarled wooden staff leaning against the wall. "All for a piece of wood."

He scratched an itch on his muscular arm. But he couldn't scratch the stronger, much deeper itch down inside himself.

Reaching for his flask, made from the bladder of a bear whose meat had helped him survive last winter, he took a swallow of water—always a scarce commodity in this realm of fire. Then, with his toes, he grasped the spit. Curling his leg, he lifted the spit up to his face, tore off a hunk of juicy meat, and chewed thoughtfully.

"You're seventeen now, Scree. Isn't it high time you left this cave—this realm—forever?" His question echoed inside the cavern. Lowering his voice, he added, "To find him, wherever he is."

He took another bite of meat. Seven long years he'd lived alone, without any sign of his brother. At first, he'd been sure that staying hidden was the right thing to do. After all, it was Scree—or the old man's staff—that those murderous ghoulacas were after. So the farther away Tamwyn was, the safer he'd be.

Turning the spit, Scree tore off another chunk. Now, though, he wasn't so sure—about that or anything else. Was this task never going to end? Hadn't he already done plenty to protect the staff? And with no—or almost no—lapses? Right now what he really wanted to do was find Tamwyn. Or at least try. But what if he lost the staff in the process? Then all those years, and all he'd done to keep his promise, would have been wasted.

He spat out some bones, which clinked against the cavern floor. "Scree, you headless troll, make up your mind!" He frowned and grumbled in exasperation, "What I need is some sort of sign."

Over by the wall, something crackled. Scree turned back to the staff, which was rippling with orange light from the vent. And also, he suddenly realized, with something else—a deeper light, from somewhere within. He watched in disbelief. The staff had never done this, or anything like this, before.

The full length of its shaft now glowed brighter, pulsing strangely. And then, for some reason he couldn't explain, Scree sensed something more than light coming from the staff. It wasn't anything so clear as a message—more like a *feeling*. Of approval, maybe even encouragement.

He sucked in his breath, then whispered incredulously, "It wants me to go! It wants me to leave the cave."

The staff flickered, then glowed even brighter.

Giving the staff an uncertain nod, he said, "I guess maybe you're not just a piece of wood after all."

He set the meat aside, then stood up and carefully wrapped his fingers around the staff. It felt different than before, though he couldn't be sure whether the difference was in the wood or in his hand. Gripping it firmly, he turned and strode out of the cavern.

Night stars glittered overhead, thousands of them, burning

like flame vents that shone through the smoky sky. Yet none of them shone as brightly as the young eagleman's eyes. For after so much time deliberating, he'd finally made his decision . . . with some help from the staff.

He glanced down at the gnarled wooden shaft, which now seemed the same as usual. No light, no feeling. Had he just imagined the whole thing?

Either way, it didn't matter. The decision was made. He would walk up to the portal on the crater's rim—right now, this very night. Then he'd plunge in, and start searching for his lost brother. At last.

As his feet crunched on the brittle volcanic rock, he said aloud, "And I'll find you, Tam. Whatever it takes."

Just hearing his brother's name made him pinch his lips together. He remembered, as if it were that very day, their final moments together, seven years before. And what had happened outside this very cavern, in the crater whose teethlike towers had swallowed all that remained of his family.

• • •

"Get off me, you ogre!" Tamwyn shouted as Scree rolled over on top of him, pinning him to the rocky ground.

Scree merely peered down at him, smirking. "Is that a command, baby brother?"

Tamwyn's dark eyes flamed—no less than the sizzling fire plants on the cliffs. "I'm not your baby brother," he spat, twisting unsuccessfully under all the weight. "You're the same age as me, ten years old, and you know it! Just because you're bigger . . ." He tried to break loose. "I'll catch up with you, though, you'll see."

His back arched suddenly, throwing his brother off balance. One arm twisted free, and just as Scree turned, a fist caught him hard on the side of his head. He rolled, but Tamwyn did the same. When Scree leaped to his feet, a leg swept under him, knocking him back to the ground. Just before Tamwyn could pounce, though, Scree swung his foot.

Tamwyn staggered, lip bleeding, and fell to his knees.

Scree looked at him, panting, then reached up and felt his own ear. "Swollen like a flaming fire biscuit," he grumbled.

As the two brothers winced, their eyes met. For a few seconds each of them tried to out-scowl the other. Then, unaccountably, they both burst out laughing.

"Your ear . . ." sputtered Tamwyn. "It's as big as a hoolah's hand!"

"And your lip," Scree retorted, "looks like a smashed plum."

"*Oooh.* Feels like one, too." The part of Tamwyn's mouth that could still move almost smiled. "But I got you just as good."

"Pure luck, baby brother."

Moments later, they were hiking up to the rim of the crater. Scree carried his staff, as always, while Tamwyn carried a new length of vine-rope to replace the snare that had recently grabbed a fire sprite, instead of the usual coal slug or cliff hare. The little beast had burned his way right through the vine, destroying the boys' snare. But even though that meant more work for them, neither held a grudge. All the fire sprite had wanted, after all, was his freedom.

"Why do you carry that stupid stick everywhere?" asked Tamwyn, as he had done so many times before. "You don't even leave it for a short walk like this."

Scree swung the staff gently and tapped him on his seat. "So I can swat pesky flies, like you."

His brother frowned. "Seriously, Scree. What are you worried about? There's nobody but us around here, three leagues in any direction. Not even any eaglefolk's nests."

Scree cocked his head at the highest tower of rocks, the one with the strange green flames at its base. "No, but there's a portal right over there, you gnome-brain. Just like the one . . ."

Tamwyn's dark eyes narrowed to slits, and he finished the sentence. "The one in the Burnt Hills."

The boys glanced at each other, remembering that portal—and that terrible moment when two ghoulacas had flown out and attacked their mother before they could do anything to stop them. Or save her life.

Scree cleared his throat. Though she wasn't his birth mother, the eagleboy had felt deeply attached to her—and deeply wounded by her loss. "At least we killed them before they could eat her."

Tamwyn just looked away.

Neither of them spoke for some time. Finally, after they had fixed the snare and were sitting on a pair of ridge rocks, watching the reddish clouds of the smoky Fireroot sky, Tamwyn said, "I'd like to try it. Just once."

"Try what?"

He waved at the toothlike tower, whose base glowed an eerie green. "The portal. She was going to teach us portalseeking—remember? She said it was good to know how to do it, for our own protection."

"No, Tam. Even just going up there is dangerous."

"Come on, Scree. How about if we just go up, take a quick look, and come back?"

"It's still dangerous. And besides, why do you want to go portalseeking, anyway?" He drummed his fingers on the wood of his staff. "Me, I'm fine just staying right here. No need to see any other realms."

"Come on, now. Don't you want to go tramping in the forests of Woodroot? Swimming in the seas of Waterroot? Climbing in the mountains of Stoneroot?"

Scree shook his head. "I just want some lunch."

"Aw, be honest. You'd like to travel, wouldn't you? There are so many places out there—as many as stars in the sky."

"Just listen to you. Tam the explorer! You sound like that man she used to tell us about. Krys . . . um, Krust . . ."

"Krystallus." Tamwyn gave a sigh. "She talked about him like she'd really met him. Really knew him."

Scree shoved his brother's shoulder. "Oh, right! And maybe he was also your father."

Instead of rising to the tease, as Scree expected, Tamwyn looked him right in the eye and declared, "Well, maybe he was."

Part of Scree wanted to laugh out loud. To remind Tamwyn that his father, whoever he was, had abandoned him even before he was born. It made no difference that Tamwyn's eyes looked more human than flamelon, for both boys had guessed that his father was just another flamelon rogue, as brutish and dangerous as all the ones they'd met down in the forests. Why else had their mother refused even to talk about him?

Sure, the flamelons were brilliant at building things in their famous Forges—especially things useful in warfare, like catapults of flaming torches. But they were always starting fights, even with their own families. Hadn't their mother told them, with real despair, that some flamelons actually worshipped Rhita Gawr over all the other gods? That they considered him not just a god of war, but also a god of triumph and renewal, who led them to new heights of power and conquest?

But Scree said none of those things. For some reason he couldn't explain, he just stood and started to trudge up to the tower with the portal.

"Well?" he called to his surprised brother. "Are you coming or not?"

● ● ●

"That was stupid," Scree now grumbled, as he strode up to the crater's rim. He sidestepped to avoid a plume of sulfurous smoke, but almost put his foot on one of those cursed fire plants, whose ghoulish fingers had scorched his legs so many times. "What a complete rock-head I was to have brought him up here!"

He climbed higher, his eyes now on the toothlike tower looming ahead. Green flames flickered at its base, bright under the night sky. But his mind's eye was elsewhere—remembering the three things that had happened, right on top of each other, when he and Tamwyn had reached the portal.

First came the instant of wonder when they had gazed into it, openmouthed, glimpsing the rivers of pulsing light that carried travelers deep into the Great Tree—to any places they wanted to go. Or, as their mother had warned them, to some places they *didn't* want to go. Concentration, she'd said, was crucial for portalseeking. That was why no infants or less intelligent creatures could do it safely, unless shielded by a magical chant. Even for adults, it was dangerous—so dangerous that many had arrived at their destinations in pieces.

Second came the heart-stopping screams of the ghoulacas as they had poured out of that portal—right into the astonished faces of the boys. This time, there weren't just two killer birds, but more than a dozen. Flapping nearly invisible wings and slashing bloodred talons, the ghoulacas had screeched with delight as they attacked.

And third came the split-second decision that Scree himself had made, knowing they didn't stand a chance to defeat so many foes: He grabbed Tamwyn's arm and jumped right into the portal! The green flames engulfed them both before Tamwyn could object, or try to turn back. And before, unfortunately, he could even begin to concentrate on where to go.

Now Scree slowed, approaching the portal once more. He peered into the green flames that rose out of the ridge. "Where did you wind up, little brother?" He kicked some cinders into the snarling fire. "Better than where I did, I hope."

He knew that wherever Tamwyn had landed, he probably assumed that Scree must be somewhere in the same realm. No doubt he'd spent the better part of these past seven years searching for his brother. How could he have known that Scree, in that instant they plunged into the portal, had concentrated on a different destination? That he had doubled back and made himself return to the crater in Fireroot?

For Scree had sensed somehow that those ghoulacas hadn't appeared by coincidence. That they were after him—or the staff. And he had realized that the only safe place for his brother was somewhere far away.

Besides, Scree's trick of doubling back had worked. When he returned through the portal, all the ghoulacas were gone. They had plunged right back into the green flames, enraged that their prey had escaped, determined to give chase. The last place they would ever look, Scree was sure, was the place where they had started.

He now gazed into the portal; flickers of green danced in his yellow-rimmed eyes. He'd waited a long time for this. Squeezing the staff tightly in his hand, he concentrated his thoughts on Woodroot. That was as good a place as any to start, since Tamwyn had mentioned that realm on their last day. And if his brother wasn't there—he'd just keep on searching. As many realms as necessary.

He raised his foot to step into the flames. "Here I come, Tam. Just you—*aaaaghh!*"

Scree jumped backward, dropping the staff. He tripped, rolled on the rocks, and finally came to a stop. Slowly, he sat up, squeezing his burned hand. The staff, glowing red with heat, lay there beside him.

"What's going on with you, staff?" he demanded, licking the burned flesh of his palm. "Are you mad? Am *I* mad, talking to you like this? For Avalon's sake, if I didn't know better, I'd think you didn't want me to go in there!"

Seeing the staff's glow fade, he shook his head in puzzlement. "And in that case, why did you seem to want me to leave the cave?"

Even as he spoke, he glimpsed, from the corner of his eye, a change in the night sky. One of the brightest stars had suddenly winked out—just like that. Probably just covered by a thick cloud of smoke.

But no, there wasn't any more smoke than usual in that spot. Scree rubbed his chin, scowling at the sky. There wasn't any doubt about it. A star had just gone dark—a star in the Wizard's Staff.

15 · Skunkweed

THIS WAY, YOU LAZY FOOLS! CAN'T YOU SEE where I'm leading?"

Llynia's harsh voice scraped on Tamwyn's ears no less than a dagger on a sheet of flatrock. He was walking through the grove of dwarf pines, whose dry upper branches brushed against his waist, tinkling the small quartz bell at his hip. Hearing her voice, he stopped and arched his neck from under the huge pile of bundles, water flasks, and cooking pots on his shoulders.

"Sure, I can see. But I told you before, the mudmoss hanging from those branches—right there, in the cedar above your head—means there's a marsh nearby. Or at least there was, before the drought. Even mudmoss that's as dry and colorless as this stuff can spell trouble, believe me. And since these dwarf pines like to grow in drier ground, staying over here is a good way to avoid—"

"Silence, porter!" Llynia glared at him, her hands on her hips. "I told you that your job is to carry bags, not get us lost. And besides, we've no time to waste."

She glanced up at the sky and frowned. Even in the midday brightness, there was no way to miss the change in the Wizard's

Staff. The gap where its star had disappeared seemed to throb with emptiness. More to herself than to anyone else, she muttered, "No time at all."

"But you—"

"Silence!"

Thanks to Nuic's herbal remedy, her face had regained most of its normal color over the last three days (except for the triangular mark on her chin). But right now her cheeks had taken on a dark shade of purple. "I said get back over here and follow me."

Henni, whose back was bending under a load almost as big as Tamwyn's, wiped his dripping brow with one of his big hoolah hands. "Just like we've done the past few days, eehee, eehee. Right, Lady Greenbeard? We've followed you into more bramble patches, peat bogs, and stickysap pits than I've seen in my whole life!" He nodded at Tamwyn, who stood just in front of him. "But at least I haven't dropped my things all over the place, like clumsy man here."

With that, he pulled the slingshot off his belt and placed a dwarf pinecone on the leather pad. Then, balancing his load carefully on his shoulders, he shot the cone right into Tamwyn's bottom.

"Yaaaaah!" roared Tamwyn, spinning around so fast that several bundles and pots flew off, clanging into the trees.

"Hoohoo, heehahahahaha. Clumsy man does it again."

Elli, who had seen the whole thing, couldn't help but chuckle. Just what that fool Tamwyn deserved! For three days now, she'd been throwing him every chore—and every insult—she could come up with. All that felt good, though it didn't even begin to make up for the loss of her harp.

"You really *are* clumsy," she jeered. "But," she added with a wink at the round little sprite riding on her shoulder, "that's just the way imbeciles are, I suppose."

Henni broke into a new fit of wild laughter, nearly dropping his own bundles.

Tamwyn just glared at the hoolah. Ever since they'd become porters, he'd wondered why Henni was still with them. It was most unlike a hoolah to travel with a group—certainly when carrying a heavy load of supplies was part of the process. But now he was sure. This accursed creature was staying around for just one reason—to torment him. And he was succeeding!

"Just you wait," Tamwyn growled, "you stinking bag of bear turds! The second I'm done with this job, I'll twist you up into such a knot, you could pass for an ogre's braid!"

A pair of purple-blossomed boughs waved a stern warning in front of their faces. Fairlyn's large eyes held them both. She was beginning to smell vaguely like a couple of crushed skulls.

"All right, then," grumbled Tamwyn. He stooped to retrieve the fallen bundles and tossed them to Fairlyn, who replaced them on his pile. "You go first, Priestess, and show us your way."

Llynia grunted in approval. "Due north, as I've been saying all along. To the Dun Tara snowfields at the very top of Stoneroot, where I believe there's a portal to Woodroot."

Tamwyn froze. "But that portal—"

"Hush, porter! You have nothing to say about this."

"But I do," declared Elli. "You said you *believe* there's a portal? I thought you knew for sure."

"I *am* sure," retorted the Chosen One. "Before we left, I had Fairlyn show me on a map which portal she came through when she left Woodroot."

"But that might not work," Elli persisted, shaking her bouncy brown curls. "Portals are quirky, you know. That one might just lead to one particular outlet, not to lots of other portals. What if it just goes back to Fairlyn's home at the western end of Woodroot? The legends say that where we want to go is way over on the other side of the realm—where the forest is deepest."

"I *know* what the legends say!" thundered Llynia. "And I don't need advice from an apprentice third class." She wheeled on Tamwyn. "Or a lowly porter."

"I suppose," offered Nuic casually, "you could just use your gift of Sight to find the way."

Llynia's eyes bulged, but she said nothing. Then she took a deep breath, trying to calm herself. "All I need is the faith of Elen the Founder, and the courage of her successor, Rhiannon." Through clenched teeth, she added, "And the patience of them both."

Nuic, on Elli's shoulder, whispered, "None of which can do much good without a brain."

Elli sputtered, pretending to cough to hide her laughter.

"Due north," repeated Llynia with certainty. Again she looked up at the stars, shining so bright—except for the one that had vanished. "And we have no time to lose."

Her face now not so certain, she turned and led the way into the cedars, her feet crunching on the dry needles. Fairlyn followed close behind, then Elli and Nuic, and the two porters.

Tamwyn shook his head. "Now I know what it's like to be a slave."

Elli spun around, her hazel eyes boring into him. "Don't you *ever* make jokes about slaves. You hear? Or I'll take that little bell off your belt and stuff it up your nose!"

Tamwyn just glared right back at her. All his sympathy for Elli had vanished after three days of her abuse. The black eye she'd given him, still bruised, swelled with rage. "Making threats, are we? Too bad you're just as lousy a fighter as you are a harpist."

She lunged at him, plowing her head right into his chest. Nuic went rolling into the mat of dry needles—but Tamwyn fell hard into the cedar boughs. Sacks, bundles, flasks, and pots sprayed in all directions. Before he could roll aside, Elli's fist smashed hard into his unbruised eye.

With a roar, Tamwyn leaped to his feet, shoved Elli's shoulder, and tripped her backward. Before she knew what was happening, he whipped the vine off his waist and lashed her ankles together. Then he tossed the longer end of the vine over a sturdy branch, hoisted her up so that her head dangled above the ground, and tied the vine around a trunk. All in a matter of seconds.

She hung there, like a caterpillar stuck inside its cocoon, struggling to free herself. Tamwyn watched her for a moment, then gave a satisfied nod. "Did that once to a bear cub who just wouldn't leave my camp alone." Gently, he touched the new bruise on his face. "But the bear didn't punch."

"That's not all I'll do to you when I get down!" She squirmed and twisted, trying to reach the place where he'd tied off the vine.

Tamwyn turned away. "At least it's going to be quieter now."

"Sure, until she gets free!" Henni, who had enjoyed the show immensely, scuttled out of Tamwyn's reach. "And then you'd better run, eehee, eehee. Or you'll have such big rings around your eyes, you'll look like a hoolah! Hoohoohoo, hohohohee."

From deep in the cedars, Llynia called: "Where are you, porters? I told you to follow!" There was a pause, some swishing of branches, and she added, "By the way, master wilderness guide, this way is perfectly fine. Imagine thinking we'd find a marsh in a drought like this! And imagine thinking that you . . . What? *Eeeehh!*"

Leaving his scattered sacks behind, Tamwyn raced through the cedars, ducking under low boughs and hurtling over broken limbs. When he reached the edge of the grove, he stopped abruptly. And stared.

Llynia had fallen face-first into a murky pool. As she struggled to stand again, thick black mud oozed through her hair, dripped down her face, and coated her arms, legs, and half her chest. A clump of marsh grass hung from her shoulder. Her mouth worked feverishly to spit out whatever she had swallowed. Fairlyn, trying to help her, was also splattered with mud. Over on the side of the pool, Henni was howling with laughter.

Into the pool plunged Tamwyn. The black ooze sucked at his legs, but he managed to find a flat stone to support his weight. He reached out to Llynia and pulled her from the murk, then led her out of the pool. At last she collapsed on firm ground.

That was when Tamwyn spotted the worms. Flesh-eating worms! Not just one or two, but dozens of them, crawling on Llynia's scalp and ears. Buried in the mud, the worms were small enough that she hadn't yet noticed them.

She would very soon, though! Tamwyn knew from experience how much the gnawing jaws of those worms could hurt. And how much blood they could draw as they scraped off layers of skin to dig themselves into a new body.

Desperately, he scanned the grove for any sign of skunkweed, the one plant whose smell was strong enough to drive off the worms. If, that is, its leaves could be crushed before the worms started digging in. After that, there was nothing to do but pull them off one by one—and tear off bloody chunks of skin with them.

Tamwyn frowned. No skunkweed! Only seconds remained.

In a flash, he turned to Fairlyn, who was just slogging out of the pool. "Fairlyn! Can you smell like skunkweed? Quick—for Llynia!"

The tree spirit straightened her trunk and eyed him suspiciously. A faint aroma of sour milk wafted from her branches.

"No, no. Trust me." He pointed at the huddled priestess, who was trying to wipe the mud out of her eyes and ears. "Flesh-eating worms! The smell of skunkweed is her only chance."

Instantly, Fairlyn's boughs snapped toward Llynia. At the same time, they released a choking, rancid, overpowering smell. It was worse than a whole family of enraged skunks.

Tamwyn jumped aside just as a mass of writhing worms tumbled out of Llynia's hair. The worms tried to burrow into the dirt, or scurry back to the pool—anything they could do to get away from the smell. Unfortunately, Llynia saw them, too. She flew to her feet and shook herself violently, shrieking at the top of her lungs. Any worms that didn't move fast enough were crushed beneath her shoes.

It took more than an hour of searching the area for Tamwyn to find even a trickle of a stream. Flowing out of a cracked stone on the hillside above the cedars, it wound down a narrow gully until it sank again into the ground. But it was all the trekkers needed for their baths. Everyone took advantage of the opportunity—except for Henni, who scoffed at the idea of washing up.

Llynia used some soaproot found by Nuic to remove the mud and the potent smell of skunks (moaning all the while that even another Drumadian bath couldn't get her clean now). Next came

Elli, who had finally freed herself from the vine, though not without getting sticky cedar sap in her hair. She scrubbed her hair in the pool, pausing only to shoot dagger-looks at Tamwyn. Last of all, Tamwyn himself washed up, removing at last the stains of balloonberries and the smell of dung. All through the bathing, Fairlyn kept her roots in the water, drinking gladly, while Nuic merely sat upstream, enjoying the feel of cool spray on his back.

Neither of the priestesses bothered to thank Tamwyn for finding the stream. In fact, neither of them spoke to him at all. But he didn't mind. At least now he felt clean.

Still, like everyone else, he remained thirsty. Even a prolonged drink at the cracked stone didn't help, for his thirst ran deeper than tongue and throat. His very blood seemed thickened by drought.

And Tamwyn's heart ached for the thirsty land around him. It didn't take a wilderness guide to see how much all these trees, grasses, ferns, and mosses needed water. So did the birds who sang plaintively from the bushes, and the newts who scurried away on the rocks. Usually, at this time of year, when new snow started falling on the high peaks, these hills sang with freshwater streams. But now the bland-colored stones and dry gullies didn't sing at all.

16 · Emissaries of the Gods

THIS IS THE NOISIEST BUNCH I'VE EVER *trekked with.* Tamwyn shook his head in dismay—though just gently, since he didn't want to drop any of the gear piled high on his back. That would only give Henni something new to harass him about. *Really, they make about as much noise as an army of gnomes.*

His dismay only grew with each passing day. Much of the time, as they tramped through forested hills and along dry riverbeds, the travelers scrapped with each other. Llynia complained that they were losing precious time; Elli often agreed and suggested that Llynia should walk faster—not exactly what Llynia wanted to hear. Meanwhile, Henni missed no chances to tease Tamwyn, Fairlyn smelled like something horrible, and Nuic grumbled constantly about how much the world (especially priestesses and porters) had degenerated over the past few centuries. Although Llynia never actually asked Tamwyn's advice, she often put him in the lead and let him guide the group north—always badgering him from behind about his clumsiness. Which, of course, delighted Henni even more.

In this way, the group trudged northward toward the Dun Tara snowfields—and the portal that Llynia insisted would take them to Woodroot, for the secret purpose that she wouldn't discuss in the porters' presence. Tamwyn had tried, for several days running, to tell her what he knew about that portal, but she wouldn't even begin to listen. Finally, fed up with her obstinance, he'd decided just to let her find out herself. The result would be quite entertaining—well worth a few days' labor as a porter.

After the seventh day of trekking, Tamwyn picked a low, rounded knoll for their camp that night. Stubby grass, faded yellow in color, covered its top. A tiny pool of water bubbled at its base, barely enough to supply the group's needs. The pool was so small, and hidden behind a fold of the ground, that Tamwyn wouldn't have seen it at all but for the family of water faeries hovering there.

The luminous blue wings of the faeries caught the light, flashing like translucent sapphires. There were five of them in all, a pair of adults and three young ones. All wore the silver-blue tunics and dewdrop-shaped shoes common to water faeries. The father also wore a belt of dried red currants, and the mother carried a backpack made from a periwinkle shell in which she carried their youngest child.

As Tamwyn approached, he nodded in greeting. *Good day to you, friends.* As always, the words to communicate with nonhuman creatures simply formed in his mind. He wondered why other humans didn't seem to use this silent language. Was it too difficult? That couldn't be right, since it felt just as easy as human speech to him. More likely they had lived for so long in villages, away from most other creatures, that they'd simply forgotten how.

The father faery lifted up from the pool with a spray of water droplets from his wingtips. He gestured angrily at Tamwyn.

You have a point, the young man replied. *How can any day be good when there's so little water around?* He listened as the faery said something else. *Well, I hope you find that spot to your liking! I've heard there are some nice waterfalls there, meltoff from the Dun Tara snowfields.*

The faery waved, not angrily this time. He swooped back to the pool, helped his wife gather the children, and flew away. Their luminous blue wings hummed softly and then disappeared behind the knoll.

Tamwyn dropped his load and started to make camp. As always, his first task was to build a fire—no trouble for him, even when there wasn't so much dry kindling around. Perhaps it was his experience as a woodsman . . . or perhaps his flamelon ancestry somehow gave him an affinity with flames. Either way, making a campfire seemed as natural as making a wish.

He started by walking over to an old hawthorn tree that he'd noticed near the knoll. One of its lower branches, broken by a storm, hung by a few shreds of bark. Hawthorn burned with lots of heat, and this branch was just the right thickness for long-lasting coals.

He stood before the tree and bent his head in greeting. Then, as was the custom of fire builders since the earliest days of Avalon, he asked:

> *Friendly tree both strong and high,*
> *Answer now in truth: May I*
> *Take your limb to warm my own,*
> *Cook my food, or heat my home?*

The tree's remotest twigs stirred ever so slightly. Abruptly the whole tree shrugged—whether from a sudden gust of wind or from its own inner will, it was hard to tell. But that was enough to break off the remaining bark, and the branch fell to the ground. With a nod of thanks, Tamwyn took it back to the knoll.

Now that he had the wood he needed, lighting the fire was easy. A few scrapes of the iron stones that he kept in his pocket, and his ball of tinder grass caught a spark. He placed it on a patch of bare soil near the top of the knoll, well away from any overhanging branches. For he knew well that the hardest part of making a fire in these days of drought was keeping it safely under control.

Once he started cooking supper—a hearty vegetable stew—only Elli made some effort to help, peeling some yellow tubers that she'd found in the forest. But she sat on the other side of the fire from him, facing the opposite direction. There was no chance she would speak to Tamwyn, let alone look at him directly—which suited him just fine.

After a while, Nuic ambled up the knoll, carrying an armful of bay leaves and garlic grass. The little sprite dropped his ingredients into Tamwyn's pot, and then sat on the grass beside Elli. Caustically, he grumbled, "If I didn't know better, I'd say that Llynia was really the child of the Dark Prophecy."

Behind them, Tamwyn perked up. He continued to make the stew, dicing and mixing in various dried vegetables, grains, bark strips, and oils supplied by the Society of the Whole. But all the while, his woodsman's ears listened with keen interest.

"I've thought the same thing myself," agreed Elli. "But she's too old—by about twenty years, I'd guess. And I heard she came from Stoneroot, not where most Drumadians seem to think the Dark one was born."

She paused, running her fingers through the low grass. "Why do they say the child was probably born in Fireroot?"

Tamwyn jolted, dropping some carrots.

"Hmmmpff. Don't you know that? Fireroot was one of the only places where there were children born that year. The flamelons refused to go along with the ban on having babies, suspecting that the whole Prophecy was just a trick by humans to get them to reduce their numbers."

"Always thinking about war, aren't they?" Elli shook her head, thick with curls. "If I ever meet a peaceful flamelon, I'll be shocked."

Tamwyn wanted to shout: *My mother was peaceful!* But he held his tongue.

The pinnacle sprite's colors darkened. "Wrong, Elliryanna. If you ever meet a peaceful flamelon, don't be shocked. Be frightened. That's so unlikely, it could well be a disguise."

Sucking in her breath, Elli said, "You mean . . ."

"Correct." Ribbons of gray and black swept over Nuic's body. "It could be the Dark child."

For a long moment, they sat in silence. Then Elli rose, scooped up Nuic, and walked down the slope.

As Tamwyn stirred his pot of stew, starset's flash of light wove golden threads into the limbs of trees and the lines of stones. Yet he hardly noticed: He couldn't help but wonder about what he'd just heard. Was he, being at least half flamelon, never going to be truly peaceful? And was that the same as being truly at peace?

Then his thoughts turned to the most disturbing question of

all. What if, despite everything he believed about himself, he really *was* the child of the Dark Prophecy? The person who would cause the end of Avalon?

No! He shook his head, brushing his long black hair against his shoulders. That was *impossible*. And yet . . . he did have a special knack for causing disasters. Whether it was losing Scree, getting banished by Lott, or destroying Elli's harp, trouble seemed to follow him like a shadow. And always had.

He stirred the stew more vigorously than ever. At the bottom of the knoll, he could see Llynia stride past Elli, who was standing by an old beech tree, and Henni, who was tossing pebbles at a raccoon that wanted to sleep. The priestess continued up the slope, swept past Tamwyn without so much as a word, and stopped only when she reached the top.

There Llynia sat down, legs folded and back straight, all set for her evening prayers. As always for this ritual, she had donned a fresh set of clothes: today's choice, a white robe embroidered with green threads, a silver sash, and a necklace of speckled brown beads. In her hands she held her volume of *Cyclo Avalon*, open to the page that began the lore of élano.

Her face seemed troubled, but Tamwyn wouldn't have guessed that right now she wasn't worried about the success of her quest, or the time they'd lost trekking. No, her greater worries now involved herself—her powers. *Just when,* she asked herself fretfully, *will my visions fully return?*

She craned her neck, looking up at the constellation commonly called the Circles—two rings of stars, one inside the other. Drumadians, though, had their own name for it: the Mysteries. This constellation, more than any other, inspired thoughts about the seventh sacred Element. The outer circle, made of twenty-one stars with hints of green and scarlet, was called Mystery of Life. It was here that Llynia directed most of her prayers; it had always reminded her of a jeweled crown. The inner circle, with eleven stars and an aura of lavender blue, was called Mystery of Spirit. It seemed pretty enough to Llynia, but cool and distant, not so inspiring.

"O Goddess, God, and all there is," she began, her upturned face washed in the light of the stars. "Tonight I pray for more than my own strength of body and purpose. Tonight I pray for all of Avalon, the Great Tree that holds our world and connects it to all other worlds."

She paused, breathing deeply the cool air of evening. "I call to you, Lorilanda, spirit of rebirth, and to you, Dagda, spirit of wisdom—my great lights in this time of deepening darkness. Please guide me . . . and help me find what I need! For only then can I lead my people through this night of torment and into a new day, a new world, when all your creations may reach their highest forms. There are those who seek to control this world, as well as others; but there are those, such as you, who seek only to give free peoples the right to choose their own destinies. And so I ask your blessing—as well as your help. And as always, I offer you my gratitude, along with my life."

Llynia focused her gaze on the Mysteries, watching the two sparkling circles with not just her eyes but also her inner Sight. As she had done every night since the start of the journey, she tried to clear her mind completely—not easy, given the persistent smell of skunkweed that still clung to her hair. But she willed herself to open her Inner Eye, to show her at least a glimpse of the future, perhaps of the Lady she so dearly wanted to meet.

She concentrated harder on the twin circles of stars. One by one, she counted them, then gazed at their hues of green, scarlet, and lavender blue. All at once, she stopped. A particularly bright star, richly blue, drew her attention. She peered at it—when suddenly it seemed to flash.

A burst of blue light filled her mind. And with it, something more: an image, as visible as the Mysteries themselves. In the center of the inner circle, she could see a wide blue lake, shrouded by swirling mist. Then, emerging out of the mist, the form of a woman, very old but still tall and vibrant. And very beautiful. Her silver hair, bunched in countless curls, fell over her shoulders onto her shawl and gown of deep, textured green. Around her neck hung some sort of amulet made of leaves.

The Lady of the Lake. It was she! As Llynia watched, breathless, the woman raised her hand, palm out, in greeting.

Llynia's heart leaped. This was the very same vision that she'd had before the Council of Elders! But this time it was much more vivid and detailed. So she'd really seen the Lady. And her powers were, indeed, returning.

Suddenly, the image blurred. Mist rose off the lake, consuming the woman's gown, her face, and last of all, her hand. An instant later, she was gone.

But Llynia clapped her hands in delight. She'd seen a vision. A vision of the Lady! And the great enchantress had welcomed her—yes, with an open hand. So she would get there after all! She would find the secret lair, the blue lake covered in mist. And whatever else happened, that meant that she would surely become the next High Priestess—and the first to meet the Lady face-to-face.

Meanwhile, at the very bottom of the knoll, another sort of spiritual experience was taking place. An experience with less talking and more listening.

Elli sat with her back against the beech tree. Its broad trunk, silver in the starlight, wore knots and gnarls from many seasons. Like all the other trees in these hills, its branches seemed brittle with dryness, its leaves bland in color. Yet the old tree still looked sturdy, and much of its bark felt as smooth as a stream-washed stone. She had started her meditation, as always, by just closing her eyes and relaxing. Breathing slowly. Listening with all her being to the living earth, the rooted tree, and the all-embracing air.

Centered now in that place, and that moment, Elli stretched out her senses even farther. As if she were casting a net, or a spider's web as light as the threads in the High Priestess's gown, she reached out to the rock beside her foot, the sprig of brown moss along its edge, and the lone beetle passing there on the way home. As her senses expanded, she could smell the dried rose hips and the stand of maples growing below the knoll. She could hear the far-off whisper of wings, sparrows perhaps, high above the beech tree. And she could feel the faint yearning for moisture in the soil, just as she could in her own skin.

Some words came to mind, words written long ago by Rhia, daughter of Elen the Founder:

> *Listen to Creation's morning,*
> *Waking all around you.*
> *Feel the spark of dawn within,*
> *Breaking day has found you.*

That was Rhia's description of what real meditation was like. It made Elli feel that she understood something about the early Drumadians' way of connecting with their world. How she wished she could still talk with Rhia! Of all the people who had been alive when Avalon was born, Rhia—or, as she was called by some,

Rhiannon—intrigued her most of all. Elli's father had told her many stories about Rhia: how she lived most of her childhood in a great oak tree in Lost Fincayra; how she saved the life of Merlin during his Quest of the Seven Songs; and how she helped her mother, Elen, found the Society of the Whole, becoming its second High Priestess. Elli had heard, too, that Rhia had resigned in a huff as High Priestess, storming out of the Drumadians' compound with a vow never to return. But if that had really happened, no one had ever been able to tell Elli why.

Something fluttered on her knee. She opened her eyes. Resting on the worn cloth of her robe sat a beautiful moth whose light green wings, rimmed with white lines, tapered gracefully at the back. Elli looked into the moth's dark brown eyes. Its feathery antennae quivered, and its wings closed together.

Gently, she stretched out a finger and brushed the moth's leg. "So, little one, you are meditating, too. And why not? You're a living creature, just like me. And you can be a priestess, too! A priestess of your own kind. With plenty to learn from the Great Tree, and lots to teach the likes of me."

A shadow suddenly fell across her robe, blocking the starlight. The startled moth beat its wings and flew off. Then Llynia's voice shattered the stillness.

"That's outrageous, Elli."

She looked up into the stern face of the priestess. And shook her head. "Outrageous? Why?"

Llynia pointed her finger at Elli's face, as if she were lecturing a child. "Priestesses must be human, that's why! Among all the creatures of Avalon, we're the only ones with the knowledge, skills, and wisdom to serve as emissaries of the Goddess and God. To carry on the sacred work of the Order."

Elli scrunched up her nose. "Is that what you think we are? Emissaries of the gods?" She stood up and faced the priestess who held the title of Chosen One. "Well, I disagree. And I think High Priestess Coerria would, as well."

The mention of that name made Llynia scowl. "You have no right to use . . . to be . . . anything! You're not a priestess, Elliryanna. Just a homeless vagabond! Someone a dottering old woman took pity on, nothing more."

Elli's face flushed. "She is ten thousand times the person—the priestess—that you'll ever be!"

"Oh? You'll never last long enough to see what sort of priestess I will be." A vengeful light came into Llynia's eyes. "That I will see to myself."

The long arm of Fairlyn, smelling of lemon balm, touched Llynia's shoulder. But she brushed it off and glared at Elli for another moment. Finally she strode back up the knoll, muttering, "Moths as priestesses. Moths!"

From his seat by the cooking fire, Tamwyn had watched their encounter. For the first time in days, as he saw Elli standing alone under the beech tree, he felt a twinge of something other than anger. Something more like sympathy. Despite the fact that she'd given him two black eyes in less than a week, and most likely deserved whatever scolding she got, he wondered whether she might actually be more than just a violent hothead. But when she turned and looked his way, he averted his gaze.

Suddenly a small object sailed out of the night, swerved to avoid the stew pot, and crashed into Tamwyn's shoulder. Whatever it was tumbled down onto his lap.

When he looked down, he saw what looked like a crumpled mass of old leaves. Then he noticed the subtle green aura that surrounded it. Touching it gently with his finger, he found a pair of thin flaps, one folded tight and the other pulled over a tiny, mouselike face with cupped ears. Wings!

A bat, then. Or some sort of bat spirit—shaped like its original host, as Fairlyn was shaped like a lilac elm, but different in many other ways. Whatever it was, it looked awfully scrawny . . . but still alive.

Gently, Tamwyn rubbed the back of the bat-thing's neck, just behind his furry ears. *You're going to be fine, little one. Picked a soft place to land, you did. A bit dirty, but soft.*

The green aura grew steadily stronger. Tamwyn could see a subtle brightening, especially in the creature's eyes. With a sudden jolt, the little fellow rolled over, shook his head, and flapped a crumpled wing.

Aglow with green light, he turned toward Tamwyn. Then he started to speak—not right into Tamwyn's mind, the way other animals did, but aloud, in the Common Tongue. And he spoke very fast, with a strange accent that Tamwyn had never heard before.

"Woojaja lika see me do do do tricksies? Me lovey do tricksies! Woojaja woojaja woojaaa?"

The bat-thing seemed so enthusiastic that Tamwyn couldn't help but smile. "So," he whispered, "you like to do tricks, do you? Great, but not right now. I'm trying to finish cooking."

"Ooee ooee ooee, manny man! I can doosy do most excellent tricksies."

"Fine, fine. But not now. My stew—"

"Stewey gooey. Watchy watch, too! Please?" The batlike creature twisted his whole head upside down. "Pleeeeeasey please? Oh, manny man, pleeeeease?"

Tamwyn glanced down at the pot, which was simmering nicely.

And smelling better by the minute. "Oh, all right then. Just one trick. But be quick about it."

Instantly, the creature's green glow swelled brighter. He flapped hard, took off, and started zipping around Tamwyn's head in an erratic pattern. Once he did an aerial roll and twirl combined—which would have been perfect except that his wing clipped Tamwyn's nose. Suddenly Tamwyn sneezed, spraying the creature, who spun out of control and landed with a splat right in the stew pot.

"Owwy wow, hot!" screeched the little beast, leaping straight out of the pot to land on the ground. He flapped hard to shake some globs of hot stew off his wings, then spun around to curse the pot. "You ucky mucky poopy pile!"

"Ah, well, sorry about that." Tamwyn tried his best not to laugh out loud. "But my stew's for eating, not for landing. Anyway, you did great up till then. What a trick!"

"It's lotsy better," the bat-thing said glumly, "when manny man no sneezy-goo all over me."

"Right, I'm sure." Tamwyn reached over to stir the stew again.

But the wacky little fellow flew up and landed on his forearm. "You really like me tricksies? Telly me truth."

"Yes, yes," he replied. "I liked them. Now let me work."

The green eyes brightened again. "Goody good good! Then me doosy do some more!"

"No," he pleaded.

"Butsy but, me do do better now. No more sneezy-goo."

Tamwyn sighed heavily. "All right, how about this? You do tricks, just over there—and I'll keep on cooking right here. That way I can watch you, but we'll have no more sneezy-goo."

"And no more poopy pile," added the little beast.

"Right," agreed Tamwyn. "So do you like this plan?"

The bat-creature rubbed his face with the edge of his wing. "Mmm . . . no! Me me no likey plan." His little mouth opened in a yawn. "Me me too sleepy now for doing tricksies."

Tamwyn shook his head. "Fine then. You go nap someplace, and I'll finish cooking."

"Nappy nap? Goody idea! Oh yessa ya ya ya. Meya Battygad, see? Battygad like nappy naps."

With that, the furry fellow tottered over to a thick bunch of grass, lay down, and wrapped himself inside his wing. From under the leathery blanket came a muffled yawn, and a small voice. "Nice and softy warm here, ya ya ya."

The young man just had to grin. Looking down at his new-found friend, he said, "Battygad, is it? More like a batty lad, if you ask me! Yes, Batty Lad—whatever you really are, that's a perfect name for you."

Tamwyn gave the stew a stir, tasted it, and added a pinch more garlic grass. Then, as it simmered over the fire, he glanced up at the stars.

So many of them . . . like luminous fields that stretched on and on forever. Even with one star less than he was accustomed to seeing, the night sky shone brilliantly. There was Pegasus, soaring with outstretched wings, flying like an eagle. Or, he thought suddenly, an eagleman.

A slight movement, barely a wink of light, caught his attention. It came from another constellation, a row of six stars not far above the horizon: the Wizard's Staff. But now only five stars gleamed there.

Another star had gone dark.

17 · Hoofprints

TAMWYN ADDED A FEW MORE BAY LEAVES to the stew, as well as the last of the bark strips, and stirred some more. But his thoughts were not on the pot below him so much as the night sky above him.

What was going on with the stars? What did it all mean?

Using a spare spoon, he nudged the glowing coals of his cooking fire. A pair of sparks flew up, then winked out, just as those two stars had done.

He turned to the small, furry creature who lay on the grass, wrapped in a leathery wing. What sort of beast was Batty Lad? Part bat, part something else . . . with those glowing green eyes, bright as sparks themselves? Well, whatever he was, he was certainly sound asleep.

Tamwyn pushed the coals together into a mound under the pot. They would keep the stew warm for a good twenty minutes—all the stew needed.

And all that he needed, as well, to do something that never failed to clear his head when he felt troubled. It was something that he'd been wanting to do all day, even before he'd seen the Wizard's Staff. No—all week.

Run.

Just run.

He peered down the knoll and gave a wave to Fairlyn, whose boughs were entwined with those of the old beech. "Would you mind stirring for a while?"

The tall maryth regarded him solemnly, light from the evening stars in her eyes. Though her opinion of Tamwyn had clearly softened since the incident with the worms, she still treated everyone but Llynia with a certain aloofness. After a moment, though, she withdrew her boughs from the beech and bent her trunk in a nod.

Tamwyn smiled. As Fairlyn climbed up the knoll, he trotted down. At the bottom of the slope he leaped over a toppled trunk and started to run up a long, rock-strewn valley. His bare feet thumped the ground at first, then struck more softly as he picked up speed. Cool night air rushed over his face and pushed his hair behind his shoulders. He loped through a stretch of tall grasses, as dry as thatch but sweet as barley, that swished against his leggings. And jumped over a tightly woven spider's web, glittering in the starlight.

Tamwyn's legs churned harder as he ran up a steep rise. He felt his heart pumping, his breath surging, with every stride. When he reached the crest, he slowed just a bit, and saw that he was running at the same speed as a fluffy white seed caught by the wind. With a gust, the wind picked up speed; so did Tamwyn. All three of them—the seed, the man, and the wind—raced ahead. They flew along, moving as one, flowing smoothly over the land.

Now he belonged to the wind.

Tamwyn ran even faster. He jumped the mound of a badger's

den, and then veered to avoid a family of ptarmigan out for an evening stroll. As he took a high bound to clear a boulder, he thought of the tales he'd heard bards sing about the deer people—a clan in Lost Fincayra who could change themselves into deer whenever they wished.

Amazing! What a thrill . . . They could be strolling one moment as men and women—then leaping the next as stags and does. According to the tales, the one great love of Merlin's life, Hallia, was herself a deer woman. And though their child, the famous explorer Krystallus, couldn't shift into a deer, the bards always held out hope that some later descendant might bear the magical blood.

I hope so, thought Tamwyn as he loped along, following a dry streambed. *I do hope so! Then the deer people from Merlin's old world might exist again . . . right here in Avalon.*

He pursed his lips thoughtfully, even as he jumped to the other side of the streambed to catch the scent of a juniper bush, its twisted boughs dotted with tiny blue berries. *But for that to be true, Krystallus must have had a child.* And though he'd heard many stories about the fearless explorer from his mother, from villagers, and from wandering bards—stories that told how Krystallus became the first person ever to find portals to all Seven Realms, the only man to reach the Great Hall of the Heartwood and return alive, the first human to dare to visit the flamelons after the War of Storms—none of those stories said anything about Krystallus fathering a child.

A scrawny little bird shot out of the sky and barely missed Tamwyn's nose. He wrenched aside, almost stepping in a marmot's hole. Then he stopped and turned to the bird, who had spun around and started to dive at him again.

What are you doing, you fool bird? Just as he threw his arms up to protect his face, he caught a glimpse of gleaming green eyes and batlike wings—and realized that this wasn't a bird after all.

"Batty Lad! You could have warned me!"

The flying creature veered sharply and landed on Tamwyn's forearm, his furry belly heaving with exhaustion. "Me do do come to warn manny man. Oh yessa ya ya ya! Bigga warning. Terri-bibble danger!"

Tamwyn, who was panting just as heavily, fixed his gaze on Batty Lad's eerie green pupils. "What danger?"

"Not to you, manny man. To others, yessa ya ya ya." He lifted his wings to cover his small face and cupped ears. "Ooee ooee . . . itsa bad, terribibble bad."

"What?" Tamwyn raised his forearm so that his nose almost touched the babbling creature's. "Tell me who's in danger. And from what."

"Everybodya ya ya!" shrieked Batty Lad. "Froma the dragon!"

Tamwyn didn't wait to hear any more. A dragon, at their camp? He dropped Batty Lad into the pocket of his tunic, turned, and started to run—this time even faster than before. Faster than he could remember running in his life. Faster than the wind.

His legs a blur, he sped back down the valley. He zipped past rocks, shrubs, and gullies, leaping over anything in his path. All he could hear was a whoosh of air in his ears . . . and the growing sound of shouts from the camp.

He came hurtling down the last slope. Just when he reached the small pool of water at the base of the knoll, he slammed his feet to a halt. There, stretched across the knoll, was a dragon.

Just then the dragon shifted its massive body. As it turned away from the now-empty pot of stew that its long green tongue had been probing, Tamwyn could see that its enormous head—three times as large as that of a horse—was completely armored with yellow and blue scales except for a scarlet bump between its eyes. That bump, he knew, meant that this dragon was still young. That still didn't make it small, though: Each of its eyes, brighter than fire coals, were as big as Tamwyn's own head. Hundreds of dagger-sharp teeth glistened in its gaping jaws. Its huge reptilian body stretched all the way down the knoll, the barbed point of its tail crushing the branches of the beech tree that Elli had sat under not long before.

On the dragon's back lay a pair of immense, bony wings. Thick blue veins ran through them like swollen rivers. Unfolded, the wings could have covered the entire knoll. But even retracted they were as large as the sails made by the water elves of Caer Ser-ella, whose legendary ships had traversed all the seas of Waterroot. Tamwyn gulped at the difference between these huge, leathery wings and the delicate ones that bore little Batty Lad.

The dragon didn't seem to notice Tamwyn at all. And it seemed equally oblivious to Elli and Nuic, who were beating on its tail with sticks to get it to leave the camp. Nor did it seem to mind Henni, who had climbed the beech tree and was gleefully trying to seat himself on the barbed tail to catch a ride.

Instead, as the dragon turned, it caught sight of Llynia, who had climbed onto a boulder near the top of the knoll. She was angrily shouting commands at the beast while shaking her fists and stomping her feet. Undeterred, the young dragon started to stretch its scaly neck toward the priestess.

Fairlyn lunged between them. The elm spirit, who smelled of smoky dragon breath, stood firmly in front of Llynia and waved her boughs wildly. Although the dragon was, fortunately, still too young to breathe fire, it simply jerked its massive head sideways and sent Fairlyn tumbling down the slope.

As its toothy snout neared Llynia, she suddenly stopped shouting. A look of terror came over her face. Even her green chin went several shades paler.

The jaws opened—not all the way, but just wide enough to nip off the head of this irksome little creature on the boulder. The dragon's tongue flicked across its black lips and rows of teeth. Llynia stood frozen with fear.

"No! Stop!" cried Elli, dropping her stick and beating her fists furiously against the armored tail.

Wider the jaws opened. And wider. Hundreds of pointed teeth, trailing shreds of meat and gobs of mucus, glistened. The dragon's mouth started to close over Llynia's head.

A high, wailing shriek pierced the air. The dragon suddenly halted. As the shriek grew louder, its fiery eyes narrowed down to mere slits. Then, all at once, it retracted its neck, brushing Llynia's cheek with its tongue.

The dragon drew its enormous wings tight onto its back. Turning toward the sound, which came from somewhere up the rocky valley, it bellowed its own version of the cry in return. At the same time, it dug huge curved claws into the ground and pushed hard. Chunks of dirt and rock flew into the air. The dragon slid forward, then charged down the side of the knoll and into the valley.

No one spoke for several seconds. Fairlyn, cradling two broken arms, hobbled back up the slope as the color slowly returned to Llynia's face. Elli stared after the departed beast, amazed and puzzled. Henni shook his head in disappointment because he'd missed his chance for a ride on a dragon's tail. Nuic, though, was looking straight at Tamwyn, whose hands were cupped around his mouth.

"How did you do that?" demanded the old sprite. His color had shifted from deep red to a pulsing yellow.

Tamwyn lowered his hands. "Oh, it's just a call I picked up . . . almost two years ago. When I tracked a family of dragons—not the biggest sort, more like the wyverns from the western caves. I watched them for almost a week."

"You?" interrupted Elli. She gazed at the clumsy porter, who wore matching black eyes. "*You* made that cry?"

Tamwyn shrugged. "It's not hard, really."

"What is it?" she asked. "Some sort of battle cry?"

He grinned slightly. "Not exactly."

"The cry of a predator, then? Something that scared it off?"

"Scared it, yes. Enough that it won't be coming back here anytime soon. But not a predator."

She stared at him, her face full of doubt.

One of his hands reached into his pocket to stroke Batty Lad's furry head. "It's the call of a mother dragon. I heard it often during that week. Means something like: *Get your scaly tail over here right now or I'll eat your innards for supper.*"

"How affectionate," grumbled Nuic, still watching Tamwyn curiously. "But you haven't answered my question. How did you do it?"

"Well," he began. "I wrap my fingers like this, then place them over—"

"No, no, you idiot!" Now Nuic's yellow color had veins of red running through it. "Not how did you make the sound. How did you *project* the sound?"

Tamwyn's brow crinkled. "It's just a trick, something I

figured out when . . . well, when I had nothing better to do." He shrugged. "Which is fairly often."

"It's not just a trick," admonished Nuic. He waved his tiny arms. "It's an *illusion*. Not a bad one, either, for a mindless beginner."

Elli, who was just starting to ask another question, caught herself. Could it be? Her crusty old maryth had just said something rather close to a compliment. And to that idiot Tamwyn of all people! A mistake, surely. Or maybe one of Nuic's games.

She stepped a bit closer to the young man, her feet crunching on the stubby grass. "Just how," she asked skeptically, "do you *know* that's what the cry means? It's dragon language, after all."

Again Tamwyn shrugged. From his point of view, she might just as well have asked him how he breathed. "I don't know. It's just another trick, I guess. Something I learned . . ."

"When you had nothing better to do," finished Nuic. Though he sounded grumpy again, there was a strange, uncertain expression on his face.

Tamwyn's gaze moved to the empty pot of stew on the knoll. "Guess I should start another supper, or we won't be eating before the middle of the night."

"Eating?"

All eyes turned to the hoolah sitting in the beech tree. Henni nodded vigorously. "Now *that's* a language I can understand! Hoohoohoo, hehe, hoohoo."

Tamwyn just shook his head. He started toward the food supplies, half of which had been swallowed by the hungry young dragon. Then, just to be sure they were now safe, he checked over his shoulder at the valley where the dragon had run off . . . and where he himself had run freely not long before.

There was no sign of the dragon. All that remained was the path of flattened soil and crushed rocks where it had dragged its enormous bulk over the ground. Nearby, in the rim of mud at the edge of the small pool, Tamwyn saw his own footprints from when he'd started his run up the valley.

And then he saw something else. Something that made his heart freeze.

There, embedded in the mud, were the prints from his swift run back to camp. Or at least that was what they *should* have been. Tamwyn stared at them in disbelief. For these prints were different. Much different.

They were the hoofprints of a stag.

18 · Absolutely

FINALLY, BRIONNA NEARED THE CANYON RIM. Though her legs shook from the strain of her long climb, she didn't even pause before starting up the last redrock cliff. Higher she moved, and higher, like a squirrel on a tree trunk. Just below the top, she wrapped her hand around a protruding knob and lifted herself up enough to throw her leg over. With a final grunt of effort, she rolled onto the rim at last.

She lay there, flat on her back, gasping for air. With every breath, puffs of red dust rose off her tattered robe. This was the first rest she'd taken since leaving the sorcerer with the pale hands several hours ago.

Before she sat up, she let herself imagine her beloved Woodroot—the forest of endless greenery that she'd now see again. Rich and lively it was, full of verdant groves, sweet-smelling fruits, uncounted creatures, and alluring pathways. Seeing it again would surely restore her soul after those three tortured days on the sorcerer's dam. For while she and Granda had been stolen away from Woodroot, bound and blindfolded, part of them could never leave those fragrant forest paths.

Though she was still panting, and her limbs felt as heavy as stones from the quarries, she forced her thoughts back to the present. She had a task to do—and a life to save. Granda's life!

She sat up. But the sight that met her gaze almost made her collapse back on the rock. The lush border forest that grew right to the canyon rim, and that marked the boundary between Woodroot and Waterroot—El Urien and Brynchilla, as Granda would say—was gone.

Gone!

For half a league along the canyon wall, the border forest had been ripped away. Torn out by the roots. Slaughtered in a massive clear cut.

All that remained of those verdant groves near the canyon, where creatures always ran free, swinging from ropemoss and leaping from branches, was a wasteland of death. Everywhere lay severed trunks, broken limbs, slashed branches, and torn hunks of bark. The very heart of this forest had been brutally hacked to shreds and left to rot. And where were the creatures—the foxes, hedgehogs, woodpeckers, and deer?

A wind blew down the canyon, whipping the surface of the white lake behind the dam, wailing across the redrock cliffs. When it reached the murdered strip of forest, though, the sound of the wind changed to a deeper, heartrending moan. She felt sure it was a cry of pain, a cry of anguish from all the trees and creatures who had once lived in that place . . . and now were gone.

The scaffolding for the dam, thought Brionna, her jaw clenched tight. *And all those logs for the barges. This is where they came from!* But the trees, unlike Brionna and her grandfather, had no chance to survive. No chance at all.

As the elf maiden lifted her gaze beyond the slaughtered

stumps, she could see the reassuring greenery of Woodroot's more distant hills—ridge upon ridge of living, breathing trees. Although the forest looked dryer, and its colors paler, than in seasons past, she knew that it was still very much alive. Within that greenery, branches still clacked and rustled and swished. Fawns still cavorted and tried to outrun their mothers. Larks still whistled freely and yellow swallowtail butterflies swooped in search of tasty blossoms. The song of the forest, one melody and many, still could be heard in those hills.

And yet, for Brionna, that song would now always carry another note. A note of pain, and loss, and the moaning wind.

She had no idea how long it took her to cross that stretch of ravaged land. She only knew that she seemed to be walking over an open, bleeding wound that could never truly heal. As she trudged across the clear cut, stepping over the hacked remains of so many innocent lives, she felt sick. Wretchedly sick. And she also felt angry—at the sorcerer, for creating this horror, and at herself, for joining in it. *How can you help that scourge of a sorcerer? What possible reason could be good enough?*

She sighed, knowing the answer: Tressimir. Granda. Despite everything she'd seen, his life was reason enough.

In time, she stepped into the living forest. As if she'd passed through a portal to a whole new realm, everything changed in the span of that single step. Her bare feet bounced on the loam, soft and rich and full of tiny creatures crawling or burrowing. Though it felt much dryer under her toes than usual, this soil seemed like wading in a pond compared to the arid rocks of the canyon.

And the smells . . . oh, the smells! Zesty resins, sweet ferns, woody bark, rich mushrooms, nutty shells, delicate lichen, tangy berries, and so much more filled her nose and lungs.

She heard sounds of chattering squirrels and slithering snakes; saw colors in bursts of green and hints of scarlet; and felt sensations of wonder, surprise, and renewal all around. For she had entered the living forest. She had come home.

At least for a while. Brionna turned west, away from the deepest groves of Woodroot, but toward a nearby portal that she knew well. She had been there many times before with Granda—who, despite his years, was always curious to learn about other peoples and other realms. The scattered races of the elves intrigued him especially, so they had traveled through the portal several times to visit the sea elves of southern Brynchilla, and once even to meet the dangerous dark elves of Lastrael.

But now—for the first time—she would take that portal to Rahnawyn. Fireroot. To seek out a crater with towers like teeth— and a wizard's staff that would buy her grandfather's life.

As she hopped across a dry streambed, whose waters had vanished along with the river now trapped by the sorcerer's dam, she pinched her lips. *The sorcerer thinks that staff, that bit of magicked wood, is so very valuable. The fool! Far greater magic is here—right here in the living forest.*

Not wishing to be seen—or slowed down—Brionna moved as lightly as a shred of mist through the trees. She carefully avoided the pathways often used by her fellow wood elves. How could she ever explain to them what she was doing? Besides, they might even try to stop her from helping the sorcerer.

She crawled through a tunnel of poky hawthorn boughs to screen herself from some elves who were busily harvesting almonds and walnuts. And she made a wide detour through a meadow of talon grass, which clutched at the hem of her bark cloth robe, just to be sure she'd miss one of the elves' largest settlements. As she glimpsed the ring of tree houses built in the boughs of eight enormous elms, her throat tightened.

Could she chance stopping by there? In the highest tree house, she'd probably find her friend Aileen, who was well on her way to becoming a master woodworker. Aileen would set aside her carving tools and make Brionna a pot of hot hazelnut tea, sweetened with honey and cinnamon, as she'd done so many times before. Just a brief visit couldn't do any harm . . .

Brionna bit her lip, knowing better. And continued on her way.

As she passed by a meadow where honeysuckle had bloomed before the frost, she stopped abruptly. There, leaning against a maple tree, rested a longbow. Carved of springy cedar, it looked in good condition, except for its broken string. Some careless archer had evidently left it there, along with a slim quiver of arrows that lay on the maple's roots. She hesitated—the archer could be planning to return, and probably needed the bow and arrows.

Not as much as I need them, Brionna thought grimly. She grabbed the weaponry and kept walking.

At last, she approached the portal, a circle of green flames that sat between two large boulders. Eerie light, shimmering constantly, danced along the sides of the boulders, and over the branches of a towering spruce.

Before entering the portal, Brionna sat down under the spruce to restring her bow with some sturdy thread from her robe. As she pulled out a loose thread (not hard to find, after her climb up the canyon wall), she thought about her plan. Or really, her lack of a plan. Why, she wasn't even sure what this staff looked like!

No matter. She'd figure it out. She just had to. Whatever it took, she would find the staff, take it from whoever guarded it, and return before the stars of the constellation vanished completely. Then she would bring Granda back home.

She had almost finished tying the bowstring when she heard an odd sound. Part rumble, part gurgle, and part roar, it seemed almost like a voice. But it was unlike any voice she'd ever heard before. Drawing her knees up to her chest, she pressed against the trunk of the spruce and sat as still as only a wood elf can.

With every passing second, the sound grew louder. And stranger. Then, to Brionna's amazement, out of the trees strode an elderly dwarf. At least he was short enough to be a dwarf— though his bulbous, potato-size nose and his unusually wide rump seemed to belong to someone bigger. Under his mop of white hair, wild pink eyes gleamed. Perhaps to cover his rump, he wore a thick woolen vest that reached down to the bottom of his baggy leggings.

The dwarf was trying to sing . . . or maybe to frighten people away. As he neared the portal, Brionna could make out his words:

> *Well, pinch me nose, I don't suppose*
> *I am a flapsy bird:*
> *Me songly croon's so out o' tune*
> *Like none you've ever heard!*
> *I withers every word.*
>
> *Now, pulls me lip, don't ever quip*
> *I am a camelump:*
> *That bump you see in back o' me*
> *Is really just me rump!*
> *Though wider than a stump.*

Just who am I? Me heartly cry—
Life's making fun o' me.
Not short or tall, not much at all,
I hates the mystery!
Certainly, definitely, absolutely.

Well, tweaks me ear, it's far from clear
I am a websy duck:
Me tries to swim are truly grim,
Just squirmsy in the muck!
A yucksy sort o' luck.

Now, strips me nude, I won't conclude
I am a stingsy bee:
Though very least I loves to feast
Insides a honey tree!
Me favored place to be.

Just who am I? Me heartly cry—
Life's making fun o' me.
Not short or tall, not much at all,
I hates the mystery!
Certainly, definitely, absolutely.

Brionna's deep green eyes opened wide. Could this be true? She had learned enough history from her grandfather to know the name of the person who, in ancient times, made famous that phrase: *Certainly, definitely, absolutely.*

Shim. The little fellow, no bigger than a dwarf, who had always insisted that he was really a giant. Just a very small giant!

He'd been one of Merlin's best friends in Lost Fincayra. Why, in Merlin's first great battle with Rhita Gawr, it was Shim's heroic sacrifice that led to the legendary Dance of the Giants—and Merlin's ultimate victory.

And in that moment of triumph, deep magic had swirled through the immense stones that were the scene of Shim's sacrifice—stones that would later become the Great Temple of the Drumadians. As a result, Shim not only survived, but grew—so large that he stood, in his own words, *as tall as the highliest tree.* As tall as a true giant.

Brionna shook her head. She'd always loved that tale. But it had happened more than a thousand years ago! Now, giants were among Avalon's longest-lived creatures. Everyone knew that. They didn't last as long as people with wizard's blood, perhaps. But they often lived for a thousand years or more, which was twice as long as elves—who themselves lived twice as long as Avalon's humans.

And yet . . . if this fellow really was Shim, how did he get so small again?

Suddenly she bit her lip. If this was indeed Shim, he would have spent a great deal of time with Merlin. The Dance of the Giants had been only the start of their adventures together—adventures that continued even after the Lost Fincayrans won back their wings and Avalon was born. Hadn't Granda said that Shim even fought right along with Merlin in the War of Storms?

And if he'd seen a lot of Merlin, he would also have seen a lot of his staff! He might know how to recognize it. Or even how to use it.

Brionna's heart pounded with excitement. In one graceful motion, she stood up beneath the spruce. The dwarfish fellow, who had been peering into the circle of green flames between the boulders, jumped backward. His pink eyes glared at her.

"What strangely creature is you, who sproutses right out o' the ground like a tallsy tree?"

"Just an elf."

"Bust a shelf, you says? Why would you wants to do that?" He scratched his head of white hair. "Maybily I didn't hears you right. Old Shim's ears aren't hearing so clearly these daylies."

Brionna caught her breath at hearing his name. "I'm just an elf!" she shouted so he could hear. "My name is Brionna!"

He bowed, so low that his bulbous nose struck a spruce branch. "I is pleased to meets you, Shionna."

"Brionna."

Shim bowed again. "Rowanna."

Giving up on her own name, she decided to confirm his. She called right into his ear, "Are you really Shim? The famous Shim?"

The pink eyes went suddenly dim. "I was, yes, a longsy time ago. Certainly, definitely, absolutely."

He looked down at his feet and scowled. "Until I started shrunkeling again! I don't knows why such a cruelsy thing should happen. But about seventy years ago, I begins to shrunkle. And shrunkle. Now I is so smallsy that lots of giants, even the ones who usedly called me Sir Shim the Brave, don't recognize me. Or don't even sees me!"

Despite her own problems, Brionna couldn't help but feel touched by his story. She put her hand on his sagging shoulder. "You're still, ah, very brave."

Offended, he pulled away. "Still a hairy knave? That's not a nicely thing to say." Then a look of determination filled his face. "I tells you what I am, though. I is still very brave."

She had to bite her tongue to keep a straight face. "I know, I told you I do."

"You stole a moldy shoe?" He shook his head. "That's not enoughly reason to enter a portal, Rowanna. Portals can be dangerously, you know."

Too frustrated to speak again, she just looked at him.

Shim's face brightened. "Now, I has a goodly reason."

"What?" she shouted.

He cocked his head. "Can I trustly you?"

Vigorously, she nodded.

He glanced warily to both sides before whispering, "I is goings to find something magical. Wizardly magical."

Brionna gripped his arm. "Not . . . the staff?"

He shook his head. "No, no, not for laughs. I is seeking Merlin's very ownly staff! It could takes me years of searching, and I isn't even surely it's in Avalon. But Merlin oncely said he might leave it behind, so it could somedayly helps his truly heir. And if that's really, truly, honestly so—it would be the only thing in Avalon with enoughly magic to makes me tall again. As tall as the highliest tree!"

It took Brionna another full hour to convince Shim that she wanted to join him on his quest. That she knew where the staff might be found. And that she could help him focus his thoughts on their destination in Fireroot.

This was no small matter. Both their minds needed to be clearly focused, or the portal would carry them to different places altogether. Or worse. For portals magically disassembled people, carried them along through the innermost veins of the Great Tree, and then reassembled them as they arrived. If their minds weren't completely clear about their destinations, so that every last particle of their beings was carried along, they could easily lose their way . . . or their lives. And even with total concentration, things could still go wrong: Some portals—especially in Airroot—seemed to have minds of their own, choosing random destinations for travelers.

In sum, traveling through portals was at best a delicate art. In the words of the famous wood elf Serella, who was the first person to journey through an enchanted portal and survive, back in the Year of Avalon 51: "Portalseeking is a difficult way to travel, yet an easy way to die."

Holding hands—the customary way to enter a portal with another person—Brionna and Shim strode into the shimmering circle of flames. The elf, her face rigid, said only one word: "Fireroot."

For his part, Shim drew a deep breath. Then he muttered, "I'll finds it, I will! Certainly, definitely, absolutely."

19 · The Smell of Resins

GREEN FLAMES BURST OVER BRIONNA AND Shim, crackling with heat and light. And Mystery.

Suddenly the two travelers were gone. Incinerated, but not burned. Swallowed, but not destroyed. For they had plunged deep inside the veins of the living, breathing Tree of Avalon.

The last thing Brionna remembered, as she entered the portal, was that loud crackle of flames. She knew, in that instant, she had disappeared not just from that particular spot in Woodroot's forest, but in a deeper sense, from herself. As pulsing rivers of green light swept her away, she joined with the Great Tree—body, mind, and spirit. If she still existed at all now, it was merely as part of Avalon's breath and blood.

Downward she fell—downward and inward. Deeper and deeper, farther and farther. She had entered the Great Tree as utterly, as seamlessly, as the tiniest drop of water, the slightest grain of soil, the smallest spark of light.

A smell, rich and resinous, overwhelmed her. It was the smell of the forest glade, the sprouting seed, the woodland mushroom, the moist banks of a rill. It blended fallen leaves and tiny shoots, old fur and newborn skin, warm bark and feathers floating on a breeze. This was the smell, she knew, of élano: the essential, life-giving sap of the Tree.

The pulsing rivers carried her, pulled her, and held her all the while. All this without motion, at least not physical motion. For now Brionna's whole being had merged into Avalon, just as a breath merges into the breather. She was both at once—air and lungs; blood and veins; heart and soul.

She was inside the Tree.

She was part of the Tree.

She *was* the Tree.

Down, down, down she flowed, moving ever deeper, always surrounded by that resinous smell. Green lights flashed, then dimmed, then flashed again. Rays of dark red and deep brown sparkled, then vanished. Spots of yellow appeared, fluttering like a flock of butterflies, before dissolving into the ever-flowing green.

Everywhere she heard a sound: heaving, surging, coursing without end—the sound of light and soil and air uniting. The sound of life first sprouting, and growing, and finally dying, only to renew itself and sprout again. Branches reach skyward—stretch, bend, or break—but the breathing continues, the breathing goes on. Again and again, again and again. For every creature, for every time.

All at once, the resinous smell intensified. Brionna felt a sudden sense of herself return, a self she had long ago forgotten. And even more strongly, she felt a pang, an ache, deeper than just her body or mind—an ache of loss for what she had been, of sorrow for what she was leaving behind.

A green light was growing. Right in front of her it swelled and shimmered, crackling loudly. So loudly that she had to strain to hear the sound of breathing, her own and Avalon's.

Flames! She toppled headfirst through the portal, along with Shim. For a few seconds she lay there, facedown in the black soil that had been charred by countless seasons of fire, unsure just where—and who—she was.

Suddenly she remembered. She lifted her head to gaze upon a landscape of spouting flames and belching smoke, fire-scorched ridges and plumes of volcanic ash. Fireroot. Not a single tree, nor even a blade of grass, grew on these cliffs. The foul smell of sulfur wafted over her.

Then, from somewhere deeper than her nostrils, she caught the barest whiff of something else—something resinous, rich, and alive. Brionna put her face in her hands and started to cry.

20 · Something Marvelous

AS SCREE STEPPED ACROSS THE CAVERN, waves of orange light from the flame vent rippled over the rock wall. And over him, as well: Since he wore no shirt, like all eaglemen while in human form, the light touched his bare shoulders, his muscular arms, and the bridge of his hooked nose.

With all the intensity of a soaring eagle studying a fleeing hare in a field below, he studied the staff that leaned against the wall. Its gnarled shaft and knotted top pulsed with light from the flame vent—but not with light from within. No, right now it looked just the same as it had for most of the past seventeen years: an unremarkable piece of wood.

Unremarkable . . . until a few nights ago, when the staff had glowed with its own light, its own inner magic.

Scree's yellow-rimmed eyes peered closely at the dark grains of the wood, the tight knot at the top, and the subtle lines along the shaft—which, in the cavern's flickering light, looked almost like the carved edges of runes.

But he saw nothing magical. Just as he'd seen nothing unusual about the staff since that strange night. Had he just imagined the whole thing? He lifted his hand, studying the charred skin and blisters on his palm. No, he couldn't have imagined that!

Though he hadn't gone back up to the portal at the crater's rim since that night, the memory of those green flames licked constantly at his thoughts. Why had the staff suddenly woken up, after all these years? Did it really nudge him to go outside that night—whether to search for Tamwyn, or to see the star vanish? And what could that change in the Wizard's Staff possibly mean?

Scree scowled, scraping the floor with his sharp toenails. Even though he'd kept the staff by his side for so long, it seemed more mysterious than ever. As did the old man who'd given it to him on that dark night long ago.

"Who was he, anyway?" he demanded aloud.

As his words echoed around the cavern, he thought about the ancient, white-bearded man who had appeared out of nowhere on that fiery mountainside. Who could change into an eagle . . . or fly straight into a wall of stone. In some unfathomable way, Scree had loved that man, loved him instantly when he looked into his eyes, at once so young and so old. And more than that, he owed that man his life.

Slowly, his charred hand reached for the staff—but stopped just before grasping it. "I still love him, too. Despite the endless chore he gave me."

He worked his fingers in the air. "But today the mystery will end. Today I'm going to find out *just who he was.*"

For Scree had a hunch—a hunch that had grown stronger with every passing year. What if that old man was really a wizard? And not just any wizard, but *the* wizard? The one whose name was . . .

"Merlin," he said in a whisper that echoed lightly in the low-ceilinged cavern. "And if that's true, then this"—he worked his fingers again—"is really Merlin's staff."

He swallowed. "Which could mean . . ." His voice trailed off, for he was daunted by the weight of his own words. "That I am the true heir of Merlin."

At that instant, a feeble light flickered along the full length of the staff. A light that came from deep within the wood itself.

Scree's heart raced. He remembered the very first time he'd touched the staff, that night on the fiery cliffs. As his small hand had curled around the wood, the old man had said, *Promise me, now, that you will keep this staff safe. It is precious—more precious than you can imagine.*

And then, in a whisper, he had told Scree about the child of the Dark Prophecy, who could bring ruin to Avalon. And about the wizard's true heir, who could bring hope instead. Both, he had said, were born in that very year—something he thought no one else knew.

Now, both Scree and Tamwyn had been born that year . . . but as the years passed, Scree had grown increasingly sure that his brother couldn't be either one. Tamwyn was just too innocent and trusting—not to mention clumsy. But he'd often wondered about himself. Could he possibly be one of the two prophesied people? After all, it was to him the old man had given the stick. And if he *was* one of them, which one? There had been times—especially after he'd made his terrible mistake and almost lost the staff—that he suspected he might be the Dark one. But in his heart, he'd always longed to be the other, who could do so much good for Avalon.

Because the old man had also told him something else: *For the child who now guards it, and for the man who someday wields it, there is terrible, terrible danger. But when, at last, the wizard's true heir appears—this staff will recognize him . . . perhaps even before he recognizes himself. When he touches the staff and says, "I am the true heir of Merlin," you will see something marvelous. Marvelous indeed!*

Why the staff had waited so long to show signs of magic, he didn't know—but now, for whatever reason, the time had come. Scree felt a drop of perspiration roll down his temple, as the staff glowed still brighter. As if it sensed his intention, its own light now pulsed to the rhythm of his heart.

He moved his fingers closer to the shaft. He was ready now. Yes, ready to take the staff of Merlin and speak aloud those words—words that would mean so much for Avalon's destiny . . . as well as his own.

21 · The Child of Krystallus

TAMWYN STOOD ON THE KNOLL, WHOSE grass shone pale yellow under the stars, looking anxiously at the hoofprints of a stag. They were there, all right, fresh and clear—and exactly where he himself had come running, heart pounding, down the valley. But were they really his? How could that be?

"Porter," snapped Llynia, seated on the grass by the smoldering fire. "Tomorrow I'll need you to show me a faster route north. We're running out of time."

Reluctantly, he turned from the hoofprints—though he glanced back again for one more look. He stepped over to Llynia, knelt by the dying embers, and stirred them with his dagger to be sure no breeze could rekindle them. Then, sheathing his blade, he sat down facing her.

"If that's what you want, then you've got to tell me exactly where we're going."

"That's ridiculous," she retorted, shaking her head of blonde hair. "You may know how to scare off a dragon, but I'm still the leader of this quest." Her voice dropped to a growl. "Even if I need a little help now and then."

Tamwyn tapped the empty stew pot beside him—a pot which, no matter how many scrubbings Fairlyn had given it, still smelled faintly like a dragon's tongue. "But unless I know our final destination, how can I pick the best route?"

Llynia's green chin darkened. "Quit gloating, porter! You already know what you need to know. We're going to the portal up north at the snowfields."

"You may not like what you find there."

"Don't try to give me any advice! All I want from you is the fastest route there, nothing else."

He scowled at her. "Then you'll have no interest in hearing that the portal you're talking about was buried under a landslide last spring."

"What?" The priestess stared at him, aghast. "Why didn't you tell me before?"

"Flipping fire dragons, I *tried* to tell you! At least half a dozen times. But no, you wouldn't take any advice from a lowly porter."

Elli, who had been walking up the slope from the old beech tree, with Nuic on her shoulder, frowned at him. "That may be true, but I don't think you tried all that hard. Were you just going to let us find out when we got there?"

His dark eyes narrowed. "Maybe so. That's just what a pair of gnome-brains like you deserve."

Her face went livid. "Don't you ever call me that!"

"Hold on, Elliryanna." Nuic's stern command was enough to keep her from charging at Tamwyn, though just barely. "He doesn't have any more eyes for you to blacken."

Tamwyn touched one of his swollen cheeks. "I don't know how you ever—"

"We don't have time for this!" shouted Llynia. "Already we've lost a precious week. And now you tell me the portal's blocked! I really don't know what to think."

"Tell you what I think," shouted Henni from the branches of the beech, where he was munching on a raw turnip. "I think you should keep on leading us, Lady Greenbeard. Wherever you like! Getting lost has never been more fun, eehee, eehee, aha-ha-ha."

Llynia just glowered at him. "Don't use that name again, hoolah!"

Henni nodded solemnly. "Yes, Lady Greenbeard." His circular eyebrows crinkled as he smirked. "Oops, sorry, hoo hoo heeheehee. Won't slip again, Lady Greenbeard. Hoohoohee, hoo-*yowwwch*!"

He nearly fell off the branch from the force of Fairlyn's swat. Despite having two of her arms splinted and wrapped in bandages made from one of Llynia's woolen scarves, she still had plenty of arms left to strike with. And plenty of anger, too, as was clear from the strong scent of broken hoolah bones in the air.

Tamwyn picked up a clod of dry dirt and squeezed it so hard that it exploded with a puff. "Listen now, priestess. I only agreed to help you because—"

"Of your clumsiness, eehee," called the hoolah.

"Because I chose to," he continued, gritting his teeth. "I can leave any time, and then the only help you'll have is that crazy beast over there in the tree."

"No way," objected Henni. "Where you go, I go, clumsy man! Life's much more exciting with you around."

Tamwyn glared at his tormentor, then faced Llynia again. "I

will help you, if I can. But if you want me to find the fastest route, you *must* tell me more. I've heard you say you're going to Woodroot, but which part? And how much time do you really have?"

Elli chewed her lip, then said to Llynia, "Maybe we *should* tell him." Before Tamwyn could show any satisfaction—or surprise—that she'd actually agreed with him, she added, "He is without doubt the rudest, stupidest, clumsiest dolt in all of Avalon. But there's still a chance he knows a better way to get where we're going." She pointed skyward, her expression anxious. "There are just five stars left now."

"I know that already," snarled the priestess. She turned to Tamwyn. "Isn't it enough that you've reduced me to asking for your help? Haven't you already humbled me enough?"

"You tell him, Llynia," Nuic said sarcastically. "Especially after he pushed you into that big mud hole, and practically forced you down the throat of that dragon."

She faced the sprite, but he'd already turned his most sympathetic shade of green. Then, before she could speak, Nuic grumbled, "Besides, any fool could figure out we're going to the Lady of the Lake."

"You idiot!" Llynia's face twisted in rage. "You had no right!"

Nuic merely glowed greener.

Surprised, Tamwyn caught his breath. The Lady of the Lake? Now *there* was an adventure—the sort he'd always thought about. Dreamed about! But could he take that much time away from his search for Scree? Such an expedition could take several weeks, or even months. And yet . . . it was sorely tempting. How many chances did a wilderness guide get to visit Woodroot, and maybe see the legendary enchantress—the very person who first uttered the Dark Prophecy?

His eyes strayed back over to the hoofprints. Under the starlight, they glowed eerily, like eyes in the soil that were staring at him. He drew an uncertain breath, staring back. Perhaps . . . he could even ask the Lady about the destiny of a lad born in Fireroot in the Year of Darkness. A lad whose name meant Dark Flame.

Llynia reached over and shoved him. "You must not reveal this. To anyone!" She grabbed him by the shoulders. "You are now bound to the Society of the Whole. Swear this to me, porter. Swear now!"

Tamwyn shook free of her grip. "All right, then. You're a damned fool! A Dagda-forsaken idiot. And a howling, hopeless, hysterical buffoon! Is that enough swearing for you?"

Llynia was so shocked, she just opened her mouth and gasped for air. Finally she found her voice, but could only mutter some lines from Elen's Humble Primary.

From the branches of the beech tree, Henni whistled in amusement. Perhaps even in admiration. But Fairlyn, standing beneath him, started smelling like smoldering flesh, so he went silent.

From his seat on Elli's shoulder, Nuic spoke as calmly as if nothing had happened. "Now that our destination is out, Llynia, can you tell us if you've had any of your visions lately? I suppose, hmmmpff, you haven't seen any more of the Lady."

She whirled on the pinnacle sprite. "As a matter of fact, I have! Just this evening, too." She pointed at him so that her finger almost touched his flesh, now a grumpy-looking yellowish green. "I had the same vision as before. The Lady welcomed me to her lair. That's right! She even raised her hand to me in greeting."

Nuic's color darkened. "She did, did she?"

"Yes," declared Llynia proudly. "It was perfectly clear."

The old sprite merely grimaced.

Elli glanced at him uncertainly, but he only said, "Put me down, Elliryanna."

With a worried look, she set him down. He walked over to the small pool in the fold of the knoll and put his feet in the water, grumbling to himself.

Llynia turned back to Tamwyn. "I'd tell you what I think of you, porter. But . . . as a holy woman, I can't!" She rose, fists clenched, and strode off toward the other side of the knoll. Fairlyn, smelling like something that had roasted too long on the fire, followed after her.

Tamwyn watched them go. Then, careful not to disturb Batty Lad (who was sound asleep in his tunic pocket), he got up and went to join Nuic. As he sat next to the sprite, he shook his head glumly. "Some quest this is."

The sprite's liquid purple eyes studied him for a moment. "I've seen worse. Not for several centuries, mind you, but I have."

The young man sighed. His mind was bursting with questions—about the Lady, the stars, and most of all, the mysterious hoofprints in the mud by the pool. Anxiously, he touched one of them with his toe, as if he could somehow feel the truth of how it had gotten there. But he felt nothing . . . except confusion.

Absently, he picked up a small branch that the dragon's tail had broken off the beech tree. Taking the dagger from his belt, he started to whittle, slicing long shavings that curled and fell to his feet.

Nuic turned his round face toward him. "So then, to get to the eastern end of Woodroot, where the Lady lives, which portal would you use?"

Tamwyn sliced off a particularly twisted shaving. "Well, to tell the truth, I'm not sure we should use *any* portal."

Elli, who had come over to join them and was now standing behind Nuic, tossed her curls doubtfully. "Not use one? What are you saying?"

Without looking up from his whittling, he replied, "Portals are unreliable. You said so yourself, days ago. But up here in northern Stoneroot, they're also scarce. There are only three that I know about—and one is that portal in Dun Tara that's now buried under rocks. The second is over on the coast, but I've been told that its only outlet in Woodroot is in the far northwest, where the elves make magical musical instruments. And if Woodroot's as big as this realm, that would be several weeks' walk—or more—from where you want to go."

"What about the third one?" asked Nuic.

"Nobody uses it anymore."

"Why not?"

Tamwyn dug his blade into the wood to cut through a knot. "Because it's down inside the lair of those dragons I tracked."

Nuic swished his feet through the water of the pool. "Hmmmpff. Our friend Llynia would just love that idea."

"Wait, now." Elli got down on one knee beside them. "Are you sure there aren't any more portals up here?"

Tamwyn rammed the dagger down the wood, slicing off a thick piece. "No. I'm not sure."

"You must not go to other realms very often."

He stopped whittling and looked straight at her. "I haven't gone to other realms *at all*. Not since I came here seven years ago."

"What? And you call yourself a guide?"

"If you must know, I've been looking for someone."

"Right. Someone you were guiding, I'll bet. And then led off a cliff."

Tamwyn's temples pounded, but he forced himself to stay calm. He sliced a few more curls of wood, then glanced at Nuic. "I thought we might try instead . . . the Rugged Path."

The old sprite's color turned as gray as many of the stones at the base of the knoll. "The Rugged Path? What do you know about it?"

"Just what I've heard from bards, really. It was first discovered back in the Age of Ripening, I think."

"Hmmmpff. In the Year of Avalon 33, to be exact. Which you humans never seem to be, until it's too late." He shifted his weight, sinking his small legs deeper in the pool. "A boy named Fergus, a shepherd, found it. Saw a strange creature one day who led him to the Path. And when he entered, he went from Stoneroot to Woodroot, or the other way around. At least that's the legend."

Elli raised an eyebrow. "What kind of creature?"

"A deer."

Nuic paused, glancing at Tamwyn, who had stiffened at the word. "A doe, pure white from head to hoof. Some bards say it was really Lorilanda, goddess of birth and flowering, on a visit from the spirit world. But if you ask me, it's all just a load of gossip. And not very reliable gossip, either."

"Why not?" asked Elli.

"Hmmmpff. For a start, the legend says the Rugged Path runs only one direction—but no one is sure which direction that is. It could go to Woodroot or from Woodroot, but not both. And if that's not enough uncertainty for you, nobody knows for sure whether the Path even exists! In all my centuries in the mountains, I heard only a few claims of finding it, none of them reliable."

"Great." Elli looked at Tamwyn with renewed scorn. "So that's the best you can do? A path that doesn't exist?"

He paused in the middle of a slice. "Oh, it exists, all right. I've seen it myself."

Nuic's color brightened slightly, with ribbons of yellow moving through the gray. "You're sure?"

Tamwyn drew a long, slow breath. "Well, no, not exactly."

Elli snorted skeptically.

He continued to the sprite, "But I'm almost sure. It's a sort of cave, you see. Way up in the high peaks, even higher than Dun Tara. I heard it called Fergus's Path by an old hedge faery I met up there—you know, the kind that's all covered with prickly fur."

"The kind that's famous for telling tall tales and stealing food from other faeries' gardens, you mean." Nuic's colors had darkened again. "And you believed what he said?"

Though he was starting to feel a bit foolish, Tamwyn nodded. "He said he was going to leave Stoneroot and start a new life."

Elli scowled. "So you speak to faeries as well as dragons?"

Tamwyn ignored her, which made her even angrier. "Then I watched him fly into the cave—and not come back."

"Hmmmpff. Probably just running away from whoever was chasing him for thievery."

"Maybe." Tamwyn carved an especially curly slice. "Look, I admit that I don't know much about these things. But I do have a theory about the Rugged Path. And it fits with what I learned from that faery."

"And your theory is?"

"Well, we know that Avalon is a tree, right? And that each realm is one of its roots. And we also know that Krystallus, after years of portalseeking, concluded that Woodroot is on the side of the Tree nearest to Waterroot and Stoneroot. So . . . what if those three realms are connected up at the top? The way tree roots connect to their trunk! Don't you see? That means the highest mountains at the very top of Stoneroot might actually be a kind of barrier—a border—between the realms. So if there really is a path up there, you could go from one realm to another."

"But that still doesn't explain why the path supposedly runs just one way," objected Elli. "Or which way that could be."

"Say," he replied in a mocking tone, "you're a genius. You have a better theory?"

"I think you're a fraud!" she shouted, waving her arms. "I think you're all those things you said to Llynia, and ten thousand more!"

A bony little wing poked out of Tamwyn's robe, followed by a pair of glowing green eyes. "Hushy shush!" squeaked Batty Lad. "Me me needsa day nap, you know. Yessa ya ya ya. Gotsa rest to go hunting all nighty."

Tamwyn tugged one of his round ears. "You're in luck, then. It's nighttime now. See? Look up."

The batlike creature gazed up at the darkened sky, his eyes aglow. "Goody good! Me hungry fora some tasty flies." He clambered fully out of the pocket, stretched his crumpled wings, and flapped off into the night.

Tamwyn was about to turn back to Elli, a new batch of insults on his tongue, when he caught sight of the Wizard's Staff. The constellation seemed to sit on the rim of the knoll, just above the dark outline of the cooking pot. It still had five stars, but one of them, at the upper end, flickered weakly. Soon it, too, would go out.

Elli had seen it, as well. She was gazing up at the constellation, her expression now one of worry. "Nuic," she asked, "what does it mean?"

"Nothing good." The pinnacle sprite looked down at the small pool of water. "I should have stayed in the mountains."

So should I, thought Tamwyn.

Elli nodded grimly. "A week has gone by already and we haven't accomplished anything."

"Not true, Elliryanna. You've given our new guide here a ripe pair of black eyes."

"Yes, well, he deserved them."

Right now she wished she could sit under the beech tree and play her harp, forgetting about everything else, feeling at peace. But now the memory of her harp just made her angry again.

She faced Tamwyn. "Looks like we have no choice now but to follow you into that fool's cave! There isn't time to find another way. In case you're too stupid to figure it out, we have to get to the Lady—and, most likely, beyond—before the last of those stars goes out."

"Shouldn't be too hard for a great genius like you," he said with a smirk.

Elli slapped at the pool, drenching him with water.

Tamwyn grabbed a couple of wood shavings. Quickly, he tied them together, then turned them in his hand. When the little knot caught a glint of starlight, he focused on that speck of light, imagining it was really a spark. Then a burning coal. Then a candle wick on fire. The wood shavings seemed to spurt into flames.

With a flick of his wrist, he tossed the knot of burning shavings at Elli. It landed on her thigh, crackling like a ball of fire.

"What? *Aaaaah!*" She leaped into the air, swatting at the flames.

But there were no flames. The knot of shavings rolled on the ground, completely harmless. Elli glared at Tamwyn, her own eyes about to burst into fire. Shaking with rage, she kicked the knot at him and strode off to the beech tree.

"Well there," said Nuic gruffly, "aren't you full of surprises?"

Tamwyn, grinning with satisfaction, watched Elli sit down hard in the roots of the beech. "Just a trick, really. But it does come in handy sometimes."

"Hmmmpff. Something else you picked up, I suppose. At least call it by its real name."

"What's that?"

"How many times do you need to be told? It's not a trick, but an illusion! You projected the image of fire onto that wood, just like you projected the sound of that dragon into the air."

"Trick, illusion, whatever." Tamwyn's toe nudged the hoof-print in the mud again. "It's not real, that's the point. Only people with real magic in their blood can change things for real."

Nuic studied him closely. "Like the ancient deer people, perhaps?"

Tamwyn's mouth went dry, for once not because of the drought. He turned to look at the hoofprints for a moment, then asked, "Nuic . . . was Hallia really the last survivor of the deer people?"

"The last in Avalon, yes."

Somewhere down inside, Tamwyn felt a sudden emptiness. But he tried to keep his face from showing anything.

"Don't you know your lore, young man?" Nuic went on grumpily. "Any child could tell you the story: How Merlin asked Hallia to come with him when Lost Fincayra became part of the Otherworld. How she couldn't bear to leave behind her people and her heritage, and so parted from him. And how, in the end, she realized that she loved the young wizard—yes, yes, he really was young once!—too much to live without him."

A lavender hue crept over the sprite's round body. "And so, with help from Dagda himself, who became a stag and led her out of the spirit world, she and Merlin were reunited at last. They were married, in the Year of Avalon 27, atop the highest mountain in the Seven Realms. Now, *that* was an event, I'll tell you, attended by all sorts of mortal and immortal beings. Even that bumbling giant, Shim, was there—holding a huge hat full of children—and a ballymag whose name, I think, was Mooshlovely."

Tamwyn nudged the old sprite. "You make it sound like you were actually there."

"Hmmmpff. Of *course* I was there, you bung-brained dolt! The wedding took place near one of my favorite bathing brooks. I had the best seat of anyone." His colors shifted to a tranquil shade of blue. "Anyway, Hallia's love for Merlin was so great that she stayed with him the rest of her days. She even joined him on a few trips to mortal Earth, the greatest sacrifice I could imagine, just so they wouldn't be apart."

The sprite made a rough sound in his throat, almost a chortle. "But of course, she had a son, Krystallus. A regular scamp of a boy, full of mischief! I should know, since I encouraged that right from the start."

"You actually knew him?"

Nuic merely grinned.

"But Krystallus couldn't change into a deer, could he?"

Nuic shook himself. "No, and he always regretted that. Made up for it by running all over Avalon, mind you! Even founded the College of Mapmakers—mainly, I suspect, to keep track of his travels. But he could never run like his mother, with the speed and grace of a deer."

Tamwyn cleared his throat. "I've heard bards saying that if Krystallus fathered a child, that child could have some of Hallia's magic. It could skip generations, the way it does with wizards—or did, at least, in the old days when we *had* wizards. But then, I've never heard anything about a child of Krystallus."

Nuic's liquid purple eyes turned to the star-studded Avalon sky. "When you live as long as I have, you get to see many things. Some of them happen only once, like the birth of our world from a single seed. And some of them happen . . . more than once."

He faced Tamwyn. "Krystallus *did* have a child." Seeing Tamwyn listening with rapt attention, he said casually, "It happened far away from here. In Fireroot."

Tamwyn's heart leaped.

"When Krystallus traveled there, he was the first person with human blood to face the flamelons since the war of the Age of Storms. Which is to say he was either very brave, or very stupid. And probably, since he was part human, it was the latter. He was captured, and sentenced to be burned to death. But on the eve of his execution, he was rescued."

"By who?"

"By a woman. A woman he loved—and who later bore their child. Their union didn't last long, mind you. For mysterious reasons, she fled with the child—no one knows where. Not even Krystallus could find them . . . though it is said that he searched everywhere, even among the stars. And that led to his final, fatal voyage."

Nuic paused, thinking. "Not many people know about all this, which is why even those who know aren't certain just who that woman was. Some believe she was herself a flamelon, perhaps part of the royal family. And others are sure she was an eaglewoman, who could carry Krystallus to safety before he was killed."

"And which," Tamwyn asked in a quaky voice, "do you believe?"

"I'm not sure. But I *am* sure of this: Their child was a son. And he was born seventeen years ago, in the Year of Darkness."

Tamwyn sucked in his breath. "So their son could be—"

"That's right," said Nuic, cutting him off. "Their son could have great powers, only now emerging. Including the power to change into a deer. After all, he would be the grandson of Hallia . . . and the wizard Merlin."

His colors darkened. "But he could also be the child of the Dark Prophecy."

22 · Death Trap

NONE OF THE HUMANS IN THE GROUP slept well that night. Or the next, or the next.

For Llynia, it was because of the difficulty of finding any flat space bigger than a ledge to lie down on, the sound of clattering rock slides that echoed all night long among the ridges, and the thinner air of the high peaks that sometimes made her wake up gasping. Not that she didn't wish for sleep, to give her some rest from all her aching muscles and scraped elbows and knees. For the Rugged Path was aptly named! And this trek up the mountain passes and glacial valleys, as Tamwyn reminded her each day, was not the fabled path itself—just the quickest way to reach it.

For Elli, the harsh terrain wasn't a problem. She began to find the challenge of climbing steep slopes hand over hand invigorating . . . although more than once she was tempted to drop a heavy stone on Tamwyn's head. She still fumed, burning like an ember herself, whenever she thought about his prank with the trick fire. And it made her even angrier when she noticed how Nuic, who rode on her shoulder, seemed to tolerate him. Even *listen* to him sometimes. As she lay on the rocky terrain each night, she tossed and turned, dreaming that she was dodging great fireballs from the sky. Most often they'd miss her, but would destroy, over and over again, her precious handmade harp.

And for Tamwyn, the nights were difficult because he couldn't distract himself from his own thoughts, as he could when he was busy guiding the group. He could only look up at the stars—and the places where stars used to be—and wonder. About Avalon . . . and about himself. Who he really was. What his fate might be. And whether he was truly destined to bring ruin to Avalon.

Each day proved more challenging than the last. They traversed a wide field of unstable boulders that shook and slid as they clambered across, using their hands no less than their feet. They hiked over a glacier, throbbing with cold rivers beneath its surface, crowned with spires of misty blue ice. And they leaped across several deep crevasses—all except Llynia, who refused to move unless Fairlyn lay down and made herself into a bridge.

Higher and higher they climbed, above the string of lakes known as Footsteps of the Giants. But like all the others they'd seen, these lakes were nearly dry. Instead of their usual turquoise blue color, they were muddy brown, their bottoms covered with webs of cracks. One afternoon, a great winged creature soared overhead, and Tamwyn peered at it hopefully—until he saw that it was just a canyon eagle, not the brother he'd sought for so many years.

As they gained altitude, the high peaks of Olanabram lifted before them. Though still crested with snow, their rocky summits were more exposed than Tamwyn had ever seen. Even Hallia's Peak, the jagged mountain where Merlin and Hallia had been wed long ago, was almost bare of snow.

Beyond the high peaks, they could just barely glimpse a series of dark brown ridges that ran northward in parallel rows, rising swiftly higher as they faded into the distant, ever-swirling mist. Those ridges, as Tamwyn knew, were actually the bottommost reaches of Avalon's trunk. For this was the only place in all the root-realms where the Great Tree's trunk could actually be seen— aside from the Swaying Sea, a strange appendage that some considered Avalon's highest root, and others its lowest branch.

As he looked at those misty ridges, Tamwyn wondered just how high the Great Tree's trunk ultimately rose. Did it support branches as vast and varied as the roots themselves? And did the trunk reach past those branches, past the swirls of mist . . . all the way to the stars?

At last, on their eleventh day of trekking, they reached the entrance to the Rugged Path. It sat near the top of a windswept ridge, shielded by a mass of jagged outcroppings that blocked it from view. In fact, the cave was impossible to see without standing almost on top of it. Stalactites, sharper than dragon teeth, hung down from the cave's roof, which made it look like a black mouth of stone ready to swallow anyone who came too near.

"*That's* where we're going?" Llynia's face, which was red with starburn (all but her chin), reddened some more. "Into there?"

Wearily, Tamwyn nodded. He set down his load, now just a few flasks of water and some dried herbs, and blew a frosty breath in the chill mountain air. Then he waved below them, at the white expanse of snowfields, glaciers, and moraines that seemed to stretch on endlessly, unbroken but for the few summits of faded gray rock that lifted out of the snow. "You can try searching down there for a portal if you'd like. Maybe you'll find a friendly snow leopard who can help."

Llynia knitted her brow. "But you don't even know if this is the right path!"

"Or if it goes the right direction," chimed in Elli. She picked up a pebble and threw it into the gaping mouth. It slid and clattered for many seconds, then all sound abruptly ceased. It had been swallowed.

"This could be nothing more than . . ." Llynia wiped her forehead on the sleeve of her badly frayed robe. "Than a death trap."

"Ooh, really?" Henni dropped his load on the rocks. Silver eyes shining, he sauntered over to the cave entrance and looked inside. "I've never met a death trap I didn't like."

"A hoolah's motto, if I ever heard one," said Tamwyn. "All right, then. You can go first."

Henni's long arms reached up high, so that his big hands could grab a pair of stalactites. He then lifted up his legs and swung there, oblivious to the danger of falling into this cave that plunged down into the heart of the mountainside. "Eehee, eehee, hoohooheeheeha-ha-ha!" he laughed, his silver eyes gleaming. "Here I go, clumsy man."

"Wait!" shouted Tamwyn. He strode over to the cave entrance. "I'm tempted to get rid of you, believe me. But just in case this really is a death trap, I'd rather you live for a little while longer." Seeing Henni's puzzled look, he added, "So I can kill you myself later on."

The hoolah giggled, swinging from the stalactites.

"So," Tamwyn continued, "I'm going to ask Batty Lad to fly in and check it out first." He shook his pocket, but the sleeping beast didn't stir. "He was out late hunting last night, I guess. Not many insects up here for his—*yaaaaaaaaaah!*"

Before Tamwyn could do anything to stop him, Henni kicked out his legs and wrapped them tight around the young man's waist. Then the hoolah lurched backward and went tumbling down into the cave—taking Tamwyn with him. There was a sound of screams, shattering stalactites, and then silence.

23 · The Rugged Path

DOWN, DOWN, DOWN PLUNGED TAMWYN and Henni, roaring wildly. The young man was roaring with rage, the hoolah with glee. But both of them shared the same fate: Now nothing could stop their fall except the bottom . . . if indeed there was a bottom.

Right after tumbling into the cave, they smashed through a row of jagged crystals, snapping them like icicles. Then, for a moment that seemed endless, they fell freely, whizzing deeper into this world of darkness. Suddenly they slammed into a wall where the passage turned. The impact drove Tamwyn's shoulder deep into Henni's chest. The hoolah screeched in pain and lost his grip around Tamwyn's waist.

Hurtling deeper into the mountain, Tamwyn thudded against a limestone column, breaking the stone into bits—along with every bone in his back, he felt sure. Down he tumbled, sliding at terrifying speed down a long chute, around a bend, and straight over a gap that could have been a side tunnel or crevasse.

Slam! Tamwyn smashed face-first into another wall. He rolled, scraping his face against some sharp stones, then spun downward again.

He fell, twirling as freely as a snowflake in a storm. Then his shoulder hit an outcropping. He whirled—and slammed into something hard, both legs twisted beneath him. He felt, vaguely, something wet running down his forehead and into his eyes.

Onward he rolled, gaining speed again, into the gullet of the mountain. *Thwack!* A sheet of rock exploded over him. The force propelled him into a dizzying spin. By now he could barely think, barely stay conscious.

Crash!

Tamwyn burst through a row of stalactites—and into daylight. He was tumbling, rolling down a hillside of something softer than stone. With a sudden *crack*, he bashed into a solid object, and stopped.

• • •

There was no way to tell how much time passed before he opened his eyes again. And felt the bolts of pain surging through his whole body. Every bone, every limb, every spot on himself, including his eyelids, felt broken, bruised, and battered.

Tamwyn tried to roll on his side, but the sharp pain in his back and thigh made him roll right back. He just lay there, eyes closed. *Nothing could make me move now,* he told himself weakly. *Nothing.*

Suddenly he remembered just what had happened to him. And he knew that, yes, there was one thing important enough, one motivation strong enough, to make him stir his broken body.

Revenge.

He opened his eyes. After wiping away the dried blood that stuck to his eyelashes, he forced himself to raise his head and focus on his surroundings. He lay on a hillside of pale green grass. A narrow cave—the bottom end of the Rugged Path—opened under the brow of the hill. Below it, a trail of dirt, broken rocks, and crystals littered the grassy slope.

Above Tamwyn's head, a tall chestnut tree lifted a delicate tracery of branches. A bird—some sort of grouse—rested on a lower bough. And there, sprawled on the tree's roots, was that blasted hoolah!

With all his strength, Tamwyn made himself roll over. He started to crawl to the hoolah, one agonizing bit at a time. "I'll get you now, you pickled pile of twisted turds! You worthless, bog-brained waste of a—"

"Oohoo, eehee, that was some ride!" Henni roused himself and pulled his red headband off his eyes. He sat up, leaning on a bruised elbow—just in time to see Tamwyn bearing down on him. He started to roll away.

Not quick enough. Tamwyn grabbed him by the collar of his sack-shaped tunic and shook him hard. "Remember what I said about letting you live so I could kill you later?"

"Yes, eehee, that was funny."

"Well, forget it!" Tamwyn growled, his eyes ablaze. "I'm not waiting any longer."

Henni just grinned, crinkling his circular eyebrows. "Good, oohoo eehee. Dying is something I haven't done yet."

"I mean it, hoolah!" Tamwyn twisted up his collar. "You went too far this time."

Suddenly a tall shadow fell over Tamwyn. He caught the smell of summer lilacs, piercingly sweet. Without releasing his grip on Henni, he turned, even though it pained every muscle in his neck and back.

Fairlyn stood above him. Though some more of her branches and twigs were broken, and bark had been scraped off her trunk, there was an unmistakable look of gratitude in her brown eyes. And standing beside her, seemingly unbruised, was Llynia. The priestess was actually smiling.

"Tamwyn," she said, "you did it."

He blinked at her, not knowing what was more strange—to hear her call him by name, instead of "lowly porter," or to see her so happy.

"I did?" he asked uncertainly. "What?"

"Brought us here, of course." She placed her hand upon Fairlyn's slender trunk. "You found the path to Woodroot. My quest will succeed, I'm sure now. And all my hopes . . ." She stopped herself. "But look at you two, you're all covered in bruises and blood."

Tamwyn took a deep breath, despite the throbbing ache of his ribs. "Oh, I'll be fine."

"So will I," added Henni, "if I'm not about to be killed, eehee eehee."

Tamwyn just growled and tightened his grip on him. Then, facing the priestess, he asked, "You're not hurt?"

Llynia smiled again. "No, no. Thanks to the sturdy boughs of my maryth here, who held me the whole way down. And to the bravery of you two, as well."

"Bravery?"

"In going down first, of course! You cleared the way for us all. That was so courageous of you both, to dive right into the cave like that."

Tamwyn traded a glance with Henni, who looked just as surprised as he did. "Er, well, we didn't exactly . . ."

"Don't be modest now," she declared. "You did a great service there, for both me and the Society. If Elen the Founder were here, she'd embrace you in thanks."

"Not too hard, I hope," muttered Tamwyn, rubbing his ribs.

Llynia drew herself up regally. "You have proved that my faith in you was justified."

"Faith?"

"Why, yes, in your ability as a guide."

Tamwyn would have laughed if his chest didn't hurt so much.

"I always knew you could rise to that challenge," she continued on in a dignified tone. "As the *Cyclo Avalon* says about the true believer's faith:

> *"Harder than stone,*
> *Stronger than bars;*
> *Deeper than seas,*
> *Higher than stars."*

She patted Fairlyn's trunk. "And even though my dear friend here didn't always share my faith in you, what you did has given her a great gift, as well. The sight of her homeland! She hasn't seen her beloved Woodroot for many years now, since she first joined me at the Great Temple."

The sweet scent of lilac blossoms swelled. Fairlyn's large eyes moved to the sight beyond the chestnut tree. Tamwyn, for the first time, trained his gaze in that direction. What he saw made him catch his breath.

Hills upon hills of forest greenery stretched before him, rising into rolling blue ridges that melted, at last, into the sky. Mist rose in twirling spirals from the trees, along with the songs, whistles, and cries of more kinds of birds than he'd ever heard before. Some of the trees had lost their leaves for autumn, while others—oaks, maples, and birches especially—wore leaves of striking brilliance. It was almost too much to believe . . . but maybe the trees here really *did* change colors with the seasons.

Ah, but there were so many colors in this forest! Nothing he'd ever seen in Stoneroot—or before that, in Fireroot—came close. Swaths of gold, orange, scarlet, and pink wove themselves into the mesh of green. There were other colors, too: late-blooming flowers, or fruit dangling from some of those boughs. *Maybe somewhere out there is a Shomorra tree, the one bards sing about that grows every kind of fruit you can imagine.*

A flock of tangerine faeries, their wings the reddish orange color of the fruit they nursed throughout their lives, lifted off some nearby branches. They glittered brightly against the blue sky, which seemed a bit more clouded and misty than in Stoneroot. Judging from the brightness of the stars, it was midmorning here. This was the first time, Tamwyn realized, that he'd ever seen the sky of Woodroot. Or, as the bards would say, El Urien.

He looked upward, scanning the stars of this realm. Right away, he was struck by the different locations of the constellations here. There was Pegasus, flying high, though he seemed to be turning a corner at the edge of the sky. The Twisted Tree still stretched out its long branches, but nearer to the western horizon. There were some new constellations, as well, forming shapes that he didn't even recognize.

Only the Wizard's Staff sat in its familiar place—and its now-familiar condition. The sight made Tamwyn cringe. What in Avalon's name was going on? Why was this happening—and why now?

He stared worriedly at the sky. Since the third star had gone dark two days ago, the whole constellation seemed to be pulling apart. Its four remaining stars, two groups of two, had a great gap between them. He shook his head: The Wizard's Staff was broken.

He turned back to the vista of endless forest—hopefully, as someone might turn to the face of a friend. But even as he breathed in the forest air, sweetened by lilac, he couldn't forget his anxiety. Stars were dying! And Avalon itself might be dying, too.

Suddenly he noticed a new sound. Beneath the ongoing melody of birds singing and branches clacking, he heard a strong but distant rumble. It sounded deep, very deep, like a great river that boiled with rapids.

He turned. There, by the horizon, he saw the foaming white top of a geyser. Not just any geyser, either. He knew from all the tales he'd heard that there was only one fountain in all of Avalon so vast and powerful: the White Geyser of Crystillia, near the northern reaches of Waterroot.

So I was right, after all! He grinned in satisfaction. *The three realms must all come together, up here at the top, like roots joining the trunk of a tree.*

"Look," he said to the others, releasing his grip on Henni at last. He pointed at the geyser, large enough that it could be seen and heard so many leagues away. "The White Geyser. And there, see that redrock canyon? That must be the Canyon of Crystillia, where the white water flows down to . . . Wait now. What's that?"

All of them stared at the large blot of white inside the canyon. On the other side of the Rugged Path, in the mountains of upper Stoneroot, he would have thought that such a wide expanse of white must be a snowfield. But here, in lower altitudes, that wouldn't be right. A low cloud, maybe? Filling the canyon to its rim? No, the white blot was too flat, too evenly spread over the canyon.

"It's a lake," declared Tamwyn. "Full of white water from the Geyser. But . . . it looks wrong somehow."

"Wrong," echoed Llynia.

Apparently Fairlyn agreed, for her smell had turned dark and smoky. Then she tapped both Llynia and Tamwyn on the shoulders and pointed with one of her blossom-studded arms to the far rim of the canyon—where the forest of Woodroot bordered the lake. Or *should* have bordered the lake.

Tamwyn bit his lip. There was also something very wrong about that stretch of forestland. He couldn't quite tell what it was, except that it looked all brown and gray instead of green. Dust clouds rose from a gust of wind; no mist twirled anywhere. And as the wind raced over that blighted spot, there came a distant sound, deeper even than the endless rumble from the fountain. It was a sound, he felt sure, of a heartrending moan.

"What . . ." he asked aloud. "What is it?"

No answer came but the long, low moan of the wind.

"Whatever it is," said Llynia, "it's wicked. A disease, perhaps." Then, with a hint of pride, she declared, "I shall ask the Lady of the Lake about it. This afternoon, or tomorrow at the latest, when we meet at last."

"Hmmmpff," grumbled a familiar voice. "Now we know which direction the Path runs."

All of them spun around to see Elli standing on the grass with Nuic on her shoulder. Neither of them looked battered, or even disheveled, in the least. The pinnacle sprite was glowing a proud shade of purple.

Llynia didn't seem pleased to see them. She scowled, for which Tamwyn felt grateful. It had been quite unnerving to see her smiling so broadly when she'd arrived.

He turned to see Elli scrutinizing him. "You're looking handsome," she said with a smirk. "A rough ride?"

His eyes narrowed. "I just wanted to get some bruises on the rest of my body to match the ones you gave me."

"Good job."

She laughed, and to Tamwyn's surprise it was a sound as sweet and lilting as a meadowlark. He'd never heard her laugh before . . . and this wasn't at all what he'd expected. How could someone so mean-spirited have a laugh so joyful?

"How did you two get here, anyway?" he demanded. "You both look like you just floated down that chute, not fell down with the rest of us."

"Good guess, master guide." Nuic's purple shade deepened. He raised one arm and flicked a gleaming silver thread off his hand. That was when Tamwyn noticed the large mass of silver threads that lay on the grass behind them, reaching almost to the mouth of the cave. Crumpled though they were, the threads still held the shape of a parachute—which he'd seen before in the wilderness, attached to windblown seeds and the backs of cloudskipper birds.

"You made yourself a parachute?" he asked incredulously.

Nuic frowned at him. "You're not the only one who can do *tricks,* you know."

Tamwyn blushed beneath his bruises.

"How do you think we mountain dwellers get from one pinnacle to another? Going up is hard enough, hmmmpff. But going down, it's much easier to float than climb."

"Look," said Elli, gazing at the rumpled hills of greenery that were so alive with life. "Such a beautiful forest."

Nuic, whose eyes had strayed to the strange white lake, muttered, "Even such beauty, Elliryanna, can hide grave danger."

"Danger?" asked Henni, looking around eagerly.

Tamwyn was about to smack the hoolah, when a tiny face, lit by green, poked out of his pocket. "Hoowah-wah-wah," yawned Batty Lad. "Me lovey do a good sleep."

"You slept through all that?" Shaking his head in wonder, Tamwyn stroked the creature's big cupped ears. "You're the best sleeper I ever met."

"Ooee yessa, manny man. But me stilla having bumpsy-umpsy dreams."

"Fine, then. Why don't you go back to sleep for a while? Where we are now, it's still morning."

"Ahoowah-wah," came the answering yawn, and Batty Lad vanished again in the pocket.

"To sleep like that," observed Tamwyn, "he must have a very clean conscience."

"Or a very thick skull," said Nuic. "So now, are we going to see this mysterious Lady, or just stand here jabbering all day long?"

"I was just about to suggest we go," declared Llynia. "Down there, in the deepest forest. That must be right."

"Hmmmpff," grumbled the sprite. "Ready to get lost, are we?"

The priestess shot him a murderous glance, then started walking down the hill, toward the thickest greenery. "Come on, Fairlyn, let's go."

The tree spirit didn't seem to hear. She was still staring at the blighted rim of the distant canyon, smelling like the remnants of a forest fire.

24 · Just Listen

HALFWAY DOWN THE GRASSY HILL, LLYNIA paused for the others to join her—though her expression was anything but patient. "Come on! Do you think the stars are going to wait for you?"

Elli came first, carrying the sprite (now dark green, like the forest spreading before them). She also bore two water flasks that she'd remembered to take down the Rugged Path . . . and a look of fascination at the rich woodland they were about to enter. Just behind her came Henni, limping slightly but clearly enthused about having new terrain to explore. Fairlyn followed, cradling her broken branches against more solid ones, emitting a rather uncertain, boggy smell.

Last of all came Tamwyn, looking less like a seasoned woodsman than a bruised and battered vagabond. He hobbled down the hill, sore in every part of his body. The quartz bell on his hip, crammed full of dirt from the Rugged Path, hardly clinked at all.

"I'm certain this is right," announced Llynia confidently. "All we need to do is head into the deepest part of the forest. Then, from my vision, I will know the Lady's lair."

She glanced around at the skeptical expression of Nuic, the worried eyes of Fairlyn, and the outright doubt written on the faces of Elli and Tamwyn. She started to say something, perhaps to ask for advice, but caught herself and threw back her shoulders proudly. "Let's go."

Down the hill they marched, with Llynia in the lead. Soon they entered a thick patch of ferns, waist-high on the humans and chin-high on the hoolah. The slope leveled out, and a moment later, sweet-smelling cedars towered over them. All of a sudden they were surrounded by such a jumble of trees, shrubs, and leafy plants that they could barely see two paces ahead. Even the sky showed itself only in rare patches between the layered boughs. Very little starlight drifted down to the forest floor, usually in misty beams that lit only a narrow slice of air, so it seemed almost as dark as night.

Llynia crashed ahead through the growth. Heedless of the others in the group, she bent branches to pass and then released them without warning, so they slapped whoever happened to be walking behind. She strode right into a clan of light green faeries, who were hovering around a stand of pear trees, using their nurturing skills to help the last fruits of the season fill with flavorful juices. But her sudden appearance frightened them, and the whole clan flew off in a frenzy.

She plowed ahead, tripping on downed branches and moss-covered stones. Suddenly she ran into a hawthorn tree hidden behind the leafy boughs of a maple. One of the hawthorn's branches poked her in the head, just above her eye.

Llynia yelped in pain. Without turning around, her voice quaking with humiliation, she asked, "Does anyone know how to get through this cursed jungle?"

"Yes," said Tamwyn with a sigh. "Listen to it. Just listen."

"Are you mad?" the priestess huffed. She swatted a maple leaf out of her face. "We need to *see* better, not hear better."

"Wrong." He stepped over to her, ducking under the hawthorn branch. "Trees and plants have their own language, just like the faeries or the . . ." He swallowed. "The deer. To learn their ways, it's more important to listen than to speak. If you want to find the deepest forest, and listen well enough . . . the forest itself will tell you."

Despite herself, Elli felt touched by his words. She whispered to Nuic, "Even an oaf like him knows more than she does."

The old sprite merely scowled. "That's not saying much."

"Here," suggested Tamwyn, pulling a tangle of vines off Llynia's leg. "Let me show you."

He moved ahead into the forest, stretching out his senses. He felt the slope and texture of the ground under his feet; noted the types and heights of the trees; and smelled the changing aromas of resins or fruit or fox's den. And above all, he listened. To the swish and clatter of branches, the undulating whisper of the wind, the footsteps of scurrying animals, the cries of birds on wing, and so much more.

This is more than a forest, he thought, as his bare feet padded over some springy bluish green moss. *This is a world—as complex and connected to itself as the world of Avalon.* He drew a full breath of the richly scented air, wondering if this land, too, had been touched by the same drought that had struck Stoneroot. Was it possible that this, the most lush and vibrant forest he'd ever seen, was actually more dry, and its colors more faded, than usual?

In a moment's time, he picked up the winding trail of a deer. Despite his many bruises, he felt a sudden, intense urge to run along it, to stretch his legs and bound. But he made himself ignore the urge. This was a time to walk on human feet.

The trail led them to higher ground. The branches grew thinner, the ground firmer, and the going easier. Soon the scent of honey fern, thick and sweet, wafted over them. They came to a glade where long grasses tickled the trunks of some mountain ash trees, still laden with berries. Near the back of the glade stood one old cherry, whose trunk bent with the weight of many seasons.

Tamwyn stretched his sore back. "Shall we make a brief stop here? Just for a little rest, or a bite to eat."

Henni, always ready for a meal, promptly agreed. So did Elli. Llynia, still sulking after her humiliation, said nothing. Fairlyn struck up a conversation with an elder faery who lived in the bole of a mountain ash—which, judging from her pleasant aroma, was going well. And Nuic went foraging around the glade.

As they sat eating berries (still juicy, if quite tart) and some spicy pepperroot found by Nuic, Tamwyn shifted constantly. With all his cuts and bruises, he just couldn't find a comfortable sitting position. So he got up and walked around a bit. Soon he noticed an odd bulge in the trunk of the cherry tree. It looked like a gnarled burl, although he'd never seen a burl with so many interesting knobs and folds.

He strode over to take a closer look. Laying his hand on the cherry's rutted bark, just above the burl, he peered closely. Suddenly he jumped backward. The burl—and the tree trunk around it—had moved!

Tamwyn watched, his eyes wide. The burl swelled larger, bulging outward like the skin on a pot of heated milk. Gradually, a narrow ridge formed down the middle. To either side, clefts sank into the bark. Deep within them, reddish sparks gleamed. And near the bottom of the shape, a thin line appeared, lengthening and drooping to one side.

"A face," he said in amazement. "It's a *face*."

The thin line of the mouth opened slightly, showing wrinkled green lips. "Not so smooth a face as yours, young man, but good enough for me, the spirit of an old tree." The voice crackled and popped like cherry branches in a fire.

Tamwyn looked around at the others over by the ash trees, tempted to show them what he'd found. But Elli and Henni had stretched themselves out on the grass, and Llynia had leaned against Fairlyn's trunk, all taking naps. Nuic, too, had closed his eyes and was resting against Elli's thigh. A thick gray mist was moving over them, covering them like an airy blanket. It almost seemed to be coming from the mountain ash trees . . . and was moving toward Tamwyn.

Turning back to the cherry, he said, "You must be very old."

The mouth turned up a bit, and released a sound like scraping bark. "Buds and blossoms, young man! Older than you, I suppose, but not very old at all. Compared to the Great Tree, I am barely a sapling! Not old enough to be wise. Just enough to be sad."

Tamwyn bent closer. He yawned, feeling a bit like a nap himself. To rest his weary body, he leaned against the trunk, careful to avoid the face. "Sad, master spirit? May I ask why?"

The old tree's branches shrugged, and its leaves rustled in a sigh. "Because, young man, in all my seasons, the winter has always been followed by the spring. But now, I am afraid, the spring may never come."

"Never come?" He felt suddenly afraid, and fought back another yawn. "Tell me why."

"Do you not yet know, young man?"

"Know what?"

The branches stirred uneasily. "A butterfly free is alive forever. But a butterfly caught is a dead mote of dust."

"I . . . I still don't understand."

"Then listen, young man!" The reddish eyes glowed. "There is right now, in this very forest, a threat to all . . ."

Tamwyn felt suddenly dizzy. He dropped to one knee, even as the gray mist flowed over him. He never heard the rest of the tree spirit's words, just as he never heard his own body collapse on the ground.

25 · Shrunkelled and Stingded

"TELL ANOTHER STORY, GRANDA! PLEASE? Just one more."

"You just don't give up, do you? A good quality, Brionna, even in a five-year-old. You got it from your mother."

"She always said I got it from you, Granda."

He just looked straight at me with those shiny green eyes. The same color eyes as I have. Yes—me, his granddaughter. And someday, his scribe . . . when I learn how to write, that is. Then I'll be *Brionna, personal scribe to the famous elf historian Tressimir*. What an honor that will be!

I smiled, sitting there on his lap. Because the very best honor of all was just being right there, right then, the one child in the whole world of wood elves to hear his stories. Sometimes before he even wrote them down! I reached up and patted his fluffy white beard. "Please, Granda?"

He pulled on his ear, the one that was more pointy at the top. Like a spruce tree on a mountain peak, as Granda liked to say. "Well, Brionna, how do I know you're going to stay awake long enough? Can't tell a story to someone who's asleep."

"I won't, Granda! Really I won't."

His green eyes twinkled. "Won't stay awake?"

"Won't sleep! At all. Ever. Ever and a half!" I smiled my prettiest smile, the one he always said reminded him of a fox who's figured out how to steal a grouse's eggs from the nest. "Please, oh, please?"

He pulled on his ear again. "Your good mother wouldn't approve, you know. She always put you to bed on time—one hour after starset, without fail. That's the right way to raise a child! And here I am, making you stay up late to hear my stories."

"But you're not making me," I squealed, tugging on his beard. "I love your stories, you know I do! And Mama would *want* me to stay up for them. Now that I'm so big." I straightened up on his lap. "See? I'm almost a grown-up."

He grinned down at me, but I couldn't help seeing something sad in his face. Somewhere down inside his eyes. He just looked at me for a while, then said, "She'd really love to see you so big."

Something about his voice, the way it shook, made me open up my arms and hug him around his middle. Granda hugged me back. Then the silliest thing happened: I started to cry. Right there, my head against his chest.

"I m-miss her-er," I said, and now my voice was the shaky one.

"So do I," he whispered.

For a long time we just sat there, quiet as a tree in winter. And then Granda stroked the back of my head and patted the wreath of ferns I'd made that morning. Finally, he spoke again.

"So, Brionna, a story. Shall I tell you the one about how Serella, the first queen of the wood elves, discovered how to travel through portals? Or the one about the Lady of the Lake—how she first appeared in the forest of El Urien?"

I wiped my cheeks on his robe—his favorite one, made from riverthread grass. It always felt so soft, and smelled like lemon balm. "No, tell me the one about the little giant who always wanted to be big."

He grinned at me, not so sad this time. "You mean Shim? Who helped Merlin become a wizard? He always wanted to be big, you're right: *as big as the highliest tree*."

"Yes, Granda, yes! That's him."

He drew in a deep breath. "Well, that story began long ago, even before Merlin planted the magical seed that beat like a heart—the seed that sprouted into Avalon. It was a strange, misty morning when . . ."

• • •

Brionna woke up with a start. She blinked her eyes, which felt oddly raw and puffy. Must have been some of this cursed dust—ash from the volcanoes, probably—that was everywhere in Rahnawyn. Even down here in the so-called forestlands. Rightly was this realm called Fireroot in the Common Tongue!

She sat up, propping her back against the smooth, hard bark of an ironwood tree, whose red needles were stirring in the first breeze of morning. "They call this a forest?" she muttered to herself. "Nothing but a few trees, some fire plants, and whatever burned-out stumps are left from the last forest fire."

Spotting a small orange blossom growing amidst the ironwood roots, she nodded. "And you, little firebloom. How could I forget you, this realm's only flower?"

She touched the pointed orange petals. Only now, after eight or nine days in Fireroot, was she beginning to see a new side of the flamelon people who lived here. Perhaps some of their fiery, aggressive culture stemmed from this harsh, volcanic land. And perhaps one reason they worshipped Rhita Gawr, god of war, was that after a fire—and, sometimes, a battle—new things began to grow. Things like this delicate little flower that thrived on ground just scorched by flames.

By her feet, she saw the remains of last night's dinner—the same dinner that she and Shim had eaten every day now for more than a week: salamanders. If salamanders hadn't been the only food they could find, she never would have done it. For eating them meant swallowing those long, leathery tails—as well as swallowing her own vegetarian principles. But having cast aside most of her principles already, she hadn't agonized too much about tasting meat.

Catching the creatures had also proved difficult. Although salamanders just love intense heat and are often found relaxing in the middle of flame vents, the heat turns their normally bluish skin bright orange, making them harder to see—and catch. Brionna and Shim had only succeeded by using some ironwood branches to flick the little beasts out of the flames.

Then came the problem of how to cook them! Brionna knew from Granda's tales that Fireroot salamanders had to be boiled, since flame vents weren't hot enough to roast them. It was Shim who thought of using a broken piece of ironwood bark, which was so hard that it resisted fire, to make a pot (what he called "a smallsy bowl"). After they'd found the bark, and a warm spring with rust-colored water, the rest was simple.

She worked her shoulders. That long cut on her back, a gift from the whip of one of Harlech's surly men, still burned. As did her hatred of Harlech—and even more, the sorcerer. Why did he stay always hidden, cowering in that cloak? And why did he want to control all that water? Couldn't he just take what he needed from the River Crystillia?

So why am I helping him? She chewed her lip, knowing the answer. The same answer as always, no matter how many times her mind ran through this circle of questions. *Granda.*

Raising her head, she peered through the ironwood needles to the dark line of cliffs beyond. All across the ridge, tongues of fire shot upward, while dark plumes of smoke belched out of caverns and crevasses and then rose into the sky. Somewhere up there, she knew from the sorcerer, she would find the crater with towers like crooked teeth. And somewhere in that crater . . . the staff that meant life for Granda.

She craned her neck and looked at the sky, streaked with reddish clouds and darkened by smoke. Yet she could still see, glinting through the haze, the constellation that haunted her every step. The Wizard's Staff now had only five stars, and one of them seemed to be flickering. Soon, she knew, there would be only four left. And very little time left to save Granda—ten days at the most.

Using her sleeve, she wiped off some soot that she could feel on her cheek. *Pointless, you elvish fool, since there's even more soot on your robe.* Then she turned to the shallow gully where Shim had slept last night.

Gone!

Brionna sprung to her feet, grabbed her cedar bow and the quiver of arrows, and stalked around to find some sign of the little giant. She didn't have to go far. Just down the hill from their campsite, she saw a small pair of legs—and a very large rump—sticking out from a hole in the trunk of an old ironwood.

As she approached, the legs started kicking wildly. The rump jumped and jiggled. And Shim's muffled voice started shouting inside the trunk.

He's stuck! She frowned. *Is this really the same heroic Shim that Granda used to tell me stories about?*

Striding over to the tree, she put down her bow and arrows and grabbed Shim's legs (not at all easy with his violent kicks, let alone his baggy leggings). She pulled and pulled, but he wouldn't budge. So she planted her foot against the tree trunk and, with all her might, heaved backward.

A loud *shhluuurp!*—and Shim popped out of the trunk. Both of them fell back onto the ground, sending up a cloud of ash. Brionna rolled over to look at Shim . . . and nearly choked.

His entire head—including his wild pink eyes, white hair, and potato-size nose—was covered with sticky yellow syrup. Honey! It dripped over his ears, across his shoulders, and down his thick woolen vest. Clumps of ash, broken needles, and shards of bark stuck out everywhere. He looked more like a strange, glistening mound of yellow goop than anything alive.

And then he spoke. He opened his mouth, licked a gob of honey off the bottom of his bulbous nose, and said, "How tastily happy is I! Something justly tells me, Rowanna, that drippingly good honey was in that tree."

He leaned forward, his hands squelching on the ground. "And you knowsy what else? This Firerootly honey is warm, like it's been all toastily." He licked some more off his nose and smiled. "I haven't felt so gladly since I started shrunkeling!"

Despite everything else, Brionna just had to laugh. "You look like a tree that honey grows on."

Suddenly his smile vanished. "A bee without any clothes on? Wellsy now! That's not very nicely, Rowanna. You maybily is beautiful, in an elvishly way, but you should learn some manner-lies."

She didn't try to correct him, knowing it would be useless. All she could do was guide him over to the warm spring and help him wash up. Or else he'd soon pick up so much dirt and bark and sticks that he'd be unable to move, stuck to the ground like a wild-eyed boulder.

But Shim had something else on his mind. He tried to scratch his head, but succeeded only in pulling out a sticky clump of hair. "A bee, you says? Maybily you're right. These Firerootly bees stingses most badly, I hears. Hot stingses, like burningly coals."

He shuddered, sending drops of honey flying in all directions. "Oh, how I *hates* to get stingded by bees. Hates it! Always have— yessily, and always will. Certainly, definitely, absolutely."

Brionna stood and offered her hand. "Come on. Let's get you washed."

He squinted at her through a layer of honey. "Gets me squashed? No thankfully. Even shrunkelled, I is too bigly for that! But now that I thinks about it, maybily I should finds that stream and gets washed."

Brionna could only glance up at the dark, smoky cliffs above them—and shake her head.

26 · Master of the Skies

HIGH ABOVE THE SMOKY CLIFFS, A GREAT black shape soared. It sliced through the red-tinted clouds like a dagger, sometimes veering to one side or the other, sometimes plunging straight down to attack its prey. Cliff hares who caught sight of that shape scampered instantly for cover. And any that heard its screeching cry—part eagle, part human—froze in fear, unable to move even a whisker. For that was the cry of an eagleman in flight: the most terrifying sound in this region of sheer cliffs, flame vents, and smoldering volcanoes.

Scree raised his right wing, banking a sharp turn over the ridge. Wind blew his long brown hair against his human head, and flattened the rows of silver feathers that covered his chest as well as his powerful legs and sharp talons. By bending his upper wing—what would, in his human form, be his forearm—he swept low across the ridge. As air rushed over his feathers, their red tips glowed as bright as the flame vents below.

How he loved to fly! To ride the wind, to sail the skies like a feathered boat that claimed no port. And knew no anchor.

"But that's not true, and you know it," he said to himself. "You *do* have an anchor."

He glanced down at his right talon, and the staff it held. That staff had been on his mind all day long, weighing him down.

Most days, when he soared above the cliffs, he thought about flight—the surge of the wind, the power of his wings, the feeling of freedom. Or he thought about finding his next meal: cliff hare or wild boar. And, of course, he thought about spotting intruders, whether they walked, like men—or flew, like ghoulacas.

But today . . . he was thinking about the staff. The gift of a wizard, entrusted to his care. He remembered exactly what had happened the moment he'd held it in that whole new way, the moment he'd spoken those powerful words: *I am the true heir of Merlin.*

He tilted his left wing, circling close to a pinnacle of black rock—so close that his wingtip nearly brushed its edge. Dark smoke, reeking of sulfur, belched from its top. He caught an updraft and climbed up, up, up toward the stars, until he could look down on everything below. The charred ridges, the smoking vents, the tallest volcanoes—all stretched far beneath him. He was the master of the skies.

He leaned to one side, catching the full force of the rising wind. And then he flapped his powerful wings once, twice, three times. His speed increased; the wind roared in his ears. Like a shooting star, he soared across the cliffs. Black ridges, orange flames, red clouds—he sped past all of them, hurtling faster than anything alive.

Free! He was truly free. Yes, even with the staff he carried. Even with everything he now knew . . . about himself, and his own destiny.

Scree cut a wide arc through some smoky clouds, his yellow-rimmed eyes gleaming. Then he arched one wing and veered again, streaking across the sky. He knew he was tied to this staff, no less than a boat was tied to its anchor. But now . . . he knew something more.

As he approached the jagged edge of the crater where he made his home, he caught a glimpse of some movement far below. Clambering up the rocky face of the cliffs were a pair of figures. One looked tall and slender, and moved nimbly over the rocks, while the other looked very short, oddly proportioned, and rather clumsy. No matter—they were two-leggeds, climbing toward his cave. Intruders!

A powerful screech—part eagle, part human—echoed across the cliffs. Scree drew his great wings tight against his body. Downward he plunged to make the kill.

27 · Prosperity

TAMWYN AWOKE IN BRIGHT DAYLIGHT. HE was lying on his back upon something soft. There was a strange taste, like licorice, on his tongue. The gray mist had gone—though a different kind of mist filled his brain, clogging his thoughts.

He sat up. He was on a couch with fat green pillows. Inside a room!

Indeed, it was the largest room he'd ever seen, larger than the whole house that he'd helped thatch in Lott's village. Windows, with fitted wooden shutters open wide, were on every wall. An immense hearth, glowing with still-warm coals, sat in one corner. Judging from the intricate stonework—deftly fitted slabs of pink granite—it had been built by a master stonemason. On one wall, between the windows, hung a richly woven tapestry of a garden overflowing with colorful vegetables. Beneath it sat a great oaken table, surrounded by a dozen chairs, on a thick woolen rug of azure blue.

Seated on two of the chairs were Llynia and Elli, joined by Nuic, who seemed quite content to sit on top of the table itself.

They were listening to an old, white-haired man who wore a gray robe with long, wide sleeves, and several hooks and pockets that held spades, clippers, plant bulbs, and seedlings. So much dirt was smudged on the robe that Tamwyn wondered for an instant whether some of the seedlings had taken root inside the pockets.

As Tamwyn cleared his throat to speak, the old man turned his way. He smiled and nodded in greeting, bouncing his necklace of garlic bulbs. "Ah, then, you've awakened."

"Have I . . . been asleep long?" Tamwyn asked groggily. "And where are we? Is everyone all right? That mist . . ."

"Yes, yes, all in time." The old fellow got up and stepped lightly over to his side. His face, round and friendly, creased in a web of wrinkles as he smiled again. "To start with your first question, you've been asleep quite some time. All last night, since I found you, and most of the morning, in fact. But don't worry," he said with a glance toward Llynia, who brightened visibly, "we've been having a lovely conversation."

"It's good you stayed asleep," said Elli with a toss of her curls. "If you'd been up walking around, you'd probably have broken some furniture."

Despite Tamwyn's scowl, the old man seemed to take this as just a good-natured jest. "Ah, but there is very little here that could break, unless he can crack oaken tables and break stones."

"You'd be surprised," muttered Nuic, his small body now a radiant golden brown.

Elli giggled at this.

The old man stretched out his hand and placed it gently on Tamwyn's shoulder. The hand, like his robe, was smudged with dirt. Every wrinkle of his knuckles and palms, and every black-lined fingernail, announced that this was the hand of a gardener. One of his thumbnails was broken, perhaps by a digging tool.

"I am Hanwan Belamir," he said in a deep, resonant voice. "Welcome to my humble school and garden."

"Come now, Hanwan," interjected Llynia. "No need for modesty, especially to my . . . er, porter here. This is no mere school! This is the Academy of Prosperity."

"Yes, well . . ." said the old man quietly. "So it is."

"And this," continued Llynia, with a dramatic wave in his direction, "is no mere gardener. You are speaking to the Academy's founder, the man many have dubbed *Olo* Belamir, the first person to bear that name since Merlin himself ages ago became Olo Eopia."

Now the fellow was looking positively embarrassed. "Such names are meaningless," he protested. "Mere distractions." He turned back to Tamwyn. "All you need to know is that I am an old man who loves nothing better than to dig around in my garden. And whose school is built upon a few useful principles."

"Hmmmpff," said Nuic, his color reddening. "Arrogant principles, if you ask me."

"Nuic!" scolded Elli, her own face reddening. "I'm surprised at you. You heard this man's letter to the Council of Elders, didn't you? You told me yourself that it helped. And besides, we're his guests! He *saved* us, if you recall."

Belamir just waved aside the praise. "Actually, that was just good luck that I happened to be out on my afternoon stroll."

"The mist," asked Tamwyn with a shake of his head to wake himself fully. "What was it?"

The teacher's face darkened. "A terrible thing, that! One of the hazards of the untamed forest—a kind of gas produced by mountain ash trees. To ward off animals who might covet their berries, I believe. Although it merely induces sleep, it can in time prove fatal. Those who succumb to it may never wake up again, unless they are removed from the spot and given the antidote, a special blend of licorice root and clover honey."

Tamwyn licked his lips, tasting again the hint of licorice. "So you did save our lives."

Belamir bowed slightly. "My pleasure. Although," he added with a wry grin, "it wasn't so easy to give the antidote to that, well, *creature* inside your pocket! It finally drank a bit, then flew off, babbling at me in a language I couldn't understand."

"You're not the only one," said Tamwyn. He patted his robe pocket to confirm that Batty Lad wasn't there. "I'm sure he's all right, thanks to you. He's probably out hunting for insects, or just napping somewhere else."

"As I said, it was my pleasure to help you. And also my good fortune." He turned back to Llynia. "How else would I have ever met the Chosen One—the next leader—of the Society of the Whole?"

Llynia blushed.

"Who promises," Belamir added in a lower voice, "to be a distinct improvement."

As Llynia beamed with pride, Elli frowned. "I thought you and the High Priestess got along just fine."

"We do." He looked at her kindly. "But there are certain . . . shall we say, *limitations* in Coerria, which someone of your youth may not have noticed."

Llynia, looking quite pleased with herself, gave a smirk.

But Elli, who was sure she had noticed *everything* about the High Priestess, shook her head. "I don't understand you. High Priestess Coerria is the very best—"

"Person for her time," finished Belamir. "But the times have changed. Dramatically, I should add. And the Society deserves better." He pinched his lips together. "As does Avalon."

His words, and worried tone, suddenly reminded Tamwyn of the warning from the old cherry tree. And that strange white lake at the canyon of the moaning wind. He wanted to tell Belamir about these things, and ask his advice. But something held him back, something he couldn't quite put into words.

"And I suppose," grumbled Nuic, "that you know exactly what Avalon needs."

Belamir looked down at his dirty hands, turning them in the light from the windows. "I know only what I've learned from my garden. If that is helpful to Avalon, I am grateful."

Elli, who still felt offended for Coerria, started to speak again, but the old man cut her off. "Come now, you must be famished! I'm sorry your other two friends aren't here to join us for a meal."

"Don't be," answered Llynia. "My maryth wouldn't eat anyway, and she's happier just being outside. And as for the hoolah . . ." She scowled. "Meals are always more pleasant without him."

"More plentiful, too," added Nuic. "But I'm sure that even now he's helping himself to some of your fresh produce."

"He's welcome to it," said Belamir. "We have plenty." He picked up a copper bell and rang it twice.

A door opened by the tapestry of the garden, and a very old servant hobbled in. He looked like an ancient, windblown tree, with scraggly hair sprouting from his chin and both sides of his head above his ears. One eye, irritated somehow, was so bloodshot that it looked entirely pink. The old man bowed, pressing together his hands, which were as black with dirt as Belamir's. "You called, Master?"

"Yes, Morrigon. Please have food prepared for our guests."

"Of course, Master." The servant bowed, then hobbled back through the door.

Seconds later, they heard a loud bustle and clatter from the next room. Tamwyn guessed it was the sound of platters, trays, and heavy containers. Feeling fully awake at last, he stood up and walked over to one of the windows—but not without stumbling against the corner of the couch. He cast a sheepish glance at Elli, but fortunately she hadn't noticed.

What he saw out the window was more than just a school . . . or even a full-blown Academy. It was an entire village, complete with houses, buildings for various trades, and farmed fields. But this village looked very different from those he'd seen in Stone-root. It wasn't just the absence of bells on rooftops, weather vanes, doorways, plows, and animal collars—something he'd come to expect in every village. No, the biggest difference was the sheer *bounty* of everything.

The houses, all painted in crisp, bright colors, had walls built of sturdy wooden planks. No thatched roofs anywhere, Tamwyn was glad to see: The roofs, too, were made of wood. Expansive vegetable gardens, with wire fences and signs labeling what had been planted in every row, flanked every house. From the look of it, the people who lived here had plenty of tools, seeds, and bulbs. And, it seemed, plenty of fruits and vegetables to show for it. Grape arbors hung with heavy purple bunches; squashes, pumpkins, and melons covered the ground; people were filling baskets with lettuce, carrots, radishes, beans, and more. Fruit trees—apples, pears, and plums mostly—grew in most every garden. And in the branches of one of them, Tamwyn saw the unmistakable shape of a hoolah, eating apples as fast as he could pick them.

In the courtyard in front of the school building, Tamwyn counted sixteen children (and several adults) playing on swings and a seesaw, running after balls, or jumping rope. Nearby, a forge echoed with the rhythmic sounds of blacksmiths' hammers and bellows, a village trading center displayed a wide variety of farming tools and handmade furniture, and a communal stable housed dozens of well-fed sheep, goats, and pigs. Surrounding the settlement were enormous cultivated fields, with corn and various grains, that ran all the way to the high wooden fences that bordered the village, separating it from the forestlands beyond.

Everything about this village felt productive. And prosperous. And bountiful, beyond anything Tamwyn had experienced. Whatever ideas Belamir had developed, they certainly seemed to be working.

The door by the tapestry opened again, and old Morrigon entered. He was followed by four men and women, all wearing brown robes covered with pockets. They carried trays, bowls, and platters full of food: melons, all sliced and dripping with juices; piping hot pies filled with roasted lamb, barley, almonds, and apricots; overflowing salads; five different kinds of grainy bread; strawberry and pear puddings; honey-glazed tarts and crusty apple pastries. To drink they brought mint, orange, and clove teas; tall beakers of freshly squeezed plum and apple juice; and a large bottle of crimson mead, which Belamir placed right in front of Llynia.

The travelers, all hungry, plunged right in. Nuic, who had sat himself in a large bowl which he'd filled with water, stuffed himself with fresh salad. Llynia and Elli both began with big slices of lamb-and-barley pie, and then had seconds. Tamwyn, meanwhile, consumed enough juicy melons to make up for several months of drought.

Their feasting continued for quite some time before anyone said a word. It was Llynia, sipping her third glass of mead, who spoke first. "Hanwan, such a fabulous meal! Tell us now, what is your secret to producing all this delicious food?"

The old gardener smiled modestly. "Simple, really. I've just never forgotten one basic rule: It is the job of humans to take care of this world, to help and protect all other creatures. That is our responsibility, and why we were created in the image of Dagda and Lorilanda."

A nice ring to those words, thought Tamwyn as he started on another slice of melon.

Llynia nodded thoughtfully. "So you're saying that humans are special—both in our gifts and our responsibilities."

Belamir beamed at her. "My brightest students could not have put it better."

Elli, though, felt puzzled. "Just what do you mean, that humans are *special*?"

"What she means," answered Nuic, who was munching on a carrot so big, he needed both hands to hold it, "is that humans are *superior*." He bit into the carrot again. "A view that is so wrongheaded that only a human would suggest it."

Llynia glared at the sprite. "Show some manners, Nuic! You are speaking to Olo Belamir."

The old fellow raised a hand. "It's quite all right, Llynia. Perhaps I didn't explain my view clearly enough." He gazed thoughtfully out the nearest window for a moment before continuing. "Humans have great gifts, as Llynia said. And also great potential—

not always realized, mind you, but there nonetheless—for helping other creatures less fortunate than ourselves. That means we need to apply our wisdom, inventiveness, and hard work to making the world a better place for all to live."

"Even if that means deciding what's best for other creatures? Making them do whatever humans want?"

"Nuic!" scolded Llynia. "How can you be so rude?"

"Wait," demanded Elli, "that's a fair question."

"What would *you* know about any of this, you apprentice third class?" Llynia's face looked as crimson as the mead in her glass—except, of course, the dark green mark on her chin.

Tamwyn wiped a dribble of melon juice off his chin. He was at least half listening to this conversation, and he thought maybe Elli had a point. He might have spoken up . . . but there was that next slice of melon, just waiting to be eaten. Besides, the last thing he felt like doing was siding with Elli on anything.

Belamir, like a practiced teacher, waved his hands for silence. He turned to Nuic. "You put it rather harshly, pinnacle sprite, but there is some truth in what you say. Humans *do* know what's best for the other creatures of Avalon. And for the landscape, as well. That is why we should always try to do what's best for the world."

"Best for humans, you mean," said Nuic icily. His color was now bloodred.

"What's best for humans is, by definition, best for everyone else." Belamir smiled graciously. "That is why so many creatures—not just humans, but creatures of all kinds—have adopted my teachings. And are living more comfortably because of it."

He stretched his arm toward the window. "You needn't look any farther than my little village of Prosperity, which has given us all this food. In a time that some are calling a drought, I might add!"

The gardener's round face became wistful. "There is no limit to human ingenuity, none at all. We can make gardens, tools, vehicles, whatever we need. Even buildings! Why, someday I predict our buildings will be so large, and so comfortable, that people won't even need to go outside."

Tamwyn stopped chewing, midslice. Not go outside?

"All things are possible," Belamir went on, "if humans just make use of their gifts. And their surroundings."

Nuic put down the rest of his carrot. "By which you mean all the world's lands—and creatures."

"That's correct, my good sprite."

"So does that mean . . . if you think it's best to keep a goat locked up, even if the goat would rather be running free, you have the right to do that?"

"Yes."

"Or to cut down an ancient tree, even the last of its kind, if you think it could be useful?"

"Yes."

"But those things are against the Drumadians'—" began Elli.

"Hush, apprentice!" hissed Llynia. "I told you that you know nothing of these matters!" She gave a sarcastic wink to Belamir. "This girl believes that even a moth could qualify as a priestess."

The old man raised an eyebrow. "Does she, now? Well, well, we were all young once, weren't we?"

"And some of us never grow up," said Llynia smugly, chortling into her glass.

Elli suddenly stood. "I think, Nuic, it's time for us to go. Don't ask me where, but away from here."

As the sprite nodded, she placed him on her shoulder. Facing Belamir, she said curtly, "Thank you for the meal." She glanced over at Tamwyn, who just looked down at his melon. Then she strode out of the room.

Llynia looked across the table at her host. "Oh, I do apologize for her impudence. She is hopeless, Hanwan, truly hopeless."

The old teacher shook his head in sympathy. "Your burdens are great, Llynia." He reached for the bottle and poured her some more mead. "Tell me, now. Just where are you going? I am sure that the Chosen One does not travel so far from the Great Temple without good reason."

"Very good." She took a slow sip of mead. Then, to Tamwyn's surprise, she said, "We are going to the Lady of the Lake. To seek her counsel."

Belamir studied her intently. "About the changes in the stars, no doubt."

"And other troubles."

"Of which I am well aware." His brow creased, like a freshly plowed field. "The Lady will not be easy to find. She works in mysterious ways."

Llynia drained her glass. "At least I've had a vision to guide us."

"A vision!" He gazed at her with admiration. "You *are* most talented."

She tried not to show her pleasure at his words, but her blush told all. Then, all of a sudden, her expression darkened. She leaned across the table and said anxiously, "Except for seeing the Lady, my visions haven't been . . . what they were. For quite some time now. They're clouded, unclear—if they come at all. Do you have any words of advice for me?"

The old man pondered for a moment. "Perhaps, Llynia, your enormous sensitivity to your surroundings—the very source of your gift—is both a blessing and a curse. A blessing for the great wisdom it gives you, and the Society you will one day lead. And a curse as well, for it probably magnifies whatever foolishness or incompetence is in your midst. Am I being clear?"

Slowly, she shook her head. Tamwyn could tell that while she didn't want to seem stupid, she desperately wanted his advice. "No. I'm sorry."

"My fault," said Belamir. "I shall be more direct, then." He breathed a sigh. "I think your problem may be the Society itself."

Llynia sat back in her chair. "Really?"

"Really." He placed his hand on her forearm. "It may be too backward, too caught up in old ways, for someone of your extraordinary skills. That, I fear, could be interfering with your gift."

She swallowed. "Are you saying . . ."

"Merely that you have an open invitation to come here to the Academy, anytime you like. You could come only briefly, as my honored guest, just to clear your mind of distractions. Or you could stay longer. Yes, Llynia! You could even help me found a new and greater faith."

She gazed at him uncertainly. "You really . . . think so highly of me?"

"Indeed I do." He smiled at her. "Well now, I believe I have delayed you long enough. Shall we gather your supplies and your . . . er, companions?"

She returned the smile. "Yes, Hanwan. And thank you for what you said just now."

"My pleasure."

With that, they both rose from their seats. Belamir extended his arm and Llynia took it. Together, they walked out of the room, without so much as a backward glance at Tamwyn.

28 · Illusion

THE HEAVY WOODEN GATES OF PROSPERITY swung open, creaking loudly. Under the strong starlight of early afternoon, the travelers filed through, leaving the village behind. Ahead of them, the massive trees of the forest seemed to whisper uneasily.

Belamir himself saw them off, flanked by Morrigon, whose bloodshot eye seemed painfully swollen. With a look of worry on his face, the old teacher stood by the gates and waved his hand with the broken thumbnail in farewell. As the travelers marched into the trees, only two of them looked back: Henni, who was already missing his time feasting in those gardens; and Llynia, who seemed to be missing something else.

Tamwyn had agreed to Llynia's request to find the highest hill around, so that she could take in the view and find something that would recall her vision of the Lady of the Lake. Normally, that wouldn't be a tough assignment for a wilderness guide. But he found himself haunted by thoughts of the old cherry tree, the strange white lake, the deadly gray mist, and his mixed feelings about Belamir. So he walked distractedly into the trees.

Thud! Tamwyn's foot caught the root of a rowan tree, and he fell flat on his face. He rolled on the mossy ground, shaking his head at his own clumsiness.

"Well," said Elli, "we're off to a great start."

He sat up, pulling some moss from his mouth. "Would you like to lead?"

"No, no," she said with a laugh. "You're much more entertaining."

Nuic, still quite red, shifted on her shoulder. "And after our talk with that *humble gardener*, we could use some entertainment."

Tamwyn grimaced, then stood up with a clink of the little bell on his waist. Remembering Batty Lad, who had flown back just as they'd left the village, he peered into the pocket of his robe. "All right in there?" he asked. A thin, whistling snore was the only reply. So he closed the pocket and turned back to the forest, determined to give Elli nothing else to laugh about.

Soon he found the narrow path of a fox run. It led them through some thorny brambles, and then, as he'd hoped, to higher ground—a narrow, twisting hill more like the back of a great serpent than a ridge of land. They followed the hill for more than an hour, though it never broke out of the trees to give them a wider view. Then, to Tamwyn's disappointment, it plunged back down again, leaving them in thicker forest than before.

Sweaty and discouraged, Tamwyn debated where to go next, when he spied a line of willows, their lacy branches waving in a subtle wind. Knowing that willows often grew by water, he turned toward them. A stream, maybe? The drought didn't seem to have reached these depths of Woodroot—not yet, anyway. So perhaps there really was a stream under those boughs.

Yes—a small, silvery spring coursed through the willows. It

glittered like a trail of shimmering stars, more luminous than any stream he'd ever seen. He stopped, gazing at the bright water.

Elli, struck by the same sight, halted right behind him. Suddenly she cried, "Look!"

As they watched in astonishment, the whole surface of the stream took flight—a liquid necklace that lifted into the air with a loud hum. Then, all at once, they realized their mistake.

"Spray faeries," they said in unison, as thousands of the silver-winged creatures—tiny even for faeries—rose skyward. In just a few seconds, the entire flock floated up through the willow leaves, like rising raindrops, and out of sight.

Tamwyn and Elli traded glances, too amazed (for the moment) to remember their old animosity. As Llynia, Henni, and Fairlyn joined them, they turned back to the stream, which gurgled invitingly. All of them knelt to take a drink—except for Fairlyn, who just waded right in.

Nuic, meanwhile, hopped off Elli's shoulder. The old sprite slid down the bank and sat on some smooth pebbles. As the cool water splashed against his back, his color changed to misty blue.

Tamwyn cupped his hands and splashed his face. "Ahhh. This is even better than that feast of Belamir's."

Elli looked at him doubtfully. "You really think so? You seemed to enjoy stuffing your face with melons."

He was about to respond, when a sudden cry startled them both. It was harsh, like the screeches of eaglefolk—but higher and more rasping. They looked up at the strip of sky above the willow-lined banks. The screeching cry came again, louder this time. And in that instant, Tamwyn remembered the two times he'd heard that cry before: at the death of his mother, and at the moment he'd lost Scree.

"Ghoulacas!" he shouted. "Run!"

But it was too late. The air buzzed with wings—transparent wings that were just blurs, bearing nearly invisible bodies half as tall as Tamwyn. Though their wings and bodies were transparent, the ghoulacas' bloodred talons and huge, curved beaks were easy to see. And easier to feel, as they ripped and slashed, trying to tear apart their prey.

More screeches echoed in the trees. Willow branches, snapped by savage beaks, splashed down into the spring. Fairlyn, who was taller than the others, tried to shield them by swinging her branches wildly. Even though several of her limbs were broken or bandaged, she still fought valiantly. Llynia, frozen with fear, huddled by her roots.

Tamwyn and Elli each grabbed willow branches and tried to fend off the attackers. But sticks were little use against those knife-sharp beaks and slashing talons. If Fairlyn hadn't been giving them cover, they would have quickly been cut to bloody bits.

Henni fared much better. His slingshot, armed with pebbles from the spring, zapped many ghoulacas—one of them right in the eye, which sent it crashing down into the willows. Even so, there were at least five more of the killer birds, all of them eager for blood. As fast as he shot at them, jumping from bank to bank to avoid their talons, it wasn't fast enough.

From his spot in the middle of the spring, Nuic surprised one ghoulaca by shooting one of his silver-threaded parachutes over its head. The bird squawked angrily, unable to open its beak through the tangled lines. But its talons ripped the air more violently than ever. It was all the sprite could do to roll down the waterway, barely out of reach.

As Nuic bumped up against Tamwyn's leg, he lifted his liquid purple eyes to the young man. "Now would be a good time," he panted hoarsely, "for one of your little illusions."

Tamwyn, who was jabbing a willow branch at a hovering ghoulaca, shot him an astonished glance. "What? Are you mad? It's no time for tricks!"

Then, all at once, he understood. Maybe, just maybe . . . with the strong starlight pouring through the gaps in the trees, he could make some fire—fake fire. And hurl it at the killer birds.

He held his branch high so that its tip caught the light. Never before had he tried to make a trick fire with anything so big—let alone while he was under attack. The biggest one he'd ever done was the knot of wood shavings he'd thrown at Elli. But he had to try! If Fairlyn's swinging arms could just hold off the ghoulacas long enough . . .

He focused on the glowing wood, willing it to grow brighter. And brighter. And brighter still. *Be a flame!* he called to it. *Be a burning star!*

The tip of his branch suddenly sparked—and then exploded in mock fire. A ghoulaca that had swooped too close screeched in fear and tried to veer aside. With a whoop, Tamwyn charged after it, brandishing his stick that seemed to be aflame. Other ghoulacas, sensing some new danger, halted their attack.

Then the fire went out. Tamwyn cursed and and trained his thoughts again on the branch. But this time he was standing fully exposed, without Fairlyn's waving arms to shield him. Hard as he tried, he couldn't concentrate. The ghoulacas were still hesitating, frightened by what they'd seen, but he knew it would not last long.

Burn, you! he commanded. Yet not even a faint glow appeared.

He threw the branch aside. "Follow me!" he cried to the others. "Into the trees!"

Fairlyn, still waving wildly, reached down an arm to help Llynia to her feet. Elli grabbed Nuic, while the hoolah grabbed a last handful of pebbles. All of them ran after Tamwyn, who had plunged through the willows. The ghoulacas screeched and attacked again, slashing their talons furiously.

In desperation, Tamwyn scanned the forest for the thickest growth. There! A stand of midsize spruces, mixed with some broad, leafy trees. He ran that way—even though he knew that a few trees wouldn't hold back their assailants for long.

Bursting through the spruce branches, he tried frantically to find better cover. Then he heard a cry from Llynia. One of Fairlyn's broken branches had caught on a tree! He turned and raced back. It took both his hands—and Llynia's, too—to free Fairlyn's limb. By that time, the ghoulacas were practically on top of them, snapping branches just above their heads.

"Look!" cried Elli. She pointed to a pair of dark, berry-laden trees among the spruces. Mountain ash! And flowing fast from that direction, a rolling bank of thick gray mist.

Tamwyn's eyes met Elli's. Both knew this was the end of their journey, the end of everything. Just as the mist covered them, Tamwyn wished he could have done better—with his fire trick, as well as his guiding. And most of all, with his short, wasted life.

Everything went dark, as dark as the vanished stars. As dark as a dead torch.

Part

III

29 · The Hand of Greeting

TAMWYN BLINKED, EVEN AS THE THICK MIST submerged him. He couldn't see, couldn't hear, and could only feel the heavy wetness of the blanketing fog. *By the Thousand Groves! I'm still alive!*

Clearly, this mist was very different from the deadly variety the travelers had met before, among the mountain ash trees. This mist was more physical, almost a solid thing . . . with a will of its own. It tugged on them, leading them irresistibly—to where, none could guess.

Tamwyn tried to pull free, to force his legs to move in a different direction. But the pull of the mist was far too strong. He stumbled along, tripping over roots and branches, his quartz bell clinking against his water gourd. This mist was taking him wherever it wanted. Maybe it didn't knock him out, as the other one had, but it still seemed every bit as dangerous.

Then, all at once, the mist cleared. Like a veil of vaporous threads it pulled apart, leaving thousands of luminous shreds in the air. Starlight, shining through the wisps of tearing mist, seemed somehow brighter than usual, and scattered into countless rainbows by the vapors. As a result, Tamwyn and the others found themselves blinking in the sudden brightness that surrounded them.

Then, out of the radiant mist, a blue lake appeared before them. Bluer than a sapphire, the lake sparkled as mist swirled around it. In its very center, a spiral of mist rose out of the still water, rising and reaching outward with long, undulating limbs, until it looked like . . .

"A tree!" exclaimed Elli. "A tree of mist."

Despite Nuic's customary scowl, his liquid purple eyes shone. So did Tamwyn's, as he stood beside Elli and the sprite. Nearby, Fairlyn's own limbs were now smelling like sweet apple blossoms. Llynia, standing by her maryth's trunk, had started to smile mysteriously.

Only Henni, who was disappointed to have the excitement of battle no longer, wore a glum expression. He cast his gaze around the misty shores of the lake, slingshot poised for action, looking hopefully for any more signs of ghoulacas.

The tree of mist, sprouting from the center of the lake, solidified before their eyes. Bark, branches, and leaves all hardened, faceted like crystals that reflected the water's deep blue. Before long, the whole tree stood fully formed.

Then, upon its glistening trunk, an image started to appear. The image of a woman! She stood as straight as the trunk, though she was clearly quite old. Long, silver hair, curling like shreds of mist, fell over the shawl that was draped across her shoulders. Beneath the shawl, her gown of textured green seemed to glitter—though not as much as her vibrant, gray-blue eyes.

Suddenly, the woman's image stepped right out of the trunk. Unlike the tree itself, she didn't look solid. They could see through parts of her flowing green gown to the tree and shore beyond. She started to walk straight toward them, her bare feet on the water, each footstep sending a slender ripple across the lake.

Elli gasped and put her hand on Tamwyn's forearm. Then, realizing what she'd done, she instantly withdrew her hand. To her relief, Tamwyn was so captivated by the strange sight of the misty woman that he hadn't noticed.

"At last," declared Llynia with satisfaction. "My vision comes true! It is the Lady of the Lake."

Her smile broadened. Any remaining traces of humiliation and fear from the ghoulacas' attack melted away from her face, vanishing like mist in the morning. In a voice both confident and proud, befitting of one whose ascension to High Priestess was now assured, she said, "She comes to welcome us. See? Even now she lifts her hand in greeting."

The vaporous image of the Lady of the Lake paused on the water, just a few steps from the shore. And then, to the wonder of Tamwyn and Elli, she did indeed raise her hand. She held it there, palm out to the travelers.

Nuic, his color a dark shade of brown, scowled at Llynia, who had raised her own hand in return. That was when the Lady spoke, her voice misty but unmistakable.

"You shall not enter." She thrust out her palm—raised not in greeting but as a command to stop. "Go away, all of you!"

"B-but," stammered Llynia, suddenly crestfallen, "you brought us here."

"I merely spared you from your attackers. But I do not invite you into my lair. Nor do I have either the time or desire to speak with you more."

She turned and started to walk back across the lake to the tree.

Around the shore, the mist began to thicken. Soon it would cover them and carry them off to another place.

"Wait!" cried Llynia. "We need your help."

The Lady's glistening form kept walking away. Watching her go, Llynia struck her fist into her palm. "It's all Coerria's fault! She tricked me into making this quest . . . this folly. Damn! She's ruined *everything*."

Elli whirled and faced her. "She didn't trick you! She gave you every chance to stay at the compound. You're the one who wanted to go—for yourself more than the Society."

Llynia's cheeks went red, then purple, while her chin turned the color of greenish mud. "You, you . . . wretch! You have no right to speak that way to your superior. No right at all! You should have stayed a slave in Mudroot! That's where you belong, groveling in the—"

Angry though she was, Elli just turned away from the fuming priestess. Before the Lady of the Lake disappeared, she had to try again—while there was still a chance. She cupped her hands around her mouth and shouted across the water, "We need your help, good Lady! To find the true heir of Merlin."

To her surprise—as well as everyone else's—the departing enchantress stopped. She turned around, standing in front of her crystalline tree. Then, her voice scornful, she demanded, "What do you even *know* about the true heir of Merlin? Or for that matter, the child of the Dark Prophecy?"

In a flash, Elli recalled the secret that High Priestess Coerria had shared with her—a secret that had come from the Lady herself long ago. How did it go, now? Something about a brother . . .

She started to speak, when Llynia elbowed her aside. "Forgive this presumptuous slave girl, your grace. Obviously, the heir of

Merlin and the child of the Prophecy are mortal enemies. Opposites. One pure, the other defiled."

The lips of the misty woman pressed tightly together. She surveyed them for another instant, then turned again to go. Reaching the trunk, she stepped inside. At the same time, thick gray mist billowed inward from the shore, covering the branches of the tree and stretching toward the travelers.

"Wait!" cried Elli in desperation. "They're not opposites!" As Llynia spun around to counter her, and thick mist flowed over them, Elli shouted: "The heir of Merlin is like . . ."

Heavy mist blanketed her, muffling her voice. With all her strength, she called: "Like a brother! *Like a brother to the darkened child.*"

The mist shimmered, then pulled apart. Bright starlight shone through, washing everything in prisms of color.

Henni stood on the shore of the lake, blinking his eyes in the brightness. He could see again! There was the glittering tree, growing out of the deep blue water. And there was Lady Greenbeard, looking wonderfully angry. How he loved seeing her all purple with rage! What, he wondered, was she fuming about this time?

Then it hit him. Llynia was there. So was Fairlyn, waving her unbroken branches and smelling like something soothing—lavender, maybe.

But there was no sign at all of the others. Elli, Nuic, and Tamwyn had disappeared.

30 · A Pure Crystal

ELLI AND TAMWYN FOUND THEMSELVES SITting on the floor of a large room. Its floor, walls, and furniture all sparkled with a moist, silvery sheen, like frozen mist. The ceiling, unlike any they'd ever seen, tapered to a point high above their heads. All at once, the truth struck home, and they turned to each other.

"We're inside the tree!" they both said at once.

"I do have chairs, you know," rang a mischievous voice behind them.

They spun around—and then leaped to their feet. Tamwyn accidentally stepped on Elli's toes, but she hardly noticed. For seated before them was the Lady of the Lake herself.

She sat in a chair sprouting out of the floor, a crystalline burl that was part of the tree itself. Under its vaporous surface, it seemed as solid as any wooden chair—maybe more so, since it looked as if it had lasted all the ages of Avalon. The woman herself seemed quite old, and yet her gray-blue eyes twinkled with youthful vitality. She studied her guests, playing with the curls of her silver hair, until at last she spoke to them in a rich, gentle voice.

"And so we meet," she declared, inclining her head to each of them in turn. "Elliryanna Lailoken. A mouthful of a name, that is! No wonder you go by just Elli." She grinned playfully at the surprised young woman, then turned to Tamwyn. "And Tamwyn, who doesn't even know his full name." She watched him shift uncomfortably, then added softly: "Although . . . I do."

Tamwyn started. He leaned forward and opened his mouth to ask her to say more, when she raised her hand. "Later, Tamwyn." Reluctantly, he shut his mouth, though his dark eyes stared at her in wonder.

She turned at last to Nuic, who was standing on the sparkling floor beside Elli. This time, she did more than incline her head. She drew her thick shawl about her shoulders and rose from her chair, as gracefully as a spiral of mist. Then she made a full curtsy to the pinnacle sprite.

"Nuic," she said. "How good to see you."

The Lady's special treatment of Nuic was, for Elli, surprising enough. But what words then came out of his mouth surprised her even more. For her ever-grumpy maryth said nothing harsh or even irreverent. He simply said graciously, "The pleasure is mine."

Elli glanced down at the sprite, whose colors were vibrant blues and greens. "You've met before?"

Nuic just shrugged. "You could say that, Elliryanna."

The Lady, watching him, fingered the amulet of oak, ash, and hawthorn leaves that hung around her neck. "Indeed you could."

Tamwyn and Elli traded glances. Then, while Elli puzzled over the sprite's strange behavior, Tamwyn turned back to the Lady.

Her eyes, so bright, with both gray and blue, reminded him of the mist swirling on the sapphire lake. And there was something else about her—something magical—that made him think of the museo he'd seen that night back in Stoneroot. Although he'd been mired in a heap of dung, that museo, and the strange bard with the sideways-growing beard, had lifted his spirits right out of the dung and into the stars.

That's how Tamwyn felt just now, for no reason he could name: ready to reach as high as he could. As high as the true heir of Merlin, perhaps—even if, as he feared, he was really very different. As different from Merlin's heir as anyone could possibly be.

The Lady of the Lake sat again, and gestured for them to do the same. Both Elli and Tamwyn found shimmering burls beside the enchantress, not far from a wide hearth that glowed steadily. But it wasn't any fire that produced the glow. It was, as Elli realized with astonishment, a cluster of light flyers—tiny winged creatures who were among the rarest in Avalon. They were crawling across the back of the hearth, their frilled wings pulsing with golden light.

"What a beautiful way to light your home," said Elli.

"And no need for kindling," said the wilderness guide next to her.

"Hmmmpff," said Nuic in his usual crusty style. He had chosen to sit on the floor, not far from the Lady's bare feet. "At least they're friendlier than the last winged beasts we encountered."

The Lady's eyes grew suddenly sad. "Ah, yes. You have met ghoulacas."

"Where did they come from?" asked Tamwyn.

The old enchantress sighed. "They are fairly new to Avalon, made by some hand I do not recognize. Yet this much I can tell you: In their blood runs an ancient evil. As old as Merlin's magical seed. The same evil that fanned the flames of greed and hatred into the War of Storms."

"But," protested Tamwyn, "that war, and that whole age, ended long ago."

"It did indeed." The elder woman drew herself up straighter. "We ended it, Merlin and I, with the Treaty of the Swaying Sea. But the evil did not die. It merely retreated to the shadows."

She plucked at one of the green threads in her gown, holding it closer to the hearth's light. At once, Tamwyn and Elli realized that it wasn't a thread at all, but a living vine. Her entire gown was woven of vines and leafy green shoots, all supple and alive. To Elli, it was almost—though not quite—as beautiful as the gown of woven spider's silk worn by the High Priestess.

"You see this vine?" asked the Lady. "Green it is, and green it will remain, so long as my will is there to support it. The same is true for a friendship, a marriage . . . or a treaty of peace."

Tamwyn gazed into the hearth. "So when the people lose their will for peace, things will happen—things like ghoulacas?"

She nodded. "And more."

He chewed his lip. "Things like weird, moaning winds . . . and strange white lakes."

"Or maybe even," added Elli, "distant stars going dark."

"Or things more subtle, that can't be seen," declared Nuic. "Things like arrogance. In a priestess, or a so-called teacher."

"True." The woman's eyes, glowing brighter than the hearth, peered at Nuic. "The same sort of arrogance that, long ago, caused Rhiannon, daughter of Elen the Founder, to resign as High Priestess and leave the Society that she'd worked so long and hard to create."

Elli started. "So that's why Rhia walked out?"

"Hmmmpff," corrected Nuic. "She didn't just walk out. She *stormed* out—shouting and hurling insults right and left. I remember well, I saw it."

"Nuic," demanded Elli. "I didn't know you'd ever been to the Drumadians' compound before last month."

The sprite eyed her grumpily. "You think all I've done with my life is sit on my ass in mountain streams? Well, think again."

Beneath the wrinkles on the Lady's cheeks, she grinned. And Tamwyn noticed, really for the first time, just how beautiful she looked. Not just radiant, and magical, and mysterious. Beautiful.

You must have been totally gorgeous when you were young, he thought to himself, speaking in his mind's private language that only nonhuman creatures understood.

To his absolute horror, she turned to him and answered with thoughts of her own. *So I'm not gorgeous now?*

Tamwyn sputtered and had such a sudden fit of coughing that he almost fell off his burl chair. As soon as he could speak again, he stammered, "You—you *are*, my gorgeous. I mean, my grace! Er, your gorge . . . No, no. Your grace. You're really—"

"Amused," she cut in, her whole face alight. She reached over and patted his shoulder. "I really am. And I'm also flattered by your comments."

Elli drew her brows together. "Comments? All I heard was coughing."

The Lady turned toward her. "With Tamwyn, my dear, you have to listen closely. Just as a good guide might tell you to listen to the voices of the forest."

Both Elli and Tamwyn stiffened. "So . . ." asked Elli, "you've been watching us?"

"Only while you've been in the forest. But that's long enough to know something else is troubling you. Something besides ghoulacas and vanishing stars." She faced Tamwyn. "What is it?"

He hesitated. "Well . . . who really *is* the true heir of Merlin? And is he . . ." His eyes darted over to Elli. "Is he really like a brother to that, that other person?"

Long and hard, the Lady looked at him, saying nothing.

Tamwyn swallowed.

"Before we talk more," the Lady said at last, "I should like to offer you a meal."

She rose, beckoning them to come across the room to a round hole in the floor where a spiral stairway descended. Elli picked up Nuic and followed, while Tamwyn came last. Down they went, stepping on the glistening stairs that seemed as delicate as wisps of mist. Soon they stood in another room, lit not by a glowing hearth but by rays of starlight that poured through knotholes in the trunk of the tree. In the center of the room sat a table and four chairs, all sprouted from the tree. As they sat down, the Lady brushed some silver curls off her brow and waved her hand in the air.

A flock of faeries suddenly appeared, flying in through the holes in the trunk. Their wings, colored the same misty blue as their flowing tunics, whirred through the shafts of starlight. It seemed as if their wings caused ripples and swirls in the light as they passed, like a hand moving through a quiet pool of water.

Some of the faeries carried slabs of honeycomb, dripping with sweet nectar; others brought apples, raspberries, blueberries, tangerines, and pears, all bulging with succulent juices. Still other faeries bore fresh green shoots, mushrooms, tubers, and tangy strips of salted chewbark. There were open shells piled high with sweetnuts and orange cream, honey-glazed walnuts, and rosehip rolls filled with sliced strawberries. And to top it all off—platters overflowing with chocolates. Made from cocoa beans and sugar cane, the chocolates had been deftly formed into the shapes of maple leaves, pinecones, and raspberries. Finally, to drink, the faeries brought wooden cups that brimmed with the simplest and most delightful prize of all: fresh, clear water from a secret woodland stream.

"Thank you," said Tamwyn as he stared at the magnificent feast arrayed before them.

The Lady shook her head. "Do not thank me. Thank the forest. For all this comes as a gift, given freely by the land."

She reached out her hands, clasping those of Elli and Tamwyn. "But first, before we eat, let us take a moment to meditate. As Rhiannon herself once said:

> "Listen to Creation's morning,
> Waking all around you.
> Feel the spark of dawn within,
> Breaking day has found you."

Elli beamed. "I just love those words."

"Do you, now?" The Lady gave her hand a slight squeeze.

"Hmmmpff," was Nuic's only comment.

A moment of silence ensued, and Tamwyn tried to think about the beauties of the forest that had produced this meal—the flowing rills, the boughs heavy with fruit, the starlit wings of the misty blue faeries. But hard as he tried, he couldn't think about such things without imagining the rills going dry, the fruit withering and losing all its color, the faeries leaving their homes in search of starlight.

That's not meditation, Tamwyn, came the Lady's gentle voice inside his head. *That's all your worries.*

He looked at her. What he saw in those gray-blue eyes was a sadness beyond anything he could comprehend. And yet . . . sparkling in the depths, he caught the faintest glimmer of something else. He couldn't be sure, but it seemed almost like a challenge. Or perhaps . . . a hope.

At a nod from the Lady, they began to eat. And eat, and eat! At some point in the meal, between the sweetnuts with orange cream and the honey-glazed walnuts, the Lady announced, "I would like to tell you a story. Keep eating, now, don't stop. Just listen to a true tale of Avalon, one that happened very long ago, before any of you—save you, my dear Nuic—were born."

She took a sip of crystal-clear water. "Long ago, in the Year of Avalon 130, a terrible blight appeared right here in the upper reaches of El Urien . . . which in the wood elves' language means *Deepest Forest.* Everything the blight touched withered and died, from the biggest tree to the smallest lichen. Some thought it was a disease spawned by the woodland marshes; others took comfort in the belief that it would never spread to other realms. But the High Priestess of the time—Rhiannon—felt differently. She felt sure that the blight was the work of the wicked spirit lord Rhita Gawr, who hoped to cause havoc in Avalon, to make this world his own. So Rhia sought help from the great wizard Merlin."

"Who was also her brother, right?" Tamwyn asked.

"Hush, will you?" Elli scolded. "Of course he was her brother! Every little light flyer knows that."

The Lady raised her hand for silence, then went on. "Merlin realized that there was only one way to stop the blight—to obtain a pure crystal of élano, which is the most powerful, and also the most elusive, magical substance in Avalon. Produced deep within the roots of the Great Tree, it is the Tree's essential sap, supporting all forms of life. Yes—even you and me! Merlin called élano *the true life-giving force of Avalon* . . . but even he didn't comprehend all its powers. What he *did* know was that, while élano needs no guidance to work its healing magic, it can still be shaped by strong wizardry."

She drew a slow breath. "There is only one place in Avalon where undiluted élano is found, with enough quantity to make a pure crystal: the White Geyser of Crystillia, not far from this very forest. Bursting forth at the uppermost canyon of High Brynchilla, this geyser carries enough élano that its water actually glows at night."

"And the water from that geyser also carries colors," added Elli. "That's why it's so white. My father used to tell me stories about it—how it flows down a big canyon to a place called Prism Gorge, and how it splits into all the colors of the rainbow."

Although Tamwyn was tempted to tell her to hush, just as she'd told him, he didn't. For one thing, he was still within fist-striking distance—no small matter, since he'd gotten enough black eyes from her already. And for another, he just liked the way she talked about her father. He wished, in that moment, that he had known his own father. Or at least known for sure who he was.

"That's right, Elli." The Lady gestured for a pair of faeries to refill her wooden cup, and they whirred over with a brimming water gourd. When they finished pouring, she thanked them and took another sip.

"So Merlin got the crystal from the White Geyser?" asked Elli.

"No," answered the Lady. "To make a pure crystal of élano, he needed to find water that was perfectly still. The geyser wouldn't work, nor would the river that runs from it down the Canyon of Crystillia to Prism Gorge."

"Is there a lake of this élano water somewhere?" asked Tamwyn.

To Elli's surprise, the Lady gave him an approving nod. "Good thinking. There was only one such lake."

"Not . . ." Tamwyn frowned. "Not that white lake we saw near the geyser? It didn't look right somehow."

"Not right at all," she declared, her brow furrowed. "About that, we'll hear more later. But in Merlin's day, there was only one such lake, and it lies far down inside the roots, many leagues below the White Geyser. Using portals known only to himself, Merlin took a remarkable journey deep within the Tree to find the lake. He brought along Rhiannon, her faithful maryth, and also her trusted companion from the Society of the Whole: a priest named Lleu of the One Ear, an old friend of the wizard from his youth in Lost Fincayra. When they finally reached the subterranean lake, Merlin conjured up a boat as white as the water itself. He sailed out to where the water was both deep and still, and inserted his staff, the wondrous Ohnyalei."

The Lady's cheeks flushed with passion. "And then a miracle occurred! The magic of Merlin's staff drew to itself the tiny particles of élano. Just as a flower with nectar draws butterflies! Even Merlin wasn't sure why it worked, though he believed that the powers of Ohnyalei were so aligned with the powers of élano that they were practically kin. So his staff *pulled* the élano from the depths of that lake, and bound it together in a very small—and immensely powerful—crystal."

Elli sighed deeply. "Amazing. A pure crystal of élano! Did it stop the blight?"

"Oh yes, my dear. Merlin and Rhiannon placed it deep in the forest, at the origin of the blight. The life-giving powers of the crystal expanded, restoring every particle of soil, every root, every leaf. It brought new life to the land, and fresh rain from the sky, leaving the forest even richer than before. Meanwhile, the priest Lleu returned to the Great Temple and gave the world a lasting gift—his master work, *Cyclo Avalon*, which sets down for all Drumadians the lore of élano."

Elli smiled, thinking how much Lleu's great-grandson would have appreciated hearing those words. "And so," she asked, "where is the crystal now?"

The Lady's gray-blue eyes sparkled. "Can you keep a secret? There are many, including the agents of Rhita Gawr, who have longed to find it."

"I can," promised Elli.

"Me, too," declared Tamwyn.

"Not me," said Nuic gruffly. "But if I ever told anyone, they wouldn't believe an old pinnacle sprite anyway."

The Lady flashed him a mischievous grin. "All right then, I'll tell you. The pure crystal of élano, the only one in existence, is . . ." She lifted the amulet of oak, ash, and hawthorn leaves that hung around her neck. As she peeled back some leaves, there was a bright flash. "Right here."

For a long moment, they gazed at the radiant crystal. Its white light, with subtle tones of blue and green, sparkled all across the room within the tree of mist. Light shone on the vaporous walls, the gnarled burls that formed their table and chairs, the delicate spiral stairway leading to the hearth room above, and most of all, in the Lady's abundant silver curls.

"How," asked Elli, "did you get it?"

The Lady released the amulet and drew a deep breath. "Rhiannon herself gave it to me."

Elli said nothing, but looked at her strangely for some time. Then, her voice hushed, she declared, "I know who you really are."

31 · The Lady Revealed

TAMWYN, PUZZLED, TURNED TO ELLI. "YOU know who the Lady really is?"

But Elli just ignored him. A shaft of starlight from one of the knotholes in the tree fell across her face, making her hazel eyes shine. And they seemed to be shining for another reason, as well. They were peering straight at the Lady of the Lake.

The silver-haired woman considered Elli for a long moment, playing with the frills on her thick shawl. At last, with a gentle smile, she said, "You are right, my dear. I can tell. And you are the first person in many centuries to guess my true identity."

Tamwyn looked from one to the other. Finally, he blurted out, "But *I* don't know who you are! Can't you tell me?"

The Lady gave Elli a sly wink. "Shall we?"

"I suppose so. If we make him try to guess, we could be here for years."

His eyes narrowed, but he kept his attention on the older woman. "So tell me, then. Who are you?"

The Lady of the Lake said simply, "In times long past, I was called Rhiannon."

As he'd done once before, Tamwyn nearly fell off his chair. "You're *who*?"

"Rhia," she declared with a playful toss of her curls. "Still alive after all these years! After all, I have wizard's blood in my veins— no less than my brother."

She laughed, and the glittering walls rang with the sound. "And I have something else, something my brother had only briefly." In one graceful motion, she dropped her shawl. There, upon her back, were a pair of luminous wings! Although they sprang from her body, just behind her shoulders, these wings were not made of flesh and bone, but of a substance more ephemeral . . . like starlight. Hundreds of shining feathers sparkled with even the slightest movement of the wings.

Elli beamed. "No wonder you decided to live in a tree!"

"Yes, yes, my dear. A tree made of mist. I made it in the image of Arbassa, my great oaken home for so many years in Druma Wood."

Tamwyn turned to Elli. "That's fabulous you figured it out."

She smiled at him—the first genuine smile she'd ever given him—and burst into her own lilting laugh. "That's not all I figured out."

Tamwyn tilted his head, unsure what she meant.

Elli just grinned at him. "I know who was Rhia's maryth."

Tamwyn's eyes opened wide. "Not—"

"Hmmmpff," grumbled Nuic. "Took you long enough."

"You mean," Tamwyn asked incredulously, "you were . . . ?"

"Yes."

"You went . . . ?"

"Yes."

"You are . . . ?"

"Yes, you knot-headed, swamp-brained dolt!"

The Lady reached out and touched a finger to the sprite's tuft of green hair. "Now, Nuic. That's enough expressions of affection, don't you think?"

"Hmmmpff. Just my affectionate nature, that's all."

He turned to Elli. "Don't get overconfident, now. Just because you made a couple lucky guesses."

Elli couldn't help but grin.

"And don't think it was just an accident, either, that I came to the compound at the same time you did."

She blushed. "You mean . . ."

"I knew you'd be arriving there," explained the Lady. "Just as I knew you'd be needing a maryth. Preferably one I could trust."

The old sprite's colors shifted to a proud shade of violet.

"Especially since," the enchantress continued, "I hoped that one day I might welcome you here. That is something I've never done before, you know."

Elli's blush deepened. The two women, one very old and one quite young, gazed at each other for a timeless moment.

Abruptly, Tamwyn turned to the Lady of the Lake—Rhia. "A while ago I asked you who was the true heir of Merlin. Is it, maybe . . . you?"

"No, my dear. It's not." She ruffled her shining wings. "But I can help you find out who it is—if you really want to know."

He shifted his weight uneasily. "I do."

"Then first, let me show you something else, so you'll understand just why Merlin's heir has never been more needed than now."

With that, she reached into the leaves of her amulet. She plucked out the sparkling crystal and held it in her open palm.

It seemed to pulse with light in her hand, much as the legendary magic seed of Avalon had pulsed like a beating heart.

Then, gazing into the crystal, she said:

> *Crystal blue and green so deep,*
> *Wake from ancient restless sleep.*
> *Show us now yon evil deed;*
> *Guide us to what hope we need.*

The crystal flashed in Rhia's hand. All of a sudden, it seemed to swell, becoming a misty sphere as big as her own head. Within the sphere, clouds swirled, expanded, and disappeared. The vapors moved with an energy, perhaps a mind, of their own.

Gradually, an image started to form within the sphere. It was a wide redrock canyon . . . with a great fountain of water spouting in the distance. The Canyon of Crystillia! Down the middle of the canyon flowed a white river, raging and pounding toward a narrow gorge—Prism Gorge. Suddenly the image changed: The river was gone. In its place, a white lake filled the canyon to its brim. Below the gorge, no water flowed, while the color had faded from the rocks. And across the gorge stood a great stone dam, half covered with scaffolding.

"The white lake we saw!" exclaimed Tamwyn. "So that's how—"

The next image within the sphere shocked him into speechlessness. Along the canyon rim, a whole great swath of forest had been slashed to death. Where tall trees once stood and many creatures lived . . . there remained nothing but torn roots, broken branches, and wasted stumps.

"Who did this?" demanded Elli angrily. "Who built that dam?"

The sphere clouded darkly, then revealed a hooded, cloaked figure standing in the shadows of a stone tower. His hands, whiter than mist, gestured, and some men cracked whips against a group of oxen, horses, deer, and dwarves, who were straining to pull huge blocks of stone out of a mining pit. The slaves—for they were clearly that—toiled to haul the stones down the canyon to a barge on the white lake. There, more slaves loaded the vessel— although one young doe fell into the water, was dragged under the barge, and drowned.

Elli shuddered. Tamwyn, instinctively, touched her shoulder, but she shook him off. In a hoarse voice, she whispered, "I know what it's like to be a slave."

Then she asked Rhia, "That slave master . . . is that the child of the Dark Prophecy? The one who could bring the end of Avalon?"

"No, my dear. The prophesied child is someone else."

Tamwyn lowered his gaze.

"But that slave master," Rhia continued, "is someone of considerable power. I can feel it clearly. And he uses his power only for wicked sorcery."

She focused again on the misty sphere. "Tell us one thing more. What does the sorcerer with the white hands need to triumph?"

A new image filled the sphere. It was a shaft of wood, gnarled and twisted. A walking stick. It lay against a wall of rock—perhaps a cave.

"The staff of Merlin," said Tamwyn. He shook his head so that his long black hair swished across his shoulders. "At last . . . I see it for what it really is."

Rhia nodded, even as the misty ball started to shrink back down in her palm. "You have seen it before, then?"

"I have." He swallowed. "For many years."

Elli looked at him with surprise.

Rhia's hand closed over the crystal, and she replaced it in her amulet of leaves. "And can you tell me why the sorcerer wants it?"

"Of course," said Tamwyn, putting it all together. "He didn't build that dam for the water—though that must be why there's been less water in the regions fed by the white river, and also less color. No, he built that dam for what was *in* the water. For the élano."

She nodded gravely. "Unable to find this pure crystal, and unable to find Merlin's underground lake, he decided to build his own."

"With slaves," spat Elli.

"With slaves. And ghoulacas. And whatever trees or stones he needed. All he lacks now is the staff."

"But," questioned Tamwyn, "why does he want to make a crystal of élano? What will he do with it?"

Rhia frowned. "No one knows, except the sorcerer himself. And, I suspect, his lord Rhita Gawr."

"He doesn't want to grow things, I'll wager. That's not Rhita Gawr's way."

"He must have some other plan," said Elli. "Some other way to use its power."

"By the Thousand Groves . . ." muttered Tamwyn. "What could it be?"

"Some form of evil," Rhia answered. Her face then relaxed slightly. "By the way, do you have any idea what the phrase *the Thousand Groves* really means?"

Uncertainly, Tamwyn said, "No."

A strange gleam shone in her eyes. "One day, perhaps, you will."

"Hmmmpff," growled Nuic. "And perhaps he won't, if he can't take ten steps without tripping over himself."

Even Tamwyn couldn't resist a grin. "How long did you put up with him as your maryth?"

"Not long," said Rhia with a shrug. "Just a few centuries." Abruptly, her face grew grim. "But we don't have that much time left now. Not nearly." She glanced upward, as if she could see the stars beyond the glistening walls of the tree. "There are now only three stars left in the Wizard's Staff."

Elli and Tamwyn both stiffened. Then Tamwyn asked, "What exactly does that constellation have to do with all this? I mean, how is *that* wizard's staff connected to the other one, the one here in Avalon?"

Rhia pinched her lips together. "They are connected, I can assure you. And in a way you'd find most surprising! But this isn't the time to talk about it. For now, all you need to know is that, when the last star disappears, so will all our hopes."

She took both of them by the hand. "To prevail, you must do something very, very difficult."

"Free those slaves!" cried Elli. "We must do that."

"Yes, that you must. But first, you must do something else. You must find the staff."

"Find the staff of Merlin true," quoted Elli, recalling the words that Coerria had taught her.

Rhia nodded in agreement, making her wings shimmer. "And in the process, you shall find the true heir of Merlin, who alone can use it."

"If you succeed," muttered Nuic, his colors darkening to nearly black.

"I know who is the true heir," declared Tamwyn. He fell to one knee before the Lady. "Scree! My adopted brother. We grew up together, those years in Fireroot. And he always carried the staff, everywhere he went, even when he flew as an eagleman." He ran a hand through his hair. "He never let me touch the staff. Not even once! Now I know why."

Elli, her voice soft, asked, "Is he . . . the person you've been searching for?"

"Yes. But when I lost him—when ghoulacas attacked us—we jumped into a portal together. And got separated! We both landed in Stoneroot, I'm sure of that. But hard as I've tried, I haven't found him."

"Hmmmpff," said the old sprite. "That's because he's still in Fireroot."

Shocked, Tamwyn stared at him. "You *know* that? How?"

"Do you think I was born just yesterday?" Nuic's purple eyes scrutinized him. "I've spent centuries in the mountains watching other creatures—including eaglefolk. Whenever they're attacked and pursued, their first instinct is to protect whoever else is with them. Their child . . . or their kin."

"That sounds like Scree, all right. But what makes you think he's still in Fireroot?"

"Because one of eaglefolk's best tricks, to shake off pursuers, is to double back. That way, the eagleman draws the pursuers to himself, and the kin—"

"Can escape unharmed," finished Tamwyn. "So Scree must have faced the ghoulacas all by himself."

"Not necessarily, you dolt." Nuic's color shifted to a slightly brighter tone. "Portals are especially difficult for pursuers . . . even ones a lot smarter than ghoulacas. They could easily have lost you both in there. And since they probably didn't have the brains to guess that he doubled back, your brother could have eluded them completely. He could be sitting there in Fireroot right now, polishing his talons."

"And wondering where in Avalon I am." Tamwyn turned to Elli, his face grim. "If he's right, you need to go to Fireroot. That's where you'll find the staff. And the true heir of Merlin."

She looked at him, taken aback. "You're . . . not coming?"

"No," he replied, lowering his gaze to the floor of hardened mist. "I'm not."

"Why?"

He pointed at Rhia. "She knows. She can tell you."

"No, Tamwyn," said the elder woman, watching him closely. "You explain."

He swallowed hard. "Because . . . I am . . . the child of the Dark Prophecy."

Elli literally jumped off her chair. "You?"

"Me. Scree's brother. Who brings disaster wherever he goes." He drew a long breath. "Now I know why my mother named me Dark Flame." Then, facing Rhia squarely, he declared: "If your Prophecy is really true, then you should kill me right now."

Suddenly Elli recalled her promise to Coerria. *You must break the Drumadians' first law.* That's what the High Priestess had commanded. *Kill the Dark one.*

Could Coerria have been right? Just kill him, here and now? Elli peered at Tamwyn's dagger—so near, so easy to reach. Her fingers twitched.

Uncertainly, she glanced over at Nuic. He shot her a strange, anxious look, his eyes alight.

Then she looked back at Tamwyn—and saw him, it seemed, for the very first time. She thought about her solemn promise. And she knew that she would never keep it. Her fingers relaxed.

Nuic turned a warm shade of yellow.

"Now, wait a moment," Elli said firmly to Tamwyn. "You may be the clumsiest, stupidest, stubbornest man I've ever met. But the great force of doom? I don't believe it."

He made a wry grin. "That's the nicest thing you've ever said to me."

She grimaced. "Don't get used to it."

Rhia then took Tamwyn's arm. "There are some things you must know, my dear. First of all, I will not kill you. Nor will Elli, or Nuic."

"Tempting as the idea may be," muttered the sprite, with a wink at Elli.

"But . . . the Prophecy! My destiny!"

"You can *change* your destiny, Tamwyn. Anyone can. Just as you can change your path through the forest, you can change your path through life. Look here, isn't that just what my brother Merlin did? Just think how he began—a boy who washed ashore, with no home, no memory, and no name. But somehow, he found a new path."

She glanced over at Nuic. "Tell me now, am I right?"

"It's true, I suppose," grumbled the sprite. "He could be even more of an idiot than Tamwyn at times."

Elli could only grin at her maryth.

"And besides," Rhia went on, "a prophecy is just a guess, a hint, of a possible future. It's merely a clue to the riddle of what a person will make of his or her life . . . and maybe a false clue, at that."

She thought a moment, as she wrapped a silvery curl around her finger. "So whether, in fact, you are destined to be the end of Avalon as we know it—the one world where humans and all other creatures can live freely together—remains to be seen. And much of it depends on you. On the choices you make. Always remember that, like Merlin himself, you have both light and dark in you."

She took a swallow of clear springwater. "And now, another thing you should know. The guardian of Merlin's staff may—or may not—be the wizard's true heir."

"But then . . . if it's not Scree, who is it?"

"You will know when he or she touches the staff. When that happens, if it's the right person, something wondrous will occur."

Elli grinned. "That's what High Priestess Coerria thought."

"She was right." Rhia watched Elli with a twinkle. "About other things, as well."

Then the elder woman squeezed Tamwyn's arm. "One more thing you might like to know, my dear. About your father."

He caught his breath. "My father?"

"He was Krystallus Eopia, son of Merlin and Hallia."

Like the walls of the tree, Tamwyn's eyes took on a misty sheen.

"And so . . . your full name is Tamwyn Eopia." Rhia paused, nodding. "I knew your father well. A braver explorer Avalon has never known! He died, as you probably know, trying to find the secret of Avalon's stars, what they really are. What you don't know, though, is that he also died of grief over losing his wife—Halona, princess of the flamelons—and their only child. You, Tamwyn."

"Why, though?" His throat felt as rough as spruce bark. "Why did he lose us?"

Rhia sighed. "Hatred between the races, the same kind of hatred that fueled the War of Storms. Right after you were born, some flamelons tried to kill you and your parents, since they thought it was blasphemy that your mother had married someone with human blood. They attacked your home in the night and burned it to the ground. Somehow your mother managed to get away, carrying you with her. She thought your father had died, because she saw him crushed by a collapsing wall. But he somehow survived! He had a powerful will to live, your father."

Her face looked suddenly older. "Then came the cruelest twist of all. Because your mother went into hiding right after the fire, Krystallus—along with everyone else—was sure that you both had died in the attack. Meanwhile, your mother kept hiding on the fiery cliffs, believing that her best chance to protect you, her only family, was to live as a peasant, in utter exile. When, at last, she discovered that Krystallus was still alive, he'd already left Fireroot—on his final expedition to the stars."

"So they never saw each other again."

"No, my dear. I'm afraid not."

Elli leaned closer to Tamwyn. "I'm sorry. I know how it feels to lose your family."

He just bit his lip.

Rhia tossed her silver curls. "You both still have family, though. Let's not forget that. Elli, you have Uncle Nuic here—the best of friends, I can promise you."

The pinnacle sprite wriggled in his chair and turned red around the edges of his face. "Hmmmpff," he declared.

"And Tamwyn, you have—"

"A brother, if he's still alive."

"Yes, but something more." She studied him with real affection, stroking his wrist. "You have an aunt. A great-aunt, actually, but that sounds positively too old! So you may, if you like, call me Aunt Rhia."

Despite everything, Tamwyn just had to grin.

Rhia glanced at the nearest shaft of starlight. She waved her hand, and the blue-winged faeries gathered up all the platters, bowls, and cups from the table. "Do you know," she said, "it's nighttime already! Time for you youngsters to get some sleep, before your journey to Fireroot tomorrow." Her gaze shifted to Nuic. "And time for us oldsters to catch up on the last few centuries."

"Hmmmpff, pretty dull compared to the old days." He waved his small arm toward Tamwyn and Elli. "Though they're doing their best to make life more exciting."

Just then Tamwyn felt a stirring in his tunic pocket. A bony wing emerged, followed by a mouselike face with glowing green eyes. "Nighty time, didja say say? Time for me to wakesa upsy! Yessa ya ya ya, manny man."

Tamwyn stroked his head. "That's right, it's time you went out for some food."

Elli shook her head in wonder. "He slept right through the fight with the ghoulacas, the mist, everything. Even dinner."

"Ooee ooee, me me go getsy me own dinner, soony soon."

Tamwyn continued stroking the little creature's head as he turned back to Rhia. For her part, she was studying Batty Lad with considerable interest. "He's, well . . . a friend," Tamwyn explained. "Sort of adopted me."

"I see," she replied with a hint of amusement. "I can only wonder why."

"Before we go," he insisted, "there's something else I just have to ask about." Seeing her nod, he pressed on. "The stars. I'm still wondering . . . after the Age of Storms, when Merlin rekindled the Wizard's Staff, just how did he get up there? And how did he bring the stars back to life?"

Rhia laughed again, and it seemed that bells were ringing inside the tree of mist. "Oh, my, you truly *are* your father's son! I can't answer those questions, my dear, at least not now." She bent her head toward his. "I will just tell you this much, though. He traveled to the stars with the aid of a powerful dragon by the name of Basilgarrad. A great warrior—and friend."

At the mention of such a mighty dragon, the little fellow in Tamwyn's pocket squeaked in fright and pulled himself back down into the folds of cloth. He stayed in there, quivering, despite Tamwyn's efforts to coax him out.

"Well, I have one more question myself," announced Elli. "I'd like to know . . . is Merlin, your brother, still around?"

Rhia smiled sadly. "Yes, yes, he's around. And he always will be, I suspect. But not anywhere in Avalon, I'm afraid. He's fully occupied these days with the problems of mortal Earth. And what problems they have! So if we are to save Avalon, my dear, we must do it ourselves."

She rose from her burl chair, her gown of woven vines gleaming in the rays of starlight. "You'll be leaving early in the morning, though I'll still be able to give you a hearty woodland breakfast. Then . . . you must seek the staff of Merlin. And find it—before that sorcerer does! So much depends on it."

She ruffled her luminous wings. "Until then, my dears, dream on this:

> *"So find the staff of Merlin true*
> *And you shall find the heir:*
> *Like a brother to the darkened child,*
> *The light of stars shall bear."*

Tamwyn opened his mouth to speak, but she raised her hand to stop him.

"No more questions," she commanded.

He looked at her, almost smiling. "Yes, Aunt Rhia."

32 · Scree's Plunge

TUCKING BACK HIS MASSIVE WINGS, SCREE plunged downward. Wind rushed against his face, blowing his streaming hair backward. He narrowed his yellow-rimmed eyes to thin slits, and clutched the staff tight within his talon. Then he screeched the cry of the eaglefolk—a cry that meant only one thing.

Death.

The two intruders, who had neared the jagged rim of the crater, froze. Just as his prey always did. Inwardly, Scree smiled. This was going to be as easy as nabbing a cliff hare for supper.

One of the intruders, the short and pudgy one, yelped in fright and threw himself behind a charred black boulder. A flame vent spouted fire and smoke right beside him, but he just huddled there, cowering.

The other one reacted differently. This one didn't run and hide, or stand still, paralyzed with fright. No, this person instantly pulled out a bow and nocked an arrow.

Scree didn't veer aside. This wasn't the first time he'd faced flamelon archers, who came up here hunting for action—or for eaglefolk meat. Even if the bowman got off a shot before Scree reached him—which was unlikely, given Scree's speed—he'd never hit the moving target. And never survive to shoot again. None of these flamelons, for all their boastful bravado, were any match for an eagleman defending his territory.

The bowman shot. Just as Scree had predicted, the arrow was easy to dodge. He lifted one wing ever so slightly, causing himself to bank to the side. Wind ruffled his feathers—and the arrow whizzed past.

Scree plunged again. Rage flooded his mind. He screeched louder than before, his cry echoing across the smoky cliffs.

By the time he saw the second arrow speeding toward him, it was too late. This bowman, whoever he or she was, was canny enough—and swift enough—to fire a second shot just when Scree banked to avoid the first. And Scree had veered right into its path.

As the arrow struck his wing, just above the joint, his screech turned into a shout of excruciating pain. He swerved, trying to pull out of his dive. But his whole right wing burned. He couldn't lift it. Couldn't pull out in time!

Towers of rock spun before him. And jagged cliffs—too close, too close! He knew, in that final instant, that he was going to hit hard. Too hard to survive.

• • •

Scree opened his eyes. He saw only dark sky—night dark, clotted with smoke. So he was on his back, then. Still in Fireroot . . . and still alive. Their mistake! Whoever had shot him should have killed him when they had the chance. He'd make sure they would regret what they'd done.

He realized in a flash that he'd regained his human form. And that he must have shifted back to human shape after hitting the ground. He could feel arms at his side, not wings. And legs, not talons.

Talons! All of a sudden he remembered the staff. He'd lost it!

Keeping silent, so as not to alert his attackers, he tried to roll over. But the instant he moved his right arm, a jolt of pain seared him. It was all he could do not to shout out loud. Then he noticed the bloody strip of bark cloth tied above his elbow. That was strange. Why should intruders shoot him out of the sky and then take time to bandage his wound?

Never mind. He needed to find his staff. Gritting his teeth against the pain, he forced himself to sit up.

"So then, you're awake."

The speaker was a tall woman, slim and strong: the one who'd shot him! She sat by a flame vent, warming her hands in the chill night air. Her eyes, not fiery orange or upturned at the corners like those of flamelons, reflected bright green in the firelight.

Scree winced against another jolt of pain as he sat all the way up. A wave of dizziness washed over him. But he held himself steady. His eyes darted about, searching for the staff. His staff.

That was when he caught sight of her ears. Pointed at the top, they were. Elf ears! He'd never seen an elf before; none lived in Fireroot. But he'd heard tales about some who came here to explore the realm's volcanoes and jeweled caverns. He cursed himself for not taking into account the possibility that his intruder might have been an elf—and an expert shot.

Then he saw the staff. It lay on the ashen ground by the elf's legs, just a body's length away. Close enough that, if he moved quickly enough, he could—

"Don't try it," she said sternly. In an instant, she stood, moving with speed and grace he'd never seen in any flamelon. Almost as soon as she was on her feet, her longbow was off her shoulder and nocked with a fresh arrow, pointed straight at his chest. "Any unfriendly moves, and I'll have to waste another arrow on you, eagleman."

"Betterly you obey whatever she wantses," declared another voice.

Scree turned to see what looked like an overweight dwarf waddling toward them. His nose, bulging like a burl on an ironwood tree, glistened with a shiny yellow coating—which seemed almost like dried honey. "She's a meanly one when she has to be! Honestly, truly, horribly."

Scree shook his head—both at this babbling idiot and at the dizziness that was gathering again. He turned back to the elf woman. "What are you going to do with my staff, you scum?"

Her green eyes flashed. "Take it."

"No!" Scree cried, his arm and head throbbing. "I haven't guarded it for all this time just so you could steal it."

"Then I really will have to shoot you." She drew back her bowstring.

With all his strength, Scree forced himself to stand. He stood before her, staring straight into the arrowhead, utterly defiant. Though his head pounded and his legs felt like broken twigs beneath him, he tried not to sway.

"Who are you?" he demanded. "A slave of Rhita Gawr?"

For the first time, her gaze wavered. She bit her lip, then replied in a slightly hoarser voice. "Who I am doesn't matter. And you won't believe this, but I'd rather . . . rather let you live than die. So now that I know you didn't bleed to death, I'll just take the staff."

Before Scree could speak again, the fat dwarf waved his hands. "Bake the staff? No, Rowanna. That would be all too splinterly!"

He suddenly frowned, pushing his finger into his ear. "Waitly, now. You didn't say *take* the staff, didly you?"

She gave a grim nod.

"But Rowanna! Isn't you some bittily confusedness? Methinks we is just going to *uses* Merlin's magically staff. Not steals it."

She glared at him, green eyes flashing. "The plan has changed, Shim. I'm going back to that cursed white lake, and taking it with me."

In that instant, several things happened at once. Scree lunged, even as dizziness surged through him. The elf woman released her arrow. And Shim wailed in anguish.

33 · A Hornet's Nest

TAMWYN AND ELLI MOVED BRISKLY THROUGH the Woodroot forest, as they had all morning, following the Lady's light flyer to the nearest portal. The luminous little creature glowed bright amidst the dark boughs and shaded roots, darting through the air along elk trails and fox runs. And yet its delicate light, barely a candle flame on wings, reminded both travelers of the fragile nature of life—and stars.

In silence, they padded through the groves. They could easily have talked, of course . . . if only about the potent smells of sweet cedar, rancid skunkweed, and fragrant dill. Or the cascades of pink bougainvillea, whose countless petals rippled like the fins of salmon swimming upstream.

But talking just didn't occur to them. There was simply too much to think about from last night's wondrous meeting with the Lady of the Lake—whose true identity they now knew, but whose mysterious ways they'd only begun to discover. As they tramped through thick groves of cedar and rowan, passing one honeysuckle abuzz with bees seeking the last drops of nectar, their heads were also buzzing.

Questions upon questions filled their thoughts. For Tamwyn, they mainly involved wondering whether he could, in fact, alter his own destiny. If nearly every creature alive knew that the child of the Dark Prophecy would cause the end of Avalon, what hope did he really have to do otherwise? Could he trust Elli to keep his dreaded identity secret? And how could he even imagine a different destiny, when he knew so little about himself and his strange, emerging powers? Sure, there was some hope in his ancestry, which included Krystallus, Hallia, Rhia—and even Merlin himself. But there was also flamelon blood in his veins . . . with all the warlike traits that made those people so feared throughout Avalon. And then there was his special knack for causing trouble.

For Elli, who trekked with Nuic sound asleep on her shoulder, the questions were different. Did she really deserve the same maryth as Rhia herself? What made her think she could find the true heir of Merlin, let alone help him prevail? Truth was, haughty old Llynia had been right: Elli was just an orphan, a former slave to gnomes, who had lucked into a role in all this. What sort of match could she ever be against a powerful sorcerer who had taken hundreds of slaves, slaughtered a forest, built an enormous dam, and halted a free-flowing river? And yet . . . something about the way the Lady had looked at her—really looked at her—made her at least hope she could help somehow.

As they entered a stand of dark green cedars, Nuic stirred. Elli reached up and squeezed his tiny hand. "Up late last night, were you?"

"Hmmmpff," said the sprite with a yawn. "I'm too old to stay up till dawn jabbering away."

"Well, now that you're awake, what do you think happened to

Llynia and the others? They weren't anywhere near the lake when we left."

"No doubt Llynia wasn't happy about being left behind—especially with a hoolah for company." His color turned an amused shade of peach. "They probably drove themselves crazier than a clan of catnip faeries."

Elli almost ran into Tamwyn, who had stopped suddenly. He was in midstep, his bare foot just above a hornet's nest resting among some cedar cones. With unusual agility, he hopped backward before his foot crushed the gray folds of the nest. But he slammed the back of his head into a sharp branch.

"Owww," he moaned, rubbing his tender scalp. He glanced over at Elli and blushed almost as red as Nuic looked at the moment. "Go ahead! Laugh."

Elli shook her head, though her eyes glinted playfully. "Wouldn't think of it."

"At least I didn't step in the hornet's nest."

"You did so," countered Nuic's gruff voice. "Just what else would you call joining this ragtag group that doesn't know the difference between the Rugged Path and a running bath?"

Tamwyn frowned slightly. "You've got a point there, old sprite."

"That I do." His purple eyes rolled upward, while his body's colors shifted to shadowy gray. "And I'll tell you something else. Two things, in fact."

Elli pursed her lips. "Good news or bad?"

"Bad, of course. What kind of maryth would ever give you good news?" He shifted his weight on her shoulder, harrumphed, and pointed toward the light flyer, who was fluttering around a towering spruce beyond the cedars. "First, the portal is right over there."

Tamwyn frowned. "That's bad news?"

"You haven't survived it yet," grumbled Nuic. "Not to mention found your brother and Merlin's staff—if they're still in Fireroot."

Anxiously, Elli twirled one of her curls around her finger. "And the second bit of news?"

"Hmmmpff. Do I need to tell you two stump-heads everything? Even show you the stars?"

At once, Elli and Tamwyn looked up. Through the tracery of cedar boughs, they could see the remains of the Wizard's Staff. Although the constellation still showed three stars when they'd left this morning, one had been fading fast—and now was gone. Only two remained!

Tamwyn winced, feeling an almost physical pain down in his chest. Another star, another light in the sky that he'd watched his whole life, had disappeared. He swore under his breath. "How can we accomplish everything we've got to do before the last two are gone?"

"Welcome to the hornet's nest," muttered Nuic.

They walked briskly through the cedars, across a jumble of spice ferns, and up to the towering spruce. It stood over a pair of large boulders, which held between them a circle of shimmering green flames. Flames that rose from deep within the Great Tree.

Just as Tamwyn approached the portal, something splatted against the back of his neck. A ripe pear! He didn't even need to turn around to know just who'd thrown it.

As juice dripped down his neck and between his shoulder blades, he grumbled. "Henni, you slimeball."

"Eehee, eehee, hoohoohooha. So you knew it was me! Very funny!"

Tamwyn shook himself, then gave Elli a wink. "You know, I really *would* enjoy killing him. But then . . . life would be so dull."

From Elli's standpoint, though, this wasn't any time for humor. She turned and asked Henni, "Where did Llynia and Fairlyn go?"

He lifted his hands, as big as cabbage leaves, into the air. "No idea. She just stomped off, right after the Lady of the Lake took you . . . um, wherever she took you. Oohoo, eehee, and was she ever mad! Hoohoohaha, really mad. Muttered something about all her plans being ruined, her life being wrecked, that sort of thing."

Henni adjusted his red headband. For a moment, he looked uncommonly serious. "I'm going to miss Lady Greenbeard, and all her pouting and ranting. She was so much fun to be around."

"Speak for yourself, hoolah." Nuic's colorful body now showed veins of dark green. "Let her spread joy somewhere else." He sighed, then added, "And yet something tells me that we will see her again."

"But where did she go?" pressed Elli, leaning her shoulder against the spruce's trunk.

"Who cares?" asked Tamwyn. "Maybe she went back to join Belamir."

Elli frowned. "Maybe. She failed at her quest to see the Lady. In her eyes, she's now a disgrace to the Society." She shook her head, bobbing her mass of brown curls. "But Belamir?"

"A perfect match," growled the sprite on her shoulder.

Tamwyn stepped closer to her, even as he studied the circle of green flames crackling mysteriously between the boulders. "They had a talk together . . . after you left. Belamir—"

"Oh, sure," she snapped angrily. "Bet you joined right in, too! Or did you just sit there and eat melons while they berated me?"

"They didn't . . . well, they did some. But then they—"

"Are we ever going into that portal?" demanded Nuic. "Or are you two going to bicker until the last stars go out?"

Elli scowled at Tamwyn, then turned to the portal. "We're going."

She peered into the green flames that smelled ever so slightly of sweet resins. Of magic. And of élano. "You know," she said thoughtfully, "the last time I came through a portal, just a month ago, it was to leave Mudroot. Forever! I never want to go back there, ever again. All those horrible gnomes! Don't even want to *think* about going back there."

"Hmmmpff," grumbled Nuic. "Then you shouldn't . . ."

Neither Elli nor Tamwyn heard the rest of his sentence. For just at that instant, Henni did something highly dangerous, absolutely foolish—and very entertaining. After all, how often do you get the chance to shove people headlong into a flaming portal?

34 · The Mudmakers

FIRST, THERE WAS A LOUD CRACKLE OF FLAMES. Then, all at once—rivers of green light, pulsing endlessly, flowing deeper and deeper . . . the sweet smell of resins . . . flashes of green, rays of rich brown . . . more resinous smell, stronger by the second . . . the sound of breathing, full and deep . . . life, death, and rebirth—all connected to the smell, the sound, the living Tree. At last, there was a new light growing . . . a loud crackle . . . and green flames again.

Tamwyn, Elli, Nuic, and Henni hurtled out of the portal. They landed on top of each other, so tangled and disoriented that it took them a moment just to figure out whose legs and arms were whose. And to realize that they lay in the middle of a vast brown field of mud.

Everywhere, as far as they could see, stretched the rolling brown plain, broken only by dozens of scattered mounds that looked like tree stumps covered in mud. The portal itself lay flat beside one such mound, its shimmering flames licking at the brown hump's base. Overhead, thick clouds covered the sky so completely that not a single star could be seen.

"Mudroot!" cried Elli in despair, as she lifted her hand from the muck with a loud slurping sound. "It can't be! We're not . . . we can't—"

"We are." Nuic, now fiery orange, brushed a clump of mud off his shoulder. "Hmmmpff. I told you it was dangerous to think of Mudroot back there . . . especially with a hoolah around! We're a long way from Fireroot."

"Eehee, I know," laughed Henni from the tangle of bodies. "But not far from the town of Hoolahome, so I could take you to meet all my cousins!"

Tamwyn found Henni's big hand and yanked it toward him. "You dung-brained dolt! You've got as much sense as a gobsken's hairy ass, you know. We could have all been killed!"

"Oohoo, oohoo, I know. Next time I'll do better, I promise. Eeheeheehee, oohoo eehee."

Tamwyn's eyes blazed. He pulled Henni's hand so hard that the hoolah flew into the air and landed with a splat in the mud. "I made a mistake not killing you after the Rugged Path. But this time, no—*yaaaaah!*"

A glob of mud, propelled by Henni's free hand, flew straight into Tamwyn's mouth. He coughed, spat it out, and leaped at the hoolah. Henni, laughing so hard he could barely stand, still managed to sidestep the lunging body. Tamwyn skidded and landed face-first in the wet mud.

"Eehee, eehee, hoohoohahahaha! You're more fun than ever, clumsy man."

"Wait, Tamwyn," called Elli, unsticking herself enough to stand. The mud oozed over her feet and came halfway up to her calves. "Don't waste any time on him. We've got to find the staff, remember? Before we lose any more stars."

"Sure, sure. Right after I kill this moron!"

He hurled a clump of mud at Henni's head. The missile splatted right in the middle of one of the hoolah's circular eyebrows, like an arrow in the center of a target. While Henni tried to wipe his eye, Tamwyn pounced on him. They fell back into the morass, rolling and kicking. Globs of mud flew in all directions.

"Lovely," snarled Nuic. "A mudfight."

Suddenly something whizzed through the air, brushing the side of the nearest mound and landing in the mud by Elli's feet. A spear! Though it was twisted and only as long as her leg, its hard ceramic shaft gleamed dully. She froze, unable to breathe. Gnomes!

Elli had seen such spears before—in the gnomes' attack on her village that left both her parents dead. And in those six years of slavery that followed, when she toiled in their dingy pits where no starlight ever reached. Even after she'd finally escaped, she still heard the whizz of those spears in every gust of wind, felt the jab of their pointed tips whenever someone touched her ribs. Only after Nuic had started riding on her shoulder, grumping constantly, had she begun to forget. And now a gnome spear had struck the ground right beside her!

She screamed. So loud was her cry that Tamwyn and Henni instantly stopped wrestling in the mud. As soon as Tamwyn sat up, looking like a mud mound himself, another sound echoed over the plains. It was a frightful mix of shrieks and howls, the sound that sent most creatures in this realm fleeing for their lives: the war cry of gnomes.

Tamwyn and Henni, covered in mud, stumbled to their feet. Almost at once, the wave of battle broke over them. Spears shot past, one of them grazing Tamwyn's muddy ear. Before Henni could pull out his slingshot, let alone load some pebbles from his pocket, a shrieking gnome tackled him from behind. While the gnome was no taller than Henni, he was far stronger, with muscular arms and jagged-toothed jaws just made for ripping flesh. The gnome battered Henni brutally in the face, then took a bite out of his shoulder. Henni wailed in pain as the gnome seized him with grimy, three-fingered hands—and started to bite his neck.

Just then Tamwyn kicked the gnome in the side—so hard that several bones splintered. The gnome howled and spun a full somersault before hitting the ground again. Immediately, Tamwyn grabbed his leg, swung him around, and let go right at the moment two more gnomes charged. His aim was perfect. The writhing body crashed full force into the attackers, knocking them flat.

"Let's go!" cried Elli. "Back into the portal, while we can."

"You and Nuic first! I'll watch your backs."

She glanced at him with a look of gratitude . . . and something more, something like real friendship. Then, scooping up the sprite, she sprinted toward the circle of green flames.

Tamwyn's feet squelched in the mud as he darted over to Henni. The hoolah's shoulder was bleeding profusely, but Tamwyn pulled him upright and shoved him toward Elli—just as several more gnomes descended.

A blizzard of spears whizzed through the air. Tamwyn heard Elli scream again, louder than before. A pair of burly arms wrapped around his neck, while someone slammed into his side. He fell to one knee, but twisted out of the neck grip and grabbed one of the gnomes. Holding the squirming warrior by the tuft of hair on his head so that he couldn't bite, Tamwyn lifted him just in time to meet three flying spears. The gnome shrieked as the spearpoints drove into his chest.

Tamwyn whirled around to see what had happened to Elli. "Nooooo!" he shouted. "Dear Dagda, no!"

She lay sprawled on her back beside the portal. Her eyes stared lifelessly at the clouds, while green flames licked her curls. A broken spear shaft stuck out of her ribs. Blood seeped steadily from the wound, staining her priestess's robe. Beside her knelt Nuic, his color bloodred, quivering uncontrollably.

In that instant, a new sensation surged through Tamwyn. It wasn't rage, or sorrow, or the will to live, though it sprang from all those emotions. And from something else, deeper than any emotion—richer, stronger, and wilder.

Power. He felt like a volcano about to erupt—not with lava, but with this indefinable burst of power. It coursed through his veins, pulsed with his heart, and swelled in his lungs. Even as he saw more gnomes pounding toward him, spears raised high, he felt no fear. Only readiness for whatever was about to come.

The power pushed its way to the surface, past bone, muscle, and flesh. It was as if he'd swallowed a star, whose light fought to shine through every pore of his skin. Across his whole body, it radiated, wild and alive.

He felt his skin crackle. And move. No—not his skin, but the mud that covered him.

Suddenly the nearest gnome let out a wail of fright. As Tamwyn spun around, something fell off his back and splatted on the ground. A beetle! Huge and hairy, the gray-colored beetle crawled across the mud, snapping its dagger-sharp pincers.

Before Tamwyn could move again, another beetle dropped off his back. Then came another, from his forearm. More and more fell off—from his neck, his chest, his thighs.

"Ugh," he moaned in disgust. "Where did *they* come from?"

He shook himself vigorously, sending another fifteen or twenty beetles to the ground. Then he thought of another, even more troubling, question: *Was that all I was feeling . . . a mass of beetles on my back?*

Meanwhile, the gnomes had started shouting—cursing, he felt sure. But the tone of their harsh, guttural voices had changed completely. They were afraid now. Already they were retreating, scattering across the muddy plains. Somehow they had gone from the attackers to the attacked.

Are they so afraid of the beetles? Tamwyn brushed the last one off his arm and looked at them crawling away. Instead of pursuing the gnomes, they just burrowed into the mud with their pincers. They really didn't seem very dangerous. Grotesque, maybe, but not dangerous. *So what scared off the gnomes?*

He turned back to Elli. At the sight of her limp form, soaked in blood, all his confusion was swept aside by a different feeling. Anguish. His stomach twisted inside him.

He knelt by her side and peered into those hazel eyes that now seemed so vacant. Elli hadn't always been easy to be around, to be sure. Yet some of that he'd brought on himself: Smashing her precious harp was a colossally stupid thing to do. He'd never really told her that he was sorry, either. And now . . . he never would.

He looked at her shoulder, where Nuic so often sat. And he could almost hear her laugh with the joy of a meadowlark when she realized who the Lady really was—and who had been her faithful maryth. No doubt about it, Elli truly loved Avalon! And lately he'd been noticing something else about her, something beyond her hot temper and savage tongue, something that made him feel . . . intrigued.

She didn't deserve to die!

He slammed his fist against his thigh, spraying Nuic with mud. But the sprite said nothing.

Hearing some movement behind him, Tamwyn turned his head. It was Henni, sitting cross-legged, his face uncharacteristically glum. In fact, Tamwyn had never seen any hoolah look so genuinely sad—about anything. At first he thought that Henni was upset about his own shoulder, which was badly torn and bloody . . . but then he realized that Henni was gazing straight at Elli. Could it be, Tamwyn wondered, that he actually *regrets* what he did to bring us here?

He just grimaced and turned back to Elli. *First my father, then my mother, then Scree. And now her!* It was all coming clear. *This is what happens to anyone who gets too close to the child of the Dark Prophecy.*

Gently, he took Elli's hand. It still felt warm with life. He squeezed it slightly . . . and then caught his breath. A pulse! A real pulse—very weak, but there nonetheless.

He grabbed Nuic by the arm. "She's still alive! Nuic, do you hear me? Still alive! Is there any way to save her? Anything we can do?"

The old sprite's bloodred color darkened. "No, no. Too far gone. Nothing can save her now, not even a mountain of healing herbs."

"Wrong you are, ancient sprite."

Nuic, Tamwyn, and Henni all jumped at this strange new voice. It spoke in the Common Tongue, but with a lilt that seemed more like music than language. And the voice sounded soft, as well, as if someone very large were whispering right into their ears. Yet there was no one, large or small, to be seen.

"Who are you?" croaked Tamwyn.

"See now you shall," the voice declared in its resonant whisper. "Behold the mudmakers."

Nuic's color flashed a surprised golden yellow, then returned to red.

All at once, the stump-shaped mound beside the portal began to bulge at the top. Its sides rippled, then started to bubble like a thick brown stew on the boil. Then, slowly at first, it lengthened, growing taller and straighter. It grew to Henni's height, then Tamwyn's, then kept on growing. Finally, when it reached almost twice the height of Tamwyn, a rounded head rose out of what seemed to be shoulders. It had enormous, deep-set eyes, as dark brown as everything else on its body. A thin, curving line opened as its mouth. Meanwhile, from the creature's sides appeared four slender arms with huge hands, each of which had three delicate fingers as long as a man's forearm.

The creature peered down at the three of them gathered by Elli's body, then bent several long fingers. "Appear rarely we do, very rarely." This time Tamwyn caught the distinct feeling that the voice was feminine.

"Yet come always we shall to greet another Maker."

Once again, Nuic flashed a surprised yellow.

Puzzled, Tamwyn shot him a glance. But the sprite just ignored him and kept staring up at the gigantic brown being who towered over them.

"Aelonnia of Isenwy am I, guardian of Malóch's southernmost portal. And these," she whispered with a wave of one great hand, "are the other mudmakers of our clan."

They turned to see dozens more tall brown figures striding gracefully toward them across the plains. As the mudmakers walked, their wide, flat feet squelched noisily. Soon they stood in a circle around the portal, swaying slowly like poplar trees in a breeze.

"Can you save her?" pleaded Tamwyn. He squeezed Elli's hand more tightly. "You said there was some way to save her."

"A way there is," answered Aelonnia. "But surely, as a Maker, you know that already."

"But I *don't* know! And she's dying! I'm just Tamwyn, from Stoneroot—a wilderness guide when I can find the work." He frowned. "And some other things you don't want to know."

Aelonnia bent her enormous body until her head hung just above his. "No." Her voice vibrated like the lowest strings on a colossal lute. "You are a Maker, a man of wizard's blood. How else could you have given life to the mud a few moments ago?"

Tamwyn's head was spinning. "Me? Life? Mud?"

"The beetles, you fool," grumbled Nuic. "Are you really so stupid?"

"Yes," Tamwyn declared. Then, lifting his face again to the mud-maker, he said, "Just tell me what to do for Elli! The rest can wait."

Aelonnia reached out two of her arms and spun him around so that his back was to Elli and the flickering flames of the portal. Gently, she turned his head slightly to the left. "That way lies the Secret Spring of Halaad, whose location is hidden to all but our clan—or a true Maker such as you. Heal your friend, it can! Yet go swiftly you must, very swiftly. For I feel her life melting away into the soil, even now."

"Hurry!" shouted Nuic, his body rippling red and orange.

Tamwyn looked out at the rolling morass before him, stretching as far as he could see, and swallowed. He knew what he must do. He just didn't know if he could do it.

35 · The Secret Spring

TAMWYN DREW A DEEP BREATH AND STARTED running. The circle of mudmakers parted to let him pass. As his feet clomped clumsily over the morass, sinking up to his calves in muck, he wished that all those enormous brown eyes weren't watching him. Now they could see what he really was—a clumsy, thickheaded man, and no more.

And yet he knew down inside . . . he had to run like a deer. Had to! It was the last chance for Elli. The *only* chance.

Stomp, squelch, stomp, squelch went his feet. No traction here. He'd run like a deer once before, in that valley, though he didn't really know how. But that was, at least, on solid ground. Here, nothing was solid! Just spongy. Every single step was a chore. His thighs were aching already, and he'd only gone two dozen paces. How could he possibly change himself to run with the speed and grace of a bounding stag?

You can change anything, Tamwyn. Anything! Your path through the forest, or your path through life. The words of the Lady of the Lake—Rhia—came back to him in a flash. She seemed very close, as if she were really riding on his shoulder, much as Nuic had ridden on hers.

He plodded on. *Stomp. Squelch.* Mud oozed between his toes, clung to his soles, caked upon his ankles and calves. At this rate he'd never reach the healing spring in time!

Desperately, he tried to imagine the way a deer would run. So fast, they bounded, and so easily, they almost seemed to be running on air. No—running *as* air. Part of the breeze, the wind. Light as the air itself.

He remembered that fluffy white seed, borne by the wind, that he'd raced in that valley. Faster he ran, and faster. His feet seemed a bit lighter now, his strides a touch easier. *Like a windblown seed.* He leaned farther forward, stretching his neck and reaching ahead with his arms. *Like the wind itself.*

Stretching . . . reaching . . . running with the lightness of the wind. His knees bent backward. His strides grew longer, surer, and stronger. *Stretching.* Suddenly he felt his hands touch the ground. Or were they really his hands? *Reaching.* His back pulled longer, as did his neck. *Running.* His nose lengthened, merging with his chin. Wide, sensitive ears pressed flat against his head, just behind his rack of antlers.

He was a deer!

With grace and power, Tamwyn flew across the muddy plains. His hooves touched down only lightly, and only long enough to leap again into the air. Bounding and gliding, bounding and gliding, he raced across the flats, feeling the wind ruffle his fur.

Moments later, he smelled something new, a scent quite different from that of wet mud. It was merely a faint tingle, not so much a smell as a feeling. And yet he knew at once what it was: the intimate touch of magic on the air.

Following the scent, he veered a bit to the right. As with the rest of southern Mudroot, there were no landmarks to be seen, just ever-rolling plains. No trees, no hills, not even any more mounds of mud that were really creatures in disguise. What sort of people were these mudmakers? And with what strange powers?

Brown, brown, brown. Even the overcast sky took on the color of this land. Behind those thick clouds, Tamwyn knew, only two stars remained in the Wizard's Staff. And he wondered whether Avalon's chances to survive this time were any greater than Elli's.

Loping across the plains, he followed the scent of magic. Stronger it grew, and stronger, until he felt its tingle not just in his nose but in his throat, his lungs, and even his hooves. Finally, it grew so strong that he could almost chew and swallow it like wet grass or juicy sprigs of fern.

But he saw no spring! No sign of water at all. Nothing but endless, rolling flats of mud.

He slowed to a trot, concentrating with all his might on the scent. He bore to the left, then a little to the right, then left again. The strange tingling swelled even more.

Suddenly, the air around him shimmered, as if he'd stepped right through an invisible curtain. There, just ahead, he saw a slight depression in the land—a depression that simply hadn't been there seconds before. He raised his large ears, and caught the unmistakable trickle of water. The spring!

He bounded over to the spot. It was really nothing more than a pool, bubbling fresh from the depths of Avalon. A little pool—nothing more. But he had no other hope, so he pushed all doubts aside.

Tamwyn moved around the edge of the pool, eyeing it closely. As he walked, his back arched upward, his neck shortened, and his hooves flattened into feet. The transition happened so smoothly that he barely noticed it until it was over. Then, with the whiff of magic still tingling his nose, he knelt by the side of the little spring.

He unstrapped his water gourd from his belt. His hand brushed against his tiny quartz bell, making it clink softly, and he wondered whether he would ever see the rocky hills of Stoneroot again. He submerged the gourd until it filled completely. Just before he capped it, an impulse grabbed him—and he took a swallow.

His eyes popped wide open with the taste. This wasn't water! This was something that sparkled inside his throat, his chest, his weary legs. A fountain of feelings exploded inside him. The exhilaration of his first climb to the ridge high above Dun Tara's snowfields. The shock of his plunge headfirst into an icy river, when he rescued a green-throated duck caught by the current. The thrilling burst of flavor when he bit into a spiral-shaped larkon fruit and tasted its liquid starshine. All these feelings and more swept through him in that instant.

He capped the gourd. Feeling new strength in his legs, he turned from the pool, stepped through the shimmering curtain, and started to run. To lope. To bound once again like a running deer.

Even faster than before he ran. His hooves barely skimmed the soggy ground. He was gliding with the speed of a stag and the grace of the wind—and before long, he saw the circle of mudmakers.

Am I too late? Did I take too long?

He bounded up to the circle and slowed to a walk. Hooves became hands and feet; he stood upright as a man. As he came closer, the ring of towering creatures parted.

Tamwyn entered the circle. The first thing he saw was the body of the gnome impaled by spears. Just the memory of those warlike beasts—and what they'd done—made his temples pound in rage. Then, by the flickering portal, he saw Nuic, Henni . . . and Elli. As he knelt beside her, he caught sight of Nuic's liquid purple eyes. They were filled, he felt sure, with something different from the usual scorn. More like hope.

One of Aelonnia's slender fingers touched Tamwyn's shoulder. "A Maker you are, my friend," she whispered in her lilting, resonant voice. "Now slowly pour it, very slowly, first in her mouth and then on her wound."

Carefully, he tilted Elli's head forward and poured into her mouth a few drops of the magical liquid. He waited a few seconds, then gave her some more. Then, very gently, he poured the water over the base of the spear that stuck out from her side. Instantly, it fizzed and frothed, spraying upward around the wound. It reminded him of the White Geyser of Crystillia that he had glimpsed from the bottom of the Rugged Path. Remarkably, wherever the spray touched her robe, the bloodstains disappeared.

A sudden spasm shot through Elli's body. She lifted her head, coughed violently, then rolled onto her uninjured side. At the same time, the spear shaft wriggled outward, pulling away from her body, until it fell with a splat on the mud. Henni reached for the spear and studied it with wonder.

Elli opened her eyes. She blinked groggily, trying her best to focus. Through her torn robe, she watched in astonishment as the gash in her side shrank, closed, and vanished.

Shakily, she turned to Nuic. "What . . . what happened?"

"Hmmmpff. You decided to scare a few centuries off my life, that's all."

"But . . . the wound? The spear—"

"Tamwyn gave you a drink," the old sprite said. Then, with his most affectionate gruffness, he added, "Not bad for a moron."

"Or a clumsy man," added Henni.

Tamwyn's lips turned up slightly. Then an idea struck him. Holding the water gourd, he stepped over to the hoolah and poured a few drops onto his ripped shoulder. There was a sudden hiss, a bubbling of white liquid—and a moment later, a full-blown smile on Henni's face. His shoulder had completely healed.

He patted the spot in disbelief with his large hand. "Hoohoo, eeheeheehee. You're too good to me, Tamwyn."

"No, not really." He capped the gourd. "I just want to keep you alive so I can kill you myself someday."

Henni burst into a howling fit of laughter, rolling in the mud. "Oohoo, oohoo, eeheeheehee! That's a good idea."

Elli finally sat up. She gasped, seeing the body of the gnome with three spears in his chest. "Who killed him?"

"I did," Tamwyn answered grimly. "With some help from his friends."

"That drink, though . . ." she said with a confused shake of her curls. "What was it?" Suddenly aware of the ring of mudmakers around them, she stiffened. "And who are they?"

"Answer I shall," whispered Aelonnia. She waved two of her four long arms. "We are mudmakers of the Isenwy clan. Lower Malóch is our home, and has been since the beginning."

"Mudmakers," said Elli in awe. "All the years I lived in Mudroot with my parents, none of us ever saw one of your people."

The tall figures around her muttered to each other, bobbing their round heads.

"Hard to find, we are, yes indeed," whispered Aelonnia, her deep voice vibrating. "As is the water that healed you. It was found long ago by Halaad, a very young daughter of mudmakers, who had been brutally attacked by gnomes. Too badly wounded was she to be taken as a slave."

Aelonnia paused, seeing Elli suddenly wince. For a long moment she watched with her huge brown eyes, then continued. "Left to die, Halaad crawled to the edge of a bubbling pool of water—magical water, rich with the most powerful substance in all Avalon."

"Élano," said both Elli and Tamwyn in unison.

"Élano it was. When she drank from it, her wounds instantly healed. And for more than five centuries since that day, stories and songs have celebrated the Secret Spring of Halaad. But magically concealed is its location, you see, so it can be found only by mudmakers." She bent toward Tamwyn, and her voice grew suddenly grave. "Or by a true Maker who comes to our realm."

36 · Something Stupid

SLOWLY, TAMWYN ROSE TO HIS FEET ON THE mud. He felt strangely awkward now, after his time as a stag with flashing hooves and bounding legs. He looked up into the face of Aelonnia, so far above him.

"Tell me, please. What *is* a Maker?"

All around Tamwyn, Elli, Nuic, and Henni, the towering figures of the mudmakers stirred. Their long arms lifted, reaching skyward, as they whispered fervently to one another. They reminded Tamwyn of a grove of ancient spruce trees, tall and dark, shaken by the same storm.

Aelonnia's brown body swayed as she bent lower. "Answer you I shall," she said in her rich, resonant whisper. "But start I must with the seed. For at first, that was all there was—one thing and all things, present and future."

She gazed around at the sprawling plains of mud. "In the beginning, there was Merlin's magical seed. Beat like a heart it did. From it arose the Great Tree, and seven great realms, all blessed with the sacred Elements of Avalon:

"Earth, mud of birth;
Air, free to breathe;
Fire, spark of light;
Water, sap to grow;
Life, fruit of soul;
LightDark, stars and space;
Mystery, now and always."

Her deep-set eyes turned skyward. "All these are the gifts of Dagda and Lorilanda, and all are found . . ."

"In élano," said Tamwyn.

"Yes, but also in one place more," replied the towering creature. "In the mud of Malóch."

Tamwyn couldn't hide his amazement. "The same mud I ran across just now?"

"Yes," answered Aelonnia.

"The same mud we threw at each other?" added Henni.

"Yes," she repeated—though her whisper sounded a bit harsher this time.

"In the earliest days of this realm," Aelonnia continued, "come here himself Merlin did. And to the mudmakers he gave a great power, a wizard's power, yes indeed."

"What power was that?" Elli rose to her feet and stood beside Tamwyn. "Can you tell us?"

Aelonnia's eyes gleamed. "The power to Make, to form new creatures from our mud. Only mudmakers do that power possess. We have used it to Make many creatures—from the giant elephaunts of Africqua, that forest of vines in High Malóch, to the tiny light flyers who live now in every realm."

"Light flyers?" asked Tamwyn, remembering the delicate creature who had guided them through the forest, its frilled wings pulsing with golden light.

"Make them we did," she replied. "Merlin himself described to us the light flyers of old who lived in Lost Fincayra, and we formed them in the same image."

Her voice, while always musical, had never been louder than a whisper. But now it grew even quieter. "To Make, ten things we need: the seven Elements, the mud that combines them, the time to do our work, and one thing more. The magic of Merlin. Only when all are present can new creatures be Made."

Tamwyn chewed his tongue. "So those beetles . . ."

"Could be Made only by someone whose very touch holds the power of a wizard." Aelonnia moved many of her fingers, so gracefully that she seemed to be strumming an invisible harp. "Hold that power you do, Tamwyn of Stoneroot. And in all the centuries since Merlin first visited Malóch, no one else who came here has been able to Make living creatures. That is why the gnomes ran from you! Thought you a wizard, they did."

Tamwyn frowned. "But . . . beetles? They were just ugly little things."

"Hmmmpff," countered Nuic. "So are you, compared to the mudmakers."

Elli giggled, then put her hand on Tamwyn's shoulder. "If you really Made new life, you can't just ignore that."

"But I didn't mean to Make anything," he protested.

The slender finger of Aelonnia touched his chin and tilted his head back so that he gazed right into her eyes. "Accept who you are, you must. It may even be that within you resides the true heir of Merlin."

Tamwyn caught his breath at that phrase. His face suddenly darkened with the memory of who he really was. He traded glances with Elli, then shook his head, dropping flakes of mud on the ground. "You've got it all wrong."

But the mudmaker merely tapped his chin with her fingertip. "Know you shall, in time."

Elli squeezed his shoulder. "Suppose she's right? Suppose you are the heir—not the child of the Prophecy? Or maybe even . . . *both?*"

"Don't be idiotic! How could I be both the greatest doom of Avalon, and also the greatest hope?"

She pursed her lips in thought. "I really don't know. But there's one sure way to find out. When we find your brother, and the staff he guards, you should touch it. Hold it! Just like R— . . . er, I mean the Lady, said."

Again he shook his head. "No chance." Lines furrowed his brow. "Don't you see, Elli? That would be the worst thing I could possibly do! If I really am the bringer of doom, then just by touching the staff I could unleash terrible power. Who knows what might happen? Nothing good, that's certain! Not just for us, but for all of Avalon."

Nuic's colors darkened slightly. "As I've said before, you two can either go on bickering forever, or go after Merlin's staff."

Elli grinned at the pinnacle sprite. "I suppose you're right," she said. "But no sooner do I wake up from the dead than you're grumping at me."

"Hmmmpff. That's how you know you're alive, you little wretch."

She turned back to Tamwyn. "About being alive . . ." She smiled at him, her whole face alight. "Thanks."

To his great chagrin, he blushed. "Er, well, that's all right." He cleared his throat. "There was something else, though. I'd like to give you this."

He held out the water gourd. "It's not as pretty as that harp I destroyed, but maybe it will be useful to you."

"What? Are you sure? It's powerful stuff, this water."

Above them, the mudmakers nodded their great brown heads.

"I'm sure, Elli." He pressed it into her hands. "I know you'll do something good with it."

She looked at him, both surprised and grateful. Then her eyes moved to the body of the gnome stuck with spears, and all the warmth in her face vanished. She hesitated, then said, "I think that first I'm going to do something stupid."

Tamwyn sucked in his breath in disbelief. "Not the gnome?"

She nodded slowly. "Something's different now—since you brought me back. When I look at him, I don't hate him so much. What I mainly feel is . . . longing. To stop all this killing. To understand the gnomes, like Coerria said. I know it's crazy, but I just have to try. Soon—before I come back to my senses."

Above them, the mudmakers whispered urgently among themselves.

"But," said Tamwyn softly, "they killed your parents."

"Right. Just like they probably killed Halaad's parents, and many other people. Too many!"

With that, she strode over to the gnome. He looked particularly ugly, with bloodshot eyes that bulged outward, a mouthful of jagged teeth, and a tuft of filthy black hair on his head. But as she bent closer to his bloodied body, she saw him take a shallow breath, and her resolve deepened.

I hope I don't regret this, she told herself as she stooped over the gnome. Into his slack mouth she poured a few drops.

The gnome stirred, flailing his burly arms. He released an agonized moan.

"You've also got to pour a bit on the wounds," said Tamwyn through gritted teeth.

Elli did so. A few seconds later, the spears popped out and smacked on the muddy ground. Before his gashes had even closed, the gnome felt them with a three-fingered hand, then sat up. Dazedly, he looked at Elli's face. Then, seeing Tamwyn by her side, and the circle of great beings surrounding them, he howled in fright and charged through the gap between two mudmakers. They watched him flee across the plains, legs churning and feet splatting, until he vanished from sight.

Elli drew a long, slow breath, then turned to Tamwyn. "I told you it was something stupid."

"Certain that is not," whispered Aelonnia with a wave of several arms. "It may be you are a fool, yes indeed. Or it may be you are a Maker yourself—though of a different kind."

Elli looked into the liquid brown pools of her eyes. "Thank you."

"Welcome you are, daughter of Malóch."

Nuic's colors shifted to fiery orange rimmed with black, and he walked over to the edge of the portal. "If we're going to Fireroot, we should—"

Whoosh! Something small and ragged, like a clump of dead leaves, shot out of the portal's green flames. It swooped upward, then swerved wildly to avoid the heads of the mudmakers. An aura of green surrounded it, and there were two glowing spots near one end.

"Batty Lad!" cried Tamwyn. He felt his tunic pocket. Empty. So much had happened since they'd arrived, he hadn't noticed the little beast was gone. "Did you lose me in the portal?"

"Noee no no, manny man. I fellsies out when Hennihoo there shoves us!"

He landed on Tamwyn's forearm, panting hard. Then he wiped his mouselike face with the tip of his wing. "Ooee ooee oo, thatsa some upsy-downsy journey."

Tamwyn stroked his big cupped ears. "You smart little fellow! You figured we came here because Elli talked about Mudroot, didn't you?"

"Yessa ya ya ya. Oh, but manny man! Before I could do follow yousa here, some elsabody comesies outa the portal. An elfy maiden, ears all pointy. Anda she carries something too too."

Catching Elli's look of impatience—not to mention Nuic's—Tamwyn gave a curt nod. "That's fine, Batty Lad. Tell me later, all right? We've got to find that staff now, before it's too late."

He started to put the little beast into his pocket, when Batty Lad flapped his wings angrily. "Thatsa what I'm saying, manny man! The elfy maiden, she carries woody staff. And she says to herself allsa proudly, *Here is the staff of Merlin*."

"The staff of Merlin! Are you sure?"

"Yessa, yessa, manny man. Allsy sure!"

Elli faced Tamwyn squarely. "If there's any chance at all he's right . . ."

"I know. We've got to check it out." He swallowed, as light from the green flames flickered in his eyes. "But I'm worried about what this means for Scree."

"Hmmmpff," grumbled Nuic from the edge of the portal. "What you *should* be worried about is what this means for Avalon."

37 · Musical Mead

TAMWYN HEARD THE CRACKLE OF FLAMES AS he fell out of the portal. He tripped on the roots of the towering spruce tree and crashed to the ground (cushioned, fortunately, by years of fallen needles). Yet the strong aroma of resins that he smelled came not from those needles, but from somewhere within the portal of green flames . . . somewhere he longed to visit again.

Muffled squeals of anger came from his tunic pocket. "Sorry, Batty Lad," he said with a smirk. "Guess you survived the journey."

The mousy little face with vivid green eyes poked out of his pocket. "But almosty not the landing, manny man. Noeeee no no! Yousa lands right on me heady-head."

Before Tamwyn could answer, Elli stepped out of the portal. Around her waist she wore the gourd that held water from the Secret Spring of Halaad, and in her arms she carried Nuic. The old sprite's body vibrated with several shades of green—no doubt because he'd bent his portalling thoughts on Woodroot. Finally, Henni skipped through the flames, his eyes so swelled with delight that they nearly touched his circular brows.

Immediately, Tamwyn and Elli started looking around for the elf maiden Batty Lad had described. And, more importantly, for the staff! But other than the twin boulders that flanked the portal, the tall spruce, and the dense Woodroot forest beyond, they saw nothing. Even on the high, grassy hill that they could see rising above the trees, they saw no sign of anyone else.

"There's no one here," said Tamwyn, disappointed. He flicked one of Batty Lad's cupped ears. "Are you *sure* you saw someone with a staff?"

"Absolooteyootly, manny man!"

"Hmmmpff," grumbled Nuic. "Just a waste of time! That's what comes of listening to a wild bat—or whatever sort of beast you really are."

Batty Lad's eyes flamed brighter than the portal, but he said nothing beyond some unintelligible squeaks.

Elli chewed her lip. "This is one time I wish we still had Llynia! Maybe she could see the future—tell us where to find the staff."

"Bah," spat the sprite. "I'd rather eat a bowlful of Tamwyn's mud beetles."

"Aw, be nice," countered Henni. "I *miss* Lady Greenbeard."

"Wait now," said Tamwyn. "Whoever Batty Lad saw, maybe we just missed her. Before we give up and head for Fireroot, it's worth a quick look around." He bent low, looking for tracks or other trail signs. "She could have gone—"

"Look!" cried Elli. "Up there."

She pointed to the grassy hill, where a lone figure had emerged from the trees below. Yet this was no elf maiden—and carried no staff. Tamwyn, watching the figure strut across the top of the hill, suddenly caught his breath. He *knew* that person, remembered him as clearly as he remembered that night outside Lott's village when he'd slid into a dung heap to stay warm.

"The bard . . ."

At that moment, the bard swayed jauntily, making his sideways-growing beard glint in the starlight. He pulled off his wide-brimmed, lopsided hat. There, atop his bald head, sat the teardrop-shaped creature with bluish skin that Tamwyn also remembered well.

"He's got a museo," whispered Elli in awe.

"Eehee, eehee," chuckled Henni. "Bet he turned blue from sitting under that ugly old hat forever."

Nuic's own colors shifted to a curious mix of blue and pink. "I wonder . . ." he mumbled to himself.

Just then the museo started to hum—a deep, vibrating sound that entered their ears, shook their bones, and echoed in their hearts. As had happened before, Tamwyn felt slightly giddy. Like musical mead, the museo's hum poured through him, stirring so many feelings that he swayed on his feet. Elli, still holding Nuic in her arms, leaned her shoulder against his, and each of them balanced the other.

The bard kept strolling across the hillside, lopsided hat in one hand and museo on his head. Then, as the humming swelled louder, he began to sing in a low, melodic voice. It was hard to hear all the words, but Tamwyn was able to catch this much:

> *Beyond endless sea, world in a Tree*
> *Holds a high secret,*
> *Vast treasure troves—*

Yet only the True ever shall view
Avalon's secret:
The Thousand Groves.

The final phrase reverberated in Tamwyn's mind. *What does that really mean? The Lady wouldn't tell me, but maybe this old bard will.*

"Come on," he said to Elli, gently stepping aside so she wouldn't lose her balance. "Let's catch up with him! Maybe he's seen the maiden—or the staff."

They raced for the hill, plunging through a mass of hip-high ferns. Underfoot, a family of silver-backed stoats scurried away, while a large hedgehog curled himself into a prickly ball. Soon they entered a grove of intertwined elms, whose slender boughs were splattered with red and yellow lichens. The terrain started to climb, and midmorning starlight pierced the uphill branches.

Tamwyn broke through the branches. Standing on the grassy slope, he looked around for the bard, but saw nothing. He couldn't hear the singing any longer, nor even the haunting hum of the museo.

"For Avalon's sake," he swore. "Where are they?"

Elli, holding Nuic, emerged from the trees. She pulled a bunch of elm leaves out of her hair. "Any sign?"

"No."

"Say, clumsy man," called Henni as he burst onto the grass. "Bet you can't beat me to the top."

Before Tamwyn could answer, let alone start running, Henni charged up the slope. He leaped over a small ravine in the hillside, then abruptly halted. "Hooee," he cried. "Come look at this!"

The others ran to join him. What they saw made them freeze in their tracks. In the ravine lay the sprawled, bloody body of an elf maiden with a honey-colored braid. Her face and arms had been slashed, and one of her pointed ears was nearly severed. Blood oozed from a deep gash in her side. She lay beside her longbow, as motionless as a fallen tree.

Tamwyn and Elli traded mournful glances. The elf had clearly died an anguished death.

"It'sa her. Yessa ya ya ya!" chattered Batty Lad, practically falling out of the pocket with excitement.

"But no staff," said Tamwyn. "You're sure about that, right?"

"Sure, sure, ya ya ya."

Tamwyn glanced up to the crest of the hill where the bard had been only a moment before. *Did he lead us here on purpose?*

Elli stared down at the body. "Whatever happened to her?"

Tamwyn pointed farther down the ravine. There lay the twisted body of a ghoulaca, its nearly transparent wings splayed wide. A single arrow protruded from its head, just above its huge, curved beak.

"They must have attacked her," said Tamwyn, his face grim. "And taken the staff."

"If she really had the staff," countered Nuic. "All we have is the word of this bubble-headed babbler in your pocket."

Batty Lad's green eyes flashed. "Me never na-na babble-abble, no no no."

Tamwyn grimaced at the mutilated elf maiden. "They attacked her just as she came out of the trees onto the open grass. It's amazing she got off a single shot."

"Good aim, too," said Henni, sounding unusually subdued.

Elli stepped into the ravine, bent down next to the elf, and took her hand. "Wait! She's still alive."

Quickly she unstrapped her water gourd. She poured a trickle into the dying elf's mouth, then dribbled some more onto her severed ear and other wounds. The elf maiden gave a sudden, sharp breath and then blinked her eyes. Even before the gash in her side had fully closed, she forced herself to sit up.

"Who . . . are you?" she asked, her voice shaky.

"I'm Elli. This is Nuic. And Tamwyn. And over there, Henni."

The elf blinked several more times. "You . . . you . . . saved my life." Suddenly she scowled. "But you should have left me to die."

"No," declared Elli with a shake of her brown curls. "Never say that."

"But it's true. I am the vilest wretch in all of Avalon." Her deep green eyes searched Elli's, then filled with mist. "Hear my story, then decide for yourself."

With difficulty, she swung her legs around and leaned against the side of the ravine. "Brionna is my name. Brionna, whose grandfather—"

"Looked just like you in his youth," interrupted Nuic. Ignoring her surprised expression, the sprite went on, "More sensible than most historians, your grandfather. Though that's not saying much! But at least he had the sense to seek me out over a century ago, asking questions about ancient times." He scratched his small tuft of hair. "Tell me, how is Tressimir?"

She answered in a whisper. "He is dead . . . or will be soon."

Nuic's liquid purple eyes seemed to harden into ice. "Tell us your story, Brionna. *All* of it."

She gave a nod. Blood-matted hair brushed her pointed ears. "Granda and I were captured. Taken from our home in El Urien and turned into slaves."

Elli shuddered. "Who did this to you?"

Brionna gazed at her for a long moment, seeing another place and time. "The sorcerer—the one with pale hands. I don't know his name. He's been using slaves to build a dam, big enough to hold back the waters of Crystillia."

Elli and Tamwyn looked at each other, recalling everything they'd seen in the misty crystal of the Lady of the Lake.

"Granda was beaten. Nearly killed. The sorcerer told me that he'd spare his life if I, if I . . ."

"Stole the staff of Merlin," completed Tamwyn. His fists clenched. "Is that right?"

"Y-yes. I went to Rahnawyn, to a fiery crater—with Shim." Reading the question in Nuic's eyes, she nodded. "The same Shim who knew Merlin long ago. I thought he could help me find the staff. But he's not a giant anymore. He's gotten smaller somehow. And deafer."

"Hmmmpff," grumbled the sprite, wriggling free of Elli's arm to stand on the grass. "He couldn't have gotten any stupider."

For the first time, a spark of something besides sorrow and remorse appeared in Brionna's eyes, then vanished. "He is stupid, yes. But loyal. I hated to deceive him."

"What about the eagleman you stole it from?" demanded Tamwyn.

Brionna's face went pale. "He was fearless, and stubborn. As well as—"

"My brother." Tamwyn fixed her with his gaze. "Did you harm him? Shoot him with your arrows?"

She looked away.

"Tell me!"

Slowly, she turned back to him. "He was diving at us, about to kill us. I had to shoot! But he's still alive. I'm sure of it."

He ground his foot into the short green grass of the hill. "He'd better be."

"Even at the end, when he tried to stop me, I couldn't shoot him again." She bit her lip. "I just shot very close to him, to make him leap aside. I knew he'd fall, he was still so weak. And then I took the staff and ran back to the portal."

Tamwyn growled deep in his throat. "Back to your master, you mean. But he tricked you, didn't he? Sent his little birds to meet you. And they took the staff! So now, thanks to you, the sorcerer has everything he needs to rule Avalon—or destroy it, if that's his plan."

She hung her head between her knees. "I told you I deserve to die."

Tamwyn peered down at her. Gradually, the lines of his face softened and his fists relaxed. "No, you don't. You were just . . . trying to save someone's life."

Elli gave him a knowing look. "That's something you understand very well."

"Right," he said, a touch of new color in his cheeks. "And Brionna—you were stupid, too. Really stupid." He sighed. "Something else I understand very well."

He straightened up and looked over the crest of the grassy hill. A few wispy shreds of clouds blew across the sky, like faded trails of smoke. He could almost hear the whistling wind up there—just as he could almost hear that painful, moaning wind near the white lake. "We're not far from the sorcerer's dam now, are we?"

"No," said Brionna glumly. "A few hours' walk."

"Well then," he declared. "Point me in the right direction."

Brionna stiffened. "What are you going to do?"

"Get the staff back, of course. Before White Hands can make a crystal of élano."

"But no! You can't fight him alone."

"We'll see about that."

Elli reached over and helped the elf maiden to her feet. "You thought his *brother* was stubborn?"

Tamwyn started to say something to Elli, but she pressed her finger against his lips. "I'm coming, too. Don't even try to talk me out of it."

"But . . ."

"I'm coming, you big oaf."

He sighed. "All right. But what about you, Nuic?"

The pinnacle sprite went reddish purple. "Think I'd let you go off alone and botch this one? No chance."

"And you, Batty Lad?"

"Me no fightsy, manny man. No fightsy ghouly-waca birds."

He nodded. "Finally, someone with a bit of sense." He stroked the little fellow's cupped ears. "I'll miss you, my friend."

Batty Lad frowned at him. "Me no leavey weave, manny man! Me just no fightsy. Rides inside your pocket, me will, me will. Yessa yessa ya ya ya."

Tamwyn shook his head, then turned to Henni, who was flicking pebbles into the dead ghoulaca's open beak. "And you? It's all right to leave, you know."

The hoolah stared at him, aghast. "Leave?"

"I mean, there's going to be some fighting. Tough fighting. You could really get killed this time."

Henni thought for a moment, twisting the woven red band on his forehead. "Sounds fun."

"No," said Tamwyn firmly. He strode across the grass and put his hands on Henni's shoulders. "It's *not* fun. And I think you've started to realize that yourself, which makes you probably the only hoolah in Avalon who understands the difference between life and death! But really, Henni, hoolahs just aren't made to fight other people's battles, are they? You shouldn't come."

Henni stuck out his chin. "I wouldn't miss it for all the balloonberries in Avalon."

Seeing there was no use arguing, Tamwyn let go. He turned back to Brionna. "So point the way."

"I'd rather show you myself." With the graceful quickness of an elf, she retrieved her longbow and quiver. "That is . . . if you'll have me."

He met her gaze, then slowly nodded. "Let's go."

"About time," grumbled Nuic, who had resumed his perch on Elli's shoulder.

Together, they marched up the hillside. Cool grass swished against Tamwyn's ankles, but he didn't notice. For his attention had turned again to the sky. To the shredding clouds . . . and beyond, to the Wizard's Staff.

Only one star remained. And it was throbbing, pulsing like a painful wound.

38 · Death on Wings

DEEP IN THE SHADOWS OF HIS STONE TOWER on the canyon rim, the cloaked sorcerer seemed just a black blot within the darkness. Only his hands, pale and smooth, caught enough light to be seen. They were stroking something with care, almost affection: a gnarled wooden staff.

The sorcerer's thin fingers slid down the length of the staff, brushing over every grain and whorl of wood. Neither the shaft nor the knotted top showed any sign at all of magic, or anything special, but the sorcerer released a thin, hissing laugh. "You cannot hide your powers from me, staff of Merlin! I can feel them, mmmyesss, even now."

He squeezed the shaft as a man would squeeze his enemy's throat. "And regrettable though it is to destroy such a powerful tool of magic, I shall destroy you. Mmmyesss! After I use you for one simple task."

He tilted his cloaked head upward, scanning the air. The bloodred talons and beaks of more than twenty ghoulacas, circling above, flashed in the starlight. Death on wings, they were. Their nearly transparent forms smeared the sky as they passed overhead, while their angry screeches echoed across the canyon, the dam, and the huge white lake.

A sharp wind gusted, wailing even louder than the birds. The sorcerer clutched at the neck of his cloak to keep his head covered. "Cursed wind," he spat. "I will be your master soon enough!"

He continued to peer skyward, past the ghoulacas and the swirls of red dust whipped up by the wind, to the stars beyond. Only one star remained in the constellation he knew so well—and it was already flickering weakly. Beneath his hood, he smiled in anticipation.

"My lord Rhita Gawr has done his work well on high, mmm-yesss. As I have done well below! Soon, very soon, the entire world of Avalon, root and branch, shall be ours."

Harlech's wide bulk climbed out of the quarry pit below the tower. He stepped over to the sorcerer, his heavy boots stained with blood, his weapons clanking against each other with every stride. Just at the edge of the shadows under the tower, he stopped.

"Everthin's ready, Master, jest as ye wanted."

"The dam?"

"Aye, Master. Jest one more line o' stones to set." He nodded at the top of the dam, where several rows of chained horses, wolves, oxen, deer, and dwarves labored to haul enormous blocks of stone into place. Their eyes looked vacant, their faces gaunt. Whether they stood on two legs or four—or, in the case of one chestnut mare with a badly swollen foreleg, three—they bent their weary backs to the slave masters' cracking whips. "They're near done."

The voice in the shadows growled, "Then we are *not* really ready yet, are we, my Harlech?"

Nervously, the warrior rubbed the long scar on his jaw. "N-no, Master."

"And my boat?"

"That's ready, aye." He pointed at the shore of the lake near the spot where the dam met this side of the canyon. "Checked it over meself."

"Its color?"

"Pure lily white, Master. Just like ye said."

There was a rustle, and the hooded sorcerer stepped out of the shadows. "A white vessel," he rasped, grinding the tip of the staff into the red rocks underfoot. "Mmmyesss, just as Merlin himself once used. Very good, my Harlech, very good."

The slab of a face relaxed slightly, and he asked, "So what's yer plan fer the slaves? After the dam's all finished, I mean."

In the darkness of the hood, a pair of eyes flashed menacingly. "Need I tell you everything? Kill them. All of them—from the biggest horse to the smallest light flyer."

Harlech's head bobbed eagerly. "Aye, Master."

The sorcerer turned and started to walk down to the road that led to the lake, then paused. "While you're at it, do something especially painful to that old elf. He *annoys* me, Harlech, with all that moaning and constant bleeding of his. I kept him alive in case I needed him to make his granddaughter obey, but he is no more use to me now."

A new gust of wind whirled across the rim, carrying dirt from the quarries and splinters of branches and bark from the clear-cut trees across the canyon. But this time the sorcerer didn't seem to notice. Grasping the staff in one pale hand, he lifted the other toward the flickering star overhead, and uttered a single word.

"Now."

With that, he strode confidently toward the lake and the white boat that awaited him.

• • •

On the canyon's other rim, near the far end of the dam, an odd assortment of spies peered out from a jumble of unused logs. But for the sturdy fingers grasping branches, the brown curls fluttering in the wind, and the shining eyes in the shadows, the companions couldn't be seen, even by the circling ghoulacas. For Tamwyn, Elli, Nuic, Henni, and Brionna held themselves as still as the stones of the dam itself.

Tamwyn crouched as close as possible to the dirt ramp that led to the top of the dam, hidden by a spray of branches and needles on a burly pine that had lived more than four hundred years before being felled. His dark eyes watched the slaves trying to move stones and scaffolding across the dam, while burly men lashed their whips. From Tamwyn's tunic pocket, Batty Lad also watched, his upright ears pink with rage.

"Terrible," muttered Elli, who was kneeling beneath the shattered roots of a hemlock. She scanned the array of crude saws, axes, and other tools that lay scattered on the ground by the ramp—as well as the body of a dead foal, its back sliced by whips, next to the canyon rim. "And those poor creatures! None of them deserved this."

"And none of them are human," added Nuic from his perch on her shoulder. His colors were all reds and browns, like the dried blood on the horse's back. "Have you noticed? The only humans here are holding whips."

"But why?" Elli scraped the last flake of bark off a branch and threw it at the ground.

"Hmmmpff. You of all people should know." Nuic paced up her shoulder so that his round form touched her ear. "Creatures almost never enslave their own kind. And even when they do, they pretend the slaves are different somehow. And inferior—so they can be forced to work."

"And some slave masters," said Brionna bitterly from behind an elm trunk, "just like to be cruel." She looked all across the dam for any sign of her grandfather, without success.

Henni, beside her, merely shook his head. It wasn't so much that he didn't approve, but that he just didn't understand how one people could enslave another. Where was the fun in that?

Keeping to the shadows of the logs, Tamwyn crept over to the others. "All right," he whispered. "Here's the plan." He glanced uncertainly at Elli. "It's not much, but it's the best I can do."

He cleared his throat. "Three things we've got to do: free those slaves, stop the sorcerer from making his crystal, and get back the staff."

"And one more thing." Brionna fingered her bowstring. "I've got to find him."

Elli, kneeling beside the elf, touched her shoulder. "I'll be there to help you." She tapped the water gourd on her hip. "With this."

Grim as Brionna's face was, it softened ever so slightly. As she returned Elli's gaze, there was a touch of hope in her eyes.

"So here's the plan," continued Tamwyn. "You two wait for my, uh, distraction . . . then make a dash onto the dam. Free as many slaves as you can. We'll create some confusion to help you. But watch those men with the whips. They'll probably have other weapons, too."

"No," corrected Brionna. "There are twelve men in all. But except for a few who carry daggers, all they have are whips. The sorcerer doesn't want them too powerful, I think." Deep furrows filled her brow. "Only Harlech carries weapons."

"Harlech?"

"The sorcerer's second in command. Big as an oak stump, he is, and . . ." Her voice trailed off momentarily. "Very brutal."

Tamwyn nodded grimly. "How many arrows do you have left?"

Brionna didn't even check her quiver. "Enough."

"Say now, what about me?" Henni thumped his small chest expectantly.

Tamwyn pointed to the far side of the lake. "You see that boat down there, just below the dam? That's for White Hands, I'm sure of it. The Lady of the Lake said that Merlin took a white boat out to deep water to draw élano to the staff. So your job, Henni, is to sink that boat."

A wide grin spread across his face. "Now *that* sounds like fun."

"Have your slingshot ready just in case."

Henni chuckled. "But of course, clumsy man."

Elli nudged Tamwyn's shoulder. "What's this distraction of yours?"

He sighed. "Well, my first thought was to make a trick fire—like the one I did with those wood shavings back in Stoneroot."

"Right," she replied with a wicked glint in her eye. "The time I almost killed you."

Tamwyn shook his head of long black hair. "*One* of the times, you mean." Then the humor vanished from his face. "But that only worked because it was small. When I tried it later on, when those ghoulacas attacked us in the forest, I couldn't keep it going."

"You've learned some things since then," offered Elli.

He shook his head. "Not enough. It takes a real wizard to do that kind of trick right."

"You mean that kind of illusion," snarled Nuic, now an irritated shade of yellowish green. "Until you realize that illusions are just as real as you are, Tamwyn, they'll always be just infantile tricks."

"Say what you like," he retorted, "but I can't count on that to work. No, the best distraction I can do is to run along the canyon rim screaming and shouting. That'll bring the ghoulacas away from the dam."

"And right onto your head!" Elli grimaced. "That's just plain suicide."

Henni stroked his chin. "Could be exciting for a while, though."

"A very short while!" Elli was adamant. "You've got to think of something else."

From Tamwyn's pocket, a small voice chattered, "Pleeease, manny man, woojaja think up somethings else?"

He shrugged. "*What* else? We're running out of time, and . . . I don't have a better idea."

"Wait," demanded Elli, shoving some curls off her forehead. "Maybe you could speak to those birds! Scare them off! The way you did the dragon, remember?"

He scrunched his nose in doubt. "That was just one creature, not twenty! And besides, I already knew the dragon's language. This idea—"

"Just might work." Elli squeezed his arm. "And keep you alive, too."

The sprite on her shoulder grunted. "For another minute or two, anyway."

Tamwyn peered up at the savage birds, listening closely to their shrieks. "Well . . . it might work."

She gave a vigorous nod. "Try it, then. And then after you've sent them away, you can go after the staff."

"One thing at a time, all right?" he said gruffly, pushing her hand away.

But the truth was, he had already been thinking about the staff. *She's right, I should go after it. Who else can possibly take it back?* But how could he tell her that he was more afraid of the staff than the sorcerer? Afraid of what might happen if he even touched it?

"Look," said Brionna, pointing to the opposite rim. A gray-cloaked figure with a staff was walking briskly down to the water's edge. "The sorcerer. He's going to the boat!"

Tamwyn pushed his doubts aside, looked skyward, and tried to concentrate. On bloodred talons and dagger-sharp beaks. On transparent wings riding the wind. On inbred anger. Hatred. The overwhelming urge to kill.

He watched the blurred streaks of the ghoulacas, concentrating all his thoughts on them. *Fly away!* he called urgently. *Fly away. Stay here and you will die!*

A new burst of shrieks suddenly rent the air. The ghoulacas flew faster, talons slashing the air. They seemed confused, or even frightened. But they were not leaving the dam!

Tamwyn glanced across the canyon. The sorcerer had stopped abruptly. He was scanning the sky, sensing something.

Fly away, urged Tamwyn. *To the nearest portal. It's your only chance to escape!*

More confusion. The birds shrieked wildly.

Go! Go now. Before you all die!

Suddenly several ghoulacas broke away and streaked toward the forest of Woodroot. Their screeches, carried by the wind, echoed across the white lake and the swath of clear-cut trees. Now more wheeled in flight. More deadly beaks and talons followed. Soon the sky above the dam was almost free of them.

"It's working!" cried Elli, almost jumping out of her hiding place among the logs.

"Hmmmpff," muttered Nuic. "Beginner's luck."

Tamwyn shot him a wink. "Just a trick, that's all." He tugged on the sleeve of Elli's Drumadian robe. "This is our chance. Let's go!"

Together, they stood and started running up the dirt ramp to the top of the dam. A stallion, chained in the lead of one group of slaves, saw them coming. The great horse whinnied, reared up on his hind legs, and kicked furiously, ripping the chain apart. Wolves, dogs, donkeys, deer, and a tethered falcon nearby halted their work, trying to learn what was happening. More of them saw the rescuers and raised their voices in howls, brays, screeches, and roars.

Surprised, the men cursed and cracked their whips, but the slaves' resistance only grew. A brawny bear snapped the links on his chains and charged at two men. A wolf-mother bit through the leashes on her cubs, then pounced on Harlech himself, just as he stepped onto the dam with Granda's limp body over his shoulder. Soon the whole dam boiled in chaos as dwarves wielded their hammers, horses their hooves, and goats their heads—all in the cause of rebellion.

That was when the cloaked figure on the far bank cast aside his staff and raised both hands above his head. Into the rising wind, he started shouting wrathful words.

39 · Strange Meetings

TAMWYN DASHED ACROSS THE TOP OF THE
dam and plunged into the fray. Close behind came Elli,
who carried Nuic in one arm like a bright red ball, and
Brionna, whose bow was already nocked with an obsidian-tipped
arrow. Henni swiftly disappeared in the melee of rioting deer,
horses, donkeys, wolves, and goats—but not before he struck a
slave master right in the eye with a pebble from his slingshot.

Seeing that some slaves were tangling themselves in the chains
that bound their necks and legs, Tamwyn grabbed a heavy stone
hammer that had been dropped by a red-bearded dwarf. He
started moving among the rioting animals, smashing chain links
until they burst apart, freeing dozens of them. The hammer rang
triumphantly as he swung blow after blow. At the same time, a
group of light flyers flew out of the quarry pit where they'd been
forced to illuminate dark places. They gathered around him, like
a glowing circle of sparks, bravely zooming into the faces of any
men who tried to interfere.

One slave he worked hard to liberate was a black mare whose

left hind leg had been so badly sliced by Harlech's sword blade that she could only hobble around painfully. But that didn't stop her, once freed, from kicking over the wooden post that tied down dozens of birds. Suddenly, their tethers released, crows and owls and cranes rose into the sky, their wings flapping with a joyous din.

Elli and Brionna, meanwhile, untied ropes, pulled off collars, and herded creatures off the top of the dam to the canyon rim. In all the confusion, they soon were separated. Elli knelt beside a goat who was bleeding from the neck, hoping to revive it with her healing water. She didn't see, though, the dagger-wielding man who came rushing at her from behind.

Brionna did. One arrow whizzed through the air—and the man fell dead, only a few paces short of Elli. Even as Brionna felt a wave of relief, she also felt a sickening twist of her stomach: But for the ghoulaca who had attacked her, and the rare meal of meat, this was the first time she had ever killed another creature.

She drew an unsteady breath, then started to rejoin Elli—when a storm of angry screeches filled the sky. She looked up, her heart frozen. For she knew that sound all too well.

"Ghoulacas!"

Called back by the sorcerer, the deadly birds sped toward the rioting slaves. Plunging at the dam, they shrieked wildly, talons and beaks ripping the air. Below, slaves and masters alike halted their battle. A hush fell over the scene; even the wailing wind held its breath.

Tamwyn, who had just freed a pair of deer, was caught by surprise. He stood on the end of the dam nearest the sorcerer's tower, peering skyward. Instantly, he focused his thoughts again on the birds. *Go back. Back, I say! If you don't, you'll . . .*

He stopped himself. The ghoulacas weren't heeding him—or even hearing his voice. Some magic more powerful than his own was blocking his words!

Spinning around, he saw the sorcerer standing on the redrock bank above the lake. The staff lay on the ground beside him. Both his arms were raised and he was chanting to the returning birds. Though his face was hidden by his hooded cloak, there was no mistaking his rage. His voice shook with anger and his words rang of death.

With the ghoulacas' return, Harlech was the first to start fighting again. Brandishing his broadsword in one hand and his spiked club in the other, he waded right into a knot of slaves midway across the dam. With one swing, he cut off the head of a great brown bear who was wrestling with a slave master. Two emaciated wolves and a young ox fell dead before he'd taken more than a few steps. His own angry roar rose above the shrieks of ghoulacas and the anguished cries of the slaves.

Brionna, seeing him, nocked a new arrow. She'd glimpsed Harlech only moments before, with Granda's limp body slung over his shoulder. Then she'd lost them both in the melee—until now. What had happened to Granda? Was he still alive? Even her sharp elf's eyes couldn't find him. But she *had* found the brute who had beaten him to the very edge of death. Grimly, she aimed straight at his chest.

Just before she released the arrow, something struck her hard in the back. A frightened colt, entangled in his shackles, stumbled right into her. Brionna went sprawling across the stones, while her arrow sailed into the air, whistling, before it plummeted into the white lake. Her bow flew out of her hand, skittering into a crowd of hooves, paws, and feet.

As ghoulacas drove down on the dam and whips cracked the air, the slaves panicked. One group of horses stampeded, crushing many smaller animals under their hooves and dragging others along by tethers and chains. Several dwarves and one stag tried to flee by jumping into the lake, but ghoulacas still pursued them, slashing viciously at any signs of life. Soon pools of red formed on the water's surface, before they melted into the dimly glowing white waves that lapped the canyon walls.

The slaves' rebellion became a rout. Everywhere on the dam lay dead and dying creatures. Some, facing the wrath of ghoulacas, chose instead to leap—not into the lake but the other way, into the rocky canyon far below. Many slaves continued to fight—and fight hard—but most of them already knew that any chance for freedom had been lost.

Tamwyn was one of those who persisted. Wielding his hammer like a hefty sword, he knocked one slave master unconscious, and threw another over the side of the dam into the lake. He found himself standing over the white water, panting hard—when suddenly he caught sight of the sorcerer.

The lone figure was climbing down the last stretch of rocks to the water's edge, one hand grasping his hood and the other holding Merlin's staff. His dark cloak ruffled in the wind like a blackened sail, while spirals of dirt blew all around him. In just a minute or two he'd reach the white boat—which was still afloat!

Tamwyn grimaced. Either Henni had forgotten about sinking the boat—just the sort of thing a hoolah would do—or he simply had never made it across the dam. But the result was the same. Tamwyn was the only one who could stop the sorcerer now.

He glanced skyward. Beyond the blur of ghoulacas' wings,

beyond all the raking red talons, he saw a single star. It glittered only weakly now, fading as swiftly as his chances.

He wiped a cut on his brow that was dripping blood into his eye. *Maybe I can still beat him to the boat! Just hope I don't have to touch the staff. . . .*

He started to run—when all of a sudden he heard raucous cries above his head. He didn't even have time to look up before the ghoulacas descended. Three killer birds landed on him at once, slashing and biting mercilessly.

Tamwyn swung his hammer hard and slammed one ghoulaca, though he couldn't tell just where. With a bone-cracking thud, the bird fell to the stones at his feet, but continued to rip at him with bloodstained talons. He kept swinging wildly, though he couldn't see his attackers well enough to fight effectively. All he could do was flail about and try to stay alive.

But that wasn't enough. Massive, curved beaks jabbed at his eyes, hands, and neck. Transparent wings battered him from all sides. He stumbled, falling to his knees. His arms ached from wielding the heavy hammer, and blood ran down the side of his neck. He tried to get up, but couldn't. He knew he'd lost his chance to stop the sorcerer.

A talon raked his cheek, just below his ear. He reeled backward and dropped the hammer. The ghoulacas' shrieks rose to a frenzy as they sensed the kill. All he could see were talons and beaks and blood.

Vaguely, Tamwyn heard another kind of shriek—deeper, not so shrill. He realized, dimly, that he'd heard that cry before somewhere. A sudden thrill ran through him. *That's the voice of an eagleman.*

"Scree!"

The winged warrior pounced on the ghoulacas with such fury that they didn't even know what struck them. Scree was everywhere at once—slashing with his talons, kicking with his legs, slapping with his silvery wings. He moved so fast that his feathered body was almost as hard to see as the transparent ghoulacas.

The birds screeched in pain and confusion. One fell to the dam, talons up. Another ended its cry with a sharp snap as a swipe of Scree's wing broke its neck. The third tumbled over the edge of the dam and splashed into the white lake.

Tamwyn's eyes connected with Scree's. As one brother rose shakily to his feet and the other hovered just above with great wings outstretched, their gaze seemed almost a solid thing, an unbreakable rope tied between them. In that moment, nothing else mattered—not their seven long years apart, not the struggles and doubts they had both endured, not the battle that continued to rage across the dam.

Everything that Tamwyn felt came together in a single word. "Scree."

"Hello, Tam."

Just as Scree started to land, Tamwyn noticed a reddish blur right behind the eagleman. Too late!

Another pair of ghoulacas shrieked wrathfully as they slammed into Scree's back. He spun through the air, out of control. The deadly beaks and talons streaked toward him. He flapped furiously, trying to right himself, but there wasn't time.

Tamwyn grabbed a chunk of stone and threw it at the ghoulacas, but missed. Meanwhile, the killer birds lunged at Scree in midair. Talons ripped at his face, gouging at his yellow-rimmed eyes. One ghoulaca reared back, about to plunge its beak into Scree's chest and rip out his heart.

"No!" shouted Tamwyn.

An arrow whizzed out of nowhere and pierced the ghoulaca's beak. It was shot so hard, and so accurately, that it passed right through the bird's head and struck the other ghoulaca somewhere on its breast. Both attackers screeched one last time and fell lifeless onto the dam.

Astonished, Scree hovered in the air, turning to see who had shot the arrow that had saved him. When he saw Brionna, standing at the edge of the fray, lower her longbow, his jaw dropped open. The elf maiden's face was full of suffering, though she stood erect and proud.

"Now we're even," she called with some satisfaction.

"Not nearly," Scree shot back, feeling his old anger swelling—along with the pain in his wing.

Brionna wheeled around and plunged back into the crowd of battling men and slaves. At the same time, the eagleman spread his silver wings wide and glided to a landing beside Tamwyn. Again, for a timeless moment, the two of them looked at each other.

"So, baby brother," Scree said at last. "Looks like you've got yourself some trouble here."

Tamwyn nodded grimly.

"Huge odds against you?"

Another nod.

"Almost no hope?"

Another nod.

Scree brushed his wing against his brother's shoulder. "Sounds just like old times."

Tamwyn smirked. "Took you long enough to find me. Were you waiting to see if I grew wings of my own?"

"No. Guess I was just waiting for someone to steal the staff."
His eagle eyes narrowed. "But I never guessed she'd lead me back
to you. Anyway, where is it now? Do you know?"

"Over there." Tamwyn pointed at the cloaked sorcerer, now
almost at the boat. "Go get it, Scree—while there's still time. But
take care! He's a sorcerer."

The eagleman's eyes gleamed at the sight of the stolen staff.
Then, turning back to his brother, he urged, "You come, too! If
he uses magic, it'll take two of us. So if I can't take the staff—you
will."

"No, Scree." Tamwyn's throat burned, from more than the
gashes on his neck. "I can't touch it. Can't."

"This is no time for modesty, Tam! You're—"

"The child of the Dark Prophecy," he finished, his voice
hoarse. "If I touch it, something terrible could happen."

Scree's yellow-rimmed eyes squinted at him. "Come on, will
you? You're about as likely to be the Dark child as I am to be the
true heir of Merlin!"

Tamwyn caught his breath. "You mean . . . you're *not*?"

The eagleman winced. "No, as much as I wanted to be. Even
said those words: *I am the true heir of Merlin*. But nothing happened! So I guess I'm just the staff's guardian." A shadow seemed
to pass across his face. "Though with the, ah, mistake I made a
while back, I'm a pretty poor one."

Tamwyn squeezed his brother's wingtip. "Whatever you did,
it can't be as stupid as the things I've done."

Scree just grunted. "We'll see. Right now, let's go get that—"

"Garr, so yer the scummy eagleman!"

They spun around to face Harlech. In one arm, his spiked

club dripped with fresh blood and clumps of fur. In the other, his broadsword, though broken at the tip, glinted dangerously. Two daggers and a rapier hung from his belt.

He kicked at the talons of a dead ghoulaca. "I seen ye kill me ghoulacas just now. Thinks yer big an' brave, don't ye? Well," he snarled, "let's see how ye do against a real foe."

The scar on his jaw shone purple. "Fight wid me, eagleman! Or are ye scared?" Scowling, he spat onto Scree's wing feathers.

The yellow eyes flashed. Out of the side of his mouth, Scree snapped, "Go now, Tam! Do what you can. I'll join you the second I'm done with this ogre."

Torn, Tamwyn hesitated. He looked from the pair of warriors to the shoreline below the dam—where the sorcerer was just about to climb into the white boat.

"Go!" commanded Scree, ducking to avoid Harlech's first swing of his sword.

Tamwyn ran, his bare feet pounding over the stones. As he neared the dirt ramp on the other side, he knew he didn't have time to climb down to the water's edge. The sorcerer would be already on the lake before he could get down there. There was no way to stop him!

Except one. Tamwyn veered toward the side of the dam, right above the boat. Even as the sorcerer raised his leg to step into the vessel, Tamwyn leaped off the high wall.

He flew through the air, legs kicking. Wind howled in his ears. At the very instant the sorcerer sensed something above him and looked up, Tamwyn landed right on top of him.

40 · Just the Faintest Heartbeat

ON TOP OF THE DAM, DOZENS OF COURA-geous horses, stags, does, and wolves fought on, locked in battle with their former masters. Whips seared the air, voices howled and whinnied, claws raked the red stones—and blood aplenty flowed. More than half the ghoulacas lay dead, many pierced by Brionna's arrows, and more lay wounded on the ground. Without the birds' help, the men found them-selves more evenly matched. What the beasts lacked in weapons, they made up for in sheer ferocity.

As the battle raged on, the golden burst of starset lit the sky. None of the creatures struggling for their lives atop the dam could pause to appreciate the luminous lines that traced the redrock canyon walls, the border forest above the clear-cut, or the wind-whipped waves of the great white lake. And yet, as rose-gold hues touched the world around them—from the highest spray of the white geyser at the top of the canyon to the deepest trench in the dry bottom of Prism Gorge—they knew that this day would end with either freedom or death.

Toward one end of the dam, two powerful warriors battled.

One wielded a club and blade; the other, sturdy wings and talons. Neither held the advantage, though both bled from several wounds.

"C'mere an' fight, ye gutless bird!" cried Harlech. The huge man jumped to slash at Scree, who was hovering just above him.

"What's the matter, old man?" taunted Scree, flapping his wings to stay out of reach as he waited for an opening to plunge. "Tired already?"

Harlech roared and hurled his club right at the eagleman's head. Scree dodged it easily. Before the weapon fell back to the dam, he dived down at the seething warrior.

But Harlech was ready. With amazing speed for such a big man, he spun aside and whipped out his rapier. Savagely, he thrust the narrow blade at Scree's chest. He missed—but cut the eagleman's feathered leg.

Scree landed on the dam, wincing in pain. Yet he didn't rest, even for an instant. Even as he touched down, he swung his wounded leg around with lightning speed. One talon ripped across Harlech's waist and severed his belt, knocking both his daggers to the ground. When Harlech glanced down, Scree swung the bony edge of his wing with brutal force into the warrior's jaw.

Harlech stumbled, momentarily dazed. Sensing the advantage, Scree lunged at him. But Harlech recovered quickly, sidestepping and slashing both swords at his foe.

Scree kicked out, knocking one of Harlech's arms aside. The rapier clattered on the stones. The warrior roared angrily, bending to pick it up—but the eagleman saw his chance. With a vengeful cry, he hurled himself at Harlech. But one of Scree's talons caught on the nearly invisible wing of a fallen ghoulaca, dragging him off balance and sending him sprawling.

Before he'd even rolled over, a bulky shadow fell over him. He stared up into the face of Harlech, whose wide mouth curled in rage.

"Yer jest . . . a rotten liddle bird, y'ar," he sneered, panting hard. "Not a real man!"

Scree grimaced, even as his golden eyes flicked to both sides, looking for some chance of escape. But there was no way! He was completely trapped.

Harlech raised both swords high. His powerful biceps flexed as he prepared to drive them down into his enemy's chest. With a heave, he thrust downward.

"Die now, ye—*aaaaagghh!*"

Harlech fell sideways, dropping to one knee. His rapier skidded across the stones. Scree instantly rolled over and bounced upright. Ready to take to the air at any instant, he stood facing Harlech, who was getting up again. Just then someone scurried over to Scree: the squat, big-bottomed warrior who had rescued him.

"Shim, you old stump! How'd you do that?"

The shrunken giant raised the stone hammer that Tamwyn had dropped. "Blue scat? What an awfulsly weapon! Even worse than this hammer I uses to smack his knee."

Scree rolled his eyes—still keeping his attention on Harlech, who was limping badly. "Guess I'm glad I brought you here, after all."

Shim's massive nose scrunched uncertainly. "Bought two beers at the ball? You're not speaking sensibensibly, not at all! But anyways, I'm verily glad you bringded me here, even with your pokily toes in me rump. Certainly, definitely, absolutely."

The eagleman's wing tousled Shim's mop of white hair. "Sorry to put you through that."

"Blue scat?" Shim scanned the ground nearby, looking disgusted. "I was hoping I didn't hears you rightly."

Suddenly Harlech roared and charged again. Scree had just enough time to knock Shim out of the way and take to the air, slashing at the burly warrior with his talons. Their deadly duel had resumed.

•   •   •

Finally, Brionna found him.

Granda lay motionless, near the middle of the dam, his back against a split block of stone. She dashed over to him, leaping over the body of a dead wolf. Her heart pounded hopefully. Oblivious to the chaos encircling her, she dropped her longbow and knelt by his side.

His frail body seemed so small. Thin trails of dried blood ran through his ragged white beard. The elf's green robe, woven of riverthread grass, was tattered and smudged with blood, yet still carried the slightest scent of lemonbalm.

Gently, she took his hand. Still warm! Yet the warmth grew less by the second. It was fleeing as fast as the gusts of wind that blew across the gleaming lake. She felt no pulse, heard no breath at all. Either he had just died or was on the very edge of death.

"Granda . . ." She bent over him, her eyes dry and unblinking. "Don't die, Granda."

Raising her head, she glanced around at the battle that still choked the top of the dam. Fighting, carnage, and death were everywhere. And courage, too: It seemed that the slaves who had not escaped or been killed were at least holding their own. One brave hawk was holding off a slave master by beating wings in his face, so that a young fawn could escape. But where was Elli? Just a little of her healing water might bring him back, as it had done for Brionna.

She cried out into the melee, "Where are you, Elli?" She could go and try to find her . . . but no, she just couldn't leave his side. Not now—nor ever again.

The elf maiden drew a halting breath. How had it come to this? What had Harlech and the sorcerer done to him while she was away? "How could I have been so stupid to leave you, Granda? This is my fault. All my fault!"

Brionna lifted his head and held it close to her chest. She kept hold of his hand, squeezing tightly. During the battle, her old whip wound had broken open and started bleeding, so a stark slash of blood now stained the back of her robe.

"Come back, Granda. Come back . . . please."

He showed no sign of life; his hand felt almost cool. Tressimir, the legendary historian of the wood elves, lay as still as the stone beneath him. It was said among the elves that Tressimir could name every living tree in the forests of El Urien—and tell the story of all the sights and sounds and smells that tree had known across the seasons. If he were to die, the loss to his people would be enormous.

The loss to Brionna, though, would be greater still. For he was her only family. Her best friend.

Her Granda.

"Brionna!" Elli's voice rang above the din of battle.

The elf maiden turned, new hope in her face.

Elli rushed over, dodging the dead wolf, and knelt beside them. She and Brionna exchanged one look, which communicated all they needed to say. Then she set down Nuic, whose dark red color deepened the instant he saw Tressimir. Seconds later, she was dribbling some of the precious water from her gourd into the old elf's mouth.

Gently, Elli tilted back his head to help him take the water. The elf's tongue was so dry that it seemed to soak in all the liquid, so she poured in some more, splattering his ragged white beard. All the while, she—like Brionna—held her breath, hoping.

Nothing happened.

Elli poured more water from the Secret Spring into his mouth. Still nothing.

In Brionna's hand, Granda's flesh grew colder. She squeezed even harder, unwilling to accept the idea he might not revive. Still no tears came to her eyes.

Elli lay her head on the old elf's chest, listening for his heart. She waited an endless moment. Just the faintest beat—that's all she needed to hear above the roars and shouts and brays of battle.

But she heard nothing. At long last, she lifted her head. She turned slowly to Nuic, whose liquid purple eyes understood right away, and then to Brionna.

"I'm sorry . . ."

Brionna just stared at her. It couldn't be true. Couldn't be. Then she held Granda's limp hand up to her face, pressed it against her cheek, and cried.

41 · A Gaping Hole

TAMWYN LANDED RIGHT ON THE SORCERER'S shoulders, crumpling him like a mushroom crushed underfoot. The staff flew out of his hand and slid across the redrock bank, rolling down to the water's edge.

For an instant, Tamwyn lay on the rocks, not so dazed that he didn't realize this was his chance to take back the staff. There it lay, the knobby piece of wood—right beside the white boat. He could lunge for it—grab it—prevent the sorcerer from ever using it.

But he hesitated. *What will happen if I touch it? All the power of the staff* . . .

The sorcerer sat up and shook his head, still covered by the hood of his gray cloak. Seeing Tamwyn, he leaped to his feet with a spray of dirt and pebbles. In one swift motion, he gathered up the staff. He stood by the lapping water of the lake, holding high his prize, as the wind howled overhead. From under his hood, he glared down at this fool who had dared attack him.

The sorcerer extended one pale hand, with smooth skin and perfectly clipped fingernails, toward Tamwyn. Before the young man could even move, a bolt of fire seared through his entire body. He shouted in pain as flames blazed inside his brain, chest, and limbs. *I'm burning! Burning!*

Calmly, the sorcerer held him like this, watching him writhe in agony. Several seconds passed. At last, the pale hand dropped. A chortle of satisfaction bubbled from the sorcerer's throat, as Tamwyn lay on the rocks, free of the flames but too stunned to move.

"Who are you, wretch? How dare you interfere with my plans?"

Weakly, Tamwyn sat up. He still winced from the intense burning behind his eyes. "Your plans are to destroy Avalon," he spat.

Under his hood, the sorcerer nodded. "Quite so." He glanced up at the sky, where the lone star of the Wizard's Staff winked with its very last light. "Mmmyesss, the end of Merlin's Avalon . . . and the beginning of another."

"I don't think so."

The sorcerer ground the tip of the staff into the rocks beside the boat. "I care nothing about what you think! Now tell me, wretch. Who are you?"

Tamwyn sat up straight, though fire still seared his every muscle and bone. "I am one of many who will fight you—and stop you."

A throaty cackle came from beneath the hood. "You believe that, mmmyesss? Well, I do not." He burst into a high, hissing laughter. "You are the prophesied heir, aren't you? Ha! So this is the best that Merlin could do! A ragtag boy with no more magic than my thumbnail."

Tamwyn clenched his fist. "I'm not the true heir. But I'm still going to stop you."

"Is that so? Well then, tell me—before I crush you like a

snail under my boot. Just how do you plan to defeat the greatest wielder of magic in history?"

Tamwyn slammed his fist into his palm. "You're no great magic wielder! Just a tyrant, a slave driver, a plague in person's form."

A hiss rose into the air and was swallowed by the sweeping wind. "Is that what you think? Well, you are wrong! My name is now a secret . . . but I am soon to be the most powerful wizard of all times, mmmyesss. And something more, my pitiable snail. I am going to be hailed in time as a great liberator, who finally recognized the superiority of humanity and built a new world around that ideal. Indeed, the day will come when I am seen as the true savior of mankind."

"Never!" Tamwyn started to say more, but stopped when he caught sight of a man and a bear, both torn and bloodied, toppling together off the side of the dam. Meanwhile, all across the dam, dozens more enslaved creatures still fought for their freedom.

He turned back to the sorcerer. "If you really were all the things you say, you wouldn't hide your name. Or your face, beneath that cloak."

The wind howled louder, hurling spray off the white lake. Beads of water pelted the rocky bank and the boat. But the sorcerer stood fast, as sturdy as the dam, while the wind swept over him and tugged at the corners of his cloak.

"Because you soon shall die, runt wizard, I will show you who I am." He thrust back his hood. "Behold, the face of the liberator!"

Tamwyn gaped in horror. For he was staring at the most mutilated face he'd ever seen—so mutilated that it seemed more the face of a cadaver than a living man. A deep, jagged scar ran diagonally from the stub of what had once been an ear down to his chin, taking out a big chunk of his nose on the way. Where his right eye should have been, there was only a hollow hole, full of scabs and swollen veins. His mouth had been burned shut on one side, leaving only a lipless gash. Much of his skin had been melted by something stronger than flames.

For a long moment, as water lapped on the shore beside them, the sorcerer studied Tamwyn with his lone, lidless eye. Then the scarred mouth sneered, "So now you see my face! Look closely, for I was not always so handsome. No, indeed! This was a gift, mmm-yesss. From the greatest source of evil in all the ages of Avalon."

Still reeling from the sight, Tamwyn could only whisper, "Who? Who did that to you?"

"Merlin."

Tamwyn scowled, almost unable to look at the face. "Then . . . you must have provoked him to do it."

"No!" thundered the sorcerer, pounding the staff down so hard that chips of stone flew. "I took no side in the War of Storms, none at all. But Merlin, in all his greatness and wisdom, thought I had. He refused to believe me—his own cousin, descended from Tuatha! So when I met secretly with a group of flamelon traders and their gobsken allies, just to barter for goods, he attacked us."

Within the narrow slit of a mouth, teeth ground vengefully. "I was the only survivor. But I paid for my will to live, mmmyesss, with centuries of sheer pain."

The sorcerer bent toward Tamwyn. "And so your master made two mistakes that day. One was attacking me, the young wizard-in-training called Kulwych. And the other, far worse—leaving me alive."

Kulwych raised the staff. It glittered darkly in the starlight of early evening. "Now, using Merlin's very own staff, which he was so foolish to leave behind, I shall remake his world . . . and win my ultimate revenge."

"You're going to make a crystal of élano," blurted Tamwyn.

The lidless eye opened a bit wider. "Very good, for a snail. But you have no idea why, do you?"

Tamwyn nodded, sweeping his shoulders with long black locks. "Of course I do," he lied, hoping to trick the sorcerer into revealing his plans. "But élano is for making life—not destroying it. So you are doomed to fail."

Kulwych chortled deep in his throat. "You know nothing at all! Mmmyesss . . . I have great plans for my pure crystal of élano. Great plans."

His slit-mouth turned down in a jagged scowl. "How unfortunate that you will not live to see them bear fruit."

He turned the staff slowly in the air. Starlight danced on the gnarled wood, even between his thin white fingers. "Élano is much more powerful than anyone, even my nemesis, has ever understood. Why, all I needed to bond the stones of my dam, to seal them tight, was a bit of this lake water—because of the élano it holds. And that is but a trace! When I possess an entire crystal . . . well, that need not concern you."

Kulwych turned toward the white boat. The scarred, melted skin of his face gleamed monstrously with the reflected glow of the élano-rich lake. "Now, before you die, I shall grant you a boon. You shall witness the creation of my crystal of power! Then you will watch me break Merlin's staff upon my knee. And then, mmmyesss, I shall burn you with the very same fires your master used on me long ago—but, unlike him, I will not bungle the job."

He made a quick motion as if he were flicking an insect off the back of one hand. Suddenly cords of rope sprouted from the air and wound themselves around Tamwyn like aerial vines. There was no time to wriggle free, let alone grab his dagger. In the blink of an eye, he was tightly bound.

Kulwych chortled quietly, then with his staff in hand, stepped into the small boat. The moment his foot touched the floor, however, there was a loud snap and splash. An entire plank broke loose! His foot went right through the bottom of the boat. Water rushed in, starting to swamp the craft.

"Maggots of Merlin!" cursed the sorcerer. He wobbled unsteadily, struggling to keep himself from falling into the boat—or the lake.

Well done, Henni, thought Tamwyn. *I shouldn't have doubted you*. He rocked wildly on the bank, trying to free himself from the ropes. But he couldn't even budge an arm.

Still cursing, Kulwych finally extracted himself. His leg was soaked up to the knee, along with the bottom of his cloak. Angrily, he jabbed a white finger at the boat, uttered a spell, and lifted his hand. The boat lifted right along with it, until it sat in the air an arm's length above the lake, water cascading out through the hole.

Keeping the boat airborne, Kulwych spat out another spell and twisted his finger slightly. The missing plank rose out of the water and fastened itself to the bottom. Finally, with a toss of his hand, he let the boat drop back down to the lake with a resounding splash.

He whirled on Tamwyn. "So much for your infantile games!" He barked out another command and jerked his hand toward the boat. Tamwyn himself was lifted into the air and hurled into the vessel. He struck the sidewall with his head, hard enough to drive splinters into his cheek, then rolled to the middle of the stern.

The hideous face of the sorcerer, splashed with water, glistened like rotting flesh. He stepped into the bow of the boat, then made a sound resembling a whistle, but throatier. The boat began to glide swiftly across the water, luminous waves lapping against the sides.

As if called by some unseen voice, Tamwyn looked up into the darkening sky. The sorcerer did, as well. Together, they saw one star, the last of its constellation, wink for the final time—then go out. Though this star was surrounded by hundreds and hundreds of others, it left a gaping hole in the celestial field. Tamwyn knew, without understanding why, that something more than a star had been extinguished. Something brighter even than light, and larger even than the sky.

The staff in the sorcerer's hand seemed to shudder. Then, from the depths of its gnarled wood, came a long, low groan of despair.

"Well, well," clucked the sorcerer in satisfaction, "now you have proof that my time has come."

He kicked Tamwyn's bound body with the toe of his wet boot. "And do not comfort yourself with delusions that the death of the Wizard's Staff is merely symbolic. No indeed! The end of those stars means a whole new beginning for Rhita Gawr—and myself. Whatever happens now, we shall triumph."

• • •

Elli couldn't watch Brionna and the lifeless body of her grandfather any longer. She rose to her feet, shaking her head.

All around, fighting raged on, though the ranks on both sides had thinned. Many slaves had escaped and run off the dam to hide somewhere on the canyon cliffs; most who remained were either gravely wounded or still battling for their lives. One of those still fighting was an eagleman who held himself aloft with immensely powerful wings and then dropped back to the dam to battle a huge man wielding a bloodied broadsword. The eagleman seemed to be holding his own, but just barely.

Could that be Scree? Elli wondered. *But how . . .*

"Look up," growled Nuic, who had climbed onto the split block of stone that supported the dead elf. His small hand pointed at a spot in the sky just above the horizon.

Elli lifted her head and stared. The last star, the final flame in the constellation that had meant so much to Coerria, as well as Rhia, blinked weakly . . . then went out. The darkness that took its place seemed dense, almost solid, as if a great black door had slammed on the spot.

"What does it mean?"

The voice was Brionna's. Elli turned to her and said hoarsely, "I don't know. Do you, Nuic?"

The old sprite, vibrating with gray and black, said nothing.

Elli scrutinized the elf maiden's face, etched with new lines of suffering. Then, noticing the bloody whip mark that ran across her back, she said softly, "I was too late to help your grandfather . . . but maybe I can, at least, do something for you." She tapped her water gourd. "That scar on your back could be healed, I think."

Brionna shook her head. The stains on her cheeks shone dully in the starlight. Pressing Granda's cold hand to her chest, she said, "It's a mark of my stupidity, as well as my shame. I will always bear that scar . . . and others."

Elli bit her lip and looked away. As her gaze moved across the glowing waters of the lake, she suddenly spied the sorcerer, standing in his boat. His face seemed wrong somehow, as if he were wearing a mask. He was holding the staff with its tip in the water, and something odd was happening.

She froze. There, tied up in the stern, was Tamwyn! Then came a blinding flash of light—and her last hope vanished as completely as the Wizard's Staff.

42 · Water and Fire

WAVES GLISTENED ON THE LAKE, BOTH from the light of evening stars and from the powerful magic within the water. As the white boat glided soundlessly to the deep water by the middle of the dam, the sorcerer, standing in the bow, nodded confidently. He snapped his fingers and the vessel instantly came to a halt. Tiny waves tapped against the sides, drumming expectantly, like hundreds of watery fingers.

Tamwyn, bound so tight that he could hardly breathe, watched his captor's mouth twist into a near-grin. He could see, behind the sorcerer, the great stone dam that spanned the canyon. Brutal fighting continued there, and amidst the fray, Tamwyn caught a glimpse of Scree's silver wings flapping in the air above Harlech's sword.

"Now," declared Kulwych, moving slightly closer to one side of the boat. "The new beginning."

He grasped the staff with both his hands, whose flesh gleamed as white as the water of the lake. Carefully, he held the staff upright over the water, so that its tip was only a hand's width over the waves. Then, concentrating on the gnarled wood with his one eye, he began to chant:

> *Hark now, élano, soul of the Tree:*
> *Seek out the magic, the staff Ohnyalei.*

Slowly, he lowered the tip into the lake. At the instant it touched the water, small white ripples bubbled up around it. They grew rapidly, growing more frothy, until the water around the staff churned and bubbled like boiling milk.

Kulwych held tight as the staff shook violently. All the while, at the very top, a shining white speck started to form. Subtle tones of blue and green sparkled in its crystalline core as it grew swiftly larger and brighter.

The crystal! Tamwyn struggled beneath the ropes, knowing that he had just seconds left to free himself. By sucking in his abdomen, he managed to twist his right arm slightly. His finger brushed against the handle of his woodsman's dagger. *Just a little farther . . .*

There! He reached the handle. Clutching hold, he nudged the dagger out of its sheath and tilted it upward. Then, moving his hand, he slid the blade back and forth like a saw.

Even as he began to cut the rope, though, he could see that he was too late. The crystal on top of the staff was swelling rapidly. Already it was as large as the one Rhia wore in her amulet of leaves.

Madly, Tamwyn moved the dagger. In just a few more seconds . . .

"At last," declared Kulwych, his voice full of pride. The wild wind howled, seeming to magnify his voice. "I have done it! I am the equal of Merlin . . . and soon his superior."

He lifted the staff out of the lake. Immediately the water ceased frothing. Kulwych stood proudly in the boat, licking the edge of his slit-mouth in satisfaction. Triumphantly, he plucked the crystal from the staff and held it high.

It flashed in the starlight—a blinding flash of deep magic. And extraordinary power.

Suddenly, Tamwyn knew what he must do. Still cutting on the ropes that held him, he bent his thoughts toward the crystal. For while the sorcerer stood savoring his plans, whatever they might be, Tamwyn had made a plan of his own.

Fire. His last fire illusion had failed—so miserably that he hadn't even wanted to try it again on the ghoulacas. But this time he couldn't fail. Couldn't! He stared at the crystal, taking in all its brightness, all its light.

He thought of Nuic's words: *Illusions are just as real as you are, Tamwyn.* He thought of his skill at building fires in the wilderness, a skill he'd never been taught but simply gleaned from the ways of wood and flame. And he thought about the strange fires that burned within him—a gift from his father, born of a wizard and a deer-woman, and his flamelon mother, whose fiery orange eyes had often warmed him as a child.

Burn! he called to the crystal. *Bright as a fire. Bright as a star!*

The crystal exploded in flames. Mock flames, yes, but real enough to cause Kulwych to shout in surprise and drop his precious crystal. A look of horror on his scarred face, he grabbed at it before it fell into the lake.

Tamwyn concentrated all the harder. *Burn! Be flames, be fire.* Instinctively, he blew a long breath of air, as if he were blowing on a spark in kindling. Meanwhile, under the ropes, he worked the dagger with all his strength.

Just as Kulwych caught hold of the crystal, a wind gusted over the water, fanning the illusory flames. The fire burst higher than his head, licking at his scarred face. He shouted again and bobbled the prize. With an agonized cry, he lunged for it.

Too far! The boat tipped sharply. Tamwyn leaned, rocking it farther. At that very moment his dagger broke through, slicing his bonds. With all his weight, he threw his body into the sidewall.

The boat flipped over. Kulwych pitched over the side with a splash that swallowed his scream. Tamwyn, too, plunged into the white water. When he came up again, sputtering for air, he was some distance from the vessel. Realizing he still clutched his dagger, he pushed it back into its sheath—and then saw, floating beside him, the staff.

He reached for it, but caught himself. If he touched it, he could ruin everything. And yet, if he didn't . . . His fingers quivered. He almost touched it, then hesitated. Behind him, he heard the sputters and curses of Kulwych as he splashed toward the overturned boat.

Tamwyn took a deep breath—and grabbed the staff. As he squeezed its wooden shaft in his hand, he felt the vaguest buzz of power down in his bones. But nothing more. No disaster. He may have been Dark Flame, and the child of a very dark destiny, but he could still hold the staff of a wizard.

At once, an idea struck him. There might be just enough time—if he moved very fast.

He swam toward the dam, kicking with all his might. One arm paddled vigorously, while the other clutched the staff. At the same time, he sent the same desperate thought to Elli, Scree, Brionna, Nuic, Henni, the remaining slaves—everyone he could possibly reach. *Get off the dam! Whatever you must do, get off it. Now!*

He glanced behind him. Kulwych, dripping wet, was trying to climb onto the overturned boat. But the hull was slippery and he kept sliding back into the lake. The sorcerer was hampered by using only one of his hands, since the other was closed into a fist.

He still has the crystal!

Tamwyn kicked harder. Gasping for air, he drove through the water like a frenzied fish. Behind him, he heard Kulwych bellowing in wrath. This time, though, he didn't take time to look back.

He swam into a dark shadow. The massive stones of the dam loomed above him, blocking the stars. One stroke, another—and at last his hand touched the hard, chipped stone. Panting heavily, he lifted the staff out of the water, pointed the dripping tip toward the dam, and spoke the chant he'd heard moments before:

> *Hark now, élano, soul of the Tree:*
> *Seek out the magic, the staff Ohnyalei.*

He heard Kulwych hurl curses—and spells. Something magical caught his arm, holding it in the air.

Tamwyn struggled to move the staff, to do the one truly right thing he'd ever done. He pulled with every scrap of strength, kicking to stay afloat. His arm moved just a bit, then a bit more.

All at once, he broke free. His arm surged forward. The tip of Merlin's staff slammed into the face of the dam with a shower of sparks.

In that instant, several things happened. The stones began to quiver and buckle. A rumble gathered from somewhere deep inside the structure, rapidly growing into a tumultuous roar. And a luminous white dust appeared on the staff, as if it had been frosted with starlight.

With the bond between the stones stripped away, the dam could hold no longer. All the water of the enormous lake pushed against the blocks of stone, seeped between the cracks, and flowed around the canyon rim—seeking to break free at last. In one gargantuan gush of water and stone, the dam burst apart. Water exploded all around Tamwyn, tossing him like an acorn on a raging river.

He knew he'd soon die, smashed on the canyon floor below. Yet even as he flew over Prism Gorge, riding a wild tide of froth and spray, he knew he'd succeeded. He would die, but so would Kulwych . . . and all his plans.

He fell faster, plunging downward. Giant waves spilled about him, slapping him with liquid limbs, spinning him in every direction. He was pummeled, beaten, hurled around with ever more force.

Then something stabbed him, piercing tunic and flesh. It felt like knives. Or perhaps . . . talons.

43 · Dark Flame

TWO DAYS LATER, IN THE DEEP GREENERY OF Woodroot, Tamwyn stood under a towering beech tree. Its branches hung so fully with leaves that they seemed to flow from the trunk like rippling green rivers. The trunk itself was so massive that ten men his size, with outstretched arms, could not encircle it. Wood elves believed it was the oldest tree in all of El Urien.

Its name, Brionna had told him a few moments before, was Elna Lebram, meaning *deep roots, long memories.* Among its bulging, twisted roots were buried all the wood elves' greatest scholars, teachers, and bards. Some thought that was why the ancient tree's bark still gleamed as smooth as a young sapling.

Today, as Tamwyn watched, those roots accepted another body: Tressimir, cherished historian of his people. Hundreds of elves filled the grove around the beech, all wearing deep green robes, all watching in silence. Nine of them, each one symbolizing a point on the wood elves' compass, lowered the body into the ground. Even wrapped in several layers of shrouds—woven from silverplume flowers, laurel roots, and leaves of everlasting—the old elf seemed very small indeed.

Brionna stood by the grave, stiff as a tree on a windless ridge. When at last the body of her grandfather had been placed among the roots, she bent gracefully, adding a wreath of fresh hemlock. She'd chosen that wreath because its fragrance was both sweet, like her memories, and bitter, like her longing.

Beside her stood Elli. Her face was grim, like that of the dark gray pinnacle sprite on her shoulder. Shim sat nearby on one of the burly roots, wiping the occasional tear from his swollen nose. Even Henni, who now wore in his headband the feather of an owl he had saved on the dam, looked subdued.

As dark loam was poured into the grave, creating a fertile mound, the elves began to sing. Their voices, more gentle than rising mist, filled the forest, weaving the varied threads of Tressimir's life into an embroidered ballad that was no less colorful, and no less luminous, than the autumn leaves around them. But while the song celebrated Tressimir's life, it also mourned his loss.

As Tamwyn listened, holding the staff that glittered with white élano, he wished he'd known the old elf. Even briefly. He raised a hand to his shoulder, rubbing one of the cuts from Scree's talons. He could still feel everything he'd felt at the very moment of his rescue: the pinch of those talons; the surprise that he wasn't going to die after all; the overwhelming relief that the dam had been destroyed; and the wonder at seeing the lake burst free at last, pour down Prism Gorge, and break into a rainbow of rivers that would bring water—and color—to many lands.

And yet, even as he'd been carried to safety, he worried that

Kulwych's evil work had not ended. Had he survived the dam's collapse? Did he still have the pure crystal of élano?

"There you are, baby brother."

Tamwyn spun around. Scree, bare-chested in his human form, ducked under a leafy branch of the beech. For a moment his yellow-rimmed eyes gazed intently at his brother, then turned to the gleaming staff.

Tamwyn held it out to him. "Time you took this back, don't you think?"

Scree scratched the hook of his nose. "No, Tam. I think you should hang on to it—at least for a while." He gave a half-grin. "I'm just getting used to life without it."

Tamwyn scowled. "You are not! I can see right through you, clear as ever. You and Elli—"

"Think you're as stupid as a headless troll," finished Scree. "Look, you may have had your eyes closed when you blew that dam to bits, but I didn't! I saw what you did."

"You mean what the *staff* did."

"In your hands." He lowered his voice to a rough whisper. "I'm not sure, but just maybe the person I was saving it for, all those years, was you."

Tamwyn shook his head. "I don't believe that. I just don't."

"Fine, then. But don't try to give it back to me. Look, for the past two days, I've been feeling freer than a fledgling! Like I'm finally done with my task."

He clenched his fist. "The only thing I want to squeeze right now is the neck of that cursed swordsman on the dam. Coward! Just when I finally had him, he jumped into the lake to get away."

"Maybe someday you'll find him again."

"He'd better hope not."

The elves' singing ended abruptly. Their ethereal tones hovered among the leaves for several seconds. Then, led by Brionna, all the elves flowed across the grove like a deep green cloud. At a sparkling stream that ran into the deepest part of the forest, they stopped.

Rows of resinwax candles lined the stream bank. As Tamwyn and Scree looked on, each elf took one candle, lit it, and placed it upon a wide, rounded leaf. In a flash, Tamwyn recognized this ceremony from stories he'd heard about the elves: It was the Procession of Flames, a tradition that dated back to the days of Lost Fincayra.

He recognized something else, too. The leaf came from the cupwyll shrub that grew all year round in the streams of Stoneroot, and apparently also here in Woodroot. The leaf's shape reminded him of the tiny quartz bell on his belt, and he glanced down at it, glad that it had survived his long journey.

He patted the pocket of his tunic, from which came a quiet, whistling snore. Batty Lad, too, had survived the journey. Sure, he'd caught a cold that had made him sneeze for most of the past two days, after their swim in the lake. But his quirky little spirit, and those glowing eyes, hadn't dimmed at all.

Gently, the elves set the rounded leaves, and the candles they held, upon the stream. The water carried them away, very slowly, like so many sparks blown from a fire. As they flowed downstream into the darkening boughs, the small flames seemed to grow taller, and perhaps a bit brighter, before they faded into the shadows.

The elves started to sing once more, a slow and somber melody. But this time their voices were so quiet that Tamwyn caught only a few words:

A candle lit, a candle doused,
a starset in the morning:
How brief the life, the love it housed
that dies while still aborning.

He thought suddenly of the bearded bard on the hill, whose fragment of a song had led them to Brionna—and ultimately, the staff. Could that have been intentional? Or just another bizarre coincidence?

As the elves continued to sing, Tamwyn heard, in his mind, not their voices—but the bard's. He heard again the song on the hill, which ended with that mysterious phrase, *the Thousand Groves*. And he also heard, from their first meeting near the dung heap, the bard's haunting description of Avalon:

A world part Heaven and part Earth—
And part what wind that blows.

Tamwyn turned to Scree, who was watching not the candles, but the elves. One elf in particular. Brionna had stopped singing and stood aloof and silent, her head bowed. When she'd bent over to put her candle on the stream, the whip cut had broken open again. Though her long locks of hair still shone, they couldn't hide the rough red slash that ran across her back.

Scree sensed his brother's gaze but kept watching Brionna. He cleared his throat. "You know . . . maybe it's possible . . . she's not quite as bad as I thought."

Trying to hide his grin, Tamwyn said nothing.

"Damn good shot, too."

Tamwyn nodded. "Not to mention beautiful."

"I suppose so," Scree said breezily. "In an elvish sort of way." Suddenly he slapped his own forehead. "What in Avalon am I thinking? I must have cracked my eggshell back there on the dam! She *hates* me. And if I had any sense at all, I'd still hate her."

He paused, chewing his tongue. "It's just that, right now, there's some part of me that doesn't really want to hate her. That wants to . . . well, help her."

"You could try."

Scree looked sorely tempted, but all of a sudden his face hardened. "Don't be crazy! The longest conversation she's ever had with me was after she shot me out of the sky."

Tamwyn put a hand on his brother's muscular shoulder. "Whatever she did to you, she did to save her grandfather."

Scree's jaw relaxed slightly. "That's true, I suppose. People will do some pretty wild things to save their only family."

"Right. Like pushing them headfirst into portals."

Scree almost smiled.

"So why don't you just go over there and say something?"

"I'm not much with words, Tam."

"Then don't say anything. Maybe just being nearby will help."

The eagleman frowned and faced him. "If you're so frill-feathered wise about these things, why don't you go over there yourself?"

"Because, brother," Tamwyn said with a twinkle, "it's your magic she needs, not mine."

He eyed Scree for a moment, then cocked his head toward the burial mound in the tree's roots. Elli was still standing there, her face solemn. "And besides, I have something else to do."

Scree smirked and shook his head. "Guess we're both hopeless."

Tamwyn, who had started to walk away, glanced back at him. "We must be related somehow."

As he stepped over the twisted roots, steadying himself with the staff, he considered Elli. So much about her—starting with those unruly curls—reminded him of Rhia, the Lady of the Lake. They were a lot alike, those two, and not merely in the way they looked.

Nuic, perched on Elli's shoulder, looked up first. His colors warmed a bit, showing some swirls of pink amidst the gray. "Well, Elliryanna," he said gruffly, "we have a visitor." Then, with a mock bow, he added, "If it isn't Tamwyn Eopia, the great illusionist."

"Trickster," he corrected with a grin. "But thanks to you, I'm learning."

"Hmmmpff. Even for a slow learner, you're awfully slow."

Elli's face was still grim, but her hazel green eyes brightened at seeing him. She wrapped her own hand around the staff, just above his, so their fingers barely touched. "You see," she said with a knowing look, "nothing bad happened when you touched it."

"You were right," he admitted.

"Better get used to saying that," snapped Nuic. "If you plan to spend time with us, that is."

Despite herself, Elli smiled. "Nuic, you're impossible!"

The sprite's colors turned to an offended shade of maroon. "I wasn't speaking about me, Elliryanna. I was speaking about *you*."

She shook her head, bouncing her curls every which way. "So how are you feeling?" she asked Tamwyn, tapping her water gourd. "All healed from the battle?"

"Mostly." He took a long, deep breath. "But I just can't stop thinking about the sorcerer. About what he said when the last star went out. He told me, *The end of those stars means a whole new beginning for Rhita Gawr and myself.* And then he added: *Whatever happens now, we shall triumph.*"

Elli looked suddenly grim again. "The stars! What does that mean?"

No one answered.

She tapped the gnarled top of the staff. "At least you still have this. How does it feel to be its master?"

He looked at the shaft, sparkling so white, and bit his lip. "I don't think anyone could really be its master. Not even Merlin." Then he frowned. "And besides, I'm still the child of the Dark Prophecy, remember?"

"Of course I remember, you buffoon! But didn't you hear what Rhia said about choosing your destiny? Don't you realize what happened at the dam?"

"I got lucky, that's all."

"Lucky!" Her face flushed angrily and Tamwyn felt a sudden fear that she'd punch him in the eye again. But she just brought her face up close to his, and declared, "I told you, you could still be *both* the child of the Dark Prophecy *and* the true heir of Merlin. *Like a brother,* in the Lady's words—but a brother to yourself. It's possible."

"No!" He twisted the staff, driving its tip into the soft moss between the roots of the old beech. "That's ridiculous."

She glared at him. "By the elbows of the Elders, Tamwyn! Have you tried to find out? Have you said those words while holding the staff?"

"No. And I'm not going to, either."

"Then how can you be so sure?"

"Listen, Elli!" he shouted, not caring that almost everyone in the grove heard him and turned his way. "Get this straight once and for all! There is absolutely no way—none at all—that *I am the true heir of Merlin.*"

A blinding flash of green light exploded from the staff, filling the grove. Before Tamwyn could even move his hand, the light transformed into thousands of tiny green sparks that crackled noisily as they rose into the leaves, as radiant as stars. At the same time, the white frosting of élano sizzled, steamed, and melted into the shaft.

Tamwyn stared down at the staff, which seemed now to glow from within. As he watched, a series of seven runes appeared, etched in the same pulsing green light that he'd seen inside the portal. And, to his surprise, he understood them instantly.

First came a butterfly, symbol for change. Then a pair of soaring hawks, wingtips touching, for bonds of the heart. Next, a cracked stone, for freedom and protection. Then came the rune of a sword, for the power of a true name; a star within a circle, for the hidden connections that allow leaps between places and times; and a dragon's tail, for the value of all forms of life, and the peril of eliminating even one. Last of all, glowing mysteriously, was the rune of an eye, for the importance of seeing beneath the surface of things . . . and into one's own soul.

Slowly, Tamwyn raised his face to look at Elli. "I guess you were right. Again."

She laughed, the spiraling laugh that had the lilt of a meadowlark. "Remember what Rhia said? *You have both light and dark within you—no less than Merlin.*" She squeezed his forearm. "Sounds about right for someone named Dark Flame."

Tamwyn smiled, though a bit sheepishly. He glanced over at Brionna, who, like all the wood elves, was watching him with amazement. Then he saw Scree, not far from her, smirking broadly. But he didn't notice Henni, who had climbed into the beech tree to try to catch some of the glowing green stars—until the hoolah hurled a chunk of bird droppings at his head.

"Hmmmpff," said Nuic with some satisfaction. "I only wish our friend Llynia, the Chosen One, were here now! She wouldn't know quite what to make of her lowly porter."

Shim, whose very large rump was resting on a nearby root, nodded knowingly. "I seeses all this happen beforely, to Merlin."

The dwarfish little fellow peered closely at Tamwyn. "I can't say for certainly, definitely, absolutely . . . but I thinks that you is lotsly like Merlin. And so be muchly careful, you hears? Because he was full of madness!"

With a chuckle, Tamwyn gave a nod.

"Oh, and could I ask justly one thing?" His pink eyes swelled hopefully. "If everly you find the wizardly way to make someone smallsy who got bigsy, then woefully smallsy, bigsy all over again, could you helps me?"

Though he wasn't really sure just what he'd been asked, Tamwyn nodded again.

"So now," asked Elli softly, "what will you do next?"

Tamwyn studied her for a long moment, then looked skyward. He seemed to be gazing beyond the leaves and branches overhead, beyond even the sky itself.

"I'm going up there," he said with quiet determination. "To the stars! The way my father tried to go. The way Merlin did, long ago—when he lit the stars of the Wizard's Staff."

Still peering upward, he grasped the staff firmly. "I'm going to find the way. Yes—and light them again. Before that sorcerer can do any more damage."

He lowered his voice and grinned. "And while I'm up there, I just might go for a run among the stars."

Elli thought back to High Priestess Coerria, and the secret they had pondered in the steaming Baths—a way to find the true heir of Merlin. At first, those brief lines had seemed impossible to understand. Especially the final line, which now, at last, rang true: *The light of stars shall bear.*

She smiled, for both Coerria and herself.

Shim, though, had a different reaction. For once, he'd heard at least well enough to get the gist of what Tamwyn was saying, and he shook his old head. "I tolds you, I didly. I tolds you he is full of madness!"

Tamwyn lowered his gaze, and his eyes met Elli's. "But first," he declared, "I have something else to do. Something important."

She raised an eyebrow. "And what is that?"

"Make you a new harp."

Elli laughed. "Yes, you will! By the Thousand Groves, you will."

Epilogue · The Encircling Shadow

FAR AWAY FROM THE GREEN GLADES OF Woodroot, in the darkness of an underground cavern, a frail light burned. Smothered in blackness, its white glow wavered, as if it were the last remaining coal from a long-abandoned fire, or a lone candle holding its own against eternal night.

Yet this was no fire coal, and no candle. This was a crystal.

Shimmering with white light, and subtle tones of blue and green, the crystal of élano sat on a stone pedestal. Though very small, it pulsed defiantly, pushing back the heavy curtains of darkness. Stray beams shot out from its core, flickering over the cavern walls, the torn strands of a spider's web—and the hideously scarred face of a sorcerer.

Kulwych scowled at the crystal, his hollow eye socket pinched in anger. "Damned crystal! Do as I command, mmmyesss, or know my wrath!"

The crystal merely swelled a bit brighter.

"Do as I say," growled the sorcerer. His perfectly manicured fingers curled into fists. "You must obey me! I command you to darken, to bend to my will. How dare you resist my spells? My magic? Do you not know that I am the greatest power in all of Avalon?"

"No," crackled a thin, disembodied voice from the darkest corner of the cavern. "You are not."

At the sound of this voice, Kulwych gasped. He spun around to face the corner, which was growing blacker and denser by the second. A sudden sizzling arose from the spot, like molten lava flowing into the sea.

Kulwych straightened, trembling, as the sizzling sound grew louder. Even the white crystal flickered uncertainly. Slowly, very slowly, a shape began to form in the darkness—a spiral, darker than smoke, coiling like a vaporous snake.

Just then a heavy door swung open and a burly gobsken, carrying a torch in one hand and a spear in the other, burst into the cavern. He started to speak, when the sizzling coil whipped at his throat, quick as a bolt of black lightning. The gobsken's body, along with his severed head, dropped to the floor. The head's unseeing eyes rolled onto the fallen torch, extinguishing its flame, and the putrid scent of burning flesh filled the chamber.

"We tolerate no interruptions," crackled the black coil. "And no failures."

"You!" exclaimed the sorcerer, rubbing his pale hands anxiously. "I, well, didn't expect, didn't think—"

"Think what, Kulwych?" spat the spiral as it floated toward him. "Didn't think that you would see me so soon? Or that I would be strong enough yet to make the journey?" The coil crackled vengefully. "You underestimate me, Kulwych."

"N-n-no," protested the sorcerer. "Never."

The dark being came steadily closer. Whenever it touched the floor of the cavern, it crackled and left a mark, charred and steaming, upon the stone.

Kulwych took a step backward. But before he could speak again, the coil lashed out at him. He shrieked and stood frozen—completely motionless except for his one twitching eye—as the spiral wrapped around his neck, not touching his skin, but only a finger's width away.

"I, I . . . have never," croaked the sorcerer, shivering with fright, "doubted you."

The sizzling shadow spun around his neck, circling slowly. At last it spoke again, its voice echoing within the walls of stone. "If you care to survive, Kulwych my pet, that had better be so."

The sorcerer could only gulp.

An endless moment passed. Then, in a flash, the coil pulled away, moving toward the crystal that continued to pulse with light.

"Now, Kulwych, you shall learn about true power."

The sorcerer rubbed his neck and nodded meekly.

The dark shadow coalesced even more, until it seemed almost solid, a rope of blackness suspended in the air beside the crystal. "First I will show you how to corrupt this crystal. Next, how to use it to defeat all our enemies. And finally, how to wield it to conquer this world."

From the depths of the coil came a snarling, sizzling laugh. "And other worlds, as well."

The sorcerer bit his fingernails. Though his voice shook, he managed to say, "Yes, my lord Rhita Gawr."

A Brief History of Avalon

AS ONE WORLD DIES, ANOTHER IS BORN. IT IS a time both dark and bright, a moment of miracles.

In the mist-shrouded land of Fincayra, an isle long forgotten is suddenly found, a small band of children defeats an army of death, and a people disgraced win their wings at last. And in the greatest miracle of all, a young wizard called Merlin earns his true name: Olo Eopia, great man of many worlds, many times. And yet . . . even as Fincayra is saved, it is lost—passing forever into the Otherworld of Spirits.

But in that very moment, a new world appears. Born of a seed that beats like a heart, a seed won by Merlin on his journey through a magical mirror, this new world is a tree: the Great Tree. It stands as a bridge between Earth and Heaven, between mortal and immortal, between shifting seas and eternal mist.

Its landscape is immense, full of wonders and surprises. Its populace is as far-flung as the stars on high. Its essence is part hope, part tragedy, part mystery.

Its name is Avalon.

—*the celebrated opening lines of the bard Willenia's history of Avalon, widely known as "Born of a Seed That Beats Like a Heart"*

Year 0:

Merlin plants the seed that beats like a heart. A tree is born: the Great Tree of Avalon.

THE AGE OF FLOWERING

Year 1:

Creatures of all kinds migrate to the new world, or appear mysteriously, perhaps from the sacred mud of Malóch. The first age of Avalon, the Age of Flowering, begins.

Year 1:

Elen of the Sapphire Eyes and her daughter Rhiannon found a new faith, the Society of the Whole, and become its first priestesses. The Society is dedicated to promoting harmony among all living creatures, and to protecting the Great Tree that supports and sustains all life. The new faith focuses on seven sacred Elements—what Elen called "the seven sacred parts that together make the Whole." They are: Earth, Air, Fire, Water, Life, LightDark, and Mystery.

Year 2:

The great spirit Dagda, god of wisdom, visits both Elen and Rhia in a dream. He reveals that there are seven separate roots of Avalon, each with its own distinct landscapes and populations—and that their new faith will eventually reach into all of them. With Dagda's help, Elen, Rhia, and their original followers (plus several giants, led by Merlin's old friend Shim) make a journey to Lost Fincayra, to the great circle of stones that was site of the famous Dance of the Giants. Together, they transport the sacred stones all the way back to Avalon. The circle is rebuilt deep in the realm of

Stoneroot, and becomes the Great Temple in the center of a new compound that is dedicated to the Society of the Whole.

Year 18:

The Drumadians—as the Society of the Whole is commonly called, in honor of Lost Fincayra's Druma Wood—ordain their first group of priestesses and priests. They include Lleu of the One Ear; Cwen, last of the treelings; and (to the surprise of many) Babd Catha, the Ogre's Bane.

Year 27:

Merlin returns to Avalon—to explore its mysteries, and more importantly, to wed the deer woman Hallia. They are married under shining stars in the high peaks of upper Olanabram. This region is the only place in the seven root-realms where the lower part of Avalon's trunk can actually be seen, rising into the ever-swirling mist. (The trunk can also be seen from the Swaying Sea, but this strange place is normally not considered part of the Great Tree's roots.) Here, atop the highest mountain in the Seven Realms, which Merlin names Hallia's Peak, they exchange their vows of loyalty and love. The wedding, announced by canyon eagles soaring on high, includes more varied kinds of creatures than have assembled anywhere since the Great Council of Fincayra after the Dance of the Giants long ago. By the grace of Dagda, they are joined by three spirit-beings, as well: the brave hawk Trouble, who sits on Merlin's shoulder; the wise bard Cairpré, who stands by Elen's side throughout the entire ceremony; and the deer man Eremon, who is the devoted brother of Hallia. Even the dwarf ruler, Urnalda, attends—along with the great white spider known as the Grand Elusa; the jester Bumbelwy; the giant Shim; the scrubamuckloving creature Ballymag; and the dragon queen Gwynnia, plus several of her fire-breathing children. The ceremonies are conducted by Elen and Rhia, founders of the Society of the Whole, the priest Lleu of the One Ear, and the priestess Cwen of the treelings. (Babd Catha is also invited, but chooses to battle ogres instead.) According to legend, the great spirits Dagda and Lorilanda also come, and give the newlyweds their everlasting blessings.

Year 27:

Krystallus Eopia, son of Merlin and Hallia, is born. Celebrations last for years—especially among the fun-loving hoolahs and sprites. Although the newborn is almost crushed when the giant Shim tries to kiss him, Krystallus survives and grows into a healthy child. While he is nonmagical, since wizards' powers often skip generations, his wizard's blood assures him a long life. Even as an infant, he shows an unusual penchant for exploring. Like his mother, he loves to run, though he cannot move with the speed and grace of a deer.

Year 33:

The mysterious Rugged Path, connecting the realms of Stoneroot and Woodroot, is discovered by a young lad named Fergus. Legend tells that Fergus found the path when he followed a strange white doe—who might really have been the spirit Lorilanda, goddess of birth, flowering, and renewal. The legend also says that the path runs only in one direction, though which direction—and why—remains unclear. Since very few travelers have ever reported finding the path, and since those reports seem unreliable, most people doubt that the path even exists.

Year 37:

Elen dies. She is grateful for her mortal years and yet deeply glad that she can at last rejoin her love, the bard Cairpré, in the land of the spirits. The great spirit Dagda himself, in the form of an enormous stag, comes personally to Avalon to guide her to the Otherworld. Rhia assumes Elen's responsibilities as High Priestess of the Society of the Whole.

Year 51:

Travel within the Seven Realms, through the use of enchanted portals, is discovered by the wood elf Serella. She becomes the first queen of the wood elves, and over time she learns much about this dangerous art. In her words, "Portalseeking is a difficult way to travel, yet an easy way to die." She leads several expeditions to Waterroot, which culminate in the founding of Caer Serella, the original colony of water elves. However, her first expedition to Shadowroot ends in complete disaster—and her own death.

Year 130:

A terrible blight appears in the upper reaches of Woodroot, killing everything it touches. Rhia, believing this to be the work of the evil spirit Rhita Gawr, seeks help from Merlin.

Year 131:

As the blight spreads, destroying trees and other living creatures in Woodroot's forests, Merlin takes Rhia and her trusted companion, the priest Lleu of the One Ear, on a remarkable journey. Traveling through portals known only to Merlin, they voyage deep inside the Great Tree. There they find a great subterranean lake which holds magical white water. After the lake's water rises to the surface at the White Geyser of Crystallia, in upper Waterroot, it separates into the seven colors of the spectrum (at Prism Gorge) and flows to many places, giving both water and color to everything it meets. Merlin reveals to Rhia and Lleu that this white water gains its magic from its high concentration of *élano*, the most powerful—and most elusive—magical substance in all of Avalon. Produced as sap deep within the Great Tree's roots, élano combines all seven sacred Elements, and is, in Merlin's words, "the true life-giving force of this world." At the great subterranean lake, Merlin gathers a small crystal of élano with the help of his staff—whose name, Ohnyalei, means *spirit of grace* in the Fincayran Old Tongue. Then he, Rhia, and Lleu return to Woodroot and place the crystal at the origin of the blight. Thanks to the power of élano, the blight recedes and finally disappears. Woodroot's forests are healed.

Year 132:

Rhia, as High Priestess, introduces her followers to élano, the essential life-giving sap of the Great Tree. Soon thereafter, Lleu of the One Ear publishes his masterwork, *Cyclo Avalon*. This book sets down everything that Lleu has learned about the seven sacred Elements, the portals within the Tree, and the lore of élano. It becomes the primary text for Drumadians throughout Avalon.

Year 192:

After a final journey to her ancestral home, the site of the legendary Carpet Caerlochlann, Hallia dies. So profound is Merlin's grief that he climbs high into the jagged mountains of Stoneroot and does not speak with anyone, even his sister Rhia, for many months.

Year 193:

Merlin finally descends from the mountains—but only to depart from Avalon. He must leave, he tells his dearest friends, to devote himself entirely to a new challenge in another world: educating a young man named Arthur in the land of Britannia, part of mortal Earth. He hints, without revealing any details, that the fates of Earth and Avalon are somehow entwined.

Year 237:

Krystallus, now an accomplished explorer, founds the Eopia College of Mapmakers in Waterroot. As its emblem, he chooses the star within a circle, ancient symbol for the magic of Leaping between places and times.

THE AGE OF STORMS

Year 284:

Without any warning, the stars of one of Avalon's most prominent constellations, the Wizard's Staff, go dark. One by one, the seven stars in the constellation—symbolizing the legendary Seven Songs of Merlin, by which both the wizard and his staff came into their true powers—disappear. The process takes only three weeks. Star watchers agree that this portends something ominous for Avalon. The Age of Storms has begun.

Year 284:

War breaks out between dwarves and dragons in the realm of Fireroot, sparked by disputes over the underground caverns of Flaming Jewels. Although these two peoples have cooperated for centuries in harvesting as well as preserving the jewels, their unity finally crumbles. The skilled dwarves regard the jewels as sacred, and want to harvest them only deliberately over long periods of time. By contrast, the dragons (and their allies, the flamelons) want to take immediate advantage of all the wealth and power that the jewels could provide. The fighting escalates, sweeping up other peoples—even some clans of normally peaceful faeries. Alliances form, pitting dwarves, most elves and humans, giants, and eaglefolk against the dragons, flamelons, dark elves, avaricious humans, and gobsken. Meanwhile, marauding ogres and trolls take advantage of the chaos. In the widening conflict, only the sylphs, mudmakers, and some museos remain neutral . . . while the hoolahs simply enjoy all the excitement.

Year 300:

The war worsens, spreading across the Seven Realms of Avalon. Drumadian Elders debate the true nature of the War of Storms: Is it limited exclusively to Avalon? Or is it really just a skirmish in the greater ongoing battle of the spirits—the clash between the brutal Rhita Gawr, whose goal is to control all the worlds, and the allies Lorilanda and Dagda, who want free peoples to choose for themselves? To most of Avalon's citizens, however, such a question is irrelevant. For them, the War of Storms is simply a time of struggle, hardship, and grief.

Year 413:

Rhia, who has grown deeply disillusioned with the brutality of Avalon's warring peoples—and also with the growing rigidity of the Society of the Whole—resigns as High Priestess. She departs for some remote part of Avalon, and is never heard from again.

Some believe that she traveled to mortal Earth to rejoin Merlin; others believe that she merely wandered alone until, at last, she died.

Year 421:

Halaad, child of the mudmakers, is gravely wounded by a band of gnomes. Seeking safety, she crawls to the edge of a bubbling spring. Miraculously, her wounds heal. The Secret Spring of Halaad becomes famous in story and song—but its location remains hidden to all but the elusive mudmakers.

Year 472:

Bendegeit, highlord of the water dragons, presses for peace. On the eve of the first treaty, however, some dragons revolt. In the terrible battle that follows, Bendegeit is killed. The war rages on with renewed ferocity.

Year 498:

In early spring, when the first blossoms have appeared on the trees, an army of flamelons and dragons attacks Stoneroot. In the Battle of the Withered Spring, many villages are destroyed, countless lives are lost, and even the Great Temple of the Drumadians is scorched with flames. Only with the help of the mountain giants, led by Jubolda and her three daughters, are the invaders finally defeated. In the heat of the battle, Jubolda's eldest daughter, Bonlog Mountain-Mouth, is saved when her attackers are crushed by Shim, the old friend of Merlin. But when she tries to thank him with a kiss, he shrieks and flees into the highlands. Bonlog Mountain-Mouth tries to punish Shim for this humiliation, but cannot find him. Shim remains in hiding for many years.

Year 545:

The Lady of the Lake, a mysterious enchantress, first appears in the deepest forests of Woodroot. She issues a call for peace, spread throughout the Seven Realms by the small winged creatures called light flyers, but her words are not heeded.

Year 693:

The great wizard Merlin finally returns from Britannia. He leads the Battle of Fires Unending, which destroys the last alliance of dark elves and fire dragons. The flamelons reluctantly surrender. Gobsken, sensing defeat, scatter to the far reaches of the Seven Realms. Peace is restored at last.

THE AGE OF RIPENING

Year 693:

The great Treaty of the Swaying Sea, crafted by the Lady of the Lake, is signed by representatives of all known peoples except gnomes, ogres, trolls, gobsken, changelings, and death dreamers. The Age of Storms is over; the Age of Ripening begins.

Year 694:

Merlin again vanishes, but not before he announces that he expects never to return to Avalon. He declares solemnly that unless some new wizard appears—which is highly unlikely—the varied peoples of Avalon must look to themselves to find justice and peace. As a final, parting gesture, he travels to the stars with the aid of a great dragon named Basilgarrad—and then magically rekindles the seven stars of the Wizard's Staff, the constellation whose destruction presaged the terrible Age of Storms.

Year 694:

Soon after Merlin departs, the Lady of the Lake makes a chilling prediction, which comes to be known as the Dark Prophecy: A time will come when all the stars of Avalon will grow steadily darker, until there is a total stellar eclipse that lasts a whole year. And in that year, a child will be born who will bring about the very end of Avalon, the one and only world shared by all creatures alike—human and nonhuman, mortal and immortal. Only Merlin's true heir, the Lady of the Lake adds, might save Avalon. But she says no more about who the wizard's heir might be, or how he or she could defeat the child of the Dark Prophecy. And so throughout the realms, people wonder: *Who will be the child of the Dark Prophecy? And who will be the true heir of Merlin?*

Year 717:

Krystallus, exceptionally long-lived due to his wizard's ancestry, and already the first person to have explored many parts of Avalon's roots, becomes the first ever to reach the Great Hall of the Heartwood. In the Great Hall he finds portals to all Seven Realms—but no way to climb higher in the Tree. He vows to return one day, and to find some way to travel upward, perhaps even all the way to the stars.

Year 842:

In the remote realm of Woodroot, the old teacher Hanwan Belamir gains renown for his bold new ideas about agriculture and craftsmanship, which lead to more productive farms as well as more comfort and leisure for villagers. Some even begin to call him Olo Belamir—the first person to be hailed in that way since the birth of Avalon, when Merlin was proclaimed Olo Eopia. While the man himself humbly scoffs at such praise, his Academy of Prosperity thrives.

Year 900:
Belamir's teachings continue to spread. Although wood elves and others resent his theories about humanity's "special role" in Avalon, more and more humans support him. As Belamir's following grows, his fame reaches into other realms.

Year 985:
As the Dark Prophecy predicted, a creeping eclipse slowly covers the stars of Avalon. So begins the much-feared Year of Darkness. Every realm (except the flamelon stronghold of Fireroot) declares a ban against having any new children during this time, out of fear that one of them could be the child of the Dark Prophecy. Some peoples, such as dwarves and water dragons, take the further step of killing any offspring born this year. Throughout the Seven Realms, Drumadian followers seek to find the dreaded child—as well as the true heir of Merlin.

Year 985:
Despite the pervasive darkness, Krystallus continues his explorations. He voyages to the realm of the flamelons, even though outsiders—especially those with human blood—have never been welcome there. Soon after he arrives, his party is attacked, and the survivors are captured. Somehow Krystallus escapes, with the help of an unidentified friend. (Some believe it is Halona, princess of the flamelons, who helps him; others point to signs that his ally

is an eaglewoman.) Ignoring the danger of the Dark Prophecy, Krystallus and his rescuer are wed and conceive a child. Just after giving birth, however, the mother and newborn son disappear.

Year 987:

Beset with grief over the loss of his wife and child, Krystallus sets out on another journey, his most ambitious quest ever: to find a route upward into the very trunk and limbs of the Great Tree. Some believe, however, that his true goal is something even more perilous—to solve at last the great mystery of Avalon's stars. Or is he really searching for the woman he loves? Whatever his goal, he does not succeed, for somewhere on this quest, he perishes. His long life, and many explorations, finally come to an end.

Year 1002:

Seventeen years have now passed since the Year of Darkness. Troubles are mounting across the Seven Realms: fights between humans and other kinds of creatures; severe drought—and a strange graying of colors—in the upper reaches of Stoneroot, Waterroot, and Woodroot; attacks by nearly invisible killer birds called ghoulacas; and a vague sense of growing evil. Many people believe that all this proves that the dreaded child of the Dark Prophecy is alive and coming into power. They pray openly for the true heir of Merlin—or the long-departed wizard himself—to appear at last and save Avalon.

Year 1002:

Late in the year, as the drought worsens, the stars of a major con-stellation—the Wizard's Staff—begin to go out. This has happened only once before, other than in the Year of Darkness: at the start of the Age of Storms in the Year of Avalon 284. No one knows why this is happening, or how to stop it. But most people fear that the vanishing of the Wizard's Staff can mean only one thing: the final ruin of Avalon.

Turn the page for a sneak peek at the next
installment of the Merlin saga:

BOOK 10

SHADOWS ON THE STARS

Prologue: The Greatest Power

DEEP UNDERGROUND, IN A CAVERN OF DARK shadows, something even darker hovered in the air. Slowly it spun—a venomous snake of smoke. As it twirled, the air around it crackled with black sparks. And wherever its tail brushed against the cavern floor, stones burst apart like trees shattered by lightning, leaving only heaps of smoldering ash.

The dark spiral floated menacingly toward a small, radiant crystal on a stone pedestal. The crystal's light, frail but still defiant, glowed white with ribbons of blue and green. As the shadowy being approached, it swelled a bit brighter.

"Now observe," hissed the smoky serpent. "I will demonstrate how to destroy this crystal of élano, just as we will soon destroy our enemies." The serpent laughed, its voice bubbling like molten rock. "But first, my pet, we will turn its power to our own purposes."

His back pressed against the cavern wall, Kulwych shifted nervously. The cloaked sorcerer chewed his once perfectly clipped fingernails, then ran his hand across the scarred hollow of his empty eye socket. "M-m-mmmyesss, my lord Rhita Gawr."

"I have but one small regret," hissed the spiral as it hardened, coalescing into darkness that was almost solid. "By now, no doubt, you have already dispatched the one who calls himself *the true heir of Merlin*. And I would have rather enjoyed making him my crystal's first victim."

Kulwych bit harder on his fingers. "Er, well, in that case, my lord . . . you'll be pleased to learn that—"

"He *isn't* dead?" spat the spiral. Instantly, it shot at the sorcerer's face, stopping only a hair's breadth away from his throat. "Have you failed me, my little magician, my plaything?"

Shivering, his head against the wall, Kulwych made a frightened gurgle.

The dark being swayed back and forth, sizzling like a tongue of lava. "You have seen my wrath before, haven't you?"

Kulwych's one eye darted to the headless corpse of the gobsken on the cavern floor. He tried to speak, but could only gurgle again.

For an endless moment, the smoky serpent hovered, crackling in the air by the sorcerer's throat. Then, with a whiplike snap, it pulled away, floating back toward the crystal. Kulwych gasped and crumpled to the stone floor.

"You are fortunate, even if you are a simpleton."

Kulwych's lone eye narrowed at the insult, but as he stood again he said only, "Mmmyesss, my lord."

"Fortunate indeed," continued the spiraling coil. "You see, my pet, I still require your services, at least until I am strong enough to take solid form. One day soon, however, I shall assume my true shape—and my true role as conqueror."

"Conqueror," repeated Kulwych, bobbing his hideously scarred head.

"Yes!" cried the smoky spiral that was Rhita Gawr, with such force that black sparks exploded in the air, sizzling and steaming on the wet stone walls. "And not just of this puny little world, this hollow hull of a tree. Once I control Avalon, the very bridge between mortal and immortal, I will soon control everything else, as well! From the Otherworld of the Spirits to mortal Earth—all the worlds will be mine."

In a quieter, almost pleasant tone, the dark being added, "And perhaps yours, too, my Kulwych. If, that is, I choose to keep you at my side."

Slowly, Kulwych straightened himself and brushed some dust off his cloak. His jaw quivered as he said, "Always your faithful servant, my lord."

"Just be certain it is *always*," hissed the shadow of Rhita Gawr, sounding more dangerous again. "Or I will do to you what I am about to do to this obstinate little crystal."

Before Kulwych could even respond, the dark coil snarled viciously, then stretched all the way around the crystal's pedestal. Circling slowly in the air, it bound itself end to end, like a noose, and began to tighten around its prey. At the same time, it grew flatter, widening so that it looked less like a rope and more like a shroud—dark enough that it couldn't be described as merely black. Rather, this shroud seemed like the essence of emptiness, so dark that nothing resembling light could ever penetrate its depths, give it shape, or touch its bottomless void.

The crystal pulsed bravely, as relentlessly as a beating heart, even while the shroud closed over it. Tighter and tighter the darkness drew, enveloping the glowing object, squeezing ever closer. Although light still pulsed beneath the shadow, and a few white rays broke through to illuminate the cavern walls, the crystal grew dimmer by the second. The whole cavern darkened.

Standing by the wall, Kulwych watched in fascination. Delightedly, he rubbed his smooth hands together. Here was power, true power, at work! And yet . . . in the back of his mind, he remained uncertain. No one—not even Rhita Gawr—had ever before corrupted a pure crystal of élano. Was it truly possible? Or would the crystal's stubborn magic prevail? After all, its magic ran deeper than anyone had been able to comprehend, flowing from the very resin of the Great Tree. Why, even Merlin, that sorry excuse for a wizard, had understood that his powers were nothing compared to élano.

The dark shroud continued to shrink, until at last it covered the crystal completely. No large openings were left, not on the top or bottom or any sides, for light to escape. And yet, even now, a faint glow still seeped through some cracks. The crystal continued to resist.

Kulwych leaned closer, his lone eye twitching anxiously. *Trolls' teeth and ogres' tongues*, he cursed to himself, *what is happening?*

Tighter the shroud squeezed, like a smothering blanket. But under its folds, the crystal glowed ever so slightly. The vaguest shimmer of light still radiated from beneath the layers of darkness.

Suddenly the shroud crackled with black fire. Heavy, rancid smoke rose from the pedestal. The darkness itself started to pulse, as if it were a fist squeezing the last spark of life out of its enemy.

The cavern's air thickened, growing steadily more foul. Kulwych choked back a cough. He felt more and more nauseated, until it was all he could do not to retch. He leaned against the rock wall for support, as the sickening air burned his lungs. Near his feet, a stray mouse lost its way, groped wildly for some way to escape, then twitched one last time before it died.

Seconds passed, stretching into minutes. At long last, the

shroud of darkness released its hold. It pulled gradually away from the crystal, forming itself again into a spiraling coil that hung in the air, slowly spinning. And on the pedestal, the crystal still glowed—but with a light far different than before.

Dark, smoky red it shone. Veins ran through it as if it were a diseased, bloodshot eye. And with every strangled pulse of its core came a repulsive odor like rotting flesh.

Kulwych took a cautious step nearer. "It is . . . done?"

"Oh yes, my pet magician, it is done." The voice of the spiral sounded drained, much weaker than before. "You did not doubt my powers, did you?"

"No, no," said Kulwych quickly. "I would never doubt you, just as I would never disobey you."

"So then," hissed the dark being, "you would obey my command to lay your hand upon this crystal?"

The sorcerer cringed in horror. He glanced at the dark red object, the color of dried blood. "T-t-touch th-that?" he stammered.

"Yes, Kulwych. Touch it. I command you."

Shivering uncontrollably, the sorcerer lifted up his arm. The sleeve of his cloak ruffled like a sail in a stiff wind. Then, gritting his teeth, he reached his hand toward the dark crystal. Closer he came, and closer. Meanwhile, the smoky spiral twirled in the air, sizzling softly.

As his hand approached the crystal, Kulwych cast a final, pleading look toward his master. But the shadow of Rhita Gawr said nothing. Perspiration glistened on Kulwych's fingers as he lowered them toward this thing that looked less like a crystal than a pulsing clot of blood.

Just as his fingertips were about to touch it, the edge of his sleeve brushed against the crystal. Instantly the cloth burst into dark red flames. The sorcerer screeched in fright and drew back his arm, even as the flames went out. Only then did he notice that the flames hadn't really burned his sleeve—but had, instead, made the cloth disappear.

Kulwych shook his arm in surprise. Where the bottom of his sleeve had been, there were no fragments, no charred threads, not even any wisps of smoke. The entire section of cloth had simply vanished.

He looked over at the smoky serpent that had commanded him. "My lord . . . do you still wish—"

"No," snarled the dark being. "You needn't touch it now. You have shown me your loyalty, such as it is."

Kulwych gulped. Then, turning back to his sleeve, he mumbled to himself, "Ironwool threads, shouldn't have burned." Facing the serpent once more, he asked, "Tell me please, my lord, just what is this crystal's power?"

A low, sizzling laugh echoed in the walls of the cavern. "Behold, the utter opposite of élano! *Vengélano*, I hereby name it: the greatest power in all of Avalon."

Kulwych just stared at him, confused.

The spiral twirled, hissing with a mixture of impatience and triumph. "Do you not understand, my foolish minion? Élano holds the power to create—which is why that scoundrel Merlin used it to end my Blight centuries ago. Or to heal—which is why a filthy little spring in Malóch can work such strange wonders. Why, even the very dirt of that realm is so rich in élano that it can bring forth new life."

"But my sleeve just . . . disappeared."

"Have you no brains at all? That is the power I have unleashed!

Where élano creates, vengélano destroys. Anything it touches, no matter how well made, will be instantly unmade."

Anxiously, the sorcerer squeezed his fingers—fingers that had nearly touched the corrupted crystal.

"Whatever flesh vengélano meets," crackled the voice, "will simply slice open, or vanish. Blood vessels will bleed without end. Healthy trees will wither, sturdy weapons will crumble, and freshwater streams will turn to poison."

Kulwych's lone eye widened in amazement. "So with this new power, we will seize control—" A sharp sizzling halted him midsentence. "Er, I mean, *you* will, my lord. Avalon will be yours at last."

The dark shape swirled around the bloodred crystal, circling it slowly, admiring it as a painter would admire the work of a lifetime, savoring its subtlest detail. "That is true, my pet. But first, before embarking on grander plans, I shall take care of one minor detail."

"Which is, my lord?"

"I shall destroy, once and for all, the true heir of Merlin."

The spiral continued to circle. "He is just seventeen years old by my count, barely a newborn to me. But his meager powers should soon start to emerge. And although the day of my triumph grows near, we have much to do before then. This young wizard could become a nuisance, a distraction. Besides, eliminating him will be easy enough, as well as entertaining. Fool that he is, I suspect that he fears his new powers almost as much as he fears me! And so, my Kulwych, I shall relieve him of his worries—along with his life."